THE MANHATTAN PROPHET

Hey Milt -

Thanks so much for all your support! I don't know how the camp industry will survive without us!

THE MANHATTAN PROPHET

Jake Packard

Jake Packard

BASCOM HILL PUBLISHING GROUP
MINNEAPOLIS

Bascom Hill Publishing Group
212 3rd Avenue North, Suite 290
Minneapolis, MN 55401
612.455.2293
www.bascomhillpublishing.com

ISBN - 978-1-935098-05-8
ISBN - 1-935098-05-5
LCCN - 2009926448

Book sales for North America and international:
Itasca Books, 3501 Highway 100 South, Suite 220
Minneapolis, MN 55416
Phone: 952.345.4488 (toll free 1.800.901.3480)
Fax: 952.920.0541; email to orders@itascabooks.com

Cover Design by Wes Moore
Typeset by Peggy LeTrent

Printed in the United States of America

This first one is for Dawn.

Thanks to Marion and Marly for all their help.

* * * * *

September 22, 2069. 12:00 a.m.

The silver haired man emerges from the forest path, crosses the moist sand and sits down on a large egg-shaped rock by the water's edge. The air is so still and the lake so smooth, the reflection of the sky makes him feel suspended once again, floating in the infinite and the vast. A meteor flames across the midnight sky, streaking in the water a few feet away from his muddy boots.

He opens his laptop as if a great omen might blaze across the screen, and when it blinks on, the computer's glow paints his wise face sterling blue in the perfect dark. He takes a deep breath, and speaks into the built-in microphone.

"My son, I am very proud of you and how you completed the final part of your intensive studies. You have learned from the so-called experts about the extraordinary events that came before your birth and compared all their opinions and theories. So now, on the eve of your departure, your mother and I feel it is time to share the truth with you, my first-hand account of that incredible time. To many it seems like centuries have passed, and nothing from back then matters anymore. But when I look into your eyes, I see promise burning brighter than all the stars that surround us.

"It is true that I have witnessed powerful evil, and some things I must tell you will horrify you and disgust you. But, in the end, I know you will agree, that somehow all of us were truly blessed during those four miraculous days."

* * * * *

1

December 21, 2047, AD, 11:58 p.m.

A single naked light bulb dangles by a bare electric cord from the center of the ceiling in a large barrack-size room. It is the only light in the large windowless area, but the bulb glows with a rich golden radiance that can almost be touched, like a soothing ointment gently blanketing the convicts, who lie asleep on small cots arranged in orderly rows. Rikers Island Jail is home to New York City's worst criminals and terrorists, but all the cell doors are opened and unlocked, and there are no guards in sight.

The only sounds are men breathing, unsullied, sonorous in the same category as infant water running in a mountain stream, joyriding on its journey to the sea.

A door slowly creaks open at one end of the hallway, cracking the unruffled hush. A black-hooded figure steps in, its bony feet click on the hard tile floor, marching to the steady beat of a dark netherdrum. Malefic whispers and giggles bristle from the fledgling goblins fluttering behind the horned one. Their caustic sniggers turn into cackles, which morph into gruntings and gutturals of lizard beasts, and crescendo into the screaming of the eternally enraged preparing for ultimate combat.

A small wooden door at the other end of the hallway opens with reluctance, as if upon a silent, irrefutable command, and a slim shaft of the deep golden light manages to reach the calm, youthful face of the lone inmate sleeping inside.

The hooded one and his hungry demons hobble in and cluster around the cot in the center of the cell. At the peak of their unworldly din, the black wraith extends one bony finger from the dank of its filthy, rotting sleeve and points at the face of the young man lying there.

Just then, from up high, almost imperceptible, a soft celestial vibrato invades the demonic chanting. The unblemished music gains momentum whirling through the discordance; a soprano tonic resonating up to its major third, up another octave and then down a fifth, and on it goes, repeating mantra-like yet never the same. The endless melody swells and surges drowning out the baneful fugue below.

The monsters beneath cringe in agony, grabbing their grotesque ears with their gnarled and deformed claws, trying to keep the beautiful song out of their heads. In anguished torment, they flee in defeat, bellowing with an unholy rage.

A moment of silence reverberates. The prisoner opens his eyes and rises to a sitting position. He detects ghostly echoes of the phantasmic battle rebounding off the hard walls that seemingly pen him in. For the last time, Salem Jones scans the blessed stillness of his barren prison cell, where he has often witnessed the bounty of so many incoming glories.

* * * * *

2

December 22, 2047, 2 a.m.

It is a bone-creaking cold night in Shantypark. Inside a dimly lit tent pitched amongst others in a dark hollow, a ten-year-old black boy named Jamal shivers. He sits on a ripped plastic tarp strewn on the bare ground, trying to stay warm next to the city-issued portable kerosene heater. His mother is copulating with vigor on a cot in the corner with a soporific stranger Jamal knows he has seen before. His baby sister is screaming and crying in his grandmother's arms as she creaks back and forth next to him on a scrap-wood rocking chair. The grandmother shakes Jamal on the shoulder and whispers, "Your baby sister is hungry, boy. She is sick; she may be dying. What are we gonna do?"

What could Jamal do? His grandmother knew his deal, born into this depravity spawned by the Exchange and ongoing eco-disasters, he has lived all his life crammed into this space that was once Central Park in a past, more opulent, New York City. He survives day-to-day in the lawless filth of this modern-day leper colony, one huge disease breeding ground excised from the rest of society.

A place from which there is no escape. His daily existence is spent treading water in the ocean of viruses that flood his world.

Now to his dismay, he is physically shaking from some searing, shiver-like shocks that wrack his small malnourished body with convulsions. These painful vibrations, erupting tonight from somewhere deep inside, threaten to tear his body apart.

His baby sister shrieks in pain from the hunger once again. His heart pounds and his skin crawls. His muscles twinge and violently contract. In panic, Jamal jumps up and, to keep himself from exploding, he kicks the stranger in his ribs who is humping his mother from the rear.

Unaware of what hit him, the man falls off and lands hard on the cold ground. Unfazed he rolls onto his back, snoring and snortling off into a drug and alcohol induced stupor.

Jamal's mother, noticing something missing, takes off her headphones and looks around. She begins to snicker, which slowly turns into a precarious laugh, a zoned-out, drugified cackle that can easily turn from pure delight to unimagined terror. A dangerous buzz like hers brought on by smizz, the latest designer drug and its ongoing evolutions, is only achieved by those who go looking for these uncomfortably high places. The chill giggle signals others around to prepare for anything.

At the height of her hysterics she sees her son standing over her and, lonely enough, she pulls Jamal down by the back of his neck, shoving her voracious and insatiate tongue deep into his throat. Disgusted, he pushes her away and she too falls off the cot and onto the strange, now comatose man. Startled once more, but seeing new opportunity, she gropes down around his scrotum trying to wake him up to have more noxious sex.

Horrified, Jamal turns to his grandmother. She says, "Oh, Jamal, honey, what are we going to do, your baby sister is sick; she is starving. She is gonna die if we don't git some food, Jamal, what are we going to do?"

Food? What food? Everything they get to eat in Shantypark comes from the city's scheduled drop-offs everyday, and the gangs, armed with legions of automatic weapons, control it all. Grandmother knows the story; you only get what they give. Jamal was born at the end of the last gang war. He knows the legends of the Shantypark marauders stalking the city government through the tunnels, like colon cancer metastasizing in the city's bowels, almost bringing New York to its knees. But the general bombed the park with the entire world watching on TV, and afterwards the mayor made a deal with the Gang Council. Now there is only one place to find food.

Jamal looks over at the tent flap and back to his grandmother. He does it again and his body shakes worse, as if one leg is running north and the other south.

Grandmother pulls the baby close to the warmth of her bosom. "Oh, no, my child, you can't go out there, boy. You don't know what's out there. It's not safe for children. They say there are hungry animals that look like people out there. Some haven't eaten for days. The taste of a fresh young kid, even skinny like you, is something they might not be able to resist. You can't go out there, Jamal. No kid goes out into Shantypark at night. That's the way it is, boy. You ain't no good to me and your baby sister as some nightcrawler's midnight snack."

A sciatic shout of "Ma, shut up" comes from Jamal's mother somewhere near the stoned man's crotch.

"Go put your damn headphones back on, you little slut." Grandma rocks on her chair like a maniacal pendulum on a grandfather clock gone wild. She stops and grabs Jamal by the shoulder and squeezes hard, staring at him with eyes edacious, her voice turning from panicked to fierce and desperate. "Your baby sister got to make it one more night so she can see him. If she can get to see him, I think she's gonna make it. I know he can make her all right. He's gonna make it all right for all of us. You too, Jamal. Now that'll give you something to talk about, right boy?"

"Ma," Jamal's mother, out of breath, pleads as she undulates uselessly on her torpid partner in a corner of the tent, "I said 'shut the fuck up.' And you know Jamal don't talk to nobody. And no fuckin' New Yawk goombah is gonna make him start now."

"Are you crazy, girl? Guido, my ass. I heard Salem Jones just might be a brother." Grandma growls at her wayward daughter groveling around on the floor between the drunk man's legs and turns back to Jamal. "Your mother is crazy, boy, and those drugs have poisoned her mind. But Jamal, you can't go out there, even though your baby sister just might die tonight if she don't get a bite to eat. So, all we can do is just sit back and look at your momma disgust up the tent. She ain't even worth a dime out in Reginald Square where some man with an extra buck would pay for a fine fuck like she used to be. But now cause of that smizz, nobody would pay her nothing except a never-you-mind. Exception being that limp dick over there who brings her the devil drugs."

As if by sick magic his mother's berserk eyes, hollowed out and jaundiced by years of addiction, appear at his grandmother's lap. She holds a serrated pocketknife, the blade resting on her baby girl's unprotected neck. One little flick and blood will pour. She giggles again. "Ma. It is so cold outside, please shut the fuckin' fuck up!'"

Appalled and melted down by the hopelessness of it all, pulsating at a critical mass, Jamal tears himself away from his grandmother and shrieking baby sister. In a brief, impulsive instant that might have gone in a hundred different ways, he leaps with determination through the door flap and out of the relative security of the family tent into the unfathomable evil of the Shantypark night.

Caught in the surreality of that moment, the baby's relentless and punishing screams pause, his mother's histrionics suspend, and his grandmother's distraught prayers halt; the tent holding its breath for an icy instant.

His grandmother, in tears, calls after him, "Oh, my darling boy, be careful, my precious baby boy." But Jamal's footsteps are already sucked up and lost to the sounds of the dangerous dark. She whispers a prayer, "Oh, please Salem Jones, be careful with my boy. Don't let anybody hurt my baby boy. Please, Salem Jones, if you can hear me, please let no evil befall my little Jamal."

The moment over, the mother howls in violent laughter and takes a long and sloppy swill from a half-empty bottle by her cot. "Screw fuckin' this" she bellows and grabs her friendly fellow, sticking several scabrous fingers up his licentious and flagellant butt.

* * * * *

3

It is dark in an upscale East Side apartment barely a mile from Shantypark, save for the boogieman-proofing nightlight that protects the luxurious sanctuary. The living space is spacious and airy, decorated sparsely with a selection of ostensibly disjointed objects that, in this case, kind of go together. In the center of the room is a king size bed, cozied between two antique nightstands and, on the one closest to the curtained window, the red digital numbers of an alarm clock radio flick from 4:59 a.m. to 5:00 a.m. A brisk classical concerto jumps out for only the briefest moment before a young woman's hand appears from beneath a colorful comforter and whisks away the wake-up.

Maria Primera, rising from her silk-sheeted bed, stunning, clad in a black thong and a white wifebeater, looks like every man's go-to imported beer commercial. She draws the curtain by her enormous bay window revealing a spectacular view of the East River and the city lights beyond. No evidence of the blast from here.

The early morning glow from the city surrounds the striking, electric-blue, silhouetted view of Maria. Mid-twenties, in perfect shape, her creamy hazelnut skin suggests a mixed waddayathink ethnic background. Una virgen que nació en Venezuela y entonces se trasladó a New York City.

Maria stretches her torso into a full body yawn, hands on neck, jutting ample breasts, head thrown back, her thick, dark brown hair hangs long behind her, with a few whirlpool locks left lazing over her clavicles. At the height of this body extension she freezes for a full beat into the sculpture of her life, which she would title, "Life is Grand," en español diría, "La vida es magnifica." Pleased, she thinks today is going to be the greatest yet in her young, but high-profile life.

Lying down on the soft plush carpeting, she starts with the ab crunches that begin her daily morning work-out. Brain always ticking, she zens into her own personal stream of consciousness.

Maria was a rare vicarious learner. Throughout her youth she demonstrated that she was unusual in that she not only heard, she listened to her parents and teachers. That fortunate gift kept her safe as an adolescent and more prone to success as an adult. As she grew, this innate skill kept her in tune to the pulse of the people, making her good at her job. After today her face should become a household icon in everyone's living room on the planet.

She rolls onto her side, head elbowed up, top leg lifting almost perpendicular to the floor. She's happy within herself knowing that everything about her is sanitary and accounted for. She has clean blood, great genes, and everything else concurrent to attract a man of a similar level and type to marry and have kids with, and maybe to fall in love with, whatever that is. In her golden years, she will surely come to grace as a leader in her sphere of influence. She'll have pure and untainted grandchildren at her feet, but most importantly, she'll have attained the mythic power of those who have entertained the public their entire lives and are able to move the media about with just the strength of their names. Her self-satisfied smile turns to a laugh. Más lentamente, estamos delante de nosotros mismos. Today it seems so close, within her grasp.

In her eclectic bathroom, naked in her perfect, warm shower, behind the almost see-through shower curtain silked with a trendy hint of just enough sparkle, the ticking in her brain continues. She reviews the major biographical points of today's story over and over in her mind, already knowing the details as if they were ingrained into her DNA. The birth, the death and abandonment, the first early signs, and the spontaneous literature, all were parts of the great picture puzzle, which, after all these months of hard work, will come to completion in a dramatic way before this very morning is through. Maria is not only beautiful, wholesome, and perfect in her health, hygiene, and bloodstream, she is also bright and does her homework.

Drying off with a fluffy turquoise towel, looking into the mirror, tilting her chin and smiling at herself with natural confidence, the main underlying thought governing all the rest was, how wonderful life could be! How beautiful! How karmic! Just point your energy in the right direction and the universe opens its doors.

Of course, Salem would say there are the doors we think we know about, but what of those we can't even begin to imagine?

* * * * *

4

The sudden burst of adrenaline quickly fades into hesitant steps as Jamal slows down and stops, tensing up like a cornered wild dog. The frigid night air adds to the exhilaration of the sudden change, but then vertigo advances rapidly. Everything outside his tent flap looks so different in the murky dark of night—especially this time of year, with the light dusting of snow turning to mist, like so many wisps of lives gone by.

Within spitting distance from where earlier he had played during the light of day, he sees a heap of diseased invalids, huddling together for whatever warmth the freshly dead in the pile could provide for the dying. Some alive are in their own death throes; others are simply moaning and shaking. Those who are unable to move just lie oddly perplexed, bearing blank witness to their inconsolable condition.

Rising out of the ragged pile of dying and deceased people, a hooded figure turns to watch him pass by and, catching the little boy's terror-stricken attention, freezes him with a dark invidious power. Extending a dank sleeve, it points a skinny finger in Jamal's direction.

Beyond terrified, the overwhelming fear of being eaten juices every fiber in his undernourished muscles and propels Jamal to free himself from the dark stranger's hypnotic gaze. Abandoning all caution, and unable to scream, he sprints off wildly into the blinding night, farther and farther away from anything he had known before.

Within a minute, whatever fear-inspired energy was left in his sickly and skinny body burns out once more. Exhausted, he stops at a junction between a couple of corrugated shacks and a patchwork tent made out of seat covers filched from cars in the dead zone, which were just far enough away from the blast that they did not melt. Trying to catch his breath, Jamal hears the chilling voices coming from just around the corner of the tent. He had almost run smack dab into one of the countless crimes that occur nightly in this his hometown—another shakedown with predators descending on the weak, reveling in the never-ending drama of man destroying life just because he can.

"What did you say? You don't believe me? Are you making a joke? You hear that, my mujahedin? I come half way around the world to be trapped in what was once America to hear bullshit from a loser like this. One whose throat I could cut like rotten fruit." The dark man doing the talking in the clearing ahead of Jamal turns to his vulturous crew behind him. Jamal ducks behind a rusty garbage can just in time to get out of sight. The man had that alarming type of accent that Jamal has heard so many times before. So cold it could blow candles out. A broken razor-sharp English dialect evolved from the wave of Kyrgisatanis, Uzbekistanis, Afghanistanis and all the other "stanis" that poured illegally into North America from the mountains and steppes of Central Asia after the Exchange, the global warming, and their ensuing continental drought.

The man wheezes out a giggle. “Funny shit, fellas, am I right? His boys mumble in agreement. “Well then, let’s look again.”

Jamal, though terrified, is unable to keep himself from peeking around the side of the corroded metal container that conceals him from the gang. In the gloomy dark he sees a man down on the ground, cringing in the mud, his tormentor standing triumphantly over his body, as four lean fiends begin to revolve around him. One of them leans over the victim and grabs his arm and holds it up in the air, the wretch barely able to protest.

The honcho pulls a small, flat electronic box with a colorful screen out of his pocket and points it at the supplicant’s hand. “I got this latest model biopod from one of my squirrel-killer amigos in exchange for a case of the finest Kentucky whiskey. Now I can hook up to the city’s databanks just like those fucking guys. The Marines are just goat shit like us, the only difference being the uniforms. But you pathetic little asshole, even you know this biopod don’t lie. It’s our friend. It helps clean up this stinking world that you’re messing up.”

He presses a button on the palm-sized wireless device, and a thin red beam of light hits the beggar’s exposed wrist. In an instant there are two small electronic beeps. The vulture drops his arm and kicks the downed man hard in the face for good measure. Within seconds two more beeps are heard and the stani looks down on the tiny screen. He laughs and shows it to his homey, who grunts and steps back into the circle lurking behind.

“I have a very funny joke for you, too, my friend. Did you hear the one about the stupid man with fuckin’ shit for brains?” The stani, Ibrahim, kicks his downed prey squarely in the balls, the victim squeals in pain. He kicks him again, harder, and again.

"You see what this biopod says. This says you are a fuckin' loser. And this info comes straight from the city that condemned you here in the first place. Your blood is not only swimming with AIDS, it tells me you are also a fucking junkie with the clap."

The addict's body convulses. "No, jeez, please, no. I promise. I'll get you the money. I swear. I just can't get it tonight, man, I'm sick, man. Can't you see I'm sick? I'll have it all tomorrow."

"Tomorrow? So, tomorrow you won't be sick? Is that right, asshole?"

"You know, don't you? He's coming tomorrow. They say that tomorrow is the day Salem will be freed to be among us. Then I won't be sick anymore. Please man, just give me one more day."

Ibrahim lights a cigarette and takes a long steady pull, his raptor eyes never leaving the twitching man on the ground, studying him, considering him. Within a slight flicker of invention in his dark and predacious pupils, the junkie's contortions quit, like a doe on the savannah, when it resigns itself to the inevitable, as the beasts in the pride slowly work their way in.

"That's it, fuckface. It's over. You did it, man. You got me sick with that bullshit miracle talk. Like somebody else is going to save you, when you did this to yourself. Besides, I think it's worth the few bucks your dead ass will still owe me." He kicks him hard in the kidneys, and the man screams. "Go ahead and make noise. Your life is over, scumbag. You are a scumbag because you suck. And you suck because you are an asshole." He kicks him hard again, this time in the head. "Besides, buddy boy, there ain't too many oxygen molecules left around these parts for us, so why waste another on a fucking loser like you." Behind him the swarming uglies snicker.

"Please, man, whaddaya saying? Don't do this. I don't want to die before he is set free. Cause then we'll all be set free. You too."

"Oh, no, no, no. Shh, shh. Don't ruin this anymore with that infidel fuckin' bullshit talk about redemption." Ibrahim bends down and sits next to his prey. He pulls the addict's head to his thigh and whispers, "It'll be alright, I'm sure. Just think about it now for a moment, before I kill you. Think that you brought this whole fucking thing upon yourself. And if there were a God, why would he want weaklings like you to possibly breed? Or, for that matter, how could he have let any of this shit happen to the world. But look, what the hell? Everybody has got to die someday, and usually sooner than later around here. But, let's consider, before you die, what is death anyway? Can it really be any worse than living like you?"

A knife appears in his hands and he slits the junkie's throat like a cardboard box, blood pours onto the ground like Styrofoam packing peanuts.

A silent jolting pause, all hold their breath until one nervous gang member babbles out, "Hey, Ibrahim, maybe we shouldn't have done that. Maybe this Salem Jones miracle guy everyone is talking about really is coming here." Ibrahim drops the body onto the frozen mud and glares at his worried henchman in bemused disbelief.

"You think so? A miracle man headed here?" Ibrahim slowly stands up, "I better run home and write my Christmas list for my Auntie Fatima."

"Yeah, that's funny, boss, and Christmas is just in a couple of days, too, ain't that right?" The gang member giggles a little, and so does Ibrahim who rubs his hand through his hair as if deep in thought, then it shoots out like a rattlesnake, grabbing the lackey gargoyle by the throat.

The man fought for air to make his words, "I'm sorry boss, I don't know what I'm talking about. There can't be no miracle shit. So, let's forget I said it now, chief, yes sir, waddaya say, all is good. Just a little joke."

Ibrahim squeezes harder, staring into the man's terrified eyes. "Too many jokes for one night, my friend. There is only one thing you need to know, asshole. Gregor's word is your law. He is our leader. He's the one who is going to set you free."

The choking man gurgles out, "Yes sir, chief, you're right, man, you're right. Gregor's the boss. He's the dude." Jamal could see the man's alarmed face turning blue in the midnight chill.

Apprehension and fear compress into a brief overcharged moment while his friends look on. Ibrahim crushes the man's Adam's apple, his head slumps forward, and all his struggling stops. Ibrahim drops the body to the ground on top of the dead junkie and turns to the other three, "Anybody else got some joke to tell me?"

The henchmen look at each other but say nothing. "Now that, my brothers, is really funny." Chuckling, Ibrahim ambulates off into the curious cold of this solstice night, leaving the consequences of the two lives as somebody else's rubbish to clean up off the ice-cold, rock-hard Shantypark dirt.

Jamal is now up and flying, his outrageous fear is making the decisions. But the night is making everything look so different, so evil, and Jamal never was allowed to go out at night. "They eat little boys out there." He could hear his grandmother's scratchy voice crying out from her rocking chair. All logic and reason was now lost with only one absolute terror motivating his little body to pump faster than any other time in his life.

A dreadful sense of being lost from everything he ever knew surges out of his heart and into his blood, numbing his already-shocked sensibilities. Thinking he discerns a strange brooding shadow to the left, he veers to the right, then down through a makeshift alleyway between ragtag and tattered hovels. Then a left turn around a clapboard lean-to, and a leap over some motionless bodies, another quick left behind the big boulder near the Sheep Meadow gate to avoid the pursuing eyes of those Shantypark ghouls prowling the after-dark on the first night of bitter winter.

Where am I? How do I get out of here? His stupefied young brain screams.

A big white tent with a dim light inside looms in front of Jamal. Without a moment's hesitation, he is on the ground and crawling under the door flap, too tired to worry about what dangers awaited him in there.

* * * * *

5

Cross-town, a voracious alarm clock bleats out 5:30 a.m. in a tiny West Side sty of a downgraded New York tenement. The little studio apartment is littered with the scraps and wrappings of the fast-food nation, reeking of stale tobacco, marijuana, corporate beer, and homemade tequila. Against one wall is a decrepit chest of drawers with a cracked mirror hung above. By the door is a small kitchenette with a tortured, rusty faucet, which drips with a nerve-wracking psychobeat into a sink full of crusty dishes. In the corner, near the door to a contagious-looking toilet is an acoustic guitar, vintage Martin, leaning into the cleft of the walls. On the floor is a lumpy single mattress, with a sleeping mass huddled under several layers of worn fabric that resemble blankets. A scarred and bruised hand claws out from under the covers, groping for the cacophonic clock. Finding the caustic little box, it slaps the sound shut with a clumsy motion that also knocks over a couple of half-empty beer cans strewn close by. The tepid contents spill onto the splintered floor. The arm pulls back beneath the ratty coverings.

But somewhere in between sleep and the working day there will be no escape from the muffled explosions and moldering shrieks of terror that suppurate in his fitful mind. Nuclear power plants on fire, plumes of rust-colored smoke belching upwards, roaring over orange flames; crumpled yellow school busses overturned along leaf-strewn roads, children scattered on the ground, some not moving, some bleeding, some staring blankly into space crying. Jump cut to a white woman floating in a pool of red blood. Jump cut running through a maze of hospital rooms, to more hospital rooms, and more, everything looking like everything else and, with nowhere left to turn, from the farthest reaches of his peripheral vision, in the corner, from amongst a crowd of the bewildered, he could see the shadow of the muzzle, pointing straight at his heart.

He tries to scream, he tries to flee, but nothing can move in his room, except the curtains by the open window, blowing in spasms with the toxic breeze from the city outside, filled with so much engine and hum.

Half asleep he knew his inertia was going to get him killed. Half awake he was shocked to learn that in his half sleep he was afraid to die. Because everyday in his waking world it seemed like God was a just a hunchbacked, tattooed little tailor, helping him to try on death for size.

The snooze alarm rings again and not too soon. This time the hand, knowing from where the culprit assailed, rips the clock from its electric outlet and throws it against the wall into the corner, just missing the guitar, banging it into pieces and scattering scraps of jagged plastic into the haphazard patchwork of garbage on the floor.

Herbie Lipton throws the rags off his shivering, sweating self and stumbles over the litter towards the shower. He pauses by the cracked mirror and peers at his strong, handsome features, somehow only slightly weathered and grayed by time and life. He admits to himself that there was that period he was more than a little depressed, but who wouldn't have been? Marty and Ira were good about giving him all that time in rehab, even though they needed his technical ability at the station. But what good did that do? His binge drinking has worsened into daily drinking, but nobody really knows and, if they do, they don't really care, so why should he?

His savage hangover starts screaming at him, taking no quarter once again this pre-dawn, jack-hammering his brain. Abandoning his reflection in the cracked glass, he stumbles into the grimy bathroom. Standing under the corrosive spout, dirty drops of water sputter forth like a shower of icy needles that stick into his skin and burrow deep. For what does he deserve this almost unbearable, eternal pain? Irrespective of what he does or doesn't do, he cannot remove the preponderance, the burden, the Herculean weight.

No matter what you want or what you try to do, the universe has its own incorruptible patterns, and we are just the infinitely tiny, totally uncertain particles in the enigmatic substance of the cosmos.

He shivers in the cold water, grabbing himself as if his body might dissolve and drip down the drain.

* * * * *

6

Jamal must have been lying there a few minutes with his face in the dirt before he opened his eyes into the dim light of the tent. But when he did, it was peaceful in there, blissful. The only sounds came from the drum machine that was his frightened little heart.

Wary, he allowed himself up. Wiping the dirt off his nose, he looked around with a burgeoning sense of amazement generated by the wealth of crates and bags of supplies organized into tidy rows and aisles inside this tent. There was a cornucopia of fresh produce, boxes of canned goods, bundles of paper towels and toilet tissue, and in some of the cartons there actually appeared to be fresh linens and towels. In his blind terror he somehow snuck into a warehouse full of everything he never had, and nobody seemed to be here. This was beyond what he was hoping for in his wild and random romp through the Shantypark night.

The feast for his eyes made his empty stomach growl, but his instincts told him this might be trouble. The only warehouses he knew about were owned and controlled by gangs. Something he just avoided and didn't want to run into again right now, even if it was one of the black gangs. People in Shantypark tried to take care of their own, but no one liked a thief. At the veteran street-smart age of ten, Jamal knew that's what would be thought of him if he were caught in here uninvited, in the late of night. Thoughts of what he just saw in the cruel alleyways of his hometown chilled him to the bone, so he turned to run. But then he heard the echoes of his crying little sister starving to death back in his tent, and he stopped.

Flustered, he hears a sweet and enthralling siren singing a simple but seductive tune from atop a stack of boxes on the other side of the tent. It was just an ordinary apple, sitting next to its open bag, shining to him as if it was an award, a trophy, an Oscar, a prize of glorious measure. The apple beckoned to Jamal. As he stared, the sweet apple melody grew into a song of allurement that swelled into a symphony of intrigue resounding deep in the chambers of his mind. He was enchanted, mesmerized by the potential, by the forbiddance. It seemed so simple to have that in his mouth, then grab a few more things and try to find his way home.

He gathered his strength. "What was the problem," he thought, "who would miss a few apples?" Unable to further resist, he skittled like a mouse up to the bag of fruit, and within an instant the apple was lodged between his teeth. Its flavor set off the fireworks at the victorious end of the brilliant rhapsody blowing his mind, a triumphant fanfare of pleasure saturating his taste buds.

But can the world be any less fair to a kid like him? To his utter disbelief, before Jamal could even chew and swallow his prize, he heard a sound that set his heart palpitating in fear. How could he have missed it? How could he have not heard it coming?

The loud drumbeat was sinister and insistent, measuring time as if it was ending. Heading his way, Jamal knew it would soon be in his face. The percussion of the gutter creeped him out, but the sounds of wild, animalistic men scared him so bad, his throat froze closed. That was enough for Jamal. He leaped behind the bag he had just pilfered, and just in time. In that instant, a gruesome parade broke through the tent flap into the space where he had just been standing.

The first to enter was a muscular, masked, and black-caped executioner, carrying a torch with one hand, the other resting on the hilt of a long, curved sword swinging on his hip. Jamal was shocked to see that he was followed by Ibrahim, who he had seen just earlier torture and kill two men without the slightest bit of remorse. Following Ibrahim was a motley gang of stanis dragging a young woman tied to leather ropes into the tent. She was clad in only a burlap sack, loosely hanging off her shoulders, one breast almost completely exposed. Some of the men were dancing and whirling about her and howling and moaning while others poked at her with wooden staves, and pinched at her with their nubby fingers. The rest of the gang poured into the tent, drumming their garbage cans with pieces of pipe, the beat heightened and pierced by their chanting. They marched up the aisle between the rows of produce rubbing past the bag behind which Jamal was hidden with the apple stuck in his teeth. They passed through into the next tent room on the other side of a thin canvass sheet.

By the flickering light of their torches, Jamal could see all their actions cast as silhouettes on the tent wall separating them. The men placed the drugged and stunned young woman on all fours upon a tall wooden platform in the center of the room. He heard them ripping the burlap bag off her panting body and howls erupted as the ghouls saw her naked body, vibrating and glistening.

The gang leader, flanked by his captains, enters through the tent flap chugging from a bottle and sucking madly on a cigar. He strides right past a hidden and cringing Jamal and into the raping area as his gruesome followers retreat before him in fierce deference, pressing back to create an opening, allowing him to pass untouched to the unholy altar.

Observing the scene with a vile impassioned eye, the leader dispatches his captains. They take their positions. Jamal sees him raise his arm towards the ceiling and it goes silent, all evil in the tent now focused on this one man. Leering, milking the pause, he strikes his fist down, producing a sudden unanimous cheer.

One scurvy captain steps up behind the victim and mounts her from behind. The girl, pierced, cries out in pain, as the men scream out their approval. He begins pounding her and his torchlight shadow looks to Jamal like a demented, mechanical rodent.

The leader with a sneering bent towards pornodrama, pounds his chest with his fists and bellows like an alpha gorilla. He casts his bottle aside, which would have hit Jamal right in the head if not for the canvass wall separating them. The gorilla's shadow invades her head, forcing himself into her mouth, her terrible screams now mostly gagged.

Crouching behind the apple crates, Jamal's every motor neuron is paralyzed by witnessing this overt bestiality. His knees seemingly can't stand, his lungs can't breathe; his skin is sweating, drenching his tattered clothes. His eyes, which can't come close to comprehending the full debasement of what they see, bulge out of his jaundiced sockets at the feral shadows only a few steps away.

The sex crazed stanis, emboldened by the carnage, are howling and gyrating, almost reaching a sick, symbiotic orgasm. The leader, a spasmodic obscuration on the tent wall, is humping at her face, screaming in primeval triumph. Splatterings of mixed fluids spray upon the canvass, causing a deep crunching desire in Jamal to vomit, knowing that if he does his fate is worth less than hers. He's dizzy, choking on the apple, fighting for breath.

Upon signal from the leader, the executioner raises his black sword high in the air in terrible ceremony. All movement stops in a maniacal instant.

Jamal dares not breathe, almost passing out as time stretches now into an unearthly, hell-drenched pause.

The arched shadow of the scepter loomed over the girl like a penumbra emanating from an eclipse between this world and theirs, quavering with the force of the eventual mercies it offered her.

A vibrating painting, spattered onto canvass, quivering in the firelight from the torches of those wicked and loathsome souls who still roam this earth and crave this kind of art. It lingered there long enough for Jamal to tattoo that picture indelibly onto his mind.

All eyes face the gang leader. He exists for this complete power to destroy. Sweeping his finger across his throat, the executioner's mighty weapon slices down. In a single sharp stroke her head is chopped off at the neck, ending her life, now gratefully departed, leaving the leader holding the severed head, fellating himself through her freshly dead lips.

He climaxes and bellows with a roar, and the gang falls to their knees in obeisance to his raging madness, their foreheads touching to the ground as one. As if a herd of primitive reptiles, together they rise back up in one long ogrific piercing cheer.

The leader strides with pride around the room, carrying the girl's bloody head over his crotch. The gang falls in step behind him, marching and shouting as they follow, parading in triumph around the tented warehouse, his temple of the unworld.

Whereupon, with great nonchalance, he knocks a bag of apples off a crate and glares down with gleeful vengeance at an apoplectic black kid, frozen in fear with an apple glutted in his mouth.

Gregor's erection points at him through the girl's decapitated head and out the hole that was her neck. Looming just inches over Jamal's head, his cum, mixed with her blood, drips with perdition down upon his horrified little face.

* * * * *

7

John Kennedy Storm became the mayor of New York five minutes after the bomb, because everyone else in the city government was dead. Things were so chaotic it took almost two years to hold an actual election. But by that time there was no doubt about it. Without his singular brand of leadership, the commanding way he took over when other powerful men were reduced to emotional rubble, all might have been lost. So by the results of that popular landslide they might have well elected him king.

Going backward in time through his incredible resume, before being so exalted into mayorhood, he was the recently elected Manhattan Borough president. Before that he was a federal judge in Foley Square, and before that a lawyer handling hate crimes and bias cases out of a storefront on Broadway across from the 145th Street subway stop. He had graduated from Columbia University Law School. He'd been an undergrad there, as well. And before that he was just a kid from Harlem delivering pizzas after public school for a little extra money. But always and at all times he was the native New York pride and joy of his dad, Theodore Roosevelt Storm.

Basketball was his game in high school. At 5'11" everybody thought Jack was way too short. But, it was his quickness, uncanny eye and, most of all, his ability to exist in the no-think zone that made him all-city his senior year. Fans of city basketball look back happily on that celebrated season, when Storm's Harlem team met with Pellet's Jefferson High Brooklyn champs for the city title. Jack's three-pointer at the final buzzer in double overtime carried Manhattan to a one point, come-from-behind victory that will exist forever in the annals of classic sport moments. Of course, being the son of Teddy, he never entertained going pro like all the others. No sir, he was going to really make something of his life. And, yes, he did.

Some who tend to mythicize say that Columbia and Columbia Law were a breeze to the mayor, although those who knew him remember that he was working all the time. Not just on his course load, which he aced every semester, but he was always moving between activist student and civic watchdog organizations that put him most definitely on the liberal side of the fence on the political map of the Big Apple. By the time he graduated top in his class, his academic and work-related resume was so strong that he was recruited by every prestigious midtown and downtown law firm in New York City. But Theodore Roosevelt Storm's son chose a small grassroots uptown firm that specialized in litigation involving civil rights and discrimination. Here at his first job he was actually happy. The reward was seeing smiles on the faces of the people his work helped to gain the justice and fair play they deserved.

Jack Storm's arresting good looks and down-to-earth disposition, his inborn charm and natural charisma, as well as an innate wisdom beyond his years, soon won the recognition of people in the government at that time. He became the youngest person ever to be nominated to a judgeship in the Second Federal District.

But being a judge was immediately unsatisfactory. In what he always perceived as an unwieldy and outdated judicial system, it was odious for Jack to base his decisions on matters of procedure as opposed to matters of justice. He hated letting the bad guys with good lawyers go free.

So he stepped down from the bench and instantly found a cozy environment in the Democratic Party's moderate left, which as everybody knows was the perfect place to be in Manhattan. Before too long, Theodore's son was blazing his very own campaign trail for Manhattan Borough president, which he won by the largest margin in city history. Oh, they were grand times, with the heartiness and gusto of good spirit and the flush of success. The world was filled with endless opportunities for him, his wife Anita, and their newborn baby boy. The blast came just weeks after he took office. Life as we all knew it was changed forever.

Some say it was Jack's single-handed vision and fortitude that kept the city from ripping itself apart in fear and burning to the ground in terror and anguish. Though he did play that large a part, it did not come easy. The personal sacrifices he had to make were as great as any other single person whose life was literally blown apart by the infamy of that day. He stood firm in his personal grief and despair, exuding the natural leadership and strength that the city so desperately needed. He worked furiously to keep the shock, bloodshed, death, and disruption from sinking New York into the depths of a physical and moral abyss.

Long years that seem like centuries later, he still rules the fractured and besieged city through daily tribulations, but now more and more with his intuition and his heart than with his well-obeyed iron fist. Still retaining most of his youthful good looks, he wears the scars of this monumental rise to power naturally, with distinction and dignity, like the graying of sideburns.

This morning he sits at his uncluttered state-of-the-art workstation ringed with flat monitors. All the information he could want from anywhere, in any language, was at his immediate fingertips. Ironic, he thought, that all this great information was never accompanied by any of the real answers he now so desperately sought. He had learned to create his own solutions, and his city and his people lived and died on those outcomes. Lately that was not enough.

One of the many landlines rings. He picks it up knowing who it is, but deliberately pauses for composure. "Morning, Sam."

Sam Gallant, his chief of staff, former Columbia roommate, and the original John Kennedy Storm supporter from a long time before the bomb. "I have the Northern Alliance, Euro-Reich, Sony, Microsoft, Digi-Bell, and Singapore, for starters, all on hold. The Union of New England City-States, as well as NYCTV and LAFox are demanding more than the feed you're allowing through ABCNN. They're screaming at me that the brownout is against the charter and, if they can't create their own coverage, they want to be fused in and allowed to broadcast the signal through their own links. They are complaining about the brutish attitude we are taking over this issue. And Jack, maybe you should run that by the general." Sam added a silent emphasis knowing that General Pellet was probably an electron's orbit away, listening in.

Storm said nothing in shrift silence, but Sam was not to be denied. "Everyone is in what you would call a very urgent mode. The Ayatollah in Basra is threatening his usual embargo . . ."

Storm interrupted, "It is all legal Sam, under the Emergency City Charter, which I enacted last night."

"I was hoping we didn't have to get into that again, Jack. You know how I feel. Even though it is legal, it is politically dangerous. It's already working against us. I don't want to see you start digging your own grave." Sam was quick to reply. Too quick.

Storm remained cool on the surface even though he was annoyed with himself. He knew it was because Sam might have been partly right. "Listen, I weighed the situation and determined that, if we went brown, it would be far less explosive and much more conducive for an unhindered release, without the complication of multiple media outlets that will try to accompany everything we do. I thought it would be better if we could distract some of the focus, then the general and I could handle it in our own way."

"But Jack, judging by the way the Alliance seems to be forming ranks over this, I think you are underestimating the power shift possibilities brewing in this situation. By making it off limits you are focusing the world more keenly on these events. I know there are influences in and around this office that would like to play down the potential value of his strength, but I feel we may just be on the verge of a volcano, and if this causes the top to blow off . . ."

"I know how you feel, Sam. Sorry, it's done, and you have no choice. Just do your job, which you do better than anyone, and tell everybody out there to keep it cool. This is my city; I make the rules. This is working out just the way I anticipated. We are at the eleventh hour and everyone's uptight. So now, I'm going to act like I'm conceding something. Tell them that I will grant a feed out from ABCNN so they can broadcast with their own sponsors, but they get no coverage of their own. Now they'll feel like they won something, the transmission goes out all over the world, but it's still under our control."

Sam pauses with just the right touch of rebellion, mixed into his unconditional and certainly unquestionable loyalty. "As always, Jack, you are the man. But may I indulge you with a little sidebar of my personal concerns? Even though this is your city right now, I think this thing has the ability to easily nosedive out of everybody's control." The phones hang up on both ends.

Several feet away, a grim General Pellet hangs up his extension. He looks at the mayor and monotones, "It is a different world one moment after the next, and that's why we do what we have to do."

"Now don't you get me started, Rodney. You and Sam are the only people left who know me from way back and can talk to me in earnest." Storm smiles like a kid for just the briefest second, then returns to the profundity in front of him.

"There aren't many who are left alive from back then, Jack."

The two most powerful men in New York sit motionless, silent, each immersed in their individual universe, gunked into some wordless glue, just watching their personal ghosts flit on by for the briefest uncomfortable gap.

Pellet broke through the frost now forming around them. "Don't worry, the brownout is sound. I will make it work. Like you said, we are giving the world the coverage and the commercial time they demand, just keeping it all under our control so it doesn't become a circus. No one knows who this dude is or even what he looks like. Or most importantly, who he actually works for. These writings of his could all be coded messages that will kick-start the jihad all over again. They could be a signal to the sleepers of al-Qaeda or Hamas or, just as bad, activate the Born Again from the Rockies who'll try once more to purge the world of sinners with their own sick form of redemption. You have to exercise your right of control in this case, Jack. Besides, if we had let them in, the security concerns at Rikers would have gone over the falls."

Storm rises to the surface from his inner dialog. "All of a sudden you are concerned for this man's safety? All month long I've been trying to keep you from turning this into another Dallas 1963."

Pellet smiles without being glad. "We have to prepare for every contingency, Mr. Mayor. That is why I am alive today. That is why you are alive today."

The phone rings by Pellet's desk and he picks it up. Sam's voice mutters laconically from out the earpiece, "It's for you. The president of the United States. On line five."

Pellet barely reacts. "Tell her I'm busy and to call back later." He hangs up the phone.

A chill runs through the room and up and down Jack's spine as he turns his eyes to an ebony picture frame placed in full view by his main personal monitor. He reaches for it and holds it by the tender edges. The picture is of him, a younger man, standing next to a beautiful dark woman with long straight black hair, holding a brown newborn infant. In the background with his arms around them all, smiling like the cover boy for Grandpa Magazine, is the very proud and beaming Theodore Roosevelt Storm. All four caught motionless in this singular slice of time, forever alive together in every dimension except one.

* * * * *

8

Rodney Pellet was officially New York's chief of police. Which was positively, a misnomer de guerre. Besides, he derided the title. As touted as they once had been, the NYPD had now become a useless burden, degenerating into a union of impotency, without the muscles or balls to enforce the rules a post-nuclear war society imposed upon itself. They were vestigial at best, and the city could not afford a distended company of corpulent traffic ticket writers, who were simply unable and untrained to deal with the massive social problems of the new world. So, when the army privatized its operations after the decentralization of the federal government, the city hired them for its defense against all its enemies—the terrorists from abroad who demonstrated time and again their hate upon the inhabitants of the Big Apple, and from the terrorists within, not so common criminals who did almost as much damage without having to come so far. Therefore out goes New York's finest, in comes the First Army under the auspicious leadership of General Rodney Pellet.

Having known the mayor for almost all his life, the corporate media had a field day with Pellet's appointment and made it seem like a perfect fit. Even the jugheads on the Alternet let it slide because New York was in desperate need of some positive news after so many successive tragedies. Life was now different than the pre-bomb society that guaranteed the personal liberty Jack had worked so hard to perfect in the beginning of his career, and the guaranteed freedom that Rodney had sworn so true to protect. But still, it didn't seem right for the people to refer to him as "General," so the puppet press titled his position "Chief of Police", an unabashed euphemism that Pellet hated as much as he hated them. It was mandatory corporal punishment for any of his recruits caught using that name.

He swung his chair around in the operations room in the armored office and took a sip of coffee, watching Jack look at that picture. He knew that Jack really missed those three. Storm's mom died in childbirth, so he grew up as the only child of Theodore. Although poor, his dad raised Jack perhaps a bit over-indulged, attended to constantly. Jack could actually pause, take his time and collect his thoughts as he grew up alone with his dad at the dinner table. Theodore doted on his every word.

Being the youngest of seven brothers and one sister, Pellet grew up in a different way. Rodney had to scream to get any attention. His parents were amongst the last of the devout Catholics who didn't flee the church after the ongoing sex scandals. They had to work all the time just to feed the kids and were hardly ever around at home to watch baby Rodney. So, the general raised himself by observing his older brothers who let him tag along wherever they went. Thereby he came to his own conclusions about life, one of which was that he had to defend himself and those he loved at all times and at all costs. He learned that early on, and he learned it well. He instinctively knew how to attain power and keep it against all odds. That may have revealed itself way back on the streets of Brooklyn where the mystery is still unsolved.

Late one afternoon Rodney and two of his older brothers were chilling out in the park by the school, which was really an area of concrete and broken glass with a couple of netless and bent basketball rims. Kids of all ages always hung out there and that's where they learned the stuff they really needed to know to survive life as it actually was. That ill-fated day, a much older badass bully with some of his big-ass friends approached the three youngest Pellet brothers with the sole purpose of removing them from whatever pocket money they may have been carrying. Rodney, being the very youngest and too small, was assumed to have none, but he still had to be held back by two of the biggest of those assholes while he was forced to watch them knock his brothers bloody around the park. Finally they relinquished the five dollars and some change they had made earlier in the day helping out their landlord. It wasn't easy work cleaning up the mess in their apartment building's basement left by that the last batch of squatters. Just cleaning up the skuzzy shit wouldn't have been so bad, but the squatter's themselves were still there, and two of them were dead, the third almost. The smell was an exponent of awful and, when the last squatter who was originally assumed dead awoke from some unconscious condition derived from some designer drug, he became extremely agitated. The Pellet boys had to go into physical combat with a zombie just to get paid a few bucks.

All in all it was just a bad day. Worst of it was Rodney forced to stand back as some misanthropes from the hood beat up his beloved brothers. Everyone from school watched and laughed after they were ripped off of their very hard-earned cash.

Later that night, Rodney seemed a little bit distracted during dinner and a little distant while helping to clean up afterwards. When the rest of the brood wanted to watch old reruns of *Desperate Housewives* in the living room, he volunteered to stay alone in the kitchen and finish. He was always such a good boy; they didn't have to pay him much mind. After the show was over, Rodney was still in there, whistling while washing up the last of the dinner stuff and putting the dishes and carving knives away. He took a shower, after which he passed through the living room where they were all still sitting watching TV, and he said good night with the dreamy tones of a peaceful sleep already in his tired little voice. He slept so well his brothers had to drag him out of bed to get him to school on time the next day.

It was there they learned that the very bully who had harassed them the day before was found in the park stabbed to death so many times that his head and limbs were scattered about like so much gutter trash. To this day they never found a clue as to who did it. However, the Pellet brothers were never bothered by anyone again. And everybody wanted to be Rodney's friend, as the shine around his special talents started to glow.

* * * * *

At 6'4" Pellet was a bigger man than Storm. In high school he was a basketball coach's power forward dream come true. Great shot, aggressive under the boards, gave good fouls and had that x-factor that makes one man a winner and the other one not. To his classmates and neighbors he was like a cross between a gladiator and a god. He seemed destined to be a media star as an NBA marquee player, so his decision to go to West Point after attending one of the most dangerous high schools, from one of the poorest neighborhoods in the city, caused a loud consternation. Like Storm, Pellet had bigger dreams of his own than just hoops. In that way they were too much alike.

After graduation, they went their separate ways. As they excelled in life, they were able to keep track of one another and their individual accomplishments through the once ubiquitous media. But then the bomb and, like everyone else, they were scrambled up in the rampant emergency and ensuing chaos. This time they ended up on the same team, playing a much different kind of game.

However, in handling this Salem Jones situation, Pellet saw something in Jack he had never seen before. There were slight but noticeable variations in the processes going on within the mayor's usually very aggressive yet very reflective form of analysis and deliberation. Now he sometimes seemed to drift somewhere else, out of touch.

Jack put the picture frame on his lap and closed his eyes. Pellet took the opportunity and gently pried, "I'm assuming you are still in the process of what is called letting go? The place you go to in your intangible moral mind that includes Theodore, Anita, and little Bobby. That decision-making place."

"Twenty-one years is a long time." Storm glared at Pellet without hearing it in his voice.

"Exactly my point." Pellet glared the same way back.

"I can't believe you are bringing this up now. Don't we have far more important things to concern ourselves than my emotional past life?"

"If I didn't think it was paramount to this moment I wouldn't be bringing it up. Dwelling in the past might be affecting your decisions right now. So let's try to stick to the present, Jack, which is more than difficult enough right now."

Chilly winds begin to blow as Storm puts the picture back on the shelf. "This compromise, this arrangement we had to make to handle this sticky mess is the worst house of cards. I went along with the brownout for one reason,

Rodney—your counsel. No one else in the administration was for it. The North American Union is against it, as is every multinational that owns a piece of this city. And, my old friend and the most powerful general in the so-called free world, what is most important in my considerations right now is that my gut instinct, which like everything else physical and visceral in this world, is evolving. I am in the incredibly uncomfortable position right now before the starting bell of not being so sure. There is a reality here. Forget about what the Alliance thinks and wants. We all can hear the voice of the people as much as we try to deny the truth of what they say. From what I gather, they are crying out that we are playing this situation a little too tough."

"Well, considering the multiple, high-level ramifications of this event to New York City, as well as the incredible lack of information we have to work with, I still think we are playing it too soft. That, my man, is also why all my clients hire me. I don't care what the computer models say are the probable outcomes of the increased pressure on the present channels of distribution and control. I don't care if the possibilities forecast deterioration all the way to level red. We have already discussed ad nauseam what could happen if it turns out this dude is really another attempt by the jihadists to perpetrate more chaos and disorder here in New York. These guys don't go away easily, and they need no justification to go forward with whatever heinous plots they can conjure up. It seems that the havoc they brew is always directed right here at us in the city of our birth, and not out there in Singapore or Brussels or Minneapolis, where all this phony resistance from the Alliance is coming from. Believe me, it's politics all over again. I know that their cash is good; I know what they really want. They want me to do this my way, even while they're complaining about some breach of charter and broken contracts. It is the game they have to play to placate their populations while maintaining market flow."

"What a joke, Rodney. If we did it your way you'd shoot him in the head on the jailhouse steps as he walks out, even though by law he's a free man."

"Not me. I wouldn't do it in front of the camera. I'd make it look like an inside job."

"You would; wouldn't you?"

"If I thought it was the right thing to do to protect my city."

A dead silent standoff between the two most powerful men in New York. The cold wind begins to turn the room an icy blue.

"You know, the way I look at it, Jack, I was the one who compromised for you, beyond what I think is right."

"Good then, General. That will have to do. Everyone needs to stay firmly committed to the strategy that is now in motion."

"But where does that get us, Jack? We have no plan after eight o'clock this morning. At that point we are at his mercy. Where is he going to go? What's he going to do? Do you think he'll just saunter into the Plaza Hotel for a massage and a cocktail? According to your plan we are just going to give up control to this complete unknown alien and allow him the first move. Didn't we learn this lesson already? How much fallout can we handle, political or otherwise, from sitting on our thumbs and doing nothing proactive?"

"Come on man, why so melodramatic? You have the most sophisticated corps of military police ever, equipped with the most modern techno-detecto gear. He can't just disappear. So we have to wait and see. You are assuming he is guilty of something we have no idea what. I think he has paid his debt to society, and most people on the planet consider even that grossly inhumane, since he never committed any crime in his life. But more importantly, I perceive same vague possibility that you might want to deviate from our agreed-upon plan"

"As you evolve, Mayor, so do I. Let me remind you that this situation is a great deal more physical than pure philosophic sport and games for your legal and political intellect. People have been pouring into this city by the tens of thousands everyday because of his imminent release. What are we going to do with all this trash? We have too many humans clogging up the system already. The extreme danger, Jack, is that these people believe in him."

"I'm sorry about that. What people believe is something we can do nothing about."

"Oh, that's great. That's real sweet. What were the last few wars that we were lucky enough to survive all about, if not what people believe? Religion, my man, religion. Millions dead, millions more agonized by fallout, epidemics, and famine, all because people believed in some fanatic who was cloaked with the irrational and zealotic power of religion. I don't think the world can afford too much more religion."

"He does not speak of religion, Rodney, but of man. He speaks of how to live together, now."

"Jesus and Mohammed also spoke about how men should live together, where did that get us? Your logic does not change the fact that people believe in this guy as an answer to all the world's problems, the same way they believed in all those past prophets. I admit that in a purely theoretical and lofty kind of way, what they say isn't so bad but, when it is taken out of the metaphysical and put into practice by the believers on this inhospitable planet with its unequal distribution of resources, the problems begin. And because of that, violence and mayhem have progressed through the centuries. Religion has interfered with the running of state, to the point where we are now looking at an extremely biodegraded planet and the real possibility of human extermination, all due to some spiritual abstractions that no one has ever been able to produce even one single piece of concrete evidence to prove. Do you believe in him, Jack? Do you think he has the power to save the world?"

"No matter what I believe, he is entitled under law to leave Rikers Island today."

"These days things go wrong and laws get broken for all kinds of reasons."

"Not on my watch, they don't."

Ancient glacial ice scrapes against the moraines that border human civilities.

"So, what am I going to do, Jack, with all these hordes of hungry transients flooding into your city, and the millions more that could be expected in the very near future, that will come to join this charlatan in building his invidious and divisive church right here?"

"I don't have the time or energy to go over this again. We will have to take it one day at a time, because that's all we or anybody else can really do. You know what I do believe, Rodney? If there is any way the world can ever climb out of the crater we now find ourselves in, we are going to have to get back to a system based on laws and responsibilities. So, as the mayor of the city-state of New York, I insist its laws, no matter how debatable they may be, must be obeyed. As public servants, I expect you and me to carry out our duties to the letter of that law. That's what we are here to do. I can't suspend the brownout now, even though I wish I could. So you got that, but the world is going to get a chance to see Salem Jones today. We need to try and engage this man in meaningful discourse to find out what it is that so many others already see in him. Then we are to try and make whatever that is into something good for this city-state and the rest of the planet. Let's just keep our heads level, stay on the common course, and see this through."

The glacier groans again and large chasms crack as it moves inexorably further towards the future, crushing all matter beneath its lifeless mass.

General Pellet stands strong and silent against the cold, salutes with numb cordiality and about faces out of the operations room, leaving Jack alone in the arctic frost of the armored office with his convictions not as perfectly frozen as his preferred, ebony framed, digital moment.

* * * * *

9

December 22, 2047. 6:30 a.m.

A well-dinged Hummer 6 hobbles down a torn-up and deserted garbage-strewn street. Like a battle-scarred, wily, armored beetle that's missing a leg, it limps around burnt-out vehicles and broken police barriers. Not even the sprinkling of the season's first snow, like a sugar glaze, can confectionize the evidence of neglect and decay. The Hummer comes to a halt at a mound of debris blocking the way.

The black man riding shotgun shouts to everyone else riding in the customized SUV, "Look what our freaky Salem Jones friends left us. She-yit! It certainly is a nice Christmas reminder that peace and joy are coming quickly to this material world of ours. Well, what are you waiting for white boy? You know the rules."

Herbie sometimes really can't stand that guy. Outside, in the wreckage, it is frigidly cold and forbidding. Inside, it is actually warm and pleasant and Herbie, who doesn't get a lot of either warm or pleasant, is remiss to relinquish it too quickly.

The interior of the vestigial flagship fuel guzzler was in direct contrast to its abraded exterior. The entire inside of the shoebox-shaped SUV was converted into a state-of-the-art mobile operational headquarters for ABCNN's New York City-State international news crew. With mobile transmitters and tracking devices to find satellites that are still operational, it could link directly through to the remaining worldwide networks—ABCNN, LA-Fox, the BBC and Al Jazeera. This made it possible to enter just about every home on the globe instantly but, of course, only with the Alliance's arbitrary blessings.

Even during those years of periodic war and disruption, the army of the faceless, with money from the corporations, kept figuring out how to keep everyone online. But after the first generation of half-life made it a little safer to move about, the Alliance cracked down with its heavy rules and regulations tantamount to full-scale autocratic censorship. A new wave of computer brains changed direction like a swarming army of attacking ants and, eureka, there evolved the Alternet.

Of course with their desire for complete control, the Alliance condemned the Alternet as subversive and made it a capital crime to be caught logged on. Whenever fresh talent appeared to give it a shot for the glory, General Pellet's touted Python Corps cracked down on their transmission sites, thinning the ranks of the alternative computer world's finest without mercy.

The real trick for the multinationals was just keeping the electricity on, because dead plankton still fueled the worldwide economy. They needed the oil to flow out of Arabia. That's why we fight, while those guys over there think it's about God.

"Do I have to hear myself say this again? You do know the rules boy, or you wouldn't be having this cushy sweet job that a brother deserves." Branford Hays is the middle-aged black man in the front seat doing the talking. His arrogance is derived from a projection of self-confidence. It is a confidence some coworkers believe is based on his own outspoken interpretation of things. But most don't think he really thought it all through.

"Yo, brother Bran, go easy on him. The sun hasn't even risen upon the land as yet. This should be a gentle time for reflection, blessings, and prayer." Jerry Gordon is the glue that keeps the crew together. As the experienced producer his main function is really to do just that. He is a portly black man in his early fifties, with the air of an absent-minded professor. Considering the extent of cynicism he confronts every moment of every day, one is astonished never to lose the sense of a jolly old soul when being with him.

"With the way this white trash ain't moving, this morning's sunlight, prayerful or fucking not, is only going to shine on him in places even its reverent self don't want to see. I advise that he just get out and move that pile of shit those hippie fags left in our way, and now! Cause, we in here have got a rendezvous with stardom. Ain't that right now my sweet, young thing?"

In the back of the Hummer 6, Maria pounds intently on a laptop connected to a couple of digital video devices, trying hard to avoid confronting Branford's explicit racism and sexism. She knows Herbie is waiting in the driver's seat for some justice she is not going to deliver. So she lets the status quo cruise for yet another while. "Go ahead, Herbie. We can't be late for this. The mayor lifted the block and says we are going global with the live link, just like we were hoping he would."

Herbie sits back for a moment and reaches under his seat for his gas mask. He takes his time to put it on, adding emphasis with a prolonged adjustment. He pulls on his disposable protective gloves with slow care and concern. Finally, with an amplified groan, he steps out into the caliginous puddles of industrial ooze hopscotching the oily street, slamming the car door behind him a bit too hard. He begins to pull the twisted pile of dreck from out of the way of the vehicle, occasionally glancing back through the windshield with an uncamoflaged look of resentment.

Jerry takes a bite of his doughnut and a sip of his coffee. Considering how many times in his life he has done that, it still registers a visible sense of joy on his erudite face. "You might go easier on him, Branford, because if he don't, and he should, I could bring you up in front of the Union Bias Board someday."

"And what civil rights of that insolent honky did I trespass upon, other than to recite what he is supposed to do according to his job description? White flight my ass, try white stampede. It's brothers that run this city. It may have taken a little time and an atom bomb, but now it's our show, for better or worse. Exception being, of course, for the fat-cat Jews who are still getting rich from our hard work. So, I'd take that racial bias summons and run it so far up your fat Black Muslim ass, you'd need dental floss on Ramadan to get the paper shreds out of your teeth. Hah, me, racist?"

"Yo, Bran, both your bosses, Marty and Ira, started out as interns years ago and worked very hard against all odds to merge the two networks so that it would survive long enough to give you the work you do to get you your Emmys and set up your family in a very fine lifestyle, which I remind you ninety-nine percent of this city-state would think nothing of slitting your throat for. So, a little appreciation maybe? And Jeez Looeez! Why is everybody so sensitive today? This could be the biggest event we ever covered without a body count."

"Doubt that, knowing the general." Branford looks over to Maria. Maria looks over to Jerry and dramatically rolls her eyes just a bit too far forwards towards the front seat. Branford enjoys the sarcasm. "I just love this girl, and she knows it, too. But, who do you think loves her the most? I'll give you a hint. It's because of her chromosomal good fortune to win those high cheekbones in the genetic luck of the draw. That's right, it is my camera that loves her the most. Notice here the operative word being "my." Since I'm the chief of this crew and all the back-up units in the NYC harbor arena, and since I personally report to our good friend the kindly General Pellet himself, you are going to have to put up with my continued freaking disbelief. And, Jerry, you can just kindly please keep your phony, liberal, Islamic ass-kissing producer's mouth shut back there. Miss Superstar needs to finish her homework so she can go get the hottest interview of this sorry-ass decade and jump on a fast plane outta New York so she can keep scrambling as fast as she can up that corporate network ladder."

Maria measures Branford with her eyes. "Oh, so it is 'my' that's the word of the day, huh? I'm impressed that you would pick such a big word with so many letters. Oh, my. Oh my, my, my. Well, try this out for a 'my.' Like, this is my gig, my scoop, and my beat. You know, this is the story I've been working on for months, assigned to me personally by Marty himself. So, if you'd rather be somewhere else, where there is more of a possibility of a body being torn apart, making for better video than a simple civil ceremony with earth-changing potential, please act like a professional and keep it to yourself. I told you not to eat sour grapes for breakfast when you're going to shoot 'my' story."

Through the mud-splattered windshield, Branford's silent chortle seemed swine-like. What's new? Herbie thought, the guy is a pig.

"My ass, sister, there's no way I'm not doing this

so-called simple civil ceremony. With the brownout effective, all the brass are gonna be chewing their fingernails looking at this charade, shot through my camera lens. Besides that homo Hebe, who thinks he owns this network, don't know shit. Pellet himself chose me personally for the honor of being the only cameraman to shoot this bullshit. So, I guess it really is 'my' show, darlin' girl, all mine."

"Would it be too lame to interject that this show is really for the whole world, and we are privileged to have the honor to report on its happening?" Jerry injected, always ready to compromise for the sake of the team. "Look, we're going to be there in a few minutes and most of it is out of our control, even the exact spot where Pellet ordered us to set up the broadcast."

"Who cares?" Branford shot back. "It's cleared by him and presented on a silver platter to us and no one else. It's obviously the best location to be. What else do you need? We can see Maria, we'll be able to see the prison, and we'll show and tell the whole world today everything they need to know about Mr. Salem Jones. It will be his coming-out party, the little queer, been sitting in prison with Bubba and the gang his whole life, nowhere to go with the little tube steak but each other's poop chutes. I can't believe he got no virus. If anything he must have the worst case of hemorrhoids. I wonder if he's gonna be walking funny." Maria cringed. "But it don't make no difference, my homeys, I still say we're living in the Dark Ages making gods out of ordinary people just to lift ourselves from the despair and drudge of our own meaningless and miserable existence. You know what I mean. Celebrities. It used to be movie stars and rock stars, now it can be just about anyone and, in this case, no one anybody has even seen before."

"No sense in cynicism. Especially for things you don't know anything about." Jerry dared to drop that in to try and soften Branford's tone in front of Maria.

"So, Mr. Producer, you have a special enlightenment thing that the rest of us can't comprehend?"

"It's about submission, you moron. You have to learn to be happy with what you have, with what you were given. It is written."

"Written? One man's gospel could be another man's cynicism," came Branford's quick retort, "It all depends on whose got the cash."

"Now that's actually the stupidest thing I've heard you say so far today," Maria interrupted.

"Excuse me, Miss Born Again and Again. But what did your boy say about the unequal distribution of ideology?"

"Actually, he has written about the lack of balance between spirituality and science." She tried to answer without looking at Branford's misogynistic provoking leer.

"Oh, I got it wrong again. I guess I'm just the seed fallen upon hard and thorny ground. So, what do I have to do now, Maria? How many Hail Mary's do I got to say to save my penitent, shamefaced, sinning soul?"

"It's hard to say, big guy, but you can probably start saying them today all the way to judgment day, because your flaming ass is sure headed downtown to that big old barbecue at the end of the world."

"Amen that, sister." The moment of mutual respect lowers gently upon them all. Jerry with relief pulls a jelly doughnut from the box.

Maria breaks the brief peace. "Listen fellas, this might be the biggest day in my life, maybe all our lives. If this guy is anything remotely close to what reports say he's like . . . "

Branford couldn't help but interrupt. "Baby M, I truly hope you ain't starting to believe this shit you're reporting. I mean it makes for a good story and all, but doll face, it is the middle of the twenty-first century and we haven't seen a sign from the Big Guy in over two thousand years."

"I don't know about that." Jerry had a quizzical expression as he wiped some powdered sugar off the corner of his mouth. "It all depends upon where you look, my faithless friend, and if you are willing to see the signs. You see, Muhammad wrote a book that was recited to him personally by God, and that was less than fifteen hundred years ago."

"And that's what he said. Big deal. You know what I say, prove it. Whichever way you chop it, two thousand years or fifteen hundred years, what's the difference? If God is real, where is he now when we need him the most?"

The driver's door to the Hummer jerks open and Herbie climbs inside, a rush of cold air following him in. He pulls off the rubber protective gloves now slimy with mung and throws them back out into street. He slams the door shut again and turns to his crew with gleam in his eyes, "Yucchh."

* * * * *

10

The prisoner's dining hall is filled with the aura and splendor of a magnificent ancient stone temple. In the center of the room is a single oblong table, and seated around it are men of all shapes and sizes, colors, and races, sentenced to life without parole in Rikers Maximum. Most have committed crimes of inhuman caliber upon their fellow citizens, but now their faces are awash in a humble and pious golden glow.

Salem Jones emerges from out of the shadows near his cell. The former criminals rise to their feet in unison, lowering their humbled heads before him. With slow intention, one by one, they approach and mumble something in his ear, each his own, tantamount to a prayer. They embrace or kiss him on each cheek, and then allow for the next to make his benefaction.

A dark man in his sixties named Esteban speaks. "Unfathomable for us to think what it would have been like here without you." The men murmuring an assent in unison, rocking some of them on their feet, sole to heel. "Our souls were devastations of the spirit and we knowingly and willingly danced with the devil. But we were never forsaken. Raising you from infancy has been the greatest beatitude we could ever have hoped for in this life."

A bald man with many tattoos named Lucas spoke next. "I was sent to this prison on trumped-up charges. The DA needed to stick something on someone to make it look like he was actually doing something good. I looked the part, so I was their man. Needless to say I was bitter. I was a human sacrifice strapped to the top of a pyramid waiting for his heart to be plucked out for some pagan god. Then you came, a miracle to us all. I don't know much, but I know this. My life now has a purpose, there is a reason I am here."

A short, grizzled and bald old man with a patch over one eye and many scars followed next. "It's time. As wherever you go, so go we." This man called Gino grabs Salem by the shoulders and they look deeply into one another's eyes. He hugs him like a brother and stands him up at arm's length. The others wait, expectant, looking up for some words.

Salem's mouth is quiet but his eyes well up with tears, like water bursting forth from an ancient stream running in the green hills of the Galilee.

* * * * *

The early morning light, diffusing in through the twenty-first century smog, made the emulsive air suspended over the entrance to the prison look particularly poisonous. Solid waste particles of a carcinogenic industrial product used to heat the penitentiary floated over the huge crowd that had been forming all night. With only a few minutes to go, they spilled out of the parking lot in front of the seldom-used front entrance of the Rikers Island House of Detention.

A garrison of the First Army surrounded the already agitated mass of devotees. The soldiers were armed to the max with the latest mob control gear, including their interlocking titanium shields with stun guns turreted to the top. Snipers with readied high-powered weapons stood by on enjoining roofs but out of sight, a concession the begrudged general acceded to facing the mayor's intransigence.

Pellet's position was near the front door of the prison's administrative wing, just outside the frame of anything Branford's camera would be shooting. He hand-picked Branford Hays for this gig because he knew from past experience the cameraman would follow his orders no matter what happened, unlike other members of the press who thought it was their duty to disrupt his work with some sudden childish and troublesome impulse to search for the truth, whatever that was. Pellet's was the best spot to see everything and still be out of the way. He had the latest communication tools in place, and from this direct vantage point he could call all the shots. His aides, as well as the mayor, argued against it as too risky, but it was his style. His troops knew that and respected him for taking chances and risking his life in the same way he often asked them to. It's where his leadership started and the loyalty to him never ended. What they didn't know was that, although Pellet looked like he took risks, he never took them by chance.

His almost-invisible mobile phone buzzes. He pats his ear to answer it, and looks at his watch, 7:55 a.m., December 22, 2047. Five minutes to go.

Approximately fifty yards away, on the west side of the parking lot leading up to the front steps of the prison, Herbie stumbles while carrying a heavy conical metal device and bangs into the side of the Hummer. Branford, who is cleaning the lens to his camera scowls at him, unable to resist any opportunity to deliver his distinctive condescending brand of social grace. "Where you been with that hook-up, you worthless piece of human shit. The whole world can't wait for your pokey white ass today. Damn, it's not even eight in the morning and this amigo has already got the shakes. I bet he don't buy those anti-hangover pills because he don't want them to show up in his bioread. Don't make a difference, you can smell the alcohol metabolizing out his skin from across the street. There he goes just grinning like an idiot and bumbling through another day in paradise."

Herbie just gives him an even harder grin as he sets the transmitter on the camera tripod and connects the antenna. He adjusts the controls manually as he has hundreds of times before, bypassing the auto locate, which takes too long. In a business of deadlines you take any advantage you can get. But he didn't really care about all that. To him it was just a distraction, a daily amusement, to find which satellite in the sky the Alliance left hot today to carry the broadcast. It was a game he played not with his technological toys but with his intuition. The Alliance knew there would always be the hackers who try to piggyback onto his signal with their own desktop broadcast, trying to angle some defiant message through their connection onto the Alternet. Indeed a suicidal game for them, because once they latched on to a signal they would always be found, and the squirrel killers would easily dispatch them off into the great ham radio heaven in the sky. So by not giving any techie geek extra time to hack in, Herbie felt he was actually saving innocent and important lives by patching in as close to the broadcast time as he possibly could.

His fluid hands glide like a pianist over the multi-buttoned and toggled metal black box, while lining up the vertices of the electric sky in his scope by eye. Confident, he punches the power button. The transmitter obeys and begins its scan for the only live satellite orbiting amongst the hundreds of others, and within a few seconds the three little beeps indicate the connection was made. Jerry, not smiling through this not-by-the-book procedure of Herbie's, appears greatly relieved when he hears the comforting success signal. "How do you always know how to find that thing?" his eyes going back and forth trying to discern the invisible thread of particles and waves flowing from the little black box to the unobservable satellite orbiting hundreds of miles away in the sky.

Branford almost pushes Jerry aside as he plugs the output of the camera into one of the transmitter's ports. "This better be good, asswipe, because we are going everywhere on the planet today that can still get TV."

"I don't build the freakin' network, big guy, I just carry the stuff around for your bitchy ass."

"Oh, listen to this. The boy talks. He exhibits such deep talent. What's up Herb, really, did they triple your dose of Prozac today?"

"Knock it off, both of you. We only got about a minute." Jerry wasn't really worried; it was just their routine. These two were always butting heads, but they were consummate professionals and never missed a deadline. "Give Herbie the remote and plug it in."

"Don't drop it, dickless." Branford hands him the wireless headbandcam. Herbie puts it around his head, while Branford plugs its receiver into the transmitter. He gazes around the outskirts of the crowd, peering into the distance, looking for crews stupid enough to get too close to the brown zone. However, the perimeter established by Pellet marking the out of bounds for competing networks was far away from the action, and even though Branford knew those crews were out there all right, their positions were so removed from the sight line they couldn't see anything even with ultra-digital zoom. For their sake he hoped they knew how easily they would end up as part of today's body count if they disobeyed the general's commands.

Although a big man, Jerry glides over to Maria at the back of the Hummer without making noise, all the time examining the screen on his biopod. She was finishing her make-up in the vanity attached to the inside of one of the back doors, now swung wide open. "Don't worry about me. I'm fine." Maria said without turning her head from her mirror.

"I'm not worried." He lied even though the biopod showed normal pulse and blood pressure for Maria, who was always a perfect specimen. "I just know how important this is to you."

"Thanks, Jerry. I really mean it. Sometimes I don't know how I could keep doing this without you and your support."

"Me? You don't need me. You're the star. I'm the company man."

"You're my friend, and that's not an easy thing to find these days."

Jerry just smiled, comforted by the thought that she was right on both counts.

"Oh, please, stop this cozy-ass bullshit. You two are going to make me throw up all over myself. I thought saccharine was outlawed last century." Branford, camera cocked on his shoulder like he was headed into hand-to-hand combat, pointed to a spot on a rise a few yards away where Herbie was standing holding the mic and the reflector. "I got just forty-seven seconds left before transmission, forty-six, so get your pretty package in front of this rig. I hope you got that opening down to less than three minutes, because that's when your young messiah is due to walk through the jailhouse doors that will be framed over your shoulder, just next to that snappy, fresh little multiracial commodity that surrounds your nose, which remember is still downstage of that microphone you hold with our ABCNN logo. At that point, my cherished, I zoom off your internationally coveted countenance, and the eyes of the world are completely upon him. God."

Herbie watches Maria flash ceramic eyes, like hot tile kilned in Castilian fire. But she stubbornly refrains from losing her focus and instead gives Branford a look that says why do you always have to be such an asshole. Branford just shrugs his shoulders and shuffles off to his tripod.

Herbie holds the metallic reflector at just the right angle to fill the shadow side of her face while scrutinizing her every move, her every nuance, with greater detail than he ever has before. He feels a queasy deja vu sensation burning in his gut of something much bigger than himself. Like a teenager driving cross country for the first time into the setting sun, adrenaline pumping with the optimism so belonging to youth, of anything and everything being possible. However, this now was so much more intense, because there was something different about Maria . . .

As the portentous red sun peeked over the garden-brown urbanscape of the East River, grazing the stars in Capricorn, signaling winter solstice and the unalterable return of the sun, a great golden light shot out of nowhere, and in that instant Herbie is volted in brilliance with Maria, transcended into a time-suspending wormhole where a direct connection to her essence put him at one with all the sustenance he needed to fathom the timeless secrets of the universe. He is caught in the most powerful of soft places, between the most spontaneous, perfect, and ingenuous moment of primeval being and Maria's eyes looking back at him.

He responds to this extemporaneous overwhelming karmic connection to Maria with an involuntary, subtle, but definite wink. Even with the most critical moment of her professional life just seconds away she fully understands that totally out of the blue she has had the singularly strongest and most significant feeling she has ever shared with Herbie, let alone anyone else in the world, and acknowledges him back with the faintest smile in return.

“Five seconds, everyone,” Jerry announces with authority. Their moment is broken and business as usual begins, but Herbie senses he’ll never be the same. “Four, three, two,” he points to her as she engages the lens, the red light on the camera flashing. Maria then begins the broadcast that she has been hoping for months was going to change her world. If she only knew.

“Good morning, world, live from New York, I’m Maria Primera. Today is a very special day, one for which we have all been waiting. Twenty-one years ago, inside this maximum-security ward of Riker’s Island Prison, a baby boy was born. Now the entire world is waiting to see him for the very first time. In these dramatic and, yes, very troubled times, when this world is so besieged with problems of extreme and dire magnitude for billions of people, you might ask why does the birth of one child merit the attention of a news hungry population? Well, on the off chance you have just arrived on the planet this morning and don’t know the back story of Salem Jones, let me present to you a short but compelling chronology of a man whose entire life has been secluded behind these prison walls. That is, of course, until just a few short minutes from now. And please remember, almost all of the facts in this story are pure supposition. Because, no one on the outside has actually ever seen or spoken to Salem Jones.”

In City Hall, Storm is engrossed on the main monitor on his desk in the operations room. Maria’s broadcast is in the little window he has placed, by his preference on the upper left, next to the spot he keeps that picture. The other monitors are dark, New York having declined to participate in the live videoconference with the member governments of the Union of North American City-States, and Microsoft-Digi/Bell. Under fire you keep a low profile. Nuclear blasts, radiation, epidemics, gang wars, famine, drought, you know what to do. But this . . . ?

Pellet stays in the shadow of the prison while he studies the areas around all the key positions, half-glancing at the broadcast on his wristwatch, listening to the feed that is mixed into his phone lines from each of his squad commanders. These boys, the ones he trained himself, the cream of the elite, the squirrel killers, like to know that he is there with them. So far, all is going as planned. If it continues to go well this is one big problem that will be over in a few minutes. But why did Jack have to make it so difficult at the end? He'll have to be worked on; he needs to come around, or else? In the distance, through his P12 multitasking sunglasses, he briefly zooms in on the newscast. His feeling of control is omnipotent, but he spent too many years in combat, in the mountains, in the desert, to take anything for granted, anything. His experienced eyes continually scan the scene for any sign of any trouble. Cities make him far more nervous than the country. There are many more contingencies lurking. But the intense firepower waiting to be unleashed at his command with just a single syllable will always take the day. Even though unpopular in this jaded period of post-Exchange, at least that gives him the time to prepare for the press conference afterwards, not them.

"Salem Jones began life here in Riker's Island some twenty-one years ago today, no one knows exactly when, but the word on the street says it was on the day of the infamous Jersey City bomb. Ironic that a soul which is known to be so connected with peace and harmony in this life, could come into the world on a such a nefarious day so recognized for immeasurable horror."

Jack inadvertently blinks at the picture in the frame

on his desktop where his family lives. Death, of what ilk are thee?

Herbie keeps his headbandcam pointing at this beautiful woman that he has been working with for years everyday but, because of his moribundity, had hardly noticed before. Even so, with his senses now more acute than ever, he can't keep his eyes from darting about the crowd, until he stops with a chill. Some creepy black-hooded figure is staring back at him with his arm outstretched, pointing a gaunt finger his direction. Herbie blinks in surprise and it's gone, melted away in the crowd.

Branford keeps his camera steady on the tripod, Pellet's voice reassuring through his phones only. This is a peach he thought. Nothing to it but a big fat payoff and the top shot at doing it again.

"Shortly after that world-changing disaster, our now famous mayor, John Kennedy Storm, declared by executive order the North Atlantic Alliance Penal System Privacy Codes, called simply Code 7, which refrained the media from any access to inmates that were incarcerated for crimes of multiple murder and terrorism. A direct evolution of the Son of Sam laws. This complied with the former Office of Homeland Security's landmark ruling quarantining the contagious in former public spaces. After the re-configuration of the federal government, the mayor's mandate was upheld by the city-state's highest court of appeals. In essence, these popular laws abrogated many of the freedoms that used to be guaranteed by the Bill of Rights. It is because of these legal restrictions, that no one outside these fifteen-foot concrete walls knows what Salem looks like."

Pellet hated hearing that. How easily laws made with the best of intentions can backfire on you.

"Today, when he steps through those doors, with the protection of the First Army, under the command of the chief of police, General Rodney Pellet, we will have our first glimpse of the man known for the revolutionary spiritual writings that have surfaced all over the globe."

"What we know of his life is scant. His mother was a convict, in for burglary and prostitution as well as a drug addict with HIV-7B, the offshoot sibling virus evolving out of the cocktails of the prior decades. HIV-7B had changed all the theories of DNA mutation, which of course changed quickly again after the blast. This type of AIDS is considered incurable, terminal, and can most likely be passed by mother to child through the birth process. His mother died shortly after childbirth and his biological father is unknown. Because of his disease, diagnosed robotically at birth, no one expected him to live more than five or six years. So, according to law, and because of his contagious condition, Salem was condemned to stay in prison for the entirety of his conjectured short life. He was placed in this ward behind me with the male inmates convicted of the most horrible crimes against humanity. It was essentially a death sentence by the authorities at that time."

"Apparently, however, these murderers and terrorists, warmed by the infant, became his surrogate parents, raising him as their own son, right there in Rikers. Instead of Salem growing sick and dying, the mandatory yearly health reports gave no signs of negative indicators. Quite the contrary, physical, mental, and emotional scores on the IQ/PP tests were extraordinarily high—off the charts high. Obviously the expectations of his imminent demise were erroneous. Health officials then noted an almost unbelievable reversal amongst the prison population in which he lived. In a group that throughout history has shown a greater percentage of infections caused by airborne and fluid borne viruses than any other modern population, the Center for Disease Control found a complete and total eradication of any disease leading to death amongst the population of inmates living behind these walls. That to many was considered his first modern miracle."

With less than a minute left to go, the crowd is vibrational in anticipation. With a subtle but discernible tension, the troops begin defensing, not so much in posture but in intention. Pellet on the horn, in every soldier's ear, guiding, inspiring and leading. Keeping one eye on the newscast on the screen embedded in his sunglasses, seeing no change there in the all-important frame.

Jack, in the strangely lonely armored office picks up a desktop phone and hits one button. Sam pulls away from the high-def wall in the operations room and spins to pick up the receiver buzzing and blinking on the oval conference table. "I'm zeroed in, Chief."

Herbie's eyes keep dancing around on the crowd, now morphing in color and pattern, people in motion in ways unnatural. Looking for the unusual, looking for a sign, yet he can't stop his focus on Maria, backlit by the rising sun highlighting her thick brown hair with gold.

"Now lately, and maybe most meaningfully, there are reports and sightings of writings and literature on, of all things, paper, surfacing even in remote corners of the world, the words of which are attributed to his teachings. The writings are simple, pure, and inspirational in a multicultural way. Uncanny, but the essences of these messages are communicated through universal symbols his believers swear they understand. Even though many printing presses and copy services have been raided by the First Army Python corps, every effort made by the multinationals and their armed forces to locate the source of this printed material has been in vain."

In one corner of the parking lot, a white woman in a black overcoat and work boots, with long gray hair braided down her back, stands adjacent to a titanium shield. She tries to turn around and, in doing so, pushes in too close to the soldier, who confused, pushes her back. From that spot of contact, the mob began to ripple and grow more excitable.

"In a world that most think is reverting back to the darkest of Dark Ages, Salem's words are giving people some hope which they might need just to survive. This phenomenon of a synchronized spiritual feeling has turned into spontaneous popular movements in regions all over the world. Now it seems, according to spokespeople of many of the multinationals, major city-states, and private armies, we may be seeing the rudiments of a worldwide movement coalescing in ways hard to predict."

A couple of Latino hotheads in the crowd start shouting. A few black boys next to them join in, pointing. Others in the crowd, Indians, stanis, Asians, whites, respond and kick up the amplitude of general chaos to another level. Maria's mic doesn't pick it up, so the world never hears it, but Pellet does. "Steady now, Hays," directing his cameraman, "Keep that frame. Keep your angle." He flicks a button on his watch, changing channels. "Look lively, boys, stay stern but calm, relaxed. You know what you're doing. In a real fight, nobody can measure up to us; we know that. You'll have your chance when I give the word."

"No place feels the physical effects of Salem Jones more than New York City, where hundreds of thousands of people have migrated over the last few months in anticipation of today's event—Salem Jones' release from prison and his first visitation amongst the people, both his followers and his detractors."

The mass was now moving in unison, wavelike against the perimeter. The soldiers stand obedient to Pellet's ultimate command, behind their six-foot-high titanium and steel mob-control shields, each braced to each other and the men behind them, making a wall of formidability. Even the heavily loaded suicide bombers were thwarted by these when they threw themselves upon them at the battle of Jericho, a few months before Jerusalem.

"Red Unit, take two steps forward, on my count, but do not move from behind those shields. This is to show we mean business, but that does not involve punishing people, yet." A click on his wristwatch back to see the broadcast and Pellet shouts, "Hays! Tilt your camera back up to that podium on the double or it's to Kansas with your ass."

Branford, mystified by his lapse of concentration and the drifting of his camera, pulls the frame away from the melee fomenting below and zooms in to the front of the prison. At that exact instant the clunky door to the prison starts to swing open and everyone just stops.

The planet paused and took a collective breath. The whole world, from the president of Euro-Bell to the lowliest nomad left alive in the Arabian Peninsula was watching what was happening on those steps at Rikers Island on their individual rectangular TV screens. Storm stared rigid. Sam tapped his fingers on the tabletop, the two connected only by the sounds of their breathing. Even Pellet took his eye off his mobile command screen and turned to see in person the mysterious, preternatural radiance emanating from behind the door. As this brilliant and mesmerizing white light spilled out onto the prison steps, Herbie had to glance up into the bloody sun, hearing high up in the gap of this supernatural silence a celestial soprano going up to its major third, and then its octave and down a sixth . . .

Maria continued her report as she, too, turned to watch history. She was thinking about that interview. "The light is so bright, you can barely see the warden on the podium, flanked on his left by dignitaries representing most of North America's city-states and regional confederations."

"Sam, where is he?" Storm said into his mouthpiece.

Sam shot back, "I don't know, Jack."

"I don't like this."

"Give it a second, Chief. Maybe he's camera shy. From zero to worldwide recognition in one second, that's tough velocity for anyone to get used to, even a twenty-first century super-shaman."

"The moment we've been waiting for is upon us, as the world now watches for Salem Jones to emerge from prison a free man." Maria more gasped than spoke the last few words because an electric pain zapped through her eardrums, and her voice disappeared to the whole world. Herbie watched her lips flap but her voice was out of his headphones.

"Where did she go, Sam?"

"You got me, Jack. This is now looking a lot strange."

"Damn it, what's going on?"

At that instant Pellet roars into his phones, and the soldiers advance. The crowd in full paranoia begins to flee from the prison, followed in pursuit by a moving wall of steel and a volley of electric shocks. People of all colors, sizes, and predilections were running in a panic that the worldwide audience could not see or hear. What they did see was a frantic warden gesticulating before the nervous dignitaries, and soldiers at the doors of the penitentiary with AK-87s combat ready.

Shadowy figures emerge from the ardent white light. One of them steps forth and with a calm expression studies the confused petty commissioners in front of him on the podium. They seem to say a few things to each other when something in the crowd catches his eye. He surveys the riotous scene with a sense of passion and looks back again at the men on stage. The inmate, bald and tattooed, says something to them once again and shakes his head.

Stepping back into the light, he retreats into the prison, and the doors start to close shut.

As the very important people on the podium look with confusion at each other, a rock flies from the crowd. It barely misses the warden and ricochets off the podium, signaling another level of bedlam. Arms and legs and bodies flail as the titanium shielding now bears down upon the crowd of believers with the full intent to cause pain. Defenseless people are caught in a vise of battering rams and tear gas billowing forth from the Mob Control units. People scream in anger and fear. Loudspeakers go off, booming orders to stay calm or else all are subject to arrest under every homeland security law ever enacted. Herbie blinks his eyes again and rubs them. What is that black-hooded man now pointing to in the back of the parking lot?

Then the gunshot. A little nine-millimeter bounces off the shields like a salivary spitball. In an instant many high-powered assault weapons in the hands of well-trained sharpshooters perched on the surrounding rooftops reply. Bodies are pierced, bones are shattered, organs are crushed, blood spills, and lives are lost. The silent TV image goes dead.

Sam goes into hyperdrive. "Jack, what's this? What's happening? Jack?"

Silence from the other end.

"Jack, are you there? Jack! Talk to me, talk to me, this is no time for that. Jack! Come back!"

The mayor in his icy-blue room is frozen like his digital picture, staring at vacant screens, fascinated by the jargon whirling around in his head.

Up by the bridge just past the parking lot, looking back upon the violence, Salem Jones pulls the collar of his long trench coat up to his ears to protect against the unnatural cold. He turns and walks away from the prison where he has spent his entire life onto an idling Q101R.

Taking a seat in the back of the otherwise empty bus to Queens Plaza, he heads steadfast into the chaotic and pulsating sprawl of New York City, on this the shortest day of the year of our Lord, 2047.

* * * * *

11

According to old Bullmoose there are only four rules in this world that you can always count on. Number one: nothing ever stays the same. Number two: everything is interconnected. Number three: you never know what's going to happen next. And, number four: there is no limit to the glory and the grace of God.

Bullmoose didn't give much credence to the popular scientific theories of the universe. He couldn't decide whether it was arrogance or ignorance that gave some so-called experts, by the logic of some abstract language invented by mathematicians, the authority to proclaim that the beginning of time was some fifteen billion years ago, when a theoretical big bang of absolutely nothing created absolutely everything in this unfathomably humongous universe of ours, all in less than a millionth of a second. He'd just grunt and say "Uh-huh, cool man." Then he'd ask, "So tell me, what was before that? And what before that?" If answered with a hypothetical shrug, he just reveled in the human mind being too small to comprehend the infinite and always.

Maybe it was that generation he was born into more than a hundred years ago. Another time, another

American war. Bullmoose did his part to avoid Viet Nam. He prevailed upon himself to smoke as much weed, drop as much acid, and engage in as much free love as possible to help protest his country's imperialism in Southeast Asia. In part, that's how Herbie's father was born.

It was during the second act of an outdoor rock concert at Watkins Glen Racetrack, when the skies burst open over the Allman Brothers, who had just lost their bass player on a highway near Macon, Georgia. The rumors about what happened to his head after the motorcycle hit the truck were hard to stop.

They found each other wandering in the mud soon after the downpour that turned hundreds of thousands of once-happy hippies into miserable, drenched, tie-dyed rag dolls. Innocent and unsuspecting, but wanting to get out of the rain, she led Bullmoose back to the Volkswagen van that her blue-blooded parents bought her as a graduation present from the Ethel Walker School for Girls. It was the first time either one of them ate LSD and they spent the evening finding out some very interesting things about each other. It was right around midnight, when the Allmans were jamming away in some furious fashion, that the unique double helix of DNA that was destined to grow into Herbie's dad was merged together with fervor. Herbie's Grandma and the famous forty-one orgasms. All purple.

The next morning, after an Oreo and Tropicana breakfast, on her way to find a place to pee, she saw Herbie's grandfather, Herschel Lipton, for the first time in the light of day. There he was off in the distance, with a halo shining over his head. Avoiding the long lines at the men's Portapotties he was squatting in the woods holding onto a birch tree for support, and dumping down hill so his crap wouldn't fall back into his tighty-whities. With a regal flair, he kicked some leaves over the evidence and sprinted off through the trees. She watched him cut across the racetrack, his long auburn ponytail blowing in the breeze, carrying with him his sacred and inseparable bong. To her, he seemed like a prince, no, a king, a king of the woodland wilds, a king bull moose, prancing eternal in his pristine forest.

The name Bullmoose stuck, but the man wasn't as constant. By the time Grandma found out she was pregnant, the relationship between the two had progressed into a deep mutual love destined to live forever but without the traditional attachments. Bullmoose was proud to have a son, but too young to commit to the responsibility. Not that he ever grew mature enough so that he could commit, but he certainly couldn't have then. Besides, he still had to become a rock star, because he knew that he and his guitar were destined to change the world in ways immeasurable. However, he did stay involved with his family, but more so as a grandparent to Herbie than a father to Henry, especially after the tragic sequence of events.

Grandma was unusual in that she never minded any of Bullmoose's random comings or goings. She actually enjoyed it, always letting him share her room when he was around, and never asking too many questions. Grandma didn't need any training in Buddhism; she was the original Zen master, one of a kind, no attitude, truly non-judgmental. She didn't have to get the enmity out of her heart, there never was any let in. When asked about her strange relationship with Bullmoose, she'd smile, shrug with a convincing moonstruck glow, and simply say that you can't be too careful with the ones you love. It was advice that was always on the tip of her tongue, funny because, with Bullmoose, she didn't seem careful at all. But for her it worked.

Once, when Herbie was a only a squeaky pre-teen, she showed him the scrapbook with the picture from the

1970s of Bullmoose in handcuffs being led away by a squad of policemen from the famous Fenway Park in Boston. It was an image Herbie could never forget, Bullmoose leering as if he were a matador basking in the glow of some bloody bull carcass.

Those being the days of the Curse, and Bullmoose being a true-blue Yankee fan living in the Red Sox Nation, he felt invincible even in their house, as he watched the Bronx Bombers take them apart that mellow summer afternoon when the world was so much younger and more innocent. Drinking a lot of beer and doing whatever drugs that were passed around in the hot sun, Bullmoose soon found himself at odds with some of the local diehards in the bleachers sitting near to him. These guys seemed to take great umbrage at something he said that hit a nerve not too gently, and retaliated in an appropriate way for inebriated Red Sox fans. They hurled him over the railing and he fell fifty feet down into the mezzanine. Somehow he landed unscathed on his ass in an empty seat near the first base line where he just stood up, cool, calm and collected, and without missing a beat, continued his harangue of the entire stadium. Especially its uncomfortable seating, which he could now attest to firsthand better than anyone, and most certainly the awful sour-tasting beer, which later he admitted he drank too much of, and of course the people, Red Sox fanatics, who he claimed looked silly in their flannel shirts in the middle of summer and smelled too much like patchouli oil. The next thing he knew he was on the field at Fenway running helter-skelter, zigging and zagging through the infield away from a swarm Boston's finest.

Hence, that all-American mug shot in Grandma's scrapbook of Herschel Lipton, King Bullmoose, tracked down upon the field of glory and being escorted to a downtown state penitentiary reserved for Yankee fans and other similar miscreants. There he waited patiently until a lawyer from the ACLU came with a barefoot Grandma and seventy-five of Grandma's single dollar bills for bail money. The singles were rolled up and bundled with a rubber band where they had been hiding behind the Graham Crackers that had gone stale months ago in Grandma's pantry. Her shoes were found nearby later the same day.

Right after Bullmoose's spectacular ejection from the stadium, the Red Sox rallied in the bottom of the eighth and went on to beat the Yankees, which started an end of the season comeback that led them that year to the American League Pennant. Bullmoose would always feel connected to that achievement. According to him, without that incident at the ball field that day, which obviously was the igniting spark to that memorable baseball season, none of the glory that happened to the Red Sox that year would have happened.

All this proved once again the four count-on-able rules of the universe. Number one: nothing stays the same, in baseball as well as in life; number two: everything is interconnected, evidenced by Bullmoose ending up as the most valuable player that season for a team that he was born to hate; and number three: you never know what is going to happen next, and for the Yankees there will always be next year. Most importantly, because Bullmoose was just drunk enough that day to survive being himself, it proved rule number four: there really is no limit to the glory and the grace of God.

* * * * *

Herbie was alone in the editing room with memories of his grandparents, now cold and gone, luckily for them before the blast. Strange that he was thinking about them after this unnatural, psychic day.

He took a long pull from the cool half pint to pass the time as the Intel chips did the math. Waiting for the hard drives to do their work, he began to wonder what Maria was doing right now. Today seemed to bring about a whole new way of thinking about things. As he washed down the last of the tequila with some lukewarm lime Coke, he heard the doorknob turn and the door to the editing room creaked open. Oh shit, he wanted to kick himself.

"What in the beJeezass is your cracker ass still doing here? I thought you'd be home tying one on by now." Not Branford, not now! "You trying to score some overtime brownie points from those Jew bastard slavemasters of ours? I always thought Marty and Ira kept you around after rehab just because part of you is descended from the same damn place as them. So Herbie my man, I've been ponderin', how many tribes of you guys were there back in Genesis when you first started out stealing land from the homeys? Twelve, right? Well, it is just too fuckin' bad that only ten got lost, cause then there wouldn't have been any of you suckers left to start that so-called holocaust in Germany over a hundred years ago. For that matter, there wouldn't have been a freakin' Israel to blow up and, by that logic, no fucking Exchange, and we'd still have a planet. It's always you Jews that keep fucking up the whole world."

Herbie ignored Branford only because it bought him some time. He made a big show of swiveling around on his chair in front of his editing console while depositing the empty bottle of tequila unseen into the open knapsack under the table on the floor by his feet. Branford was so caught up in his own ignorance he didn't even notice Herbie's.

"I thought you already took off for that radioactive slum you live in, white boy." Branford stared at him with his usual rancor, but Herbie detected a subtle hint of weakness in there, and he thought he knew why. So he called his bluff, staring back at him with equal toughness.

"I'm doing a little something, big guy, that might shed some light on this morning's mystery." Checking himself, he actually wasn't pissed off that Branford was able to take him by surprise while daydreaming about his grandparents. Maybe this will prove to be good timing.

Branford shoved his head into Herbie's personal space by the computer, intent on seeing the little icons on the screen. Each one indicated a video clip, a thumbnail of the podium set up at the entrance to Riker's Island.

"What the fuck? You're in my files, you dipshit asshole." But Branford had an uncharacteristic sheepishness creeping in to the sound of his voice, and Herbie, upon hearing the wavering sound, looked up again into his eyes and realized that there was some genuine guilt trying to hide in there. This added to the strength of the evidence he was pretty sure he was going to find in those complex equations almost finished compiling on his desktop.

"Wrong. I'm in 'our' files, Chief. Like in 'our' shoot, like in what 'our' team recorded today, like in 'our' transmission. I guess the question that is being examined is why the footage you shot this morning, while in and around all kinds of hell-breaking-loose, show nothing of that."

Branford stayed silent. Both of them watched the little hourglass on the screen flitter and jitter, until a rendered thirtieth of a second flickered on the monitor for an instant, displaying on the screen a still frame of the confusion in the crowd at the parking lot that morning. There was a burning white light streaming out from a partially opened prison door in the background. The computer went back to its number-crunching gyrations, and the picture disappeared into its electronic file.

"Wait a minute. What was that?" He looked at Herbie with a startled glimmer, which included the possibility of a surprising newfound respect. "That wasn't what I shot."

"I know, even though it should have been. I'm applying a little program I figured out in the past before the blast. It's a basic animation logarithm. Something they used to do for movies fifty years ago when they wanted to animate an object in a computer-generated universe. Granted this is much more difficult and time consuming, because it is trying to recreate a three-dimensional environment with interactivity, and with a whole lot less data." Branford was now looking dumbfounded, his mouth hanging open but no insults able to be emitted. "These results might look a little low res, but they will show us something very revealing."

Again, no Branford comeback, so Herbie stayed on the attack. "Basically, by putting together two different points of view, one from the video recorded by my headbandcam, and the other from your dumb ass camera, including the important few seconds when you drifted off the podium, this animation engine, with the factors I had built in, is able to predict and recreate in 3D, with a high degree of accuracy, the actual events that were going on in the riot, which you were supposed to be shooting."

Another dense Branford pause. They exchanged wary glances at each other, suspicious for different reasons. "So maybe now you can explain that to me. How did you miss that, Chief?"

"We were there to shoot Salem's release."

"We were there to shoot the news. The news means that there is no script or prefabrication of the actual events. We are professional reporters and are supposed to report what actually happens. Not what somebody who is paying you off behind the scenes wants to see."

"What are you implying here, big fella?"

Herbie pressed on. "We are supposed to work with

what is called professional ethics. But, I guess that's not the kind of news General Pellet had in mind. And don't look at me with those blank eyes. How did you become so incredibly obvious and stupid today of all days? I wonder what Marty and Ira are gonna think if they find out about this breach of conduct."

"Marty and Ira don't run this show as much as you think they might."

"Oh, really? This is getting more interesting by the minute. Well, how about Maria and Jerry? They may not be your bosses, but they are on your team. They already know how you left their asses out on a sling this morning. And you know what else I think? I think they already know who you really are, even if they haven't really thought about it."

Branford could not reply with his usual imperiousness, but tried. "No need to get sarcastic with me. Pellet gave me orders. You can't mess with him."

"No shit. You are really in this deep. All right for you, but I can't leave my sense of morality and professionalism out of this like you have. For my own personal curiosity I want to know what happened out there, because I felt it. There was something very unusual going on, but thanks to you, the empirical data is sketchy at best. However, maybe this little animation will help."

As if on cue, the computer suddenly beeped three times, signaling its task was complete. The screen blinked back to the desktop displaying a small window with video controls. Herbie reached for the mouse. "Waddaya think dude, want to take a look now or, would you rather keep your head in the sand, your ass in the air, and those butt cheeks spread open wide for your boyfriend, General Rodney Pellet?"

"Go ahead, I got nothing to be afraid of. Who's gonna believe all this shit anyway from a drunk like you?"

The interface was simple. Center screen was the

virtual video, which was the computer-interpolated version of the event. Around it were smaller screens from the actual sources and the virtual sources the computer had to construct to create the final three-dimensional version. The genius was the interactivity. The operator could change the point of view of the virtual cameras, thereby getting a full forensic three-dimensional perspective of a partially recorded event. The computer filled in the gaps. At least two real recorded points of view were the necessary input for the program to work and Herbie hoped Branford's unusual mistake gave him enough footage to work with.

He clicked the play button and the movie started. Herbie began the clip from Branford's original point of view, but with the perspective zoomed in as if it was originating from on the podium itself. On the center screen the doors of the prison were opening, with the white light pouring out. Some strange-looking men emerged. There was one in particular, patch-eyed and noticeably bald, who approached the officials. He seemed somewhat condescending but sincere in his interest to help them. He said something, but what it was would take many more hours to calculate. The computer would have to sift over and over again through the thousands of sounds that were recorded at the same time on the single track of audio, and then commit to the mammoth task of isolating what it was he was saying from the thousands of noise sources pinning the volume meter into the red. Herbie made a mental note to remember to do a re-render overnight to include that audio separation.

The man shifted his good eye down towards the crowd in the parking lot. Herbie hit a key and the point of view of the clip on the screen switched to a virtual camera turned completely opposite of that of Branford's, so it would match what the patch-eyed man on the podium was seeing. Although the image was a bit fuzzy, it was clear enough to be able to see a white woman in a black overcoat with long braided gray hair, staring the opposite way towards the back of the parking lot, absorbed, motionless, not looking or even caring about what was happening back on the podium. The people all around her were doing the same. They were turned away from the advancing soldiers and the charade going on at the front of the prison, and were facing the back end of the parking lot transfixed on something over there.

Herbie jumped on another button that gave him the virtual point of view of the gray-haired woman in the crowd. The computer showed a great mass of people frozen in their tracks, astounded and spellbound. Off in the distance, there was a small, but noticeable yellowish haze shining with a distinct glow.

Confused, thinking maybe it was a computer-generated error, Herbie hit another button and pulled the camera position far back enough to observe the entire scene in one lateral view. In the way back, up by the ramp to the highway, there was an unexplainable amorphic fog, radiating with an uncanny golden gleam. The computer froze.

The animation over, both men stood agape, staring at the screen, and made speechless by the weight of thought now blossoming in directions incomprehensible to their conscious minds.

On instinct, needing to change the space, Herbie stepped back from the frozen image on the monitor and over to the room's only window. Reality check. He glanced at his watch, 4:40 p.m., December 22, 2047. That was right. He looked around the room as if to make sure he was still in an editing suite at the ABCNN building on 62nd Street, one block in from Shantypark, overlooking the no man's land that separates it from the rest of the city. He was. Branford was there, too, standing by Herbie's desk, alternately looking between the computer screen and back at Herbie. He was visibly perplexed, disturbed, searching for some physical footing, looking for something to say out loud, to get back for himself the superiority and control he felt he needed to carry into each situation.

Desperate for some fresh air, Herbie opened the window and stuck his head out, leaning way forward into winter's first twilight, brisk and reinvigorating on the back of his neck. Branford, unwelcomed, followed him, poking his head out the other side of the same open window. The two constant enemies watched each other with monition from the edges of their periphery, the mist from their breath dissipating into the evening cold.

Nighttime was falling on New York, covering most of its major architectural scars with darkness, electricity outlining and creating sparkle and glitter to the obscured shapes of the injured buildings that in the light of day seemed so much more harsh and foreboding.

Herbie's common sense was trying hard to disregard whatever tricks the computer had created with the day's inexplicable events. Maria, the wormhole, the music, the fog, memories of Bullmoose. However, tonight, off in the distance, clear-cut and plainly manifest, suspended over the forbidden turf like a pillar of light, a well-defined yellowish fog emanating a soft golden glow was fixed in the air over some small patch of ground in Shantypark.

"It's just some low-level clouds out there, Herbie," Branford said, almost whispering, almost hoping, "just a lot of mist on the ground. Some damn fool in Shantypark must have gotten hold of some black market pyrotechnic junk and lit the shit up. Making everything look spooky."

Herbie stared at the distinct golden glow shimmering not that far away in the early winter evening. He was thinking how much he wanted another long stiff drink.

* * * * *

12

The twilight zone just after sundown always had a freakish holiday feel in Shantypark. To some it's the celebration of being one more day alive. To others it's the anticipation of the action and danger that nighttime provides. But tonight in Reginald Square, at the beginning of the longest night of the year, there is something else. Like an invisible breeze sifting through the trees, making what was left of the leafless branches whistle in the wind, like something new settling in.

At this time of early darkness, night which was still day, Reginald was filled with its usual; revelers, mendicants, hookers of all kinds and their pimps, the drug buyers and the drug dealers with their runners, and the makeshift kiosks of the black market, mostly boards supported by empty milk cartons. People bought and sold disks, batteries, cosmetics, disposable phones, and any other obtainable contraband smuggled in through the tunnels. And of course, there was the ubiquitous sick and the almost dead, beginning the nightly challenge to see if they could make it through to the next morning.

Several months after the initial radiation killed off so many, left thousands of others sick and scores of thousands of others homeless, one of the dying gasps of the federal government was to give states the rights to create refugee camps on public land. Countless homeless, infected, and those already terminal with the new strains of AIDS and bodily-fluid-borne cancers, flocked to Central Park and dug in. They put up tents and shacks and called it home.

During the first truce between the gangs and the city, Mayor Storm quickly formed the New York City defense team. Basically they were a ragged consortium of surviving city police units, National Guard, firemen, and sanitation workers. Through the mayor's inspiration and leadership, they quickly and effectively put up huge concrete and steel walls around Central Park in Manhattan, which at that time was already inhabited by thousands of the dispossessed. The barricades simply followed the old stonewalls that bordered the park for generations.

The walls were only a nominal symbol of division and restraint for the controlling criminal elements. The elaborate system of tunnels that had been burrowed under the city centuries before for the purposes of bringing water, power, and transportation to the municipality, were now used as underground passageways where terrorists could easily travel to and from Shantypark with ease. From within these tunnels they staged brazen raids on the so-called legitimate society for which they had great contempt. This created a new kind of homegrown fear, which over time grew in size and proportion leading to the second great gang war.

After the deployment of the First Army as New York's principal organ of defense, the violence was quelled when every building in the park was bombed into rubble. This led to the second truce, when the enactment of Code 7 made it a capital offense for Shantypark residents to be found outside the walls. The proliferation of biopod technology made it easy for the army to identify the perpetrators. The death sentence was quickly administered to those apprehended and without appeal.

These days the tunnels were used only for smuggling goods and drugs into Shantypark for sale on the black market. The known entrances of these tunnels were patrolled by squads of squirrel killers, but most of them had a tacit understanding and looked the other way, creating an underground economy that in its own corrupted way helped keep the peace.

Reginald Square was the area just north of the mall, right by the old bandshell. It was named after the gang leader who was one of the original founding fathers of Shantypark, Reginald Deforest, undisputed and self-anointed imperial gangster. He was instrumental in the turnover of control of Shantypark from the mayor to the gangs. He was a very bad man. But in his own sick, violent, perverted, and egomaniacal way, he helped Shantypark find a way to coexist in its own unique cultural diversity.

During the bombings, when those who wanted to survive bad enough had to find shelter underground, Reginald went on a violent murderous spree. Through brute force, a multitude of brazen grisly assassinations of rival gang leaders, and other macabre terror tactics he learned growing up watching the western media and surfing through the Internet, he was able to force together a coalition of gangs by establishing territories for each, thereby creating what is still the ethnic map of Shantypark.

He was killed early one morning by a jealous girlfriend high on smizz, who ripped his testicles off with her teeth. He bled to death as he slept while she tried to tape them back on. They named this de facto meeting ground and makeshift bazaar near the bandshell after him.

The loyalties within the coalition shifted from issue to issue, sometimes by popular will, sometimes by the wishes and vagaries of the individual gang leaders, and sometimes by the consensus of the Gang Council. This in turn kept the tension level in Shantypark as close to explosive as humanly possible. But in Reginald Square, this is where their turf touched, their elbows rubbed, and where their deals went down.

At this hour the gangs prepare for vigilance. They cruise through Reginald showing their strength, lighting up drugs, displaying automatic weapons, sizing up their share of the black market business going on, and making sure no one steps too far out of line. They pull up the collars on their winter coats, readying themselves for another night amidst the dying and the recently dead.

The one consistency of creation is continual change. Life in Shantypark for all its anguish and misery was no exception. But tonight, in the last fastly fading snippets of sunlight, there were some Shantypark residents in Reginald lifting their eyes to the sky, sniffing in some new and vibrant color that was blowing in the wind.

* * * * *

13

The final gasps of the first winter sunset reflected off the humpback storm clouds swimming menacingly in the sky. Disconsolate, Maria closes the drapes on her bay window, snuffing out the remnants of the day, and steps away from her beautiful view twenty-two stories high up off the East Side streets.

Her day was an utter disaster. Salem's no-show led to a riot, which led to the unapologetic, cold-blooded, and repressive modern-day version of riot control. Easy for Pellet to get away with this since society no longer had any official instrument in place for a legal review or even a reprimand. This allowed Pellet's unique rapid-response division, the famed Python Corps, to be brutally effective once again without recrimination, and this time even bloodier than most New York citizens would expect to have to tolerate. They responded with vengeance, leaving sixty-three dead and no army casualties. What was even more frightening was that the enraged mob at the prison was most likely just the tip of the iceberg worldwide.

Since Maria was the sole authorized newscaster on the site today, her report was the only one. It played again and again all over the globe, of course to over-the-top ratings. But after seeing the edited version she was embarrassed to be a part of it. ABCNN only showed her opening, cutting away to the podium when Salem did not appear. There was no indication of the pandemonium in the parking lot, or that golden fog.

According to Ira and Marty, who were the prime recipients of the profits, all was good news. Whatever happened to their idealism and their love of the esprit de corps amongst journalists in the heat of the hunt for a story? The only other video even closely resembling what happened today was a fuzzy slide show from some geeks on the Alternet who cut away to some of their shaky and fuzzy homevids shot from who knows where and how many miles away. Their audio track of some pseudo Salem gibberish was so garbled that even the Pythons wouldn't be able to figure out who made it or from where it came. Even then they dared not blog on it for too long, for the response would have been swift and terrible. Many a hacker was left with his guts spilled on the ground for hanging around a transmit site too long.

The weight of Salem's non-appearance was indeed heavy on all counts. In and around the recycled interviews of experts playing on the TV stations the Alliance allowed back online, the supporting story with the best ratings other than her own report from the prison was also out of New York. A rumor was circulating about an incident that happened in Times Square, of all places. Because of the intense security guarding this last glittering bastion of capital opulence, only the army could have gotten any guns into that sector. But somehow, this ostensibly crazy lady sneaks in under the radar with a wooden one-shot. Of course Pellet wouldn't allow any of the interviews from the eyewitnesses who swore to the story to go to air. But they all had said it was almost evangelical the way the woman, brandishing her virtual peashooter, preached the writings off a printed piece of paper as she was cut clean in half by multiple scatter bursts from the AK-87s. Squirrel killers.

Back at the ABCNN New York bureau, filing her report was worse than torture for Maria. It wasn't just disappointment over that exclusive interview with Salem that never materialized. There were those nagging questions about the footage that Branford didn't shoot, Pellet cutting her audio, and then the blacking out of the entire video transmission. And what was that with Herbie?

Nothing could be done or said now to alter the feeling of failure that controlled her every action and dominated her every thought. Failure wasn't a word she ever before associated with her career. Now home alone, she felt dysfunctional, weak, and at a loss as to what to do in her own privileged living space. Like a doting dog with no one home, lonely, in need of petting. This wasn't even that kind of a one-time failure, a battle lost, yet the war still able to be won. That kind of failure now seemed simple and easy to deal with. This was a failure of a far grander missed opportunity. The consequences for her life and the little plans she had for her conquest were now in the obscure realm of the unknown.

She needed to get out of this sorry, loathsome self. In her mind, she put herself in a scene out of the ancient soap operas still playing as reruns in most areas of Brazil between Sao Paulo and Rio when they had electricity. The ones she had the opportunity to view when passing by the monitors in the origination center, on the rooftop of her Lincoln Center offices, in the early days before her rise to prime time, when she video-jocked for different areas in Latin America, in between the global disasters and the subsequent brownouts.

Keeping in character, but with a far too dramatic flair, she opens a bottle of red wine and pours a glass, her luscious lips taking a sumptuous sip. The scorned senorita slowly turns her head towards the seduction that loomed, in an aspect ratio of 16 to 9, deep within the plasma of her desktop monitor, her gigolo feigning sleep, with steady sensuous breathing. Entwining her fingers around the bottom of her glass, she salsas across the floor to a spotless, polished desk. With a flamenco stomp she kicks off her expensive mules and reclines with attitude in her favorite chair, bought on impulse, overpriced in a Sotheby's low-radiation close-out. She savors some more wine. Out of her conscious control, her eyes lock onto the video-answering device, throbbing, chimera red on the seventeenth century imitation French country desk, bought as part of the set that had sat together in a fringe area townhouse for a long enough time until it was safe to take out and bargain off. The original owners now gone forever, relatives unable to be found. So many stories, so little time.

Did she dare or did she not? Torn between intellect and instinct, control and curiosity, she finds herself unable to resist. She hits the recall button on the machine. A brief relief as the first graphic page to pop up indicating the time, place of call, and the face of the caller, promised to be another round of syrupy support. Jerry's friendly face blinks into the speaker's window.

"I'm sorry to bother you at home, kid, but I do know your recognition codes. What can I say that I didn't already say a million times at the office, but I am truly sorry today turned out the way it did for you. However, on the brighter side, that doesn't mean it wasn't great news. Not only were the ratings on our live transmission a grand slam, but the reruns and follow ups are being demanded at all-time highs. Your agent will like those numbers, so will your accountant, so will Marty and Ira. Some say it was the most watched news clip of all time. Even more than Zapruder, or when Armstrong stepped on the moon. The estimates are that everyone in the world saw your face within five hours of the original transmission. Granted it's not your father's Internet, but in today's world it's outstanding. I know I'm showing off my fossil collection, because I do remember when it was instantaneous. Except of course for your boy, Salem, who's spontaneous and even with paper, which is wild, and in my opinion that should be your next angle, and immediately. Anyway, right now this mysterious disappearance is playing out to big-time exposure, more than we dreamed about, even if he cooperated and showed up to the interview to answer your questions. But don't you worry; you are still right smack dab in the center of it. That's why I'm calling. Contrary to what I know you are thinking, the word at the station is that Pellet had nothing to do with his disappearance, and supposedly that comes straight from City Hall. And speaking of the mayor, his office has been trying to reach you all day. So what's up with that? Please, get back to them immediately. I have a feeling this is big, and this comes from a friend as well as the producer of this show."

Unconsoled, she hits the pause button, freezing Jerry's face in an inopportune moment. The contortion on his lips and nose was much less than flattering. Maybe its time to change those recognition codes. She pours a new full glass of wine and takes a healthy draught. Jerry was a mentor to her in this business and still one of her best friends. He taught her how a person should hustle for what they wanted in an assertive yet patient way to get better than just instant results. His presence added a touch of humanity to everything she did. He gave her the sense of urgency to keep her performance more real than that hype tone of voice that every newscaster sounds like who graduates from Broadcast 101. Without his help and his trust, who knows where she might be today? Forgiving him, she re-hits the pause button, his face free to move beyond its last unlovely grimace.

"The squirrel killers are out there now, combing the city for him. Pellet promises results. Without any way of identifying him, they have to conduct a reverse search, canceling out the positive responses to isolate the negative contact in the outside population. In this growing city of over thirty-five million mostly displaced souls, that's like looking for that last drop of unpolluted water in the Atlantic. It's a quantum problem; just observing the event changes the outcome. So, as the producer I suggest you have a glass of wine," she takes another healthy swallow, "relax, and have a hot bath."

She scrunches her eyebrows; did he really say that? "Did I really say that? What dreadful oversight on my part, please don't tell Human Resources." Scrunch morphing into smile. "Most importantly, please take care of yourself. Tomorrow is another day. I'll see you bright and early. Remember, that's why it is called the news, because it always is."

That was too easy, even for Jerry. And, what's up with this Storm thing? What does Pellet really know? The reporter in her was now fighting back through the gloom and doom of defeat. Or was it the wine? Only upstate New York, but not bad for the only thing you can get sometimes. The distribution of goods was always a big problem, nowadays compounded by the Exchange, which changed the world forever. However, Maria was so young at that time she really can't remember what it was like before.

The next graphic page was also too easy. "Hi, honey, it's me. Daddy and I saw the whole thing this morning and can only imagine how awful you must feel. Not to restart any old battles, but you are working with prison people on this, not exactly reliable if you know what I mean." Ma, please shut up. "But we have gone over all this before, so I'll just shut up like I'm sure you want me to. I'm just calling to let you know we're here if you want to give us a call and talk, and who can you talk to if not your own mother? If we are not here you'll know where to find us. Love you, honey." Love you, too, Mom.

Maria grew up well. Sus padres eran pobres muy rica, from a long line of Caracas oil money, who got out before the Shining Path moved into the Venezuelan fields in order to avoid becoming somebody else's breakfast news headline from another regional terror war. "Please pass the Frosted Cheerios, honey, and did you see on the news that the Primeras and their two-year-old baby daughter Maria were slaughtered, then mutilated and decapitated by violent communist Taoists in control of the cocoa crop in Northwestern South America? Oí que rellenaron sus órganos genitales en sus boca. Sounds so bestial. Can you pass me the Lactaid now?"

The Primeras were proud survivors. With the help of her father's money and her mother's family connections, they succeeded in fitting into Miami, their newfound land of freedom. Just days after gaining U.S. citizenship, on a venture out of town to buy real estate in the panhandle, they survived the South Beach biochemical attacks.

At first it was so confusing, so many people dying in such a short, gruesome time. No terrorist group took responsibility, but Homeland Security broke it down to the Islamic Jihad operating out of Havana, attacking another international symbol of American decadence and sin. The Feds were always after Cuba and here was a way to hit it, hard. The way Washington was thinking, right or wrong, any reprisal had to be right. American justice reverted to biblical, and in the spirit of one eye for another, several hundred thousand Cubans, whose only defense was an old and useless vaccine stored decades ago by an impoverished Castro government, died grotesquely from a virulent re-engineered strain of smallpox.

The Primera family ended up this time in New

York with an intro letter from an uncle-in-law who had some friend. Her dad started to do well again, this time with a string of Volvo dealerships in the Tri-State area. Her mom enrolled her into the best prep schools and Maria was on her way. But everything had to change with a small nuclear bomb going off on the other side of the river, and as the epidemics evolved so did most parents.

The world was now beyond the point of simple cautionary paranoia, and became obsessed with viruses, and bacterium that cause disease. These included of course the pandemic mutations in HIV and those new nasty cancers that, after the radiation, became airborne and waterborne, spreading like rampant crabgrass in some populations. The advanced stages of contagion in certain communities led to an enflamed social crisis all over the U.S. and the world.

An entire new class of ultrarich arose, made up of people of all countries and colors who could afford to live as germfree as possible. They quickly reverted from the Saturday night society of the casual goodnight blowjob, back to the one that sacrificed virginity only upon an altar. Male or female, being chaste until marriage became the absolute ideal. No one with a real life wanted any micro-ganistic invaders to attack their body through their lips, skin, or genitals, from friends great or not so great, close, casual, or anonymous.

But most people didn't even have a chance for a real life, so the sexual behavior of the rest of society continued to mudwrestle in the Gomorrah-like gooze it is today.

No, it wasn't easy being ultrarich parents. The competition in society worldwide for untainted, healthy human product went to the extreme. People these days could not afford to make mistakes. Bags of bones could not hide anymore in hallway closets. The proliferation of the new biopods, which instantly analyzed and diagnosed an individual's health-related and blood-related factors using portable lasers, while cross-referencing the information against worldwide databases, helped cause the "anything goes and you can reinvent yourself at anytime" mentality to go up in smoke.

There didn't seem like much left to believe in to instill the desire to have children, especially after those few months of acute madness. But when the jihad simmered back down to a more regional and resource-based struggle, it was rediscovered that the human drive to procreate is just too strong, or at least the going through the motions part of it. There was actually a baby boom a little more than nine months after Ellis Island was taken out. Maria's mom always thought that made sense, but she was glad she never had anything to worry about with her daughter.

The video answering machine beeped and the next page appeared on the screen. First Maria saw the seal of the city-state, then onscreen the troll woman Vera blinked like a gecko.

"Miss Primera, I'm calling for Mayor Storm, but of course you know that, don't you? I'm sorry we superceded your right to privacy and suspended your recognition codes, but of course, all within the law according to the Cities Emergency Regulations. The mayor called a meeting with you at 7 a.m. tomorrow. I'm assuming you're going to be there so no need to call back to confirm. So, dear, please be punctual, we've heard about you."

She felt instant hate for that homely bitch. It was bad enough Maria had to listen to that surly voice, but she had to look at her too. The eyeball recognition technology utilized by the new security codes made these video answering machines insufferable.

* * * * *

14

Herbie fumbled through his two police locks and kicked open the apartment door. He flicked on the light and large cockroaches scattered when he banged the paper bag onto the tiny, greasy countertop. Bless that little agave cactus and the termination of its copyright, cause this magical moonshine was homemade right here in the Big Apple, and only by the best surviving Mexicans. Herbie went way back with this hood. Farther than that, he did not like to remember.

His wizened leather bomber jacket hits the floor, aviator glasses follow, landing nearby. Unscrewing the plastic bottle cap, the first odors tickle his nostrils tinkering with the chemistry in his brain. He puts the bottle to his mouth and takes a huge gulp. Swallowing, Herbie opens his mini-fridge and catches a half-finished bottle of Corona before it could spill onto the cracked linoleum. See, those old reflexes are still sharp as shit! He pours the remaining beer down his throat, chasing the tequila down to a place where it can do the most good. He grabs a crumpled cigarette from a twisted Lucky Strike pack, also hard to find, and lights it with the gas stove, using his free hand to keep his hair from singeing in the flame. He pulls an unopened can of Budweiser from the mini-fridge and kicks the door shut hard enough to hear the cans and bottles inside clink and clang. He grabs for the brown paper bag.

Settling on the dusty floor against the unpainted sheetrock, for the first time in years Herbie reaches for the old guitar propped into the corner. His fingers begin playing with the strings, hitting a note, sliding up an octave, picking back down a fifth, doing it again, making some already familiar music that appeared to him today, from where he could not say.

* * * * *

15

Maria watched the last little drop of Upstate Merlot drip out of the overturned bottle suspended above her Waterford goblet. She looked up at her Howard Miller antique grandfather clock as it gonged midnight. She would sleep a little later tomorrow, forego her usual workout to a head too woozy from sulfites. But she still needed to relax to go to sleep. Maybe that hot bath.

She puts the glass down in her stainless kitchen sink and walks to the bathroom. Turning on the hot and the cold, she pours aromatic bath salts into the tub, which is perched on a throne of marble and ringed by sconces that looked Egyptian.

She flips on the satellite radio already tuned to her favorite light jazz station, which is playing a sexy little walking bass and muted horn, the back beat undulating it along. In the soft light she examines herself in the full-length mirror covering one wall. She unbuttons her silk blouse, one of scores she has in her closet that are perfect for work, on or off screen, and tosses it into the hamper in the corner, genuine Brazilian bamboo. Without taking her eyes away from her own reflection, she turns three quarters to look at her back, lifting up on her toes the way Western women have been doing for years to show the shape of their extended calves and up perched butts. She unzips the fly to the skirt and lets it drop to the floor, revealing a beautiful behind uncovered save for a white lace thong hiding in the crack between her tush cheeks. The space between the tops of her thighs, the pristine target where all human creation takes aim. She turns back to the mirror and, in profile, removes her bra, cupping her breasts in the palms of her hands, rubbing the nipples with her thumbs. They instantly extend and become hard. Removing her hands, the breasts remain firm, pointing forward in maximal protuberant strength. She turns fully frontal and gazes at the curves from torso to waist to hips to knees, down through her rare, elegant calves to her long, delicate toes in French pedicure. Almost naked, the girl in the mirror is a complete knockout.

She turns off the running water just as the tub fills with thick, luxurious bubbles and steps in, the liquid warmth an instant signal to unwind. She sits down, removes her tiny panties, and drops them soaked upon the Costa Rican terracotta, soap bubbles rinsing over the hand painted dots on the tiled floor. Her eyes close, her hands reach for the trimmed patch of decorative hair above her vagina. She starts to rub her inner thighs and outer lips, her mind relaxing, her nerves unwinding, the radio now playing a soft celestial soprano skipping up an octave, and then down a fifth, and up another, and starting all over again . . .

* * * * *

16

Halfway around the planet, yet he could still hear the muezzin's plaintive air calling the faithful to their afternoon prayers. Wild-eyed men in black robes gathered by the bullet-ridden mosque, submitting themselves to their intractable version of Allah. On their knees, weapons at hand, they made ardent pray for their own martyrdom in battle against the infidel, their zealotic will exponentialized by the last few decades of religious war. A few miles away, nervous Christian soldiers in what was left of Fallujah patrolled their compound, awaiting the next attack.

No surprise that the Middle East was the flashpoint. The Arabs and Jews were at each other's throats ever since the creation of Israel. The ongoing mistrust and endless intifadah grew more murderous everyday. A Palestinian population was now in its own land but with an irreversible refugee mentality based on the extermination of its neighbor even if it meant their own. The Israelis kept doing what they thought they had to do, and received the first blow. The suitcase bomb, smuggled in from Natanz through the Hezbollah delegation in Tehran, was set off in downtown Haifa, instantly immolating scores of thousands and rendering literally dead the area from the city center outwards for almost a mile. The act of mass murder was conceived, planned and worked on for years, committed in a ferocious instant by a single man who believed he was on a mission from God, roaring towards his version of the hereafter on a flying carpet of high horror perpetrated upon the anonymous. This atrocity, the imams preached, will most likely win him far more than the requisite seventy-two virgins when he finally stands next to Allah and Mohammed, who'll surely be waiting for him in heaven to receive what's left of his incinerated ass. God is great.

The Arab world from Egypt to Indonesia was seen celebrating the annihilation in a frenzy of joy. There were so many horrific images of dismay broadcast for the rest of the world to witness over and over again. The western media made it look as if Muslims everywhere were dancing in the streets with pure jubilation over the cremation of so many Jewish bodies now melted into the rubble.

The shocked and bereaved elders of Israel could not hold back their monstrous grief and revulsion. In retaliation, two similar devices were lobbed back, one into southern Gaza and one deep into the West Bank, where Muslims now lived in the old Jewish settlements. In a blinding instant, tens of thousands of Palestinians were taken out in revenge.

A collective hush fell as the entire planet held its breath. That evening, the firmament over the eastern Mediterranean, which had been obscured with dirt and sand blown high into the atmosphere from the atomic bombs, was somehow cleared by an arctic steamroller of chill, clean air, which charged into the vacuum created by the hellish heat. By early morning, when the sun rose into an icy blue sky, all eyes were turned upon the Holy Land. In that awful dawn we saw a great gasp of fire race towards the heavens leaving a mushroom cloud roiling diabolically in the desert sands over the once sweet and fertile hills of Jerusalem.

Everyone, Muslims, Christians, and the few remaining Jews, all those descended from the artifacts of ancient monotheism, lost forever their chance to know the true nature of the divinity that was first witnessed on this historic soil. The dispute over this ancient real estate, which had been based on completely conflicting versions of what God had said and to whom, would never be settled. Bang. In one terrible moment, it was gone.

Maybe it could have ended there, had the people who wielded power had any of the right stuff. But the world was at an utter loss for true leaders for the longest time. In the East, the wave of extremist Muslim fundamentalism had replaced any sense of reason in a secular sense. In the West, the unremitting force of the omnipresent media driven by hollow capitalism had lowered the bar to allow an elected class of mediocre, power-hungry bureaucrats govern the democracies. The impotence of the current presidents, prime ministers, dictators, and kings was embarrassing at best.

In the chaos, the psychotic and pathological leaders of Hezbollah smelled blood in the water. They released stores of enhanced anthrax that had been smuggled in from Baghdad during the second Iraqi war and stored secretly in safe houses in North Africa. It spread quickly through the devastation in the land of milk and honey, preying upon the unfortunate survivors, both Israeli and Arab alike. Once again, the Israeli Defense Forces retaliated with a short-range missile. The somewhat larger warhead touched down ever so perfectly on ground zero Cairo, leveling everything. The pyramids, once a timeless wonder of the ancient world, were turned into acres of radioactive stony rubble.

The entire Musilim world was now united in jihad for the final extermination of Israel, and the surviving remnants of the mega-paranoid Israeli Defense Forces were poised to light up the rest of the Middle East like a verse out of Revelations. Somehow the heads of state from all around the world arranged with great haste a global peace and unity day. They set the date for November 26, 2026, Thanksgiving, in North America, the 250th anniversary of the U.S. Declaration of Independence. They placed the grand ceremony on Ellis Island, for centuries an icon of freedom for populations in distress and a symbol of racial and international harmony. Here the planet would come to its senses and rally under an unfurled emblem of world peace. It made so much sense to just mourn, clean up the mess as best they could, and then move on. Everybody had lost something, an enormous something to be sure, but what could be gained was a new understanding, a new tolerance, based upon this mutual disaster. It seemed so real, so natural, and everybody so wanted it to work.

That day the entire world watched the proceedings live via satellite from the grand harbor of New York City as the so-called leaders of the world made frantic gestures of hope and said their empty words of peace. But al-Qaeda, on the run for years but waiting in the wings, detonated an antiquated dirty bomb planted years ago deep below the water line in a decommissioned freighter docked in Jersey City, sitting under our nose, ready and waiting for an opportune moment like this.

The world once again was traumatized in horror, apoplexed in panic.

A few hours later, a single Stealth Bomber based on a carrier near Perth, refueled somewhere over the Indian Ocean on its way unchallenged across the Arabian Peninsula, and decimated Damascus, the new home of al-Qaeda since they were ejected out of the Kashmir. On its way back, another bomb was released over Mecca for good measure. The pilot, flying low to the ground to avoid anti-aircraft response, swore in debriefings that he could see former Bedouins of the Naj, out in the scorching desert, ripping their clothes, tearing their hair and gnashing their teeth.

With seemingly nothing left to lose, the remaining terrorist cells, fueled with weapons procured from the black market, went wild in the U.S. and in Europe. They shot their atomic wad in misbegotten jihad, taking out millions in DC, San Francisco, Moscow, London, Paris, and Milan.

Soon after, during one very dark night, from submarines in several seas, long sinister missiles with large reprobate warheads were launched. They ended life in many Arab and Muslim capitals.

That morning, with a coordinated level of movement that almost seemed rehearsed, the Marines and the First Army stormed in and took control of the Saudi and Iraqi oil fields, instantly making the U.S. Armed Forces the richest oil-producing corporation on the planet, provided there was going to be any technological society left to sell oil to.

However, the Muslim theocrats still alive, who had hijacked the religion to do its part in the horror, recoiled in the face of the destruction from their extremist policies. Besides, they ran out of bombs. From that time on the scale of the carnage dropped back down to the terror levels before the Exchange. The weapons of mass destruction unleashed since were acts of an angry environment, triggered by years of negligent industrial policy, now accelerated and magnified by the nuclear blasts.

Western civility with its Christian virtues that evolved from a cold, stony continent, and Mid-Eastern hospitality based on Islamic culture that came forth out of the hot, sandy desert, finally combined to scorch the world. Each religion left their followers no chance to come closer to understanding the glories of eternity they had so readily been promised.

Even so, around the oil oases where Christianity still meets Islam, the war continues, albeit on a smaller destructive scale, but every bit as savage and hateful as before. Memories of terrorized cities in flames and the bodies of charred loved ones smoldering in the debris kindled murderous impulses on both sides. Revenge was the law; hate begat hate, and violence led to more. That's why the gunships keep flying in during the night, bringing what was needed to keep the troops in Iraq alive.

From firing positions behind heavy fortified earthworks, the Marines could do nothing but watch their captured comrades hang from the crosses erected in the squeamish blackness of the night before. Now, crucified in the broiling midday sun, their horrific screams rebounded off the sand, echoing in with the enemy's prayers across the bloody desert. Pellet remembered this all too well. His perceptions about war were reinforced during his tours of duty. Nothing had changed except the technology. The bestiality was still of biblical proportions. As far as he was concerned, there was only one truth important and relevant to sustain life. Those with the bigger and better guns seize the day and survive to write its history.

That's how he explained it to the hopefuls who volunteered for his Marines. There were always enough people in America who thronged towards military life, the regiment, the team, the thrill, the army of one. Now that there were so many men and women with nothing better to live for, they flocked in lemming-like droves to the enlistment offices, choosing to work for the only company that seemed to wield any real power. In a world filled with daily violence and imminent war, Pellet's army was the safest place to be. They had threes squares a day, good shelter, and a purpose. They could defend themselves, and they looked out for one another.

However, the elite First Army had to turn most of the volunteers away, because there was only room for the best men. Pellet ran his boot camp to determine who those deserving lucky ones were. Every minute was carefully planned, to rip them apart from their individual identities, in order to form an unstoppable team, a killing machine, capable of fighting a foe brought up from birth in every way to die in combat for his individual account of Allah.

Pellet had a standard opening-day speech to inspire the rookie recruits. After making them wait in an overheated auditorium, sometimes for hours, he arrived through the back of the house and strode confidently down the center aisle, creating a hush across the room. By the time he stood before them with a single spotlight trained upon him on an empty stage, they were silent, awed, and completely captivated.

He was one of them. He came from where they came, and he rose through all the pain, hardships and obstacles in his way to become the man of great power and position. They could work for that man who stood alone on the stage and promised them great strength and security. They could die for that man in the spotlight on which every eye in the room was glued. Maybe someday, if there was a someday, they could be like that man, or maybe even be him.

"There are three types of men in this world," Pellet always began his speech. "The way we find out who they are and what they are made of can be found in the spontaneous reactions they reveal when presented sudden and surprising stimuli."

Silence. All eyes and ears upon the general.

"Consider this scenario. You're driving with your honey on a dark country road; the top is down on your convertible Corvette with a full silver moon shining high in the sky. As you cruise by, late summer crickets serenade you along with that MP-12 you bought to plug into your soundboard. Everything you can touch and feel seems like it is all go for love and romance." A few snickers could be heard in the crowd. "When suddenly, a squirrel dashes into the road right in front of your wheels. What would you do? How would you react? In that automatic reflex lies the essence of who you really are.

"One type of man would hit the brakes and swerve, avoiding the collision. A noble act indeed, trying to preserve the sanctity of all creatures, no matter how small or meaningless in the scheme of things. But perhaps, through circumstances, this avoidance action forces a change in direction, which ends up injuring an innocent bystander, yourself, or your girl. That would certainly end any chances for getting lucky with this lady at the end of the night."

A few louder laughs, high-fives, and "yeah baby's" heard in the room. Pellet's pause is perfect before continuing.

"A second type of reaction causes a man to freeze, for a moment leaving him indecisive. Unable to parlay sudden and potentially dangerous information into action leaves the consequences of the situation completely out of his control. I guess that's okay for some people, maybe they believe in destiny, that a man has no choice. Perhaps they believe it is all pre-written, pre-determined."

Here he stops and slowly scans the auditorium, each man believing that Pellet is looking into his eyes only. With their total attention he brings it all on home.

"I say we can make choices in this world! We can do better than merely survive, for we are literally the captains of our ship, and truly the masters of our own fate. We can win and we most certainly can have it all!" By now he would be roaring. "What I am saying, gentlemen, is that these are the men I want in my Marine Corps! I want you, the third type of man. I want the man with no questions or qualms! The man who will put that pedal to the medal without a moment of hesitation. The man who will drive his car straight at that miserable little rodent and squash its ass out of existence. Because it is that man who will drive on down the road and fuck his baby's brains out of her head all night long! That's who I want in my command! I want the squirrel killers in this room in my Marine Corps!"

At this point the men always jumped up, shouting and whooping, certainly squirrel killers every one. Over the next eight weeks the training Pellet had in store for them told him which small percentage of them really were.

In this early morning, alone in his soundproofed bedroom, amongst the barracks that house his boys, Pellet ponders yesterday's developments, preparing for tomorrow's plans. In his mind he knows what to do. But there are always contingencies, and even for him, there are still those he has to answer to. Yet he has his sources, which help keep him ready. You never know what is going to happen next.

A secured cell phone rings and ready, he takes the call.

* * * * *

17

Gracie Mansion, New York City's renowned mayoral residence, now housed hundreds of transients instead of the mayor and his family. Jack preferred to live uptown anyway, because he had no family.

For months after Anita, their baby boy, and his father Theodore were extinguished together in one single instant under the shadows of the Statue of Liberty, Jack lived alone in his office in the same Armani suit he was wearing when the bomb went off. It was considered small for a nuclear explosion, and the freighter it was stored on below the waterline miraculously limited the range of the blast across the river to mostly New Jersey, but it did kill off his family, most of the leaders of the world, and thousands and thousands of others who thought they were lucky enough to get a ticket to be at the event in person. The explosion also wiped out the last elected mayor of New York and most of the city officials presiding as hosts. This made Jack, who was left back in Manhattan to run the city government during the Ellis Island extravaganza, the acting mayor. His first job, from in the bunkers, was to deal with this unfathomable and overwhelming tragedy and its immediate ongoing catastrophe of radiation, fallout, and chaos. There was no time to change his clothes.

The world being turned upside down was not the right analogy. It was more like it was shoved into a wood chipper and tossed into a satanic storm. The scale of human disaster expanded worldwide during the next few weeks of the Exchange that followed. It was hard to mourn for the dead properly when there was so much devastation left to deal with for the living.

When the initial emergency slowed to a constant droning exhaustion, Sam forced him to move into this apartment on 122nd Street, near Columbia, near his old hood. Sam had it furnished with some of the stuff from his old apartment with Anita, and decorated it with things from Jack's childhood with his father. Although surrounded at all times by squirrel killers for security, it was as close to normal as Sam could make it for the man he loved like a brother and a leader he would follow anywhere. But that couldn't keep the voices from drifting in on Jack and the tides of soapy waters from washing him over.

Lately Jack wondered if he lived a complete delusion. It seemed right to want to do the right thing. He wanted simple acts of kindness on a day-to-day basis to be the foundation of governing. Instead, he contorted the basic human freedoms he was brought up to believe in, and interpreted them back as something totally necessary in order to restore society into something remotely resembling life before the bomb. Was he right? Maybe, for back then. These days he was so introspective, soul-searching and full of doubt.

Unlike America before, during the post-Exchange there wasn't the slightest pretense of social justice and equality. The gulf between rich and poor was an untraversable chasm. The glue that used to keep the great society of immigrants from all over the world together was missing, whoosh, sucked up in a mushroom cloud, goodbye.

Security was the only concern. In order to give the city any chance to come back after the attack, Jack had to create a fascistic form of pseudo-democracy. There were still elections, and he always welcomed a rival candidate, but he's been the only mayor post-bomb. When the City Emergency Regulations were enacted, as they were now, he had absolute power. Every democratic principle Jack grew up with was subverted.

The New York story, how it was able to crawl out of the crater back into some semblance of control and prosperity served as a role model to a world beset in disaster. Jack knew his Machiavellian policies toward population restraint in the face of catastrophe was what brought them up to the top. It is that fact, and not his heart, that has been applauded and imitated around the globe. Deep down inside, somehow he still believed in the basic goodness of humankind, even as a firsthand witness to horrors of unspeakable dimensions.

Now he keeps hearing these whispers from all different places, and he feels that this power he had to protect the city he loved so deeply was being changed by something way out of his control.

Jack always believed there were many points of view to any issue. He listened well and formed his strong opinions accordingly. Then he fit them into the new reality that constantly had to be relearned in the neverending spiral of the constant evolution of all things.

Adaptability was the key to survival. In this way he had kept his city from tearing apart. Change, like all other immutable laws of the universe, is inevitable, as it is in the evolution of the human condition. Therefore, Jack still believes that, although mankind is barely a microscopic part of an unbounded universe, life on earth still had to be a part of the endless struggle between creation and destruction, light and dark, good and evil.

According to General Pellet, Jack still believed in those old Hollywood endings too much, where Will Smith triumphs over intergalactic evil in every scenario imaginable and ends up on some other planet with an incredibly gorgeous and amazingly brilliant babe on his arm that truly loves him and whom he truly loves. But if the good guys always win in the end, why has he seen so many good men die such horrible deaths?

In the dark hours during the civil twilight, unable to sleep, alone in his solitary world, there comes a hushing, and an irresistible sigh heard just in time. He pulls his tortured soul back and just lets himself go, swirling around and around in the heavenly eddies of pure and deep cleansing waters.

* * * * *

18

The sunrays broke through onto the moist leafs in spotted brilliance and the morning dew bounced their rainbows back like pigmented spraylets, liquid light, of a divine kind.

Herbie climbed up the hill immersed in the smell of the damp autumnal forest, each breath inhaled through his lungs went straight to his heart, carrying the healing of an abundant and unscarred earth, mother to us all. Almost to the top at the clearing around the beautiful white mansion, he stopped and lifted his head in reverence to hear the chorus. Perfect as always, the same and yet never the same, the inimitable instant changes in beat, tempo, and rhythm, predictable only by its being heard. Silhouetted in the rising sun and haloed in its refractions, the magnificence of the edifice beckoned him in.

He entered a windowless high-walled hexagon, Pisa-like in its list toward the sky, the ceiling one huge skylight. The building was tilted and rotating to follow the sun. The great room was nuzzled in earthlife, the white and rapturous walls were a siege in glow. He felt nourished by the ebullience and connected to all things within this emulsion making them all as one, the same as the other but easily differently the same.

Herbie lifted his face up high to the apex where the walls lavished in light and all around and through that enraptured room flew endless possibilities. With a casual fluttering of his hands he floated upwards into the great height of the hall, each motion of his arms winging him higher, and with just a tilt of a wrist or the flick of a finger, he could change direction at will.

He looked back down to see the great hall now filled with people living together without exploitation, and he heard them cheering in unparalleled harmony. He knew at once he could never let them down.

A toothy jaw smiled up at him, and pointed with a bony finger.

Doubt. Fear. His arms cramped and tired. You can't fly with fear.

The skylight fatigued and slowed, and shadows fell over the smooth veneers of the once living walls now gone geriatric, rigid in rigormortic decay. They were cracking and peeling, revealing cobwebs in the corners built by scurrying arachnids of unusual intrepidity.

He careened off a wall and the crowds below began running away, fleeing in terror. Falling into a straight nosedive, plummeting to the surface, the war drums of the netherworld pounding the beauty of the celestial melody. He watched his own crash and burn moments just before the floor rushed up to his face and at the exact instant of impact his eyes slam-jerked wide open.

The alcohol had worn off, but the hangover just begun. It was 4 in the morning, a bad time to be awake if you didn't want to think about death. His body and blankets were drenched in sweat and his head was glutted with ghosts. The pipes in his building rattled and grumbled as if they were cholestorized arteries denying the lifeblood to a body in advanced decay. For a few minutes he lay petrified, not so much in fear but in disbelief, not knowing what it was that was dying. He tried to curse his always-absent angel that it was he that still breathed under the soaking bed stuff. But he couldn't even find that strength.

He closed his eyes, in dread of the wakemares of the dead of night. His sweet little Sophie in the green hospital robe, hair fallen from her head, eyes drugged for pain, hands reaching for his fingertips on the untouchable other side of the treated safety glass darkened by the lead. "Mommy's home," he could hear himself say, "She's not feeling well, but I'll go get her now." "Please Daddy, don't go, I'm scared; I'm so scared." You are sacred; you are so sacred. "Don't worry, honey, nothing can happen to you. I won't let it."

Back home the EMTs pulled Mommy's bloodless body out of the bathtub, and the terminal grief almost suffocated him while he filled out government forms for an apathetic emergency crew that had seen this so many times before.

Sophie slipped away, probably at the same moment as Danielle, before he made it back to the hospital to be by her side while she died. Three more ruined lives in and amongst the billions.

He buried his wife and daughter on the same day in the family plot in Putnam Valley, very near his mother's and his grandmother's graves, overlooking three beautiful hills, whose verdant leaves were already showing effects of the recent fallout. He gazed with well-practiced grief at the graves of the previous generations, those of the wombs through which his life had passed, and now the fresh new holes in the ground.

But Herbie couldn't take these thoughts anymore, so he hobbled out of bed into the dilapidated shower stall to let the cold water spark his toxic body back to life. He leaned against the cracked tiles in pure despair and broke down. He cried and wailed and screamed into the forsaken night, anguished tears mingling with the rusty water washing him over. For some reason he did not know, he began to pray for the first time in years. Please, oh God, he pleaded, make the world live. Make the world live. Stop the pain and make the world live.

* * * * *

19

Jamal woke up to an ugly pungency, causing him to gasp for air in uncontrollable paroxysms, which hurt because he was staked down spread eagle to the frozen ground. His clothes were gone, replaced with a burlap bag with holes cut out for his skinny arms and legs.

Gregor was on his knees inspecting the tumors developing around the glands below Jamal's ears. His skanky breath wafted into the boy's nostrils and made Jamal vomit the digestive juices from his otherwise empty stomach. Some droplets of that essence of Jamal sprayed upon the shirtsleeves of the evil gang leader, so he smacked him one time hard on the side of the head to shut him down. "This little shit's no good," he announced, "he's got AIDS."

Ibrahim, who was munching on microwave popcorn and swilling whiskey for a late night snack, couldn't have cared less. To him the boy wasn't even close to an abstraction of a human life. "Let's get rid of him."

"Better idea. We take him to Reginald. We gonna put this out in the open."

* * * * *

Horns sounded and drums were on the approach. Everyone in Reginald Square turned their heads.

In these graveyard hours before dawn, all the people hanging around Reginald were engaged in some form of perversion or fetish that could only go down during dark hours like these. Besides the trafficking of black market goods through the tunnels and this business noir, there was no real work in Shantypark. This welfare economy underscored the pervasive helplessness and hopelessness, which were the founding themes of Shantypark in the first place. So, upon the first sounds of the fanfare, the modern-day lepers looked with great glee to the oncoming spectacle. What better way to kick off a holiday season than a beheading?

Gregor's horde came from the east like their ancestors of the ancient khanates, ascending from out the Asian steppe, marching westward towards rape and pillage, taking no quarter along the way. By the time they reached Reginald, the crowd had grown larger, congealing into groups of like colors that offered the most safety, leaving the middle of the square free and unopposed.

A bearded brown man wearing a simple dishdasha appeared out of the southeast corner of the mall, leading his mullahs. They silently grouped on the edge of the action like birds of prey descended from giant reptiles, many eyes looking as with one head.

On the northern fringe of the square, a large bald man with no eyelashes led a band of white men onto the pavement, their bodies draped in leather and fur, wearing motorcycle boots, and showing many piercings and tattoos.

Black men materialized from the south, and so the darker-skinned people in the crowd drifted in that direction, some very bald, others with kinky hair and some Rastafarian.

All packing pieces very visible.

The stani gang broke through the ring of jerry-rigged tents and dilapidated shacks that bordered Reginald. They marched in procession flexing their power as the onlookers melted out of their way. They stopped in the now barren turf in the center of the square and encircled the area, standing off any would-be lunatics stupid enough to attempt a breach of their circle. A motley stani man in ragged robes raised a horn to his impious mouth and blew forth a truculent trill and, within the ring of warriors, the altar was placed.

Mysterious apparitions appeared, infiltrating with ease into the crowd, mixing unnoticed since they had no colors of their own.

The stanis remained implacable in the center of the Square, focused on their barbaric and psychotic ritual. Everybody else was passing pipes, bottles, and vials, and disjointed pockets of cryptic laughter bubbled up along the surface, turning the crowd ever more fantastical. In Shantypark, an execution is always a good reason for a party, and the people were busy dizzying themselves for the pageant.

When the first light of morning showed phosphorescent blue in the eastern sky, Gregor stood up on the platform. The crowd hushed. He held Jamal up by his throat before them and announced with his gravelly voice. "This little nigger is mine." He laid the boy down on the chopping block, Jamal's young Adam's apple bobbing wildly in fear. "This little bitch stole from me and will pay for his crime my way."

A tall, young black man, dressed in black clothing, walked out of the crowd and stopped just shy of the ring around the platform, a few yards from Gregor's face. "Your choice of words sickens me, Gregor, almost as much as the sight of your stupid and repulsive face. You are a pagan and a pig, and I spit on your very existence."

"You amuse me Marcus, but you don't fool people around here. If it's a question of who's got the goods and who's got the guns, I win." Gregor's stani lilt making a nursery rhyme out of a deadly threat. "But if you got something to say, this is the time; so make me laugh."

"My people have been here for centuries, so Gregor, to me you are an intruder. We were conceived in slavery, weaned on Jim Crow and subjected to lynching and harsh segregation. But now, dude, we run this city; we run the show. I, for one, am personally disgusted by your illegal alien ass terrorizing my brothers and sisters."

There were murmurs of assent and a few shouted affirmations from the black people behind him in the crowd. Gregor's face grimaced and snarled, showing his rotten and diseased teeth, yellowed and brown. He shouted back at them, "Shut the fuck up!" The people cringed backwards in fear, leaving Marcus particularly isolated and vulnerable against the invader horde.

Gregor was just beginning revving himself up. "That's the trouble with you Americans. Everything was so free and easy. That's why all this shit happened to you. A fucking open society can't exist forever because of what comes in and what goes out. You assholes had it made and you let it go to shit. Your morality sucked, like here man, here you are, go fuck my wife, go fuck my daughter. You are all sick fuckin'pimps and whores. What do you know about honor, Marcus, when all you ever cared about before was yourself, what kind of fancy car you drove, and what kind of running shoes you wore?"

"There are good people in Shantypark, Gregor, who, given the opportunity, would work for a living, earn their dignity in a society of law, not like animals, not like you."

"Laws! You call those fucking things you lived by laws? Don't make me laugh too hard, shithead. The only law I see in America lets killers walk free and child fuckers work in kindergartens. Your law lets oil companies start world wars and pollute my planet. Your law lets the Internet be filled with your sister's faces covered with cum. And your leaders, your fuckin' lawmakers who made these fuckin' laws, lie openly to you. They hire other liars, actors, and similar prostitutes who inject their bodies with silicone and steroids to convince you to buy into shit you don't need or believe in, and you treat them like gods in your full-color glossy world. While men who rhyme and shake their hips steal the money out of your children's pockets and stick drugs up their veins. America's laws, fuck that bullshit!

"But you know what Marcus? Where I came from was no fuckin' better. My people were proud once. We lived on our land in dignity and were taught to protect widows and orphans and give charity to the poor. Men from my village were honored for their strength and their willingness to submit to a merciful all-knowing Allah. That got totally fucked-up. Now my brother's sons are trained to kill themselves in the name of some new vengeful god invented by assholes calling themselves the true protectors of the faith. These pretenders sucked the real wealth out of our country, our children, while leaving grandmothers and widows to starve like diseased pigs in shit-strewn streets.

"Bad enough got worse after the bombs. Now this fucking lousy world locks me in behind walls with you rotten infected scumbags So, fuck that! Now wherever I go in Shantypark, I make my own rules. For you see Marcus, I am the law here! I am the lawgiver! Do you savvy? Whether you like it or not, these are my rules and Shantypark will live by them because I say so. This little nigger stole from me, and my rules say, 'thou shall not steal from Gregor.'"

Marcus felt an evil potent force just below the

surface of this spontaneous display of Gregor's derangement. He wanted to minimize the damage. "He's just a little boy, Gregor. He was lost and frightened. He was cold and starving."

"Kiss my ass! For breaking into my tent and stealing my apple he will be made an example for all you freaks, cause now he will be dead, and that will be one less thieving nigger kid to look out for." He pointed to the executioner, who on command pulled his well-oiled sword from its ornate sheath. "And Marcus, there ain't nothing you or anyone else here can do about it."

The crowd's thickened hush resonated like a metal gong in reverse, sucking in the nearby energy like a black hole on earth.

Jamal was alone on the chopping block, his life in Gregor's grimy hands, which at the moment were busy picking his weather-beaten nose as he stared down Marcus with his creepy-calm, raptor eyes. Taking his time, making sure he got it all, he flicked some green mucous on to the ground.

With a smirk at Marcus he swept his filthy, scabby fingers across his neck like a knife slicing a throat. "Kill him."

The crowd tensed; this was the moment. The executioner, doing what he was trained to do, raised the sword high in the air, every muscle in his powerful body coordinated into a ceremonial position that ended lives. Reaching the height of his mighty back swing, he poised over Jamal's outstretched throat like a glossy photo for the textbook cover of Terrorism 101.

In that perfect moment, as the dark hooded legions of wraiths waited for blood, a strong but soft voice called out from the wilderness of the unruly mob. "Woe unto this monstrosity."

The swordsman froze, physically unable to move

a muscle. He stood shivering in place, stuck in his horrid posture, his grisly face in deep and dreadful panic.

"Enough of this evil." Said the lean young man, alone in the middle of Reginald, glaring with incredulous steadfast strength. "You must give the boy to me." His dark curly hair edged over the collar of his long brown trench coat as he took several steps towards the atrocity in front of him. The people in the crowd stepped back as he moved through, and those standing close felt their fear turn to a curious wonder. The killer backed down and lowered his sword, barely looking at Gregor.

"What the hell are you doing? You fuckin' assh-ole! Kill the kid! Kill that fucking kid!" Gregor screamed but the trained assassin stood literally petrified, his body quaking, unable to move a muscle. His killer eyes, gone now from great arrogance to great fear, sent shivers running through the skin of the onlookers.

Someone in the mass of people shouted, "Its Salem Jones!" and the entire mob vibrated in recognition that a great reckoning was now before them.

Gregor's muscles and veins strained to break out of his skin when he realized he too was incapable of moving. He could only manage muffled screams, hellish and grating, like mummies emerging from ancient crypts. "Ibrahim! You! You take that sword and kill that fuckin' kid." Ibrahim, unsure of what was going on, made a stumbling move for the sword.

"Become like the child and you too will see salvation." Salem said to Ibrahim, moving closer to the stani stronghold. "Then you will have nothing to fear." Ibrahim froze like a vile and helpless serpent, lost in a very cold shadow, unable to avail upon the energy of the sun.

"What are you waiting for, you fuckin' idiot?" fumed Gregor who still couldn't move, but his insides were on fire. "Kill him. Kill the boy. Kill the fuckin' nigger kid."

Everyone in Reginald was motionless, stunned, suspended in a slice of elastic time that stood still but kept stretching out to far reaches. In their center, upon a primitive wooden altar was Jamal's pathetic little body, trembling.

"Ibrahim," Salem said "bring the boy to me."

Gregor, convulsed in an internal seizure, was unable to countermand this sublime, soft force that superseded his power.

Ibrahim, in a trance, as if summoned, untied the leather straps that bound Jamal's wrists and, heedless of Gregor's rantings, lifted the boy off the chopping block and carried him towards the wavy-haired man in the crowd.

Jamal, unable not to look into his savior's eyes, will never forget that instant, blinding light.

"What is this bullshit? Ibrahim, you asshole, kill that fucking nigger kid, now! Do what I say, for I am the fucking law here." But incapable to resist Salem's easy command, Ibrahim stepped down from the altar and carried Jamal to him, passing in front of Gregor who was still unable to muster a single fiber of muscle to move.

A black hood slipped away from the crowd.

Ibrahim stopped before Salem Jones and gazed up at him. He looked like any ordinary Shantypark youth in jeans and work boots, except for his eyes. Salem looked down upon him with a tender mercy. "Ibrahim. You must free yourself from the evil that howls deep inside your heart, strangling your soul."

Salem Jones extended his arms and Ibrahim gently placed Jamal into them. Jamal looked up once again into the radiance in his eyes, then curled his head against Salem's shoulder, exhausted, spent, in full submission, exposing the telltale AIDS-7 melanomas behind his ears.

Gregor's baleful laugh lingered and echoed in the scuttling night. "Whaddaya gonna do with that little shit nigger now, big fuckin' shot? Can't you see his blood is all fucked up, man? He's gonna die in a few days, ya know!"

Salem smiled at the boy, patted his head and stroked his hair, ears, and face. Jamal looked back up in wonderment as his body fully absorbed the depth of this contact. No one had ever touched him with such incredible warmth.

Curiously, with none of the abhorrence others were sure he deserved, Salem looked upon Gregor and said to him, "Even you have time to turn from your evil ways. Then maybe you will have a chance to live."

"Are you threatening me asshole?" Gregor screamed out at Salem, his gang tittering behind him. "Are you threatening me? I am Gregor! I am the law! Who the fuck are you?"

Salem Jones turned his back on the angry horde and walked away with the boy through the immense gathering of the astonished, all now dazed and amazed, eyes filled with tears and mouths dropped in awe.

As he passed through the multitude, a high celestial soprano lilted up an octave and then up a melodic sixth and many turned towards him. A great movement then swelled and followed Salem as he walked away through the detritus of Shantypark.

The first rays of the rising sun broke through the clouds, sliced through the brittle twenty-first century smog and deflected over Reginald Square. A marvelous golden glow appeared above, like an umbrella, like a shield, bringing shelter to this haggard city, filled with so many afflictions and troubled tents.

* * * * *

20

Bullmoose was a world traveler. In his prime nothing could keep him back. He first got the calling years ago while driving taxicabs in Boston when he should have been enrolled in M.I.T. Sitting in the taxi pool at Logan Airport, during an innocent time pre-Oprah, waiting for suburbanite customers who could pass for starchy vegetables, he figured he should give into this calling now, when he was young, before he was tied down to a successful rock-star career.

One fine morning, after driving cabs all night, snorting whiteys and smoking pot, Bullmoose dropped in at the passport office in Government Center with his birth certificate. Grandma, Bullmoose's perpetual yet unattached squeeze, received it from Bullmoose's family right before their son who was destined to be Herbie's father was born. Grandma had called asking Bullmoose's mom to send it soon after Bullmoose first started mumbling about his newfound wanderlust. Grandma's thinking was in case he never made it back she would have some kind of proof for her infant son that he had a father that actually existed. Rule number two kicked in; everything is interconnected, and often in ways that most of us can't understand. Although it was actually something he absolutely needed to get out of his country and into another, Bullmoose never even thought about it until he saw it sitting in the pile of mail on Grandma's kitchen table. Then it dawned on him. Grandma and he were a good team that way, interconnected, and that's how they got things done.

After several weeks of amphetamines and Coors Light, driving cabs all day and all night, he saved up enough money for a round trip airplane ticket to Bombay, which was what Mumbai was called, back then, Pre-Exchange. It was the early 1970s and Bullmoose was going to India to find himself.

For the first time ever on an airplane, Bullmoose picked just about the longest ride possible for his maiden voyage, a trip halfway around the lonely planet. But, of course, Bullmoose went prepared. When the stewardess came around with the drink cart, he washed down a couple of valiums with a few airplane bottles of vodka. He popped another couple when she came back around again with more vodka. He would have bought even more but he couldn't believe how little money he had left, and he wasn't even out of the airplane yet.

At one significant point, on his way back from a much-needed trip to the toilet he became fixated on a well-shaped female, about nineteen years old, with a perfect behind packaged in tight sexy blue denim wiggling up the aisle just in front of him. As it turned out she was sitting in the middle four seats of the widebody jet with some friends equally as female and scintillating. Bullmoose, being as he always was, entertained them with his you-really-wanna-let-me-inta-your-pants kind of charm that came by him naturally in situations like this. The stewardess rolled through again and he found himself buying those very expensive tiny bottles of vodka for her and all her libidinous friends. Everybody laughed harder as the party grew heartier, until Herbie started staggering and falling into people seated all around. He remembered the chuckling sounds as someone very kind and gentle guided him back to his seat.

Before he knew it he was standing alone in a customs line in the Bombay airport handing his singular, unique proof of existence to the Indian customs man, whose eyes kept darting from the sleepy young man in front of him with only a knapsack and a guitar, to the passport picture of a ponytailed hippie, eyes black and widely dilated from speed, staring off the document. To him Bullmoose looked like a twentieth century suburban Buddha, daring his karma to take him, and bring him back to, wherever he thought he deserved to go. Which really wasn't going to be very much further since he spent most of his money on tiny bottles of Smirnoff while trying to pry the panties off of some random honey in row 37 so that he could gain entry into the exclusive mile-high club. Of course Bullmoose had never even heard about the club at that point and nobody was sure if it was even invented yet, but assuredly Bullmoose would not have minded being one of its first and founding members.

The poor customs man, not knowing what to think, probably believed that a well-sodden Herschel J. Lipton from Canarsie, New York, standing before him, smiling cockily under his Boston Red Sox cap, was just another modern-day would-be white shaman with vast resources of spiritual power backed by lots of American cash, rather than the hungover, horny, and almost broke pothead he really was. Because of Bullmoose's well-concealed self-doubts about his outward presentation and personal intentions, he was actually let into India.

Elated yet confused, inspirited but insecure, Bullmoose drifted out of the terminal into the halogen Hindu night without the vaguest idea of where he was and what he was going to do. The first things he noticed stepping outside the terminal building were the jumbo mosquitoes and other ravenous giant flying insects. They buzzed with a fearful droning around the few electric lights in the passenger pick up area in manic anticipation of a sudden blitz upon unprotected human flesh.

In the distance by the taxi stand, he saw proud but idle sons of the Raj hanging around and talking, disregarding his appearance as another unremarkable manifestation of Shiva on earth. They intuitively knew who could and who could not afford to pay them for a ride into the city. At best they were going to be no help.

Advancing towards him came the inevitable bedraggled hordes of beggars, omnipresent upon the Indian landscape, with their children at the vanguard, many maimed and missing limbs. Each clamored to be the first and the most worthy of alms from the newly arrived foreigner, whose financial status suggested he really should have been joining in with them to beg for money from those who actually had some. They spilled into his breathing space, quickly filling it up, reaching out, touching him, pulling on his shirt sleeves, begging in human sounds that were as unintelligible as their smells. Their cluster behavior began choking off his air supply; he felt weak, shaken, fatigued. He thought he was going to be devoured by a double frontal attack of bugs that resembled the Nazi air force, and people who resembled bugs.

There he stood at the spread-open and beckoning portals of the exotic and intriguing Far East, the beacon of light during the short spiritual reawakening in America in the early 1970s due to the popularity of LSD, mescaline, peyote, and other psychedelic drugs in vogue at the time. Bullmoose was alone, almost broke, and halfway around the world in a time before iphones and emails. Wavering, he forgot all about the count-on-able rules he had followed with all his heart to the other side of the world. He already had enough and wanted to turn around and run as fast as he could straight back onto that airplane and head his ass right back home to Boston.

There, at his darkest hour, a little vision hit him like an epiphany. It made him realize once again number four; there is no limit to the glory and grace of God. It was that perfect female body painted into those faded denim jeans that adorned the nineteen-year-old nymphet he so beguiled on the airplane with his irreproachable lecher routine. She just happened to be attached to a group of other American college kids traveling on a semester abroad, who just happened to fly into India on the same aircraft as Bullmoose. They must have told him that fact earlier when he partied with them in the airplane, but he probably didn't hear them because he was just too high.

Following his natural self, he sidled up alongside her once again. She looked like she actually enjoyed the attention, probably because of that talented I'm-so-cute-you-want-to-get-naked-with-me sensitive rap he laid on her before he fell on his face in the airplane aisle. He followed her towards an antediluvian school bus that was pulling up with a groaning screech, late as usual, as things were done in that country at that time in history. Without much thought, and without a word, with the guitar case strapped to his back, Bullmoose mingled in and, just like that, they oozed him onto the bus like another American college kid on a semester abroad in India. The kids immediately accepted him as one of their own and nobody asked questions, all the way across the country, for several weeks on a whirlwind tour of India's holiest sights, until they got to Madras and, thereupon registering at the dorm, they realized he was a fraud.

After a few less-than-friendly handshakes and some firm nudging by the administration and faculty, the next thing he knew he was hitchhiking on the only road south of town, headed to a coastal area where rumor had it there was a nine-hundred-year-old temple on the beach where, the kids told him, it was easy to score dope and buy beer. He could lie in the sand all day long and do what he did best, just get a big huge buzz on and basically get his head together.

That's exactly what he did. While his prep school friends were back home in the cold at Yale or Harvard or Brown reading Nietzsche and Pinter and Freud, he woke up to the sunrise on the Bay of Bengal, played music, hung out, got high, often times getting some, and slept under the stars on the beaches. Each day it started all over again.

Life was a beautiful dance. He had to come to the other side of the planet to find that he was a divine cosmic dancer, like Shiva Natraj, infused with the reality and joy of creation. When he moved with veneration through the several manifestations of divinity he too could experience the truth, the good, and the beauty that is God, as long as he held onto that return ticket back to Boston in case his money completely ran out.

One morning he awoke on a beach he knew he had not been on before, because all around was this clink-clink-clinking stone-like sound. It was as if the tides of alcohol and cannabis upon which he nightly sailed dropped him like driftwood on a dune. Towering above him, at the convergence of sea, sky and land, as if it were a sandcastle made by giants, an ornate and ancient structure stood guard on the beach, its gopuram reaching for the heavens. He had found the ancient temple.

With nothing better to do, Bullmoose sat on the beach and strummed his guitar at the juncture of the endless motion of the universe, jamming to the melodies of life.

Upon hearing the Bullmoose music, an old man emerged from inside the temple, wearing the traditional orange of the Hari Krishna. His long gray hair was soaked in sea salt and matted to his head in impenetrable knots; his arms were outstretched and his fingers were gyrating, and he was mumbling in an ancient language Bullmoose had no idea what.

The orange man entered very close into Bullmoose's personal body space and began what sounded and looked like praying. He made great swirling shaman-like circles occasionally picking up sand and letting it blow gently from his hands into the wind. The singing jumble of invocations all sounded very convincing to Bullmoose.

The orange man reached into his pockets and pulled out things he must have collected along the way. He sorted through the riffraff with great concern, throwing aside cocktail napkins, buttons, matchbooks, broken beads, bottle tops, a ripped notepad, leather strings. Finally he found it. A little wire ring. It was made from a single strand of copper wrapped in such a clever way that even under close inspection it was hard to tell where was the beginning or the end.

With grand ceremony and great gesticulation the orange man placed the ring on the fourth finger of Bullmoose's right hand. "Hey, careful dude," Bullmoose said to him with cautious timidity, "That's my pickin' hand, ya know."

He giggled and stepped back to admire the King Bullmoose. After a couple of pious and profound moments he extended his palm outstretched in front of Bullmoose's face. "Waddaya want? Some money for this thing?" Bullmoose queried him.

With that the old man jumped into action, bending and postulating and pointing to the ring on his finger and saying in broken English, "It's for you. It's for you. It's for you!" When Bullmoose looked back at him with a blank and confused expression, the orange man became excited in an almost insulted, over-animated way. "It's for you. It's for you. It's for you!" He literally spat the words into Bullmoose's face.

"Yes, sir, I know it's for me and it is very nice." Bullmoose thought he was doing well not to hurt the guy's feelings.

However, the little orange man was not to be denied and certainly wasn't going away. He stood in Bullmoose's face and repeated again, "It's for you. It's for you. It's for you."

Exasperated, Bullmoose pulled out his last money. It was a fifty rupee note that he knew was not worth very much, but was much too much to give a beggar, even one who acted like a holy man or whatever. Before he could ask where he could get some change, the old man grabbed the bill and stuffed it down into his pocket with all the other trash. He grabbed Bullmoose in a big bear hug of gratitude, giving him a first-hand chance to discover the orange man's mighty body odor that had been gathering for years.

Before Bullmoose could manage the will to extricate himself, the orange man pushed him aside and ran back towards the temple from which he came, patting his treasure pocket where he kept his fifty-rupee reward from heaven. It would probably last him all year long down by the taverns in town near the lagoon. He turned just before entering the temple under the tower at the juncture of all the churning earthly elements, and gave another supplication to the sun or the wind or the sea or all three on Bullmoose's behalf and, in an instant, disappeared inside.

Bullmoose stood in silence, except for the constant clink-clink-clink. He immediately liked this place. He turned up the beach, walked a hundred yards, and found a spot in the brush where the sand met the jungle to call his own. He settled in at Mahabalipuram, in the shadows of the ancient gopuram, a major milestone in his soulful sojourn.

That afternoon Bullmoose started making back a few of the rupees he had sacrificed to the gods through the orange man. He strummed his Martin and sang a few songs in the Mahabalipuram main square, which was really just the intersection of a few dirt roads and a couple of shabby-by-western-standards hotels. The guitar case was open at his feet for handouts from German and Japanese tourists, whose parents had lost World War II but they still had all the money they needed to travel. He soon made enough spare change to eat that night. Clink-clink-clink.

After dinner and a few shots, he headed back to the beach. On the dirt road he heard a rowdy and coughing car creep up behind him. He hadn't heard the sound of an engine all day. It was an old Indian-made Ambassador, white not black. Even by twentieth century Indian standards this car was not great. Its engine was on the horsepower par of most American's backyard appliances that cut grass. He stuck out his thumb and the car stopped to pick him up.

The only taxi driver in town was an enterprising young man his own age. He was a Muslim and told Bullmoose so right away, as if Bullmoose should understand that Muslims were, of course, far superior, more intelligent, and more worldly, than his neighbor Hindus in the jungle. Pranan listened to him play his guitar earlier in the day in the town square and knew at first sight they were going to be great friends. He gave him a ride to introduce him to Sivan, who owned a little restaurant down by the beach. Like all the cafes in town, it was a little thatched hut with simple cast-iron furniture strewn about in the sand. Pranan told Sivan that Bullmoose would be playing his guitar there later that night. Sivan just shook his head side to side, which in America means no, but in India means yes.

In a few days all the cafes in Mahabalipuram wanted Bullmoose. After he played a few tunes for their happy guests, they invited him into their kitchens to select his favorite catch of the day, caught by the tribe of local fishermen who lived near him on the beach. Every morning Bullmoose watched them defecate into holes they dug in the sand, and then paddle out to their dinghies docked on the tide to catch the fish that kept them all alive. Yes, everything everywhere is interconnected. Clink-clink-clink.

It took Bullmoose a few days to figure out what was going on. Not only did he stumble into the holiest of exotic Hindu shrines, with the wealthiest of European and Pacific Rim tourists, but Mahabalipuram was also the center of the statue-making industry in India.

Durga Works, old man Durga riding the tiger, had the monopoly. Every statue of Shiva, Vishnu, or Brahma, that hundreds of street people tried to sell to tourists everywhere in India, was pounded out right here in Mahabalipuram by a small army of apprentice sculptors. They were really kids conscripted from the neighborhood, mistreated like slaves and forced to work sixteen-hour shifts in abysmal conditions for hardly any pay. The Durga Gestapo ran deep. There were rumors that street vendors selling statues not bearing the Durga logo would be found later in compromising positions, very dead, with their non-Durga statues protruding from various orifices. Durga kept tight control over everything he owned and kept those kids working round the clock, chiseling away at lumps of rock. The sound was so loud it competed with the surf. Clink-clink-clink, there goes a Shiva for a tabletop in Tokyo.

Regardless, Bullmoose had found himself; he was in Brahmaloka, with all the splendors of earth. Great weather, plenty of beaches, a fair share of tourists who threw plenty of coins in his guitar case, and an occasional fraulein or geisha daughter mixed in with the Hindu ladies. He was an avatar, prancing in shit. But, number one: nothing ever stays the same.

He first sighted the little Gypsy on the beach, as a silhouette in the rising moon. Waves pounded on the jetties guarding the temple behind her, sending fountains of spray into the sky refracting the moonbeams like fireworks made from salt water. Although wrapped in dark shadows he could sense her sharp eyes perceiving him, burning through her veil.

People walked this part of the beach for all reasons all times of day and night, but this was something totally different. Maybe it was the shimmering moonlight reflecting off the ocean's incessancy that sent his blood flowing. Whatever it was, shock waves of desire rippled through him, but not without consequences that would change his life forever.

A couple of nights later he saw the little Gypsy at Cudalore Cathy's Cafe. Birdlike as the most delicate of beauties, the little Gypsy's eyes were fire-piercing brown. Her petite round face was garlanded by the bounty of her lustrous black hair. Her smile was like the ageless Shakti, the mother goddess, the energy that powers the universe. She smiled at him. He stood to invite her to sit, and she was gone. He turned his head for only one instant and she was zip, gonzo, dissolved into the palm-shadowed Mahabalipuram night.

Later, when he played for money as he did at the end of each evening, when the German tourists left their wives snoring and came to Cathy's to get drunk and then some, Bullmoose swore he could feel her watching him. There from behind a palm frond, no, there near the screen door to the kitchen, but no. He wondered if his mind was playing tricks with his eyes. If she was real, why was she doing this? The surreal game of hide-and-seek aroused him. Clink-clink-clink. Another new Vishnu for a mantel in Düsseldorf.

He hung around later than usual that night, hoping she'd come back to him, but no. Eventually all the patrons stumbled away to sleep it off in expensive mosquito-netted rooms. Bullmoose was alone, sitting at a little wrought-iron table in the sand. The sounds of the sea and the sounds of the stones were all that were left. Cathy sidled up alongside him, rubbing him high up on his thigh, to see if there was something he wanted to buy that she could sell. But no thanks, Cathy, and no insult suggested. None taken.

He packed up his guitar and headed off to the ocean. He trudged along on the beach past the temple. Disheartened, and a little stoned, he laid out his sleeping bag on his spot twixt two flowering hibiscus at the point where the jungle brush gave way to the sand. He lay down and gazed into the unfathomable, voluminous universe. It was just him, the rhythm of the waves, and clink-clink-clink.

Not long after, he was in a large purple room playing chess with an attractive woman with uncommonly short hair. Actually she was bald. And she was bored, very bored playing with Bullmoose. She was kicking his wimpy ass. They sat on a thick rug with a low cocktail table of ornate chess pieces between them. The pieces were not of the conventional sort, but something more like those gimmicky chess sets where the pieces are figurines of the Revolutionary War or the Rockettes or dinosaurs or, as in this case, the New York Yankees, and of course on the other side of the board, the Boston Red Sox. The fire in the fireplace roared next to them. The bald woman moved her knight, who looked a whole lot like Ron Swoboda did in his prime on the Mets, and placed it near Bullmoose's king, which looked exactly like Carl Yastrzemski, which made sense since he was the clean-up hitter for the Red Sox. Her smile was wicked. "Check."

At that moment, a huge man, maybe nine feet tall, broke through a brick wall and demanded that everyone stay still while he searched the room for hidden recording devices. It was then that Bullmoose realized he was sitting in a very fancy living room where an avante garde party was in full swing. Loud, but very cool, jazz modulated through the buzz of the partygoers. Behind him on the circular staircase, two flat-chested lesbians were engaged in an oddly balanced oral sex situation.

The giant brought with him some agents who were now ripping the place apart, checking for concealed bugs that might be tapping the room. They sliced open couch cushions and slashed behind picture frames. One of them was getting head from a bimbo on the floor who thought it remarkable that his penis was so long, and blue, and covered with sharp and prickly thorns like a rosebush. "That sure will hurt a lot," Bullmoose heard her say.

Bullmoose moved Yaz one square over to his left and smiled at the bald woman who looked exactly like Grandma. Before Bullmoose had a chance to figure out what he was doing with the Red Sox as his team, she immediately slid Mel Stottlemyre into position on the square directly in front of him, protected by Thurman Munson, who looked funny dressed in drag. "Checkmate."

"Nobody leave!" The giant boomed in a menacing deep bass that echoed off the brick walls. Instead, the party grew ever more frenzied. People were snorting drugs on the fire escape and then some jumped off and flew away; some were smashing their glasses and other breakable objects into the fireplace spraying glass chips and glowing embers all over Bullmoose. Grandma just sat there and laughed, while others in the room were undressing. Some exhibited mixed gender body parts while others were simply exquisite with divine proportions. The giant bellowed again. "Nobody can leave until we figure this out. Somewhere in here is the piece we need."

Grandma looked over to Bullmoose from in the midst of a roomful of naked people gyrating about in an orgy of lust, booze, and drugs. She smiled her most moonful and purred, "In the end, all we want is love." Bullmoose wondered why she didn't say, "You can't be too careful with the ones you love." As she leaned forward to kiss him, her breasts, which were meaty and bouncy, became exposed when her silk shirt unbuttoned.

It was starting to get good when the giant grabbed him by the neck, hauled him outside onto the fire escape and dangled him over the railing. People around him started pouring their cocaine down his nose and Bullmoose started choking and fighting for breath. There was so much white powder he couldn't breathe and, just when he thought he was going to suffocate and die, there came the crashing of the waves and the clink-clink-clink, and in this instant she was upon him, surprising him with a girlish laugh, dripping a light stream of sand onto his face to wake him up.

As he sat up spitting out the sand from his nose and mouth, she jumped on him and pushed him back down. She sat there giggling on his chest, her hair glistening in the Tamil balm. The fragrances of jungle flowers, sea salt, and Hindu pheromones swept into his nostrils, stimulating his gonads and pouring into his erection. Even totally unprepared, Bullmoose had a way of playing every situation with the same course of action. She sensed his dick growing full speed towards her so with one coordinated coy move bounced herself from his chest, and sat on the sand next to him. She lightly teased his dick now at full attention under his jeans, with playful brushings of her fingertips over his zipper, more with fascination than cock-teasing flirtation.

She talked to him in flowing rivulets of tantalizing Indian English, about the sand, the sea, and the stars. She had followed him home that night but was with some silly friends, so she didn't stop to talk to him even though she wanted to. Her father would kill someone, probably Bullmoose, if he knew where she was right now, but he could never find out, because he was always at work and she was always at play.

She was all light and very bright. He felt a grand déjà vu, much greater than the feeling of being here before or knowing her from a past life. It was more like he remembered her from a future life spiraling back, reversing time and splaying it open to all avenues and feasibilities.

He could barely answer her back. He was too infatuated with her sensuous youthful face ripe with wisdom, and her intelligent voice lush with passion. Mostly, he was riveted by his boner that screamed to rip out of his jeans. She sensed the discomfort he was in from desire. "No, I don't think we can do that. I hardly know you," she murmured into his ear. Waves of sumptuous jet-black hair fell onto his face. Clink-clink-clink, another Ganesh for a bookcase in Gyoza.

They went on like that for some time, Bullmoose barely able to communicate while in full combat against an unruly ejaculation. Sometime in the dead of night she stopped talking, laid her head on his shoulder and fell asleep with her arms wrapped around him, which slowly gave him respite without unmanly embarrassment.

He woke up several hours later as the sun tickled the night with its first turquoise light. She was unzipping his fly. "You've been such a good boy all night and I feel so bad. I'll give you some head to make you feel better before I have to go." Before he knew it his pants were down to his knees, her mouth engorging his dick, no barbs or fins thank god, her hand gently massaging his balls. It wasn't long before he exploded in her face. She gagged a little and giggled, "Oysters."

* * * * *

That was the part of the story Herbie didn't understand. During an odd period in Herbie's late teenage years when kids think they have become of age, and Bullmoose was back from somewhere who knows, he insisted it was time for Herbie to learn how to drink like a man. Learn from the best, he would say, and there was born yet another Bullmoosian platitude to be emblazoned across the heavens and gilded to the sky. One time he got a little buzzed and told Herbie about his travels, including a vague mention of the little Gypsy from India. Upon hearing it retold by Herbie, his cross-dressing poser middle school friends looked up from their Blackberries and remarked that Bullmoose had to be full of shit and the Gypsy was probably just a street hooker he spent too much money on. The blowjob Herbie understood, the falling asleep while embracing he did not.

According to Herbie, most people don't really touch when they sleep together. During the sex part, okay, the sleeping part, nah. It's not that they don't want to; it's that they probably just can't. But, not Danielle. She was the only woman in Herbie's past who could, and did. His every night for the last thirteen years was living proof of his constant loss of this one principal comfort, which was robbed from him when the world went completely insane.

It wasn't that he intellectually couldn't allow himself a relationship; he was just physically and emotionally incapable of having one, any type or kind, intimate, sexual, or whatever. His personal torment was too excruciating and was the cause of an arduous self-induced celibacy. Except, of course, for those several shameful times when he was so drunk and miserable he risked health and fortune with some wretch of a gutter whore who seduced him into an opprobrious sex act in some dirty alley on his way home from somewhere depraved.

He remembered sex to be great. He used to be all for it, every bit of it, and whenever he could. There was the first-time sex with a first-time partner that he practiced often in college, and the few years afterwards when he was going through the internship at the station. The freshness of the new experience always inspired people to perform at a higher level of intensity, men looking for high grades, women heightened by the excitement of the unknown, the newness inciting. Sometimes if the girl was hot enough and or the sex was great enough, Herbie arranged a second or third encounter where that little bit of added familiarity made the motion even more acrobatic.

That wild stallion behavior galloped to an even more happening level when he landed his first primetime crew assignment. Ira, in person, said to him that it was a big break that he got, that many an intern would sell their soul for it. Marty told him the hours were much better; he'd get a lot more money, and thereby be a cooler Herbie, with ta-dah! more chicks, end of chapter, beginning of story. He bought it; he loved it.

Now Herbie, from deep inside his scarred and scabbed psyche, was real glad he met Danielle before Jerusalem.

By the first part of the twenty-first century, American sexual behavior degenerated into profligate indiscriminance. Anything went on anywhere, anytime. Pornography flooded the Internet. Personal sex clips of all kinds and combinations abounded. The pharmachemical giants had pills for everything. Anonymity was an advantage.

The opposite was true for the Muslim world. The Saladins on that side of the planet decried that kind of behavior as undeniable evidence of Satan on earth. References to Sodom and Gomorrah were replete in their sermons to the kneeling faithful, whose spiritual leaders controlled every aspect of their daily lives. As their governments fell under wave after wave of fundamentalism, mosque and state became one, and the sexes were more and more segregated. As the West was getting it on, the East was getting none. The two sides were tearing away from each other at lightwave speed.

Of course, nothing stays the same. Down came the nuclear bombs, the mutations and epidemics. In the States, as the government cracked and society fragmented, the enlarged lower and poverty classes commenced fucking like there was no tomorrow, because in many instances there wasn't one, or certainly didn't seem to be one. Sex, drugs, and rock and roll, what else was there to look forward to? Black market cialis derivatives poured in as steady as the smizz.

The middle class, reduced drastically in size, put a Victorian blanket over everything, grateful to the rich for whatever crumbs they could get. They smothered their children in chastity, and those that erred lost their chances of marrying up.

The rich, always with the most options, took advantage of the emerging technologies while reverting to a Middle Ages morality. Like royal families, they used sex and marriage as a way to control their wealth and make themselves richer.

Herbie was blessed not to be alone in this world of woe. He knew how lucky he was, thrust into that dwindling middle class after the Exchange, already in love with a gorgeous woman who loved him back. A woman who couldn't fall asleep without him rubbing her, massaging her, tickling her. Her delicate limbs would clutch for his warmth as she tried to find a peaceful dream in a wicked world. It was the mother of his daughter who showed him the joys of partnering with a lover, a best friend, a soulmate, amidst the fetid stench and erosion of the modern world.

She was an angel who kept his life together after witnessing the horrors first hand and surviving. Everyday he raced as fast as possible to each successive tragedy, important that ABCNN be the first to get it to air. When he finally returned home, he would find his private blessing, ready, waiting to take him back in whatever twisted shape he was bent into. She would nurse him back to health all through the night so he could get back out there, straight and strong, and do it all over again.

It seemed like a good idea to sublet the apartment and move to Westchester so Sophie could grow up somewhat holistic. He, on his rare days off, could at least catch his breath and savor the reason he worked so hard. It was to be a new beginning, the start of a new life, a good phoenix rising from the nuclear ash. But number three: you never know what is going to happen next.

With the attack on Indian Point Nuclear Power Plant, which was perfectly timed and performed so that the maximum amount of radiation could be spewed out over the largest population, he lost everything he thought he had managed to save in one terror-filled afternoon.

Now because sex was linked to memories of a ruined woman floating in a bathtub of blood, it was the furthest thing from his mind. Those images did no good for an erection. Instead he consumed enormous amounts of alcohol to ease his daily suffering.

That's why this morning it seemed so strange that he couldn't get Maria's smile out of his mind. It stimulated this old familiar tingle at the base of his balls.

* * * * *

Herbie caught himself in a frozen pause by the entrance of his apartment building. For how long he was standing there deep in a personal trance he did not know, but when the psychic roadmap shook, he swerved around a strange cloverleaf that eventually brought him back to his empty lobby on the West Side of Manhattan. Luckily there were no puzzled witnesses to this strange private moment of his, lost in time with Bullmoose.

He opened the door and stepped out into the curious cold. It rushed onto him and clung to his face as he descended the several steps of the aging concrete stoop and turned towards Broadway, walking in the direction where Central Park used to be. The working world rushing to industry sidestepped around him as he made his unsteady way to work.

There were a couple of ordinary squirrel killers, constantly moving, lighting smokes, nervously looking about, giving him a never you mind. Yesterday they would have seemed more reassuring, but today they seemed ominous.

There were the same silent, angry families sleeping on the air vents coming up from the subway. Their blood was clean enough to keep them out of Shantypark, but there was nothing else left for them, except this warm, ventilated patch of sidewalk they guarded with a vicious urban vengeance. Huddling together for warmth, they barely looked at him as he walked by. They too gave him pause to ponder. Yesterday they would have been part of the landscape; today they seemed neglected.

He was invisible to the anonymous now rushing past him. The sun glassed, the faceless, jockeyed around him on the sidewalk, readjusting their earphones, keeping cadence, as if he wasn't there.

He could only describe their emptiness, which was never so clear to him before, as simply, thankless. Yet how different were they than he? Not much, he reflected if this was yesterday. But it wasn't, it was today.

Adding to his uneasiness was the undeniable golden fog still hanging in plain view somewhere over Shantypark, which the thankless, marching briskly away in their hurry to oblivion, didn't even notice.

* * * * *

21

Monday, December 23, 2047, 7:05 a.m.

Maria walked through the inner security checkpoint at City Hall. The last few press conferences she attended here in the large atrium were jammed, packed solid with veterans from around the world. Today the City Hall lobby, usually bustling with reporters and crews, was empty.

The guards were pleasant, recognizing her from the news reports. One even asked for her autograph after she passed through the screens but, as she was signing it, the troglodyte that the mayor used as a receptionist flashed Maria a faint wan smile, which was worse than no smile at all.

Maria took the high road and ignored the contempt. Her Prada footsteps echoing off the hard tile floors, she lighted her svelte self onto a red, leather couch on the other side of the atrium perched beside the armored door. She wasn't in a good mood; her head was woozy from drinking too much New York State red, and she just didn't like that nasty spinster biddy squatting at the reception desk, especially her insipid little facemails.

The steely grey armored door to the mayor's inner office glistened in the fluorescence with a metallic sheen that looked like perspiration. Mayor Storm installed the door during the last gang war after one of his deputy mayors was kidnapped during a daring daylight raid and eventually beheaded. The atrocity was televised live on ABCNN with the highest of ratings, much to Marty and Ira's eventual enrichment. At that time Maria was only a middle school brat getting straight A's and trying to evade the parental blocks on her Internet browser.

Hostilities had subsided years ago with the formalization of the territories within Shantypark and the arrival of the First Army to put muscle behind that unwritten understanding. At this point everyone thought the armor on the mayor's office door was probably not even needed. Jack, while in intermittent moments of great attention to the smallest of details, alluded to the day when he was going to remove the ominous entryway with the heavy metal plates, because it didn't seem pleasant or diplomatic. But he hadn't yet, probably because you never know what's going to happen next.

Maria sat somewhat self-consciously, although confident enough to know her designer outfit fit her perfectly, making that Neanderthal at the reception desk entering data into her iMac look slightly worse than a Peruvian wood lizard. She barely had time to start feeling uncomfortable about anything when Jerry pushed through the outer door into the grand hallway. It troubled her that she didn't look herself, and that he knew it too. But she also knew this wasn't the time or place for him to ask. So they both wrote it off to the red wine. Thank God, he didn't pull out his biopod.

A red light started blinking on a control panel on the anthropoid's desk. She picked up a phone, listened, looked up with an icy glare, which Maria took as jealousy, and pushed a nearby button. The armored door began to grind. Maria stood up next to Jerry, waiting for the door to slide open wide enough for them to step in to the mayor's inner sanctum.

Behind the solid steel wall was an operations room. It was much bigger than expected. Huge banks of monitors lined the walls, ready for anything from worldwide teleconferences to aerial reconnaissance of street-to-street combat. It also was hard linked to the city's central database and continual real-time updates from thousands of detectors situated in strategic sites throughout New York. A decade ago they ran a war for the preservation of the city's very existence right from here.

Once inside, Jerry blustered his overly gracious good mornings, but Maria went straight to a side table with a simple but generous coffee service. She poured hers black into a white coffee mug that had the new city-state logo of a red apple with two bites taken out of it, one from each side, under which the words read "I still luv NY." She always loved the mayor's brand of reality mixed with optimism.

Joining Jerry, already sitting opposite the mayor, his chief of staff, and the general on the other side of a mahogany conference table, she took a sip of her coffee and burnt her lips. She hid the pain and annoyance quite well, except from Jerry, and waited in the awkward silence for a gravid moment, as they observed her, each coming to their own impressions about this sudden luminary, this internationally known supernova TV star. Maria was surprised by the calm and steady beating of her heart and her subsequent realization that it came from a place deep inside, where she felt alive and without constraint; right now she couldn't put on an act for them even if she wanted to.

Sam broke the ice. "Okay folks, it is now 7:11. We have clearance at 7:18. So I suggest we move this on to the chopper forthwith. We can conduct the briefing once we are airborne."

She gave Jerry a quick what's up glance. He shrugged, and they tried not to appear too dumbfounded.

"Don't worry, people. Only good things are waiting for a global all-star TV reporter and her ever-faithful watchdog producer." The armored door banged shut behind them punctuating Pellet's not-too-subtle sense of sarcasm. They now were essentially locked in the operations room as it locked others out.

"What's with the riddles, General?" Maria's snap was plainly transparent despite Jerry's deepest wish that it was not.

"Riddles?" Pellet took the cue, stood up and moved forward to face them, always the believer that a good offense is the best defense. His quiet demeanor belied his personal ferocity, and he spoke with a soft and intelligent voice. "You call this a riddle? Yet I think it is you, Ms. Primera, that is the enigma here. That you could even express a mote of effrontery as I am about to offer you the opportunity of a lifetime—when I could just as easily crush your career like a troublesome mosquito—is beyond my understanding."

Jerry cringed. Maria had to use every bit of psychic strength to stand firm. Pellet could have nailed her right then and there, but for the moment he needed her, so he lowered his voice even further and shook his head, smiling with an ostensible true sense of paternal sweetness. "I am going to choose to ignore your impertinence and write it off as immaturity, even though I see this look in your eye that wants to blame me for what happened yesterday to your lost interview. So, I will leave you with one more question to reflect upon during this morning's journey and that is: in what way conceivable, Ms. Primera, would my lack of knowledge as to Salem Jones' whereabouts aid in my job in protecting this city and its inhabitants from any further harm?" Maria could swear the subtitles read, "Be sure that I'd kill him with my own bare hands if I could."

Sam broke the jagged silence again. "I suggest we take this upstairs. It is a two-and-a-half hour flight all said and done, which should get us to the meeting exactly on time."

Jerry finally jumped in. "Where are we going? And Your Honor, if it involves us and it's newsworthy, why can't I have my crew?"

The mayor smiled. "We can't use cameras where we are going. Not yet. It is too high-level confidential. No one outside this group knows. This trip will be much-needed background for you."

Sam started handing out flight jackets and helmets from a closet near a mechanical sliding door. He pushed the button for the elevator that will take them eight flights up to the helipad on the roof.

* * * * *

The helicopter lifted gracefully from the roof of City Hall into the winter sky. Sam, as usual, was at the controls with no copilot by his side for these secret flights. In the cabin, Maria stared out the window into what was actually a beautiful sight. Their height above the earth diminished the visual impact of the garish wounds that had been perpetrated upon Manhattan, blending the city below into a broad google map of greater appeal.

Once they had left the city airspace behind, Sam put the controls of the aircraft over to autopilot and walked back into the noisy cabin. He took an empty seat and pointed to the button on his helmet. Maria understood and pushed the button on hers and could now hear his tinny voice. "Listen up. We are going to be flying low to the ground to this meeting. This chopper has been manufactured with the latest of stealth technology, so no one out there is going to know where we are or where we are going."

Maria caught Pellet's eyes, confident, smiling. He seemed to be operating from several different agendas. She wondered what kind of pornography he liked. Was he one of those dirty pictures on the forbidden websites, in full parade uniform standing hunched in front of some kneeling naked teen whose head he forcibly held with mouth gaping wide open? She also wondered which sex would that teen be. She never trusted him before but now for some reason he began to disgust her.

Sam handed her some documents. Maria, shocked by her own triple X-rated reverie, was glad he could not invade her thoughts the way his voice invaded her ears. "Read these, Maria. They'll give you the skinny on where we are headed. And these," he handed her a thicker booklet, "will tell you about whom you are going to meet."

* * * * *

22

All morning Jamal drifted in and out of an effortless slumber with long revolving dreams. A satiny place of pure softness, like immersion in amber mist. The downy bed cushioned him against all the pain that wracked every muscle, bone, and joint in his thin little body. Voices glided in and out. Gentle, resonant tones emerged from hoarse, desolate places.

"My people were starving and angry, ready to kill, but now they don't seem to want to fight anymore."

"They all had heard about it. They were all talking about it but, of course, none of them could have believed it would really be like this."

"Yesterday I could never have sat down with you, without pointing all my guns at you."

Once the sounds of velvety feet came into his tent to assemble all around him. Through half-open eyes he saw faces of many men, some dark like his, some white, some with lots of hair, others hardened and scarred now merciful and mild. All gathered around to witness in silence, to view his life with great endearance.

Other times he saw women unlike any he had ever seen before. They had sympathetic, loving eyes that probed for his sorrow, for his pain, yearning to take away all that hurt.

One time he found himself floating out and above in the air looking down over the tents, people converged around the perimeter, hoping for a healing touch, hoping for just one glance. Glimmets of speech, murmural, effusive, reached Jamal's ears.

"My uncle stopped doing smizz. He's taking a shower for the first time that I can remember."

"Yes, my brother, it's unreal how clean I feel."

"This baby girl is almost a year old and it's the first time I have ever seen her smile." Jamal looked down in wonderment at his grandmother holding his baby sister in her arms. The little girl was simply all smiles, one after another, and chubby baby healthy.

Floating out there just far enough away was the sun, golden and strong, burning forth the life.

Jamal opened his eyes and saw Salem through the tent flap, breathing in the words of all those who reached his ears. Sometimes his expression was genuine and glad, often his eyes seemed hollowed by pain, but always they glowed with a light of their own, embedded far behind the realm of human history, centered in the spiral of creation.

Jamal crawled out of his cozy bed and sneaked over to the tent flap. He peaked into the connecting tent where Salem was sitting, surrounded by men and women of all colors and kinds. A thin black man, dressed in black clothes, who Jamal thought he had seen before, stood up to talk.

"I don't know where to begin. You got this joint all turned around, man, and that is good. Oh yes, all good. But, I have to say it again because this is beyond good, man, it is incredible." The people around him vocalized assent. Marcus continued. "In a few short hours we have the leaders of the strongest gangs in New York gathered peacefully in one tent actually hearing the word "truce" being spoken many times. This is it. This is the Council. It don't get better than this." Marcus looked about the tent and his voice turned bitter. "But Gregor ain't here. None of us like his stinking ass anyway. Those stanis came in here organized. They were very good at being very bad. Gregor himself is one very sick dude. We don't know who he is, but he can't be one of us."

Salem shook his head like a gentle older brother and smiled. "Let it go Marcus. Whatever time it is, we don't have much." And then the room smoothed, and the feelings soothed, and there was nothing left in that immediate space that had any room for opposition.

* * * * *

23

The helicopter landed in a clearing in the middle of the mountains on the shore of a beautiful blue lake, just beginning to ice over for winter.

The Adirondack Mountains were far enough away from the nuclear explosions for any direct environmental consequences. Of course the socioeconomic fallout was worse than awful. People, just scraping by then, were now totally impoverished. During the restructuring of the economy and the waves of population migration, many original Native American inhabitants who had been resettled in nearby reservations started drifting back.

Cranberry Lake was tucked away in a forgotten corner of the Adirondack State Park. There was a violent windstorm here back in the mid-1990s. It's recorded as a natural disaster, but there are those who say it was an act of some great forgotten spirit who could see long into the future. The storm knocked down thousands of acres of trees closing all the trails into the area, denying any access to the interior. The state was forced to close that area of the park for the longest time. After several decades, just as the new hardwood and evergreen forest made its magnificent come back, the Exchange hit. As the reality of limited nuclear war settled in around the globe, the descendants of the six Iroquois tribes scattered around these mountains in Canada and the Northeast USA, upon instinct migrated back here to Cranberry Lake to become a nation once more. They went back to their old ways before Europe trespassed onto their continent with spurious claims to ownership backed by some Christian god who blessed his followers with superior weapons of destruction and village decimating diseases.

In a world gone insane, these Native Americans had seen it before and chose a simple, ancient way to raise their children. They liked it remote and inaccessible. The Great Spirit had prepared for them the way back. Everything is interconnected.

Jack Storm, the mayor of New York the city, had taken control of New York the state, from the ex-governor, because the state had no funds and no ability to raise taxes, and therefore no real economic power. It did not offer much of a consumer base to the multinationals, who thought of everything as direct market share. Without commerce, the rural provinces in this snowy area were going to wither, die and rot. But Jack came from a different sort. He wasn't able to just sit back and bear witness to the problems of his neighbors without reaching out with a helping hand. Besides, he did have his city to look out for, and its watersheds extended deep into those mountains. Being the wise man beyond his years that he was forced to be, he made many well-publicized arrangements to cover the clandestine ones that really counted. This gave the progeny of Hiawatha much greater autonomy than at any point in time during their centuries of relationships with unscrupulous white men.

Their goal was self-sufficiency, but at this point in history they were not going to be fools to reality. Jack soon became a friend. He gave them as much aid as he could in return for uncontested access to watershed areas, and for the safe house here on the southern shore of the lake. Hidden in the mountains, he could use this place to transfer his government in case of another imminent attack from a weapon of mass destruction. The log house up on the bluff rising from the lake, if not quite palatial, was more than adequate. It could house his staff and provide systems for him to direct the action from this great distance, while waiting out the initial intensity of any future nuclear, biological, or chemical attack on New York.

As the helicopter settled back down onto the earth, Maria saw a few dark-skinned men dressed in simple, warm clothing come out of the house and head towards the helicopter. Obviously, she thought, they were Haudenosaunee—what she just learned the Iroquois called themselves. Maria was good with a briefing; she usually remembered everything she read. Maria was also good in a meeting; but the extraordinary nature of this one made her skin goosebump.

Sam cut the engines as she stepped out of the chopper. The motor noise faded and the city people found themselves snared in winter silence. Maria instantly sensed the stillness as foreign, yet inspiring. Her life in New York was external combustion, chatter, noise, and chaotic bustle. But this place was clear, beautiful and pure, and it settled around her with a soft hushness. The lake waters beside her reflected the sapphire sky and bathed deep blue against the red earth.

The nimble man who was in charge, and she could tell by the way those around him acted, scampered with great verve down the path from the big house. As he approached, Maria could see that he was actually quite older than she originally thought, but he carried himself with the boldness of youth and the vitality of a great life force. He had the countenance of a sage, with skin weathered by the years. His bright brown eyes briefly met hers and twinkled with the light speed of the morning star.

He came toward Jack with the deepest respect. "Deganawida," Jack called to the Iroquois chief who, looking deeply into the mayor's eyes, pulled him in with a great embrace for a long fraternal moment. They pulled away, searching each other's eyes for the vast strength of character they always recognized inside each other.

"Mayor Storm, my good friend, I am honored once again by your presence"

"My humblest thanks for this imposition at such short notice, Chief Deganawida. I hate to have to burden you with our world's sudden and dangerous problems."

"Not at all. I have been waiting for this."

"How are you and Desidera, and your seven children and sixteen grandchildren?"

Deganawida chuckled as he thought of his growing little nation. "They are all well, Jack. The littlest one, Tadodaho, is already chasing after the others. He will be the one to grow up the mightiest hunter and serve his clan mother well. But I am concerned about you, Jack. There is something in your eyes like a shadow descending."

Pellet butted in. "Chief Deganawida, excuse me, sir, but our time is limited and our guests must be waiting."

"Aah, General Pellet, always so officious." Deganawida, never hiding his annoyance or his personal feelings about anything, turned towards Pellet. He looked deeply into Pellet's eyes and mumbled something no one could hear but everyone could understand. Returning to English he stayed true to his gracious protocol. He smiled, "Everything in its time, General. Come inside my guests, and let's get warm."

They all ascended the stony path back up the bluff to the log house. Once inside, the warm natural interior of wood and stone comforted them. As pleasant young

Iroquois men and women attended to their winter coats, Maria could see through a wall of bulletproof glass into a room with a long wooden conference table. The most powerful people in the surviving technological world were seated there.

* * * * *

24

If Bullmoose was obsessed with her before, after that night with the little Gypsy, he was now disturbedly rabid. She left immediately after the famous blowjob on the beach, in the nautical twilight before sunrise. Bullmoose lost sight of her as she skipped past the temple where her goddess-like form blurred into the obscure Indian Ocean mist.

That day was long and agonizing. Clink-clink-clink, a dancing Natraj off to a countertop in Kyoto. One hundred degrees in the shade of the palms, Bullmoose, sweaty and flushed, jotted lyrics like a madman into one of his ragtag notebooks. When the heat of the day became unbearable, he took a long swim in the Bay of Bengal, being careful as he walked upon the hot sand to avoid the little holes of shit left by his fishermen neighbors earlier in the morning.

Time took umbrage and scraped itself by, like crossing a street of broken glass barefoot while trying to avoid an oncoming bus. Even Bullmoose's usual fructiferous inspiration was begrudging. He strummed a few chord changes on his guitar, trilled a few notes and slapped the body of the Martin in beat with the invisible band he could hear in his head. But he just couldn't get that B string in tune. He tightened it and loosened it and tightened it again, his body pouring off sweat onto the guitar in the struggle, until the string snapped. He cussed and swore and unwound it from its tuning peg, knowing now why they call them the blues.

Around sunset Pranan came by to give him a ride to Cathy's, and he could immediately see on Bullmoose's face how the harmless fantasy for a mystery woman had progressed overnight into a crazed and frothing animal-like disease. As they drove into town, Bullmoose sat in the bouncy Ambassador, babbling and spilling his heart out.

Along the dusty highway they passed a ten-foot-high chainlink fence topped off with loops of barbed wire that surrounded a compound. Inside, groups of little children were sitting and chiseling large chunks of stone set upon splintery wooden tables, clink-clink-clink. Pranan gave the little slaves a lingering glance and tried to relate this living metaphor to his cavilous buddy riding shotgun. Life could be much worse than being in romantic love on a southern Indian beach when you are young, carefree, and without a responsibility in the world.

Although he started drinking shots early in the day and was working on quite a buzz, later that night his music was particularly crisp and strong. None of the drunks trying to get laid at the bar could actually tell the difference that he was only playing with five strings. Once in the jolly madness he looked up and saw the orange man dancing by himself in ecstasy. At one point, obviously inebriated, he was kneeling in front of Bullmoose and air-guitaring along with the song, occasionally looking up to the sky as if in prayer.

All Bullmoose could think about was the little Gypsy. He looked for her in the bushes by the path to the ocean, no, by the post with the burnt-out lantern near where the lightweights threw up their cheap Indian vodka, but no. Maybe by the kitchen where the freshly dead fish caught by his very regular gastrointestinal neighbors stared back with no eyelids at those who were about to eat them. No, she was not there, either.

In the murky hours between closing time and dawn, Pranan let an inconsolable Bullmoose out of the Ambassador near his little sweet spot in the sand, Clink-clink-clink, off goes a Brahma to Berlin.

He couldn't believe it was only twenty-four hours ago she was sleeping here with him, her head on his chest. It seemed so much longer. He listened for her closely in between the sounds of the stones and the sounds of the sea, but he heard nothing but clink-clink-clink. He was beginning to feel a gnawing apprehension that maybe he wasn't ever going to see her again. Maybe he never really did see her; maybe she was a hallucinatory byproduct of living in India, a mere manifestation of a love goddess in the chimerical madness of Mahabalipuram.

As a waning crescent moon cleared the horizon over the muezzin sea, as if from out of the point of exact nothing between the waves and the breeze, she appeared. This time he was ready. They slowly moved closer towards each other, their faces within inches of their most intimate breathing spaces, her eyes moist, twinkling, their lips finally finding each other. Instantly they locked into a long and immersive kiss, as deep as the universe has ever gone to spawn a space where it could recreate itself.

They clutched each other recklessly as they fell to the sand. They made love all the rest of the night near the temple on the beach in the town where tender young children fashioned the gods with their indentured and innocent little hands. Clink-clink-clink.

This continued with ignorant bliss for a few weeks. Every morning Bullmoose woke to find her long gone. He spent his day lonely for the girl he hardly knew except for the deep excursions through each other's body to find each other's soul that always occurred late at night shortly before the Bengali dawn. By day he'd kick around town, smoking weed with Pranan, or chattering idly with the orange man, who always eyed Bullmoose in a strange intoxicated way. At night he sang a few songs at Cathy's, made some jokes, did some shots, all in anticipation of that magic time twixt the night and the day when his every romantic fantasy came true on the sacred beach by the temple made of sand.

Sometimes after lovemaking they lay spooned, her thick black hair blowing in the sea breeze into his grateful nostrils. He listened to the waves and the clink-clink-clink and could swear he was off in some other time somewhere else. It was here at the root of all creation where he was Brahmin; at the heart of human life consciousness he was Vishnu, and swirling about a pageant of newborn galaxies he was the cosmic dancing Natraj. He was an avatar prancing in shit.

Lying on the beach, their limbs entwined, their fragrances and juices, their breaths in and out, their continual arousals, peaks and then peace, he seemed to forget two sure things you can always count on: nothing stays the same, and you never know what's going to happen next.

It all changed the day Pranan finally brought him a new B string from a music store in Madras. He restrung his guitar and took it down to the temple and played in E minor for an hour or two by the ocean, with the orange man close by, occasionally clucking some anonymous supplication to the endless motion of the eternal sea. But when he returned to his little spot near the jungle, he was taken aback. All his belongings, what little he had, were scattered about, his guitar case ripped and splintered, as if some mad ninja Hindu karate god brought an undue and uncalled-for vengeance to this little spot Bullmoose called home. He was perplexed but not pissed off, because he always carried his stash of weed and his pipe with him everywhere he went, so very little was actually lost that could not be replaced. He just wrote it off to dogs, or vandals, or beggars, because every paradise has to have some thieves running in the night.

But she didn't show that night at Cudalore C's. Neither did Pranan, which was unusual. As a matter of fact, Cathy's was completely empty. No philandering ex-Nazis at the bar or heaving Samurais by the lantern post. It was totally empty, and that never happened before. Cathy, always the businesswoman, tried again to sell him a good-natured suck and fuck, which he politely refused. She laughed and gave him a grilled grouper to eat, a blanket to sleep on and sent him home, making a joke about his stepping in shit, which was funny because it was a constant reality of his life on the beach that he worked hard to avoid.

Back at his spot, he took off his sandals and spread the blanket over the sand awaiting his lady, his moonlight goddess, his Scheherazade of a thousand nights. Clink-clink-clink.

The stars were especially bright on this clear night of the new moon. Fantasizing about making love in weightless space, smoking a bong, he drifted off into the most vivid of abstracted sleeps.

He was in a restaurant, empty of people, noticeably so. The room was filled with empty banquet tables covered in lime green linen, adorned with rich pewter table settings, as if he had arrived early for an elegant yet offbeat medieval ball. Suddenly, out from the kitchen, burst four clean-cut waiters, all with short haircuts like his high school football team; wait, they were his high school football team: Knuckles, Pea-Brain, Elmo and Zanzanelli. They smiled at him with obvious recognition and then, in unison, they looked at each other, shook the tension out of their fingertips, leaned backwards and started to sing in perfect harmony like a barbershop quartet. It was the song he wrote in the heat of the day after his first night with the little Gypsy. "*Only you can make me feel this way*" . . . Over by the window with the sun streaming in on a bed of pastel flowers, her back turned towards him, was a dark-skinned, long-haired beauty, her lustrous black tresses draping over the luscious curves of her lean and naked body . . . "*Only you can take my breath away*" . . . where did Pea-Brain, who slept through all his classes during his sophomore and junior years in high school, ever find the talent to learn to sing that well? Then Bullmoose found himself sitting on the bed behind the dark goddess, so close he could smell exotic perfume. She turned to look at him and it was the little Gypsy with her athletic breasts bared and her face partially covered with a pink silk veil. He felt Peewee Bullmoose start to look for a way to escape from his underwear. "*Only you can wake with me each day-ee-ay*" . . . and the way the sun reflected on the back of her head, sending up spectral cascades of color refracting off the long pearl earrings that dangled in the locks of her ebony hair, she was Parvati, the consort to gods . . . "*Only you can make me feel this way*" . . . and finishing as strong as they had started, his high school buddies took a deep and appreciative bow, waved goodbye as if they would see him tomorrow in homeroom and exited stage left, yo Z'zanelli it was good to see you here in India my bro', and good luck on your new job as a consultant sanitation removal specialist. The love goddess little Gypsy parted her ruby lips as if to say something, but Bullmoose could not hold himself back. Before she could speak he reached down and grabbed her beard and kissed her with the greatest of yearning and starving passion. She started to squirm, trying to pull away, gagging and choking, and what was with that beard? He woke up as Pranan shoved his face away and they both spit into the sand, "Yucchh."

"Oh, Jeez, sorry man, I thought you were my love goddess. I was dreaming actually." Bullmoose said.

"Your love goddess? You pathetic dumb fuck! It really is time for you to wake up." Pranan spit again onto the sand with great disdain.

"Hey, dude, I said I was sorry."

"Fuck you. You really don't know how sorry you are."

Pranan never talked to Bullmoose like that before. "What's up with you, man? I mean, I really don't know what you are talking about."

"I'm talking about the little Gypsy, turkey shit, which she isn't. I found out she belongs to old man Durga who owns this entire town and who now has everybody and every stone statue in this area on his side and getting ready to cut your balls off. It's going to be like a lynching, like something your country used to do regularly to black people."

"Hey, wait a minute. If this guy has anger issues, man, like if he can't keep tabs on his old lady, what the fuck, someone has got to check her oil, and I know you know what I'm saying, my fellow male chauvinist pig. It's like the future now, dude, it's 1971. Ya' know what I mean? Hasn't he heard about woman's lib?"

Turns out old man Durga had not. And it turns out the little Gypsy wasn't his wife, she was his daughter from a third wife who he adored, who died giving birth to the little Gypsy. And it turns out she was only thirteen. And it seems Bullmoose had gotten her pregnant down on the beach that was dotted with the little holes of shit surrounding the sacred temple made of sand at the center of the universe. Daddy Durga, the richest and most powerful man in town, who couldn't give one twink or a nod about female liberation, was after Bullmoose's balls with a vengeance, and a posse.

Bullmoose, getting it, moved forthwith, rapidly following after Pranan, sticking to the shadows of the palms along the beach until they reached the Ambassador. Bullmoose threw his guitar in the back seat as Pranan fired the little tin car up. It roared like a mighty lawnmower, and they were out of there, albeit a bit on the slow side considering the situation, but being the only automobile in town it had to be faster than anything Durga could chase them with.

So far everything was quiet, but rule number one, nothing stays the same. There was only a single road out of town, and it had to go by Durga Works.

The morning sun was on the rise when, out on the highway up by the Durga compound, they saw a big ominous cloud of dust rise into the sky. As they got closer they could see that a huge flatback wagon filled with little statues of Hindu gods had just left the gate at the statue factory. It filled up the road, creating a roadblock, as if they knew who was approaching. Bullmoose imagined himself strapped to one of those wooden worktables while little Hindu children hacked away at the little personal statue of his manhood that caused all this panic in the first place.

Pranan seemed possessed. He jammed the gas pedal to the floor and the little car picked up speed. He made a quick right, swerving into the ditch by the side of the road to avoid hitting the heavy open wagon topped with stone. As they passed, Bullmoose looked up at the driver's seat and lo and behold he saw the old man Durga himself, and his lovely daughter; both saw him back. They had equally odd expressions on their faces for opposite reasons that he could well understand. Confronted by the imploring look in the little Gypsy's eyes and the unbelievable panic in his own heart, he knew through this inescapable manifestation of the count-on-able rules that he, in his brash insignificance, was toying with the immutable laws of the universe.

"Step on it!" he shouted over the din of the antiquated engine. Pranan for some ungodly reason was laughing like a maniac as he steered the awkward, brittle car out of the ditch and back onto the road, emerging in front of the statue wagon. He began shouting to Allah about how great he is and how amazing it all was, and the Ambassador took off down the hill, leaving the stunned wagon in the lurch. The little bumpy car leveled out at the bottom and with a bounce disappeared around another curve.

The wagon was out of sight behind them and the road ahead looked good to go. But number three; one never knows what is going to happen next.

Just around the next bend came the awful and unthinkable. The little tinny Ambassador started quivering and shaking and then snap and pop! It was a metallic wrenching, stomach-sickening sound. They turned around just in time to see through the rear window an indiscernible piece of metal bounce out from under the car and onto the road behind them. Pranan screeched the wounded vehicle to a stop, jumped out and sprinted back to retrieve the disjointed automotive part. Recovering it, he ran back and dove under the car, muttering that they were going to kill him now also, and why did he have to help this infidel idiot white man in the first place? Bullmoose waited with anxiety, his hands deposited in his pockets guarding his balls, realizing that he left town without wearing shoes and that it would be a mighty long walk back to Madras bare foot, and bare balls.

"Shit!" Pranan screamed and climbed back out from under the stricken Ambassador. "It's the damn lock to the driveshaft, man. It split in two. There is nothing to hold it to the wheel box." He flung open the trunk of the car and started rummaging frantically about for something he could fix it with, throwing things onto the side of the road that he didn't need. A stack of unused egg cartons, four long skinny bags filled with Styrofoam coffee cups, greasy mechanics gloves, but nothing that would hold two rotating pieces of metal together.

In the meantime the ox cart ascended the hill behind them and pulled around the bend into view. In that instant Durga recognized that he had almost caught up to them. He screamed loudly for his oxen to go faster, as a score of skinny little statue builders jumped out from the back of the wagon and started running downhill towards the stricken vehicle with weapon-size statues in hand. Bullmoose quivered when he envisioned the stone image of Vishnu embedded into the place where his Johnson used to be.

"American, where are you going to run now?" shouted old man Durga, holding up a menacing iron contraption that looked like two small shovels welded together at their handles. "Do you know what this is, American dog? I use this to geld the weak rams in my flock that are not worthy to breed with my ewes. I put these in the fire and when they become red hot I use them to burn off their balls. Do you see this, American? It's for you. It's for you. It's for you!"

What did he say? Where did Bullmoose hear that before?

"It's for you. It's for you. It's for you!"

Then it struck him.

He dove under the car and immediately located the dangling drive shaft and the lonely wheel box. He slipped off the ring the orange man gave him that fateful day when they first met on the beach and he was swindled for fifty rupees, and slid it over and onto the separated bolt of the primitive transmission. Not only did it fit exactly, but it easily slipped over the beveled edges and locked perfectly into place. He scrambled out from under the car, and Pranan, looking frightened and bewildered, jumped into the driver's seat and turned the key. The doughty little putt-putt fired back up.

Bullmoose dove into the passenger seat just as the first wave of statue assassins struck, smashing the windows of the vehicle with their little holy idols. The Ambassador, spewing sprays of broken glass and black diesel smoke, sped off just in the nick of time and just fast enough to keep ahead of the wave of Durga's little guerillas. The legion of lethal child sculptors raced behind them in their dust and exhaust, as Durga shouted after him, "It's for you, American. It's for you!"

They didn't stop until they got to the Madras airport, where they left the Ambassador at the sidewalk of the passenger drop off, the same spot where, many weeks earlier, Bullmoose had staved off blitzkriegs from squadrons of brobdingnagian mosquitoes and vanguards of cannibalistic supplicants.

Pranan dove under the chassis and retrieved Bullmoose's magic ring. Everything falling into place, they both marched barefoot onto an airliner bound for Boston as the doors were closing. Just like that, Bullmoose departed India, Mahabalipuram, his love goddess incarnate, and his paradise on earth, gladly calling it a fair trade to leave with nothing but his guitar, a new best friend and, most importantly, his balls.

He was half way back over the continent of Europe on his seventh tiny bottle of expensive vodka that this cute divorcee from Manhattan was buying in appreciation of his I'm-so-cute-and-don't-you-know-we-can-make-room-for-two-in-the-bathroom routine, when he realized he had been having sex regularly with an underage child and was most likely the father of her baby.

Herbie's father hated that part of the story, because he knew he might have a half Hindu brother whom Bullmoose was already paying more attention to in his mind than he was ever going to give to him. Grandma tut-tutted her son Henry and told him to mind his manners, that it was with the unbounded glory of the grace of God that his father was able to return to them with his most precious of possessions without which Henry himself would never have been born.

Bullmoose always just smiled at the end of the story and looked quite cocksure of himself, as he explained that nothing stays the same, which could be similar to saying things ain't always what they seem, and that everything is interconnected, even though in ways vast and mysterious, and that you never know what's going to happen next or, for that matter, you never know which part of the puzzle is the going to end up being the key.

* * * * *

On that latest Bullmoose thought, Herbie swiped his ID card and entered the editing suite, the darkness of the room matching his mood. It was a good sign that the computer was in sleep mode, because that meant the rendering of the audio animation was complete. Without hesitation he threw his jacket over the back of the chair as he pushed the mouse an imperceptible tinge of an inch in order to wake the screen up. Herbie pounced on the waiting playback controls.

He fast-forwarded through the first few minutes until he saw the doors to the prison start to open, the white light beginning to pour out. He reverted to the original point of view and the image on the main screen popped up as the bald man with many tattoos emerged out of the white light and approached the waiting government officials. Herbie played with the audio controls and, suddenly, sounds of chaos spewed out of the speakers. There were shouts and screams, which must have been coming from the parking lot, that drowned out everything else. He toyed with the program's concentric locator and moved its position onto the podium. Instantly the crowd sounds diminished and the muffled voices from the dignitaries on stage became audible. Herbie raised their volume.

"Congratulations on your freedom and we welcome you to New York, Mr. Salem Jones. I admit you look a lot older than your reported age of twenty-one."

The bald man look amused, and then spoke. "Older? Older than who? Today is your birthday, my friend. Mine too. We are all the same age; we're all as old as life. Happy Birthday."

The dignitaries on stage were tongue-tied, discombobulated. High-pitched sounds broke into the audio track. Herbie knew that they were the initial outcries from the crowd in the parking lot in reaction to the first big push by Pellet's riot control units, his Pythons, beginning to tighten their grip around the spectators like they were rodents. The bald man looked into the crowd with a mixture of curiosity and compassion and back at the panjandrums on stage. "Of course sir, you must know that I am not Salem Jones. I'm not even worthy to untie his shoes. You see my friend; today your society was to set him free from this prison. But you should know, he always has been free. And so, he has already moved on."

Herbie pounced on the video directional and immediately reversed the point of view to see what the bald man saw. The officials on stage looked confused and helpless. He raised the computer's eyeline to look past the podium and out into the riot now being pitched on the parking field below. There, off in the distance in the animation was the golden fog that he'd been watching now perched over the skies of Shantypark.

Up in the audio landscape pulsing out his computer, amongst the shrieks and caterwauls, lilting along the sky, confounding yet confirming all that was challenging Herbie from within, he heard the distinct celestial soprano singing a note up through its major third, and then skipping up an octave, down a sixth, and over again . . .

* * * * *

25

There was ruffling along the tent wall, some scuffling sounds from outside, and then a shout of "You can't do that." Within an instant Gregor and Ibrahim burst through the flap into the inner sanctuary, brandishing their not too polite AK-87s. All the men in the room jumped to their feet grabbing their weapons. For the second time in a few hours, Shantypark saw Marcus and Gregor enter into a stare-down; any miscalculated blink could sentence war.

"You trespass here. One more step, Gregor, and I will separate your ugly head from your blasphemous body."

"Empty threats, Marcus. This is a Council meeting where we swear not to shoot each other. So why the fuck wasn't I summoned? You know there is no Council without me."

"You didn't seem like you wanted to talk the last time we had the pleasure of seeing you."

Gregor ignored the sarcasm. "That's because your boy over there hypnotized everybody with his magic tricks."

"Strong magic, I'd say. It kept your sorry ass frozen for sure."

"I didn't see or hear too much out of you, Marcus, as a great leader of men. Here you are now. You can't beat 'em so you join 'em."

"The difference between me and you is that I believe Salem Jones is bringing good for all of us locked up here in Shantypark. For that I will gladly give myself up to him for redemption."

"And what's with this fucking holy born-again routine, Marcus. You're a killer and a thief, not some fucking disciple of new-age horseshit."

"That's old news, Gregor."

"Listen, fuckface, you need me, so get that through your stupid head, otherwise we would have killed each other a long time ago."

"This is good, for in your own way you two have begun your search for peace." All the people in the tent of the Council laughed and looked towards Salem as he spoke. He sat in calm repose, legs crossed upon the ground.

Gregor turned on Salem and erupted. "I am sick of this faggot dude who talks like a woman. Can't you all see through this bullshit? Who do you think I am? Do you think that I'm a stupid son of a Kyrgstani whore? That I don't know all the bullshit rumors about this Salem Jones? I am a great warlord descended from generations of mujahedin who brought honor and glory to their tribes and their homelands. I know who I am. So, answer me, who the fuck is this guy? How do you know who the fuck he really is? Anybody in this sick fuckin' world can say he's Salem Jones cause nobody ain't ever seen a Salem Jones. This guy could be some undercover squirrel-killer dick for all we know, probably sent by the city to infiltrate us, divide us up and cut off our nuts."

Marcus leaned towards Gregor and, in almost a whisper, asked, "Why do you mock what you can't believe, Gregor? Why does that cause fear in you?"

"Don't fuck with me." Gregor pulled a sawed-off shut gun from his belt and pointed it two inches from Marcus' head. "Give me one good reason why I should believe this is who you say he is, and I won't have to blow your fucking shit for brains to hell."

All focus in the tent was upon Salem, who was quiet, with a supple determination, at once adamantine and easy. He looked back and around into the eyes of the people who were gathered unto him under the Council tent, representatives of every gang and clan in Shantypark, every race, creed, color, and all combinations thereof.

He stood and moved with grace amongst them, touching those he passed on the crown of their head or the points of their shoulders, each bending toward him as if they were fragile flowers reaching for the life-giving light of the sun, gaining strength through him from some unseen transference of spirit. The room's energy flowed towards Salem with such great magnetic force that Gregor once again was thrust into a wordless stupor in the presence of this effortlessness.

"My brothers and sisters. So very, very long ago, there was no darkness and there was no light. There was only the is. Science attempts to determine exactly when the universe began, but can't. Even the most dedicated scientists say that, according to their most extensive calculations, at that first millionth of a second of creation, their comfortable mathematics simply break down and become worthless. Apparently the closer we get to the beginning with these theories, the quicker they all come to an end. The question looms so large, what was before that millionth of a second, and what was before that?

"Let's assume that an instant of awesome majesty came from nowhere – where there was not one thing before, now there are millions of galaxies, with billions of stars, all of which burn with the glory of such amazing fuel that they blaze forth atoms across the infinity of time and the expansion of space to right here, this spot, this world, where they became the stuff of life.

"As the earth cooled we were formed to fit this place, and hence, our bodies were fashioned. We found ourselves in the middle of colossal forces, given sweet life and bathed by the glory of the heavens, yet stricken with hunger and fear in the darkness and the cold. We knew not where to turn.

"Longing for answers, we conceived a Creator in the image of ourselves, and under the assumed protection of these primitive beliefs, civilizations of men and women began to spread over the planet. For those who didn't believe, we made rivers run red with young blood, and carved huge holes in the earth to fill with the bones of their martyred sons.

"However, echoing from deep inside, we all can feel that one spirit, and hear that one voice, if we so choose. As every man and woman is a child of that spirit, those who care to live in its glory must seek the light of truth that comes from within."

As he talked he taught, and as he walked he seemed to swirl, touching each man and each woman just slightly, enough to lighten their countenance and lift them up.

"How incredible is the torment for souls on earth today? Have we created so much spiritual debt that it's too much to ever repay? Harmony envelops the entire universe, yet here in humankind we cower with fear in a world whacked out of balance.

"The battle between the darkness and the light rages here amongst us upon this hallowed ground. We must learn to give this world up, my brothers and sisters. The time is now at hand."

A great murmur rose within the tent and the people looked about at one another, astounded. As Salem went about the room he came face to face with Gregor and Ibrahim. He looked upon Ibrahim and saw the demons he possessed inside. Salem reached out his hand and placed it upon Ibrahim's forehead and squeezed, and his truth bore deep into the craven yellow eyes of the evildoer. He commanded, "Get thee back, Satan."

Ibrahim fell to his knees with a groan and, in a rush, dark shadows seemed to pass from deep inside of him. Salem took him by the chin and lifted his face to look into his eyes. "Be of good cheer man, your sins are forgiven." Ibrahim looked up at Salem in palsied relief, feeling clean for the first time in his life. He cried in absolution and prostrated himself before Salem like a newborn baby. The Council, giving witness to this mighty act, was filled with wonder and awe.

"All the children have this great power burning within them. It is from the power to forgive that comes the source of all healing. So I put forth now to the Council; it is true healing that we in this world really need."

The tents all around surged with ease, and with joy. With no room for opposition, the men dropped their weapons in epiphany, and all fell to their knees before Salem. Except for Gregor who, upon feeling Salem's deep searing eyes of truth fall upon him, fled the tent in fear.

Jamal rose from his hiding spot behind the tent flap, scratching his ears. The blood dripped off the incensed tumors now growing larger and more furious up and down the length of his neck. He entered the great and awesome tent, the light in which was now so dazzlingly bright, that he had to shield his meek eyes from the glare, with his long-suffering and bloody little hands.

* * * * *

26

Maria felt stronger than ever, sharper, centered, as the helicopter lifted off from the shore of Cranberry Lake. Her head was overflowing.

The meeting was short, but splendid. Maria loved roller coasters. Especially when riding with royalty. After the introductions, the chancellor of Euro-Reich kicked it off with a long piercing stare that made her shiver, which then turned into a stony cold smile that didn't even try to mask his personal consternation. The Sony CEO, who was a Korean national, spoke first. He was most clear and succinct . . . events of the past several decades have left western man in no position to clamor for the individual liberties and personal freedoms in which they luxuriated before . . . life has to be restricted, limited, regulated . . . and most importantly, the media has to be controlled . . . it causes too much fear . . . it causes too much chaos and discordance . . . the pace of the Exchange proved all that . . . people were glued to their TVs as horrific events of enormous magnitude unfolded all over the planet . . . and the media with its own self-interests put their own spin on things . . . this makes the daily challenge of control and distribution of the resources that keep people alive very difficult . . . we live in a post-Exchange world . . . any moment another huge disaster could take out millions and put the entire planet into advanced economic aftershock . . . society depends on trade and the buying and selling of goods and commodities . . . any danger that threatens the super-corporations and the allied states must be removed . . . the Alliance of was not prepared for a worldwide movement that enhanced the spiritual, de-emphasized the material and advocated a return to simpler ways . . . the leaders of the world agreed; Salem was bad for business.

The others of the Alliance at the table had heard this speech before, but seemed to admire the eloquence and ardor with which it was delivered once again. Yet it was the woman who ran Singapore who was the best. She was smooth, like a tree snake clinging to the bark without any apparent effort, blending into the environment, putting both prey and predators off guard. She rose from her chair, walked slowly around the room to where Maria sat and, leaning on the magnificent conference table, propped herself right in her face. She took Maria's hand gently in her own and looked long into her eyes. Maria was the one they trusted . . . they watched all of her Salem Jones clips of the last six months . . . they knew the story because of her efforts, her research, her passions . . . now they needed her . . . they needed her to help the world stand against the ignorance and the fear.

Pellet, operating with apparent ease amongst the corporate czars, interjected. He thought Salem was still in New York, probably in Shantypark. The lawyer for the Microsoft delegation intervened to applaud Pellet's hypothesis. Everyone seemed to agree.

The curious woman, part Asian, part Caucasian, leaned deep into Maria's face. Her voice was now quiet, but even more forceful, almost whispering, her face so close, the breath from her words moved tips of Maria's hair . . . my dear, one newscast could change the way the whole world thinks . . . could change the whole world . . . broadcast live over every station in every part of the planet . . . and when contact was made . . . the exclusive interview . . . unprecedented exposure in a world of monstrous precedents . . . the opportunity of a lifetime.

Pellet agreed; she was the one woman for the job. She already had the sympathies of the entire planet; people connected to the story through her.

The pale, thin man from Digi-Bell, who Maria thought was middlesex when she first saw him, agreed with the general and added that the location of this newscast was key.

"Right outside Shantypark," said Pellet. Broadcasting from there would show the world that that they had nothing to fear because they, the powers that be, had everything in control. The rest of the room vocalized a collective agreement that sounded like "Aah", but John Kennedy Storm was unusually quiet.

After that business was done, they were through with her. Waiting for the mayor and the general to finish, she gathered her coat and wandered out the door. She left Jerry, who had a great reticence for the cold, back in the lodge by a cozy fireplace. She carefully made her way back down the steep path towards the lake, her head so filled with promises and dreams.

She stood at the water's edge, near a boulder. The lake, several inches away, barely licked the sand on which she stood. Noon, she knew looking up into the Adirondack sun. Her aura was awash with the incredible possibilities waiting for her, yet she somehow found focus centered right here on this spot, trying hard to imagine how many countless times the planet had rotated this lake to this vantage point under the winter sun.

"It is said this is the boulder by the lake where the clan mother came to birth her children, and there…" he said pointing to a cluster of white birch on a rise near where they stood, "was found the remains of a longhouse she used hundreds of years ago to guide her people, her warriors and farmers, in the ways of the Great Fathers and the Creator Mother."

Maria turned to see Deganawida seeking her eyes. He didn't startle her, but how did he get so close without her hearing him? She smiled; his eyes said it all. They stood in silence looking at the world over each other's shoulder, she at the cluster of birch at the top of the hill, and he out at the lake waters, reflecting the light of the sky. He began to pray in a tongue she didn't understand but it stirred her.

The ancient chanting and the mantra of Deganawida's melody were still swirling in her head a couple of hours later when Sam guided the stealth chopper down into a perfect landing onto the helipad on the City Hall roof. Without a moment's thought or hesitation, Maria jumped out on the run.

* * * * *

27

The Hummer was parked across the street from the mayor's office in the security zone, Herbie as usual in the driver's seat. When he saw Jerry and Maria step out of the side entrance and on to the street, he threw it in gear and moved the vehicle right along side the curb to pick them up. They popped into the back, Herbie noting the voltage in his body when eye contact came with Maria through the rear view mirror.

In and around all the excitement she was feeling with her career about to skyrocket, Maria knew it would be hard work to ignore Herbie. She longed to talk with him, when the time was right.

Branford was back to his cocky and conceited self, like yesterday never happened. "Eighty-ninth and Fifth Avenue, cabbie, and get the asphalt out of your asshole buddy; we are in a hurry."

"How did you know where we were going?" Maria shot out at Branford.

"The general called me himself. Wanted me to look out for the crowds of homeless encircling Shantypark. Doesn't want them in the video. Funny, first time he called himself 'General.'"

The drive uptown was quick. Pellet had posted squirrel killers on every corner, waving the Hummer through the traffic. The closer they got, the thicker the crowds grew, which was opposite the norm. Most people always kept as far away from Shantypark as they could.

Herbie pulled the Hummer up near the old engineer's gate, across the street from the now abandoned Church of the Heavenly Rest. He couldn't help but feel the irony. They were going to broadcast from the front of the old Guggenheim Art Museum, now desolate and bullet ridden, standing like an empty monument to ages long past, when man's artistic expression of his universe and of himself were acts of creation simply for creation's sake.

Maria jumped out of the car before Herbie could even put it in park. He found it hard to take his eyes off her. How could he never have seen her like this before? He didn't move, riveted to his spot behind the wheel. He knew he had to set up the transmitter but he felt compelled to watch over her.

She brushed some of the wavy raven hair off her forehead and stood in wonderland as she watched people emerge from every wrinkle of this debilitated part of the city. They were slow, tentative, coming out of the abandoned luxury apartments, doorways, alleyways, and burnt-out vehicles on the streets around, all moving towards Maria. There was recognition there; they understood who she was. They had seen her before on the newscasts, but their eyes were seeking more, as if nearness to her gave them more of the answers they were desperate for. She stood amazed, feeling light-headed, almost tipsy, as they came closer. Despite Jerry's admonitions of danger, she found them childlike in their gentle approach. Like munchkins discovering Dorothy after she landed in Oz.

But Branford found them cult-like, with the vacant eyes of deer caught in headlights. "The squirrel killers would have a field day just plowing into these guys. There wouldn't be enough medals to hand out to cover the body count of these lemmings." Doe-eyed people continued congregating around Maria, but with great deference, wanting to reach out to touch her to see if she was real.

"Geezuss, look at these freaks. The general was right about this, your boy must be inside that shithole. If you were the Manhattan Prophet, whom would you walk amongst? The rich and well bathed who look at you with fear and scorn and want to see you dead? Or amongst the sick and miserable, the wretched and the doomed, the ones who really need you the most?"

The crowd thickened to the point where Jerry became uptight. Sticking to the safety of the Hummer he spoke with urgency. "Do not go too close to those Shantypark walls, very bad men are in there."

Branford scoffed back, "Yo, big balls, don't you see this squadron of squirrel killers right here spread out all around us with heavy duty automatic weapons. Can you see the museum headquarters just a couple of blocks away? We are surrounded by the good guys man and besides, there hasn't been a raid in over ten years."

Maria's eyes glowed with delight as believers continued to encircle her. She didn't feel Jerry's paranoia, for in these people's eyes she saw no hostility. Instead they seemed innocent, almost helpless, as though lost in the woods and trying to find their way back home.

An armored truck pushed its way up the avenue through the thickening mass of humanity congealing around the shoot site. The people in its way complied peacefully and parted a path that allowed the vehicle to pass. Soldiers jumped out of the back in full battle array and herded the people away from the Shantypark walls, and away from the camera. The intent was to show the world that a situation of control existed in New York.

What it looked like at the moment resembled a renegade cattle drive of acolytes.

"Pellet don't want these hordes of freaks messing up his video, that's for sure." Branford chuckled, as he set up the tripod to take the satellite hook up. "Oh, shit! Herbie, waddaya doing now? Get your ass out of the truck and jack my ass into this whole wide world."

Herbie didn't move; he saw it before at Rikers Island. In came Pellet's best, the Pythons, rodent killers of another sort, trained in crowd control. They entrap their prey, stun it and strangle it. They were fanning out quickly behind the armored vehicle carrying their titanium shields, locking them together and pushing people as far away from the camera focal point as possible. It was a chaotic mess, because so many of the enchanted Salem proselytes were already all over the site. The soldiers were having trouble removing those devotees who were caught on the inside of the perimeter they were trying to establish. Herbie knew he had to get moving with the transmitter, but was stuck in limbo, just sitting and staring at Maria from behind the steering wheel.

A black BMW sedan with dark-tinted windows moved in behind the Pythons. Jerry sounded relieved. "There's the general now. We can get this interview going and get the heck out of here."

All attention was turned to Pellet's bulletproof Beemer moving slowly through the crowd, when a single burst of an AK-87 dropped a squirrel killer standing only ten yards away from Branford's tripod. Time collapsed as the soldier buckled and fell to the ground like a bad toy.

Suddenly screams. Shouts. Rapid spatterings of automatic fire. More squirrel killers shot, dying. Men in ski masks with automatic weapons rappelled over the barricade from Shantypark, others burst out of the ground from manholes. Those neophytes closest to the camera, so docile and acquiescent before, were fleeing in terror. Some fell victim in the crossfire as squirrel killers began to spray lead back from the direction it came. In an instant the camera crew was isolated, exposed, and vulnerable.

Jerry, in shock and disbelief, was still standing by the open passenger door of the Hummer. He shouted, "Everybody over here . . ." but never finished his sentence as a bullet struck his throat and another his heart and he crumpled.

Branford, standing next to Maria took a bullet in his chest and went down into the tripod, knocking the camera onto the ground, his body convulsing.

Maria started to run towards the Hummer, but tripped over the collapsed tripod and fell to the street.

Herbie leaped out of the driver's seat into the erupting bloodshed, the automatic fire pounding his ears, punctuating the declarations of many sudden deaths. Somehow he reached her without being hit himself just as several thugs in ski masks poked out of the sidewalk from a well-camouflaged hole in the ground, like deranged groundhogs invading from hell. Without hesitation, Herbie instinctively dove on top of Maria, physically covering her body with his, trying in the last way possible to keep her from harm.

The raiders from Shantypark converged on the helpless pair huddling on the pavement clutching each other for safety, picked them up, pulled them apart and threw them back down into the hole. They jumped in after, closing the tunnel behind them.

As instantly as it started, it stopped. There were shattered people left lying in the street, and shell-shocked soldiers moved about them, tending to their wounded.

Pellet emerged from his protected vehicle and walked the scene of the slaughter. Cell phone on, he surveyed the damage as he listened with great heed to the voice in his ear. He looked at his cameraman groaning in the street, writhing in a puddle of his own blood, pleading to the general for help. Pellet pulled his pistol from its holster and put a bullet through Branford's head.

* * * * *

28

The padding of little feet scampers by like wood sprites but not so innocent. Infant demons, dervishing around and above, giggling. Abruptly they scatter this way and that, before the coming, heralded by waves of tyranny and fear. Bats fly by, screeching, talons distended, and rats run forever, mouth in chew, scurrying over the bindings, leaving their droppings. The inertia was so deep, and the gravity so fierce, that the weight of the incoming mass was incalculable to ordinary human senses, let alone these so very drugged.

Occasionally a man's face, like that really hideous one, the one missing many teeth and an eye, or that pierced and scarred one covered in tattoos, quickly glances in. Staccato popping like soundtracks of old movies about newsrooms with prop typewriters, splatches of men's laughter, skin slaps, little smacks of dripping water leaking from some slit in something somewhere. All the senses in the skin gone now without a trace, unable to move, or to feel. The wind tunnel roared, drowning out any chance for a discernible cry for help into the locusted and many-tendrilled night.

At one point her mother came through an open window and sat on the sill, consoling and soothing, and said, "Honey, things that were meant to be are meant to be. No matter what you do, I love you dearly. But stay away from bad people, like my old friends, malos amantes, you know, the ones you talk about on TV all the time. Your dad says you look much too serious, demasiado, todo el tiempo. He loves you, too, but he wants to see you happy, mas alegre, married already, casado ya." And then, at the commercial break as she got up to leave with her Chanel and her Jimmy Choos, she introduced the angry counterfeit seraph who shot up Maria in the leg with more spoon-cooked smizz.

Time stilled again. The ugly one was standing guard when Jerry came to pay his respects. Affable, like he just had his third jelly doughnut and a caramel macchiato. Not too foppish, because she knew him better than that, he gave her a big wink, indicating with his Breitling black on black that it was all the time he had and toodle-ooed out the window. Branford following after, hands in his pockets, shuffling his feet and shrugging his shoulders.

The Alliance skimmed in on crystal blue water, paddles at rest, asking all the right questions she knew the answers to, but Maria had not enough time or energy to muster the words. Shots rang out, and people screamed, and bodies fell . . . and that saving scent wrapped around her, embracing her in the hour of darkness, the memory of which has kept her alive up to here . . . now, that almost gone, there is nothing left in the dark but that seething, bogus angel.

An acrid, malicious odor from something breathing close by rankled her nostrils. Unable to scream, she was sure a hell-born monster was sniffing at her neck and examining her behind the ears.

* * * * *

29

Monday, December 23, 2047, 6 p.m.

Seismic shock in the ABCNN New York Bureau. The murder of an entire news crew was a nightmare. Losing Maria Primera, a globally recognized reporter only one year into her ten-year contract was devastating. Not to mention her connection to this Salem Jones story. Even without actual footage of the raid, the exclusive coverage granted ABCNN by the city on this skyrocketing story created a staggering record-breaking income in the media industry for a twenty-four-hour period. Revenues in sales to the blacked-out networks were triple the average, and spots for their non-stop news channel were going for many millions a shot.

Right after the Exchange, the Alliance cracked down on competitive news distribution. They placed powerful homeland-security measures on the vassal city-states, giving broad terms to the war emergency powers of the local governments and private security forces they controlled. This forced many of the hundreds of TV stations worldwide to go belly up. With just a few channels, what was left resembled something like the USA in the early days of television, the difference this time being there was no real competition or watchdogs. The leftover field was small, still giving some illusion of free press to the surviving billions desperate for info, making it easier for the multinationals to control what news was allowed out.

As the proliferation of desktop computing increased along with the power of its processors, alternatives to these traditional avenues of news coverage evolved with the Alternet and privatized satellites. The controlling parent companies were powerless in keeping hackers from broadcasting surrogate frequencies alongside those reserved for the multinationals. Their technology was based on string theory applications to accelerated microwave transmitters, which was akin to graffiti paintings in the subways whose messages roll along with the trains, invisibly appearing and reappearing no matter what vigilance was placed on wiping it out.

If it wasn't for the army's continual war waged upon these alternative news forms, with savage punishment doled out to perpetrators they smoked out of the confused cyber landscape, all the media corporations would have been forced out of business from the bottom up. But the remaining few were sitting on top of the world dropping the information down; their assets and revenues were amongst the highest in the United States Alliances.

All of it was due to the good graces of the First Army, a very powerful player in the corporate northern hemisphere. They were the controlling party in what used to be OPEC, and received cash payments, like blood money, to protect the countries that bought their oil. True, it was a challenge to be always fighting Muslims, but dead soldiers were easily replaced by good kids who needed jobs.

So Ira Fine and Marty Gold walked the tight line between ethical journalism and pleasing the powerful hands that fed them. They reported what news they could in this restrictive environment, while running one of the most lucrative corporate ventures in the 2040s. As they put away personal fortunes that guaranteed them and their ancestors the most comfortable lives available on earth for generations to come, they rationalized it all by saying to themselves that there hasn't been any real moral principles in the news for decades. It was just a bizarre entertainment venue, real life made into scary video. It was all profit-motivated from the beginning. Besides they couldn't make a decent living any more producing reality TV about radiation victims from the Ellis Island bomb now that they all died off and the dead zones were being reopened for gentrification.

They smiled at each other sadly by the only monitor in the control room on West 66th Street with a picture moving in the frame. It showed an empty ABCNN podium with the seal of the First Army draped behind, an eagle carrying an olive branch in its clenched talons. Ira remarked that it should have been a dead rodent in the eagle's fist. He was right; the Army didn't care about political correctness anymore. This morning two employees were shot dead and two were missing and presumed dead, but this next press session, well, it was guaranteed to bring in millions.

The studio next door was filled with the buzz of chattering news people who quickly quieted to a hush as General Pellet approached the podium, elegant, almost swanky, his uniform cut and pressed, the essence of control. He stepped to the mic and he was as good there as in a command center.

"In lieu of the tragic circumstances surrounding this afternoon's intended newscast, I'd like to make a short statement; then I'll be open for a few questions. At approximately 3:30 this afternoon, December 23rd, 2047, on the corner of 89th Street and Fifth Avenue, a band of heavily armed, terrorists originating from inside Shantypark attacked a peace-maintaining unit of the First Army as they prepared to secure a video transmission location near the area. The combatants surprised the troops with automatic fire and grenades, killing seventeen soldiers and thirty-six bystanders, including two of the news crew from ABCCN, two others of which were abducted and presumed dead. Before the army could respond in a coordinated effort, the assailants fled."

A low jumble of mumbling moved through the room. A man in a brown tweed suit, with a burgundy bowtie, scratching notes on his tiny qwerty, raised his hand, and stood up. "General, and we all agree," indicating his fellow journalists, "that we are honored in calling you General, which we believe is the appropriate title for your position."

The crowd of paparazzi burst into a short laugh. The general's smile was pleasant because he knew he could squash them all like small mammals.

The reporter continued, "Considering the events of the past few hours, including the positioning of troops around the perimeter of Shantypark, why is there no official response from City Hall to this attack on your men?"

"Ronald, as you know, the mayor is still unavailable, involved as we speak in top secret talks with the leaders of the free world, which shows you how serious this new threat is. Ten years ago when we were called in by the people of New York City to free them from the ravages of gang war and terrorism, Shantypark became an established, yet necessary, evil in society. A city-state with laws such as ours can't exist in a state of anarchy. We also cannot abandon the helpless and the truly innocent whose diseases keep them locked up with these blatant criminals. However, we also can't allow these elements in our society to infect the healthy. We are a professional army hired by the multinational corporations who underwrite this entire city. We train every day to do our job to protect their investment according to their evaluations. We have done our part to keep the peace. During my command, things have stayed stable between our society and that which is confined to Shantypark, until now. It is obvious to me that something new is causing this first direct outbreak of violence from the gangs in more than ten years."

The reporters, smelling good juice, jumped to their feet, each clamoring to ask the next question. Pellet pointed to a familiar face. The others, disappointed, sat back down grumbling.

"General!" exclaimed a lady in a blue dress, white cardigan, and wearing a grass hat, waving her Blackberry VI. "Are you saying that the disappearance of Salem Jones is connected with this violence; and as a follow-up, do you think he is now inside Shantypark as popular sentiment seems to feel?"

"Simply, Marcia, the answer is yes, and yes." The ostensibly erudite roared to its feet loudly vocalizing its excitement over these succinct but powder-kegged assumptions. The grass hat kept the floor.

"If that's the case, does the First Army have any intention of reversing Mayor Storm's historic agreement by making an incursion into Shantypark."

But Pellet, already walking away, didn't even bother to give a no comment.

As the mad tapping of palm-sized wireless technology began beaming words through an orbiting satellite, the only TV camera allowed in the room was shut down upon Pellet's quick and sharp departing glance.

Back in the control room, Marty and Ira, with yet another sad smile, knew it was meant as a direct warning to them.

* * * * *

30

Theodore Roosevelt Storm believed it was good for a boy to get a job and earn his own money. He practiced that belief on his son. So at the age of ten, John Kennedy Storm was delivering pizzas for Sharif and Hussein Konakli, two Turkish brothers who bought a small Italian eatery on Morningstar Avenue, a couple of doors down from the apartment he lived in with his dad. Young Jack liked the feeling of having his own money, buying his own stuff.

It was not an easy neighborhood for a ten-year-old to work in. Home to mostly hardworking decent folks, however, there were robberies and shootings every night. Hookers, gangsters, gamblers, and drunks were common pedestrians on the thoroughfare, tripping the light fantastic past the omnipresent drug dealers on every savage corner. Several times when Jack was out on a delivery, a gang of middle school dropouts mugged him at knifepoint, kids he knew from school, what their names were, and where they lived. They robbed him of his money and then, for fun, they rubbed his nose in the hot, oily mozzarella cheese he carried.

Some of his friends and neighbors in the hood thought Theodore was way over the top, sending a ten-year-old boy out there in the night all alone. But Theodore would always slough off their reservations with a strong rebuff, saying that it was good character development; the boy would learn how to fend for himself. He was proud that his son, John Kennedy Storm, was more then capable to be out there in the dark world, young and alone. Ironic when you look at how alone little Jack always felt now.

Years after the catastrophic loss of loved ones, and after much hard work, most people finally can get used to the loneliness. Mayor Storm really never had the chance. The need to make sense out of the mystery of life and death, why some survive and others die, had to be shut out from his consciousness early after the disaster so he could save the city he loved. He had no opportunity left to save the family he loved, and he had no time to grieve.

Sam said it was the forced subjugation of these heavy traumatic emotions that gave rise to these recurring blackout events later in Jack's life. Of course, a great friend, but no frigging Sigmund Freud is Sam.

The blackouts start like an echo, maybe an indistinct memory of a sound, a hushed inhalation of satisfaction breathing from his past, a snuffled sneeze, a baby's gurgle. They continue with voices, somewhat recognizable, parts of phrases, catches of music, caught in the drift of an elusive energy. Then the ensuing struggle to react, to proact, but frozen by forces other than his own.

Luckily, it has not yet interfered with the running of government, and nobody but Sam knows, even though lately they seem to come when he needs himself the most, when his city-state, his people, turn to him to pull another rabbit out of the hat. It's getting harder and harder to hold the blackouts back, and what frustrates Sam, what downright drives him nuts, is that Jack now admits he sometimes doesn't care, he likes his thoughts being cleansed. However, watching Pellet's emergency newscast today, while he was stuck in a teleconference with the multinationals, really put him in a spin.

Jack is alone once again, late at night, no one else in the armored room. Locked away from everything. Alone with his computers and megabands, he could go anywhere, but his eyes gaze only on the picture next to his monitor. It's the only image of his family he allows in this place. He looks at it hard and wishes it could bring him back to that slice in time scientists swear still exist in the abstract equations made out of chalk dust fading on their blackboards.

Today's meeting made him feel like he was a kid again getting his face rubbed in pizza. How long has this conspiracy existed? And how far has the set-up progressed? Now what's going to become of that poor girl who was offered up as a sacrifice earlier today? What was the entity Deganawida saw in my eye? And why am I running out of steam in this most crucial of times?

The washing machine kicks into another cycle and his thoughts go sudsing around and soon they all became so richly clean, leaving him incapable but to breathe, and the light opens in the center, swirling, and the soft lathering glow causing tears to trickle from his eyes, now able to see only very far off and away. Familiar smiles in the photo on the shelf start singing tender hymns, of the place across the river, in the rolling fields of redemption, in the land of milk and honey.

* * * * *

31

At the bottom of the hole they tore Herbie away from Maria and knocked him unconscious. The first thing he realized coming to was that Maria was nowhere near to be seen. The second thing he realized was that he was naked and tied to a cross, lying on his back on a thick wooden beam with his arms outstretched to each side. Around him he could hear the jarring tones of MP12s banging out gutter hop downloaded from the Alternet. There were pinging sounds, like popcorn in a microwave, coming from the other side of a canvas divider. The smell of human excrement from untended outhouses permeated the walls of the tent in which he was shackled down.

Then he got it. He was in Shantypark. In a tent. Maybe even one he has seen before from the window of the editing suite on 62nd Street. The chances were one hundred percent that on the other side of the canvas walls surrounding him was the gang who had attacked them at the shoot site, and then forced them down here. Now they were gathering around flatscreens watching bootleg mini Blu-Ray 4s, and midnight snacking on popcorn and Jack Daniels provided by the keenest of these guys' sources, smuggled in through the tunnels when the squirrel killers looked away. The good whiskey could fetch a better price than homegrown smizz, but they'd rather keep the best stuff for themselves.

Herbie felt so tired, drugged; he didn't have much strength to keep from falling backwards into that iron-walled subconscious state from which he had just managed to escape. A place where he had no recollection of sound or living substance.

Off in the distance he heard a drumbeat and the dancing of hooves. Percussion so evil it could clear angry rats out of sewers. A chill wind blew in from under the tent and his skin shivered. It seemed to be coming towards him.

How long he could not tell, he fought the fading in and out, straining himself to stay awake, the drumming clinging to the periphery of his senses. The drugs relentless, the fatigue numbing bordering absolute, but he must keep eyes open, must stay alert. His arms stretched out on the cruel, splintered cross were bloodless, empty, and the cold settled down upon him complete and total, his entire body gone numb, wanting nothing more and at the same time nothing less, then sleep.

Coming from all sides they were upon him, lifting him on the cross into the air over their heads. Out of the corners of his eyes he could glimpse a procession of unbathed men, chanting and grunting and moving in ways robotic to the funereal beat, like all the Internet pictures of filthy-looking gangs that ruled the world in Shantypark, but this was not a plasma screen, this was real and, carrying sticks and staves and spears and poking away at a defenseless young girl . . . and then his body flailed against the ropes, his bound mouth screaming in futility, the gags ripping into the corners of his lips.

The gang was dragging Maria into the tent, barely dressed in a burlap sack.

The disguised demon walking with her upon this

ignominious path grew wan, and withered away as the last blast of drugs they gave her faded. Surrounded by these frenzied animals her bewilderment was giving way to something inside her stupor that maybe things were not okay.

They dragged her to the raping station and set her upon it, kneeling on all fours. They ripped off the burlap bag exposing the perfect skin on her perfect body and a horrid cheer dinned her ears. She waited, naked on her knees for the devil.

Herbie, lifted on the cross above the mob, was so close he could see each of the tiny exquisite hairs flourishing along the grove of her holy arbor, about to be bloodied and defiled.

The men milling around her were drunk with the vulgar euphoria that accompanies the worst kind of evil, which in this purest form of degradation was inconceivable to Herbie, his body heaving against the excruciation of the bindings holding him to the cross.

They flipped her over on her back, her breasts jouncing. They tugged her legs apart. A captain with facial maculation held her head, laying her neck vulnerable to the executioner's long black sword unsheathed in striking position.

Maria's mind was still incapable of formulating anything but a notion, her body unable to motivate its own muscular response. She couldn't understand the mixed sounds and visual fluctuations which caused her wild heart beat. And what was that creepy guy in the black hood doing with that sword?

A path parted within the sea of demons, and the beast stepped through, stopping in between her widespread legs.

Gregor unzipped his pants and the gang roared. He began to masturbate in preparation of shoving it into her waiting and helpless vagina.

A brilliant celestial harmony invaded the rancor and muffled the fury, singing up a fifth, and then a sixth, as another path revealed itself through the tortured creatures. Untouched, a small black boy lead a calm tall man by the hand through the cringing crowd of miscreants, until Salem Jones stood face to face with Gregor, petrified between him and the girl, blocking the way.

"Get back, Gregor, you are faithless and perverse," commanded Salem, and Gregor stepped back in awe, as did his stani horde. Herbie heard the astral tone continue up another octave, and then again, ripping the beasts intent on this wanton evil apart from their common degeneracy while freezing their leader, belittling him.

Salem Jones went up to the altar of pure evil. He removed the long trench coat he wore and covered her body, lifting her off the unholiest shrine. Surveying the silent stani gang, his eyes on fire like eruptions on Mount Sinai, his bellow repercussed all the way through to the furthest alleyways on the street map of time. "Shame falls upon you all!" The gang recoiled as if ducking volcanic debris.

Salem looked up at Herbie, stunned and tied upon the cross. "Bring this man to me." The cross was laid back down on the ground and Jamal helped Herbie rise to his feet, naked and spent, and they followed Salem as he carried Maria out of the tents of inspired sin.

Gregor, hunched and seething amidst his horde of cowering gangsters, was left holding his little shriveled penis in his hand.

* * * * *

32

Tuesday, December 24, 2047, 6:58 a.m.

The monitors blinked on in the armored office just as Jack Storm stepped out of the bathroom, freshly shaven, in a pressed suit, polished shoes—looking dandy, Sam said. Three hours of shaky sleep on the office couch, two cups of joe, one minute in a cold shower, ready to go. It's going to be a busy day in offices everywhere in the world.

Already in the sound booth, Milos hooked up connections with the other geeks working techie in high places throughout the world, making sure things were right for when the big guys do the talking.

Sitting down in front of his camera, Jack could just imagine the palace in the Hague, where the chancellor would most certainly be. Storm-troopered to the max, the Euro-giants sipping tea and shooting brandy at little round tables with spotless white tablecloths, while pre-pubescent ballerinas pirouetted for their pleasure on checkered tile floors. Two blocks away standing by campfires burning synthetic logs donated by Seattle, Inc., which inherited the Pacific Northwest after the Cascadian tsunami, were cro-magnons of the Green army. In outposts socked in by the fog all the way to the canals, in constant vigil, they stared daringly at the opulence, but too cold and hungry to put on a good fight that night.

Claire, the tree snake from Singapore, pinged onto a monitor in the bottom left quadrant of Jack's array on the wall. She was seatbelted in the lounge of her Lockheed 57 about to take off, the wide-angle lens made her fishbowl face look worse. Not yet back home from across the Pacific, just one short stop to lay a wreath at a ceremony in LA. She looked up into the armored room in New York City as her printer came to life with the copy of the brief.

Other quadrants flickered to life as the most powerful players took their seats. General Pellet entered punctiliously at 7 a.m. and took his place next to Jack. His own separate camera. To anyone watching the conference they could have been a world away from each other as opposed to almost brushing elbows like they really were. Before they could begin, the middlesex man from Digi-Bell was the first to remark. He saluted hello into his camera, "Good morning again, General." Pellet saluted back without changing expression and opened the meeting with an official air.

"Good morning to all the members of the North Atlantic Alliance. Good afternoon to those in the European Union, Abu Dhabi, and the Emirates. For those of you on the Pacific Rim, it is tomorrow. This emergency session of the voting body of the League of Democratic Alliances is called to order. We are gathered to deal with this new and very real threat, now fomenting in New York City, with extreme implications for all of us. We have been following this situation for several months in anticipation of Salem Jones' release from prison. Few could have predicted the turn of events that brings us to where we find ourselves today. The message of peace and understanding that was the thrust of his worldwide popularity has been replaced with reckless lawlessness and senseless aggression. Yesterday's unprovoked act of violence, tantamount to cold-blooded murder, is an indication of just the beginning of what will probably be a serious offensive. What we can expect in the days ahead is anybody's guess. I have my own apprehensions.

"According to psychological surveys administered robotically from Rikers Island, and considering the success he must feel with the affirmation of his message, especially if measured by the huge amount of the attention he has garnered through the media up to this point, all evidence strongly indicates that Salem Jones is the worst kind of terrorist, a megalomaniacal fanatic who believes he has a direct link to God as the source of all his convictions. He is loose and operating right now unhindered in New York's Central Containment Zone. That area everyone calls Shantypark. My sources clearly indicate that he is forming alliances with the local gangs in preparation for further armed incursions."

The Ivy League Korean from Sony jumped in. "General. Let me be brief. My patience for this matter is growing very thin. The situation is very clear. So may I ask what preparations have you been making for a counterstrike? Preferably a quick preemptive sortie that could sever the head from the body so to speak without actually doing too much damage to anything else but the head." The members murmured their agreement from transmission sites all over the world, their individual anxieties over the issue as clear to each other as their high definition images.

Claire, waiting to be hurled into an arc high in the sky over the Pacific, murmured something about Salem being less then a mile away from Pellet's troops and the incredulity of their inability to zero in on him with the latest of their GPS technology. The Sony guy reminded her how the human density in Shantypark threw the heat sensors out of whack. The tree snake uttered back that it was still hard to believe that this was the reason he didn't come up on any of their scopes.

The mayor spoke with his usual soft strength. "If I may interject a measure of delicacy at this juncture." A pause gave them time to look into the many windows that faced them and see how uncomfortable everybody else was with what they all expected to hear next. Jack continued, "As all of you know, it has always been my contention that it benefits the greater good if we can be in a position of communication with this person, Salem Jones. His influence on the thoughts and moods of our populations has obviously risen to a point of undeniable significance. These are extremely difficult times, and there are many more ahead. However, there is no direct evidence at this point that Salem or any of his people were involved in yesterday's attack. We need to reserve the military option until all our attempts to engage this man in fruitful dialogue have been exercised."

"Noble indeed as always, Mayor Storm," said the Euroreich chancellor who wiped his eyeglasses with ill-concealed irritation. "But our position has always been—absolutely no negotiation with terrorists. We all know that no matter how much damage is done by suicidal fanatics, they will have done less if we acted earlier to exterminate them."

Storm jumped in, "Chancellor, I ask you again to reassess the situation. Yes, there was an unprovoked act of violence committed on this city and the First Army, but there is no proof whatsoever of any involvement by Salem Jones. The last time we were confronted with a violent uprising from Shantypark, we were overly hasty and much too heavy-handed in our response. This century's wars against insurgents should remind us that military force will not work without the clear support of our policies on the ground at the friction point."

Pellet interjected before the contentious faces on the screen could reply. "Mayor, no one here is advocating for any kind of force at this point."

"C'mon, General, how else do we sever heads from necks?" Jack stared into the camera lens even though Pellet was sitting an ant's snowball toss away.

The Sony Korean had to keep silent here, knowing how the forceful takeover of Japan's industries by his mother country after the superquake fit perfectly into the category of beheadment.

In the uncomfortable pause, Jack continued, "I agree that the policy of no negotiations should be applied for terrorists. However in this instance I don't see it. Quite the contrary. There are no hard facts to support that there have been acts of aggression connected to any of the known camps of Salem Jones supporters. Treating this movement as a terrorist force could actually turn an otherwise peaceful movement into a hostile dilemma. I believe we should sit back and watch this play out. No matter why Salem Jones disappeared in the first place, I can understand why he would be reticent to come out now. Let's try to contact him and see where that dialogue goes."

"Rubbish." The chancellor's reply was immediate. "For all we know, the next thing that could happen is that this Salem Jones will make some preposterous claim of divinity, or perhaps a direct genetic lineage to Mohammed or Jesus or some other popular religious prophet. This so-called peaceful force could turn into a global cartel armed with the conviction that whatever mayhem they produce is in God's name. Then what kind of a mess are we going to be in, again? How long this time do we wait to find out we waited too long? The carnage created from the last religious conflict is proof enough that the time to cut off the potential for more is now."

* * * * *

33

"Hello," she said to the wavy haired man seated calmly at a small card table at the foot of her bed. She woke up from deeply layered dreams when he arrived, as if he came through a wisp in a wrinkle in the air, photon by photon.

She felt disoriented because she felt so clean. Her hair smelled like it was recently washed and brushed. She was wearing different clothes, more coarse and common than would have been found in her plenteous closet, but they were dirt free and practical, rustled up by the Council and donated for her within minutes after the word went out. She felt like she was being taken care of now, with loving hands.

She also had distorted memories and strange sensations of being in an incredibly vulnerable and perilous situation before this man saved her life. Should she be embarrassed by her nakedness? Nevertheless, she felt secure right now being alone with him in this simple drab tent. However, she knew this interview should not be conducted from a bed; so, she slid herself off and sat down across from him at the table on a folding chair that was waiting for her.

His eyes were soft, absorbing her every move. As she took her seat, an awesome power of acceptance and ease draped around her like a protective cloak. She looked over at him, and it seemed his body was composed of light, of an ethereal non-substance that she could reach for but not touch. She had to blink more than once, but yes, there he sat, smiling as if time didn't exist and neither did pain. But she knew that was crazy as vague recollections flashed on the flat screens of her blurry memory, gruesome faces in homage to some heinous deity, images of Jerry's Adam's apple blowing out his neck.

She swallowed to clear her throat and make sure her voice was still working. "Who are you?"

Unblinking, he leaned in for a closer look at her eyes, enabling her to get a closer look into his. Her eyes were like a suspicious sun rising with caution over open water. His were green like forests, observant with vast intelligence.

She felt like she was outdoors, back in the Adirondack Mountains, and that spine of mountain peaks that seemed to tower behind him were now warm and flush with spring.

"Is this my interview?" he asked with splendid flecks of autumn changing the colors in his eyes like maples bending in October winds. The sun came up and spread its rays across the snow-tipped mountains far away behind him.

"No, you are right. I am sorry. What am I saying? I should be thanking you, Salem. I thank you for saving my life." Her cheeks flushed cherry red.

"You have had a very long night and I know you need to sleep." His smile was an unshaven Buddha, his words the swift mountain stream. He opened a bottle and poured its contents into a paper cup. "Here, drink some of this, it will help you relax and sleep some more." She looked at it with hesitation. "It is a good wine, an old recipe, one that will sustain you and carry you forward." She tasted its sweetness and felt refreshed.

"I hear that people want to know more about me, that some actually think I'm God."

Surprised, she gagged a little on the wine and tried to suppress the cough that followed. "I must be dreaming," she heard herself say, "for months I have been waiting and preparing for this exact moment and now that its here, I have no composure." She looked away and through the flap in the tent she saw the multitude that was camped all around. She looked back to Salem and the mountains she perceived behind him were shining from the empyreal glow of starlight generated billions of years ago. "I'm confused, a bit shaken. And, I am more than somewhat humbled."

"Please, by all means, relax, and be of peace. I am just a reporter, like you, telling the story of what I see. It seems we need to talk for a moment, so please tell me, how do we begin?"

"I guess I just have to ask. So please, tell me, are you?"

"Scientists suppose that if we could travel at the speed of light, we would be energy in its purest most life-giving form. As we slow down to take form, the energy becomes particles, then more and more like matter. Soon we take on actual mass, which eventually, over eons, evolves into individual human identities for our ever-seeking souls. But as we do that, some of us can still go faster than others. So maybe you can just think of it as a question of velocity.

"In earthen form, these tiny, individual identities impact the entire universe. In that way I am representative of that which put us on earth. It is the potential we all have. We have different tasks no doubt, yours, Herbie's, and mine. Everything is interconnected."

Herbie's smell, smoldering in her sense memory, bursts forth at the mention of his name with a feeling of safety, this individual identity. She tugs back her heart. "If you were human, by all scientific measure, you should have been dead by disease years ago."

"What else can you rightly say about the science of men? One can learn to control the improbabilities that are only remotely possible. The one time in a trillion that the positive attracts the positive, use that to kill a virus."

"What about your writings, on paper, millions of people abandoning what is left of their lives to find some meaning or salvation with you?"

"Codes, symbols, that are waiting within us to recognize, like they always have been, for those spirits who are ready to see."

"And the power to heal, the so-called miracles?"

"If the force we call Satan was not so powerful here on this planet, this type of strength would not be needed."

"Excuse me, Mr. Jones . . ."

"Please call me what my fathers called me, Salem."

"Okay, Salem. By Satan you don't mean what I think you mean?"

"Yes, I do." His bubbling stream came to a valley on the side of an emerald green mountain, and collected itself into a pool of dreams, vibrant yet still, with pink and violet wildflowers ringing one lovely golden lotus growing on its shore.

Maria felt so serene her eyelids started to droop. "I'm starting to feel so drowsy. I must lay down." She stood up and found the mattress and laid her head upon the pillow. "But, I am so glad, so very glad, we had this time to talk."

"I must thank you, Maria Primera, for the sincere pleasure of my first interview."

"But I didn't know that, you can't mean that, I wasn't ready. I had no laptop, no video camera." She was so sleepy, but tapping the strength of a grace deep within she managed to utter one last question. "But you never answered me. You never told me. Who are you? Who are you, Salem Jones?"

A heavenly soprano embraced the tent skipping octaves and thirds as Maria saw the sky behind him turn brilliant blue, with a saintly golden glow giving sanctuary to the holy mountains. She closed her eyes and the vapors of this gentle image faded on the back of her lids. As she slipped into the all-forgiving mercies of sleep she heard his soft whisper in her grateful ear.

"I am who I am."

* * * * *

34

"Grandma?"

"Yes, my child?"

"Is that you?"

"Yes, my child."

"What's it like being dead?"

"Are you thinking about your mom and dad again?"

"Yeah. And Grandpa Bullmoose. And you. I always wonder."

"Yes, I'm sure, but don't you think everybody does?

"Everybody wonders?"

"Yes, my little silly, everybody wonders at some time about what it's like being dead."

After the incident, Grandma often thought about what it's like being dead. Bullmoose was inconsolable and, like he often did, he shut out the rest of the world. Eventually he just took off, the world traveler, to work out the grief alone. But Herbie was a baby, and Grandma had to stay and fight to keep their lives together. She had to raise him, and life for her became very complicated. But it wasn't always so.

Life in Cambridge, Massachusetts, in the early 1970s was idyllic for a woman like her. Here in a small city surrounded by the bastions of academic liberalism, she and a small army of people like her settled down to change the world. Optimism as a color in youth is very becoming, and in senescence it's outstanding. To Grandma, it always came naturally.

Soon after Watkins Glen, she settled back to gestate and give birth to Herbie's dad, in her little two-bedroom house in a backyard on Perry Street near Central Square in Cambridge, with her prep school roommate, Lorraine, a committed counterculturist. Grandma's mother was indignant about her situation; Grandma was just nineteen, a college dropout, pregnant and unmarried. Her mother made a lot of noise about it, but really would never have been happy about a marriage between her daughter and Bullmoose. She just didn't like the idea that her baby girl was going to have a baby of her own out of wedlock. Good Golly, Miss Molly. And what's this about no doctor and no hospital and no painkillers? What are you crazy?

Grandma had the baby her way, up in her attic bedroom with lots of candles and incense burning and a bevy of freewheeling midwives, boogieing naked and howling at the liberated moon. Herbie's dad, Henry Lipton, was born into a coven of hippie-era feminists. Thirty years later, faces paralyzed by Botox, they popped Vicodin in upholstered ladies rooms in suburban country clubs all over America, while sipping martinis and laughing out of the sides of their faces with other fifty-something cosmetic queens, whose silicone implants give them backaches late into the night. Nothing stays the same.

Lorraine was a piece of work. Slim, dirty blond hair, sparkling blue eyes, lithe and tight, luscious boobs, and smooth, pale skin that seemed to always have a seductive glossy sheen in summer. She loved Southern Comfort and Camels with no filters. And she had this thing for guys on acid. Especially musicians. It was like a 1970s kind of love 'em and leave 'em, as if the pill was invented for her personal sexual revolution.

Herbie used to think his grandparents' entire generation only thought about two things, sex and drugs. They probably did back then, but then, like everything, they changed. They started caring mostly about mutual funds, long-term care, and cosmetic surgery, while forgetting how to protest against American presidents who sent armies into needless wars. Even with all that, her generation is all dead.

He wishes he could talk to Grandma now, when he really needs her. He wishes she would tell it to him straight for once. But too late, his eyes open and he's in a tent again. It looks like he'll have to wait a bit longer for any answers to his questions about the afterlife, because here on earth there are so many other pressing ones to ask.

* * * * *

35

The monitor from Abu Dhabi blinks out on the expatriate Saudi princes, who still cannot go home due to the heavy debt built up in half-life, both radiational and political. Yet they still have plenty enough money to slug Glenfiddich and frolic with blond Norwegian models ready to spread their outlandishly long legs in exchange for weekends in gilded palaces. To insure their survival the same princes covertly fund what is left of the moderate Muslim media. The media in turn stays alive amongst the extremists, by constantly inciting public reaction against these very princes with stories of their degenerate hedonistic existence. Everything is interconnected.

Working all night, glad to now be going home, Milos, the mayor's main techie, wonders how his own Latvian ancestors could kill so many Jews and then quickly convert from Nazism to Communism to democracy and back again. He shuts the light switch in the control room and slowly steps out through the heavy atmosphere in the armored room of so many now-blank video screens.

"Breaching Shantypark with an armed force is out of the question."

Pellet stares silently into his camera, now powered down, observing his own oddly distorted reflection on the lens. How to put this gently to the mayor? But did he really care anymore? So he lied. "No one, Jack, wants a confrontation. If there is a way around one, I'll take it. But can I remind you that we have seventeen military funerals to attend this coming week?"

"Rogue elements continuously operate within Shantypark, however the Gang Council has always been able to eradicate the threat in their own fashion."

Milos, loyal to the end, but wanting to go home to his wife and kids, hustles out the door hoping no one notices, closing it behind him with an almost inaudible click.

"Jack, my sources indicate that's not happening now. Far from it. They say there has been an almost instantaneous transformation of power. The entire Council has been in session since yesterday morning, sequestered in a complex of tents that are now completely controlled by Salem and his followers."

"What are you talking about?"

"Apparently his network was greatly underestimated while hiding behind the protection of Code 7 while in Rikers. Terrorists have uncanny ways of turning a system's strength into a lethal weakness. Now he's working carte blanche in Shantypark, worming his way into control by taking advantage of existing power structures and using the present legal system as the perfect cover to his operations. This has got to stop."

Storm took a deep breath. "Rodney, your talk is junk food, too packaged up and ready to go. You were my strongest ally, and closest confidant for the longest time. Why are you bullshitting me now at a time of such incredible intensity."

"I don't know what you are talking about, Jack. It's embarrassing to me that you are getting so maudlin and melodramatic. But thank you for not dripping this all over the international scene. I greatly appreciate the compliment of trusting me with your innermost emotional turmoil, but when you start to say things that encroach upon my loyalties and moralities, you make it very hard for me to stay in synch with your government and your policies."

"It is still too early in the morning for this, Rodney. In a better world, one where everyday decisions don't concern the life and death of millions, you and I might still be best of friends."

"This is exactly what I mean. Where you are going with this does nobody any good. Personally I am done with your philosophic meanderings. What I need here are hard and fast decisions in order to parlay this extremely dangerous situation into our advantage, even if I have to make the decisions myself. I am officially sick and tired of being your foil for the rest of the planet. So in case you didn't hear it quite correctly before, as of now, the world is putting you on notice. This is your last call, Jack, get your act together or suffer the consequences."

* * * * *

36

After a brief nap, Marcus ushered Maria, still a little unsteady on her feet, into the large tent. When she saw Herbie they both jolted with a warm honey color that drew the attention of everyone present. Some nonverbal interpersonal communication can stun a room without a sound and, for reasons unable to be explained intellectually by either person involved, this was one.

Marcus led Maria over to a long table where Salem and the Gang Council were meeting. He sat her in an empty seat next to Herbie, who was seated far to Salem's right. Herbie looked into her eyes, and she looked back. He had to fight off the urge to grab her and pull her close in to him and tell her how worried he was about her and how glad he was to see her. She wanted to do the same. In that instant observed by all, they forgot for a second where they were, whom they were in the presence of, and how close to horrible death they had quite recently been.

Ibrahim stood up from his seat at the far end of the table, next to Salem, and addressed the Council. "Our posts have reported a significant increase of regular army moving into position in No Man's Land, surrounding us and blocking off all known surface exits from Shantypark."

Marcus spoke. "We are not ready to meet this challenge head on. If we had time to prepare we would put up a good battle, but now Salem you seem to have us going in a different direction."

Salem, still sitting, had all eyes upon him. "It is true. The time is now. Bring me the boy."

In a moment, a loving elderly woman brought Jamal into the tent. He was bathed and cleanly dressed in a new dashiki. His grandmother delivered Jamal to Salem, and bending before her prophet, she tenderly kissed him on both his feet. She slowly backed away as Salem's eyes registered a warm surprise. He stood up.

"For centuries men have looked for answers. They probed far into the miracles of this world. They explored deep into the ocean and the earth and far out into the sky and the stars. They developed incredible machines from out of the insights they gained about how the universe is put together and how it will always work." He paused and looked around the tent, looking at each person there as they gazed back at him. His soft command of their complete attention all-powerful. "But once again it is time for the world to see the pure power of faith."

The Council and the people seated around whispered amongst themselves, unsure, confused, yet all accepting and ready to follow. Salem looked across the table, "Herbie Lipton."

Surprised, Herbie replied. "Here I am."

"I am told that this is yours, it was in your jacket when you were delivered up to Shantypark." Herbie looked curiously at the headbandcam that Salem held up, and found it hard to believe he had been here less than a day. Salem continued, "We cannot make a direct transmission with this unless approximately thirty feet from a receiver, am I right?"

Surprised by Salem's sudden shift to technology, Herbie rose to his feet and took the tiny camera. Somehow he knew where Salem was going with this. "You're right. This antenna is only good for about thirty feet. I could jack it to fifty or maybe sixty more with some tinkering around and some copper strands, but, I'm sure there isn't any receiver close enough to here where it could reach. However, I can rig the memory key so it can hold about two minutes of low resolution footage and then transmit at another time."

"Exactly." Salem smiled and passed the video recording device across the table. "Please attend to that Herbie and with haste." He turned and fixed his eyes upon the thin black man, "Marcus, my brother Marcus."

Marcus was ready, "Here I am."

"If you would be so kind to please give Maria your biopod." Marcus nodded and handed it to her without hesitation. Maria, puzzled, took the device.

The crowd in the tent waited with a whispering hush as Herbie took the few dexterous moments he needed to adjust the headbandcam.

"It is time now for our new friends to escort our little ambassador of possibilities to the world waiting outside these walls. But first we must make sure that he is recognized out there for who he really is. Jamal come beside me." Jamal drew himself close, very comfortable in Salem's warmth.

"Herbie, I assume that your headbandcam is set to the same world clock as that biopod." He nodded yes. "You start recording and then, Maria, you administer the standard biopod blood tests on Jamal while telling the camera everything you see."

Herbie looked at Maria and again he somehow knew . . . "I'm rolling."

Maria, the consummate professional, immediately fell into character, alert and inquisitive, however everyone noticed the new level of warmth and genuine concern. "This is Maria Primera live from inside Shantypark, where by the grace of Salem Jones, I am alive to report to you today. This young boy's name is Jamal. He was born here in Shantypark and, like most native kids his age, has never been outside its walls. I have been asked by Salem Jones to administer the standard biopod blood exam to Jamal and report the results to you."

She turned to Jamal and focused the laser part of the instrument on his hand and pushed the button. A little spot of red light appeared on the skin of his wrist and then disappeared. After a brief pause the biopod beeped twice.

"The connection has been made to the central data base in New York, which has received the examination and will e-message us back momentarily, with the results."

The biopod beeped twice again. Maria gave a tentative glance towards Salem, who stood in self-contained radiance. She looked down at the device and could not hold back her sudden unprofessional gasp. She tried to force back her tears as she read the results on the little color LCD.

"The Center for Disease Control says that Jamal is infected with HIV-7B, and the amount of virus in his blood indicates that it's going into its final phase."

The silence in the tent inspissated, like arteries clogging in arrest.

Salem gestured to Jamal, picked him up and hugged him.

Maria managed to continue, "You now see Salem Jones hugging Jamal. He is smiling at him and Jamal seems very relaxed. Now Salem is bending Jamal's head to the side showing us the AIDS melanomas behind his ears." Herbie zoomed in on the malignant pustules, as close as a weak stomach would allow. "Oh my god, oh mercy, I can't believe my eyes, but Salem Jones, as you can see, is kissing them. He is kissing Jamal's tumors, with his mouth, each one, one by one. I swear," she said choking out the last words, "I have never seen anything like this."

Neither had anyone else. Herbie, true to the task, continues to record until the drive is full. His eyes crane with incredulity towards what is happening with Jamal. As the heavenly tone skips up an octave and then up a major third, the little boy is stunned into a dazzling rapture as Salem caresses his highly contagious terminal disease with his tongue. The surrounding Council and its attendees in this marvelous tent, people born into suffering and torment, plague, poverty, and sorrow, all stand agape at this unspeakable, but spectacular act being performed before them, filled with so much abundant love, the most tender of mercies, and boundless, neverending faith.

From within his brightness Salem spoke to Herbie. "You must go forth and show the world what we have done here."

The tent was abuzz with wonder, but Herbie looked speechless over at Maria, who too was at a loss for words. Finally he spoke, overcome with his own banality. "I'm not sure what to do, Salem, where to go, or for that matter how to get there."

"Ibrahim will take you towards the tunnels. All you have to do is watch over Jamal. You will know when you get there. Have faith, for I will always be with you."

* * * * *

37

The concept of the news desk in television hadn't really changed much since the beginning of the industry. An intelligent-looking actor who could read off a teleprompter without blinking, with a few pictures either keyed in over the shoulder or full-screen cutaways to video, was basically what you have. The look of the broadcast studio, the graphics employed, the dynamic lighting that was created, everything had been tried and will go in and out of style again as all things in vogue will do. ABCNN had settled for years on a predominantly blue high-tech look, with moving streaks of light in subtle but constant motion detailing the background. This was Marty and Ira's favorite look since even before the Exchange, and the one they continue to use during their nightly primetime show.

It was a few minutes before six-thirty, at the end of another Christmas Eve broadcast sugarized neatly to please the Alliance. The streaks of studio light were zipping behind Marty, as he began to segue his now captive audience into their nightly wrap-up. At the same time the security guard at the front desk of the ABCNN building, Alphonse Guerrero, a native New Yorker who was crippled years ago when he stepped on a homemade landmine buried on the center strip of Park Avenue, was the first to notice the ghosts walking through the metal detectors and flashing their ID cards. The land mine had utilized forks and knives stolen from the Waldorf Astoria as shrapnel. It took five hours for the doctors to get the cutlery out of his leg before they decided to amputate. He was given this cushy desk job because the real security started way before him out on Columbus Avenue. How did two dead news people and a skinny little black boy he didn't recognize get past those squirrel killers on the corner?

"Guerrero, my man, what is happening my brother?" Herbie greeted him with a firm handshake and a warm straight-on smile, as if he just returned from R and R in Barbados during a more tranquil time in the century.

"Wait a minute. Herbie? Is that you? You look different. Fuhgeddaboudit. You ain't supposed to be here. Even if you were alive, you ain't supposed to be here. That's the rules. You know the rules."

"This is different, Guerrero. The union doesn't have jurisdiction about this. We've got to go in there; so that's where we're going. But thank you very much for your concern."

"Ms. Primera, is that you?"

"Buenos dias, Alphonse. Como esta Juanita y su hijos?" With a wink and a smile she breezed by the startled security guard amputee who didn't know what to do about this because he thought they were dead. That's what the news was saying for the last twenty-four hours, but they seemed so much more alive than he had ever seen them before.

As they made their way down the long fluorescent corridor on the way to the soundstage, ABCNN employees popped out of cubicles and doorways to gape at them. Nobody said a word or tried to stop them because of the definite immediate purpose that surrounded the three. They entered the studio, stepping over cables and stands. They passed big cameras on hydraulic pedestals and startled camera operators. Flabbergasted gaffers and grips looked up at them, muttering things like, "Maria? I thought you were gonzo; wha's goin' on?" As she emerged onto the studio stage, the bewildered anchormen who were her bosses, the owners and the operators of one of the few remaining television companies in the northeast, were struck speechless on stage in the middle of their show, so amazed were they by Maria's unheralded appearance.

"Hi Marty, hi Ira. Say hello to my friend Jamal."

Ira, although still on air, was in a state of dumbfounded shock, and only able to mutter with in an involuntarily reflex, "Hello Jamal."

"Jamal and I met this morning in Shantypark."

"That's nice." Marty said. Like his partner, his stupefaction made him look pretty stupid, acting like an intern production assistant grunt, very wet behind the ears, not like the cutthroat media exec he really was.

"Jamal doesn't talk. At least no one I know has ever heard him talk. However I think he has something very important to show you. We have a video Herbie Lipton shot of Jamal this morning and I'd like to play it. Yes, that's right, there's Herbie, over there by the technical director, yeah, and he's alive too. Hi, Herb, say hello to New York." All three cameras that were focused on Maria and Jamal onstage suddenly swung around 180 degrees, fighting to see Herbie, who was waving from the control booth. The contract techies around him were in obvious agitation and muttered to each other, "That's Herbie? Not the Herbie we knew. When did he learn how to smile?"

These images broadcasting out over the greater NYC viewing area made Pellet, riding in his limo, furious beyond the purely physical. He barked orders into his headset for the immediate dispatch of several platoons of

SKs to the transmission area.

Sam, in the mayor's office, found himself laughing as if this Herbie was a twist in a movie that he should have guessed was going to happen a few minutes before it actually did.

Jack caught it all in real time for a change in the armored office, in a little window on the monitor next to his digital picture. This event broke into that loss of concentration and, in an instant, he flicked the button on the ABCNN live feed to see it full screen on his SHDTV 66 inch.

Maria continued, "This is a standard issue biopod. It is unable to be edited, and is backed up in two central data storage locations, making the information tamper proof. Here guys, please, be my guest, check Jamal out for his last signature data entry." Neither Marty nor Ira could yet move, so they signaled Lorenzo, the stage manager to get the biopod. Lorenzo looked around the studio for a sign of disapproval from any of the many producers standing by. He found none, they were too caught up in the drama on stage. He took the biopod from Maria and plugged it into the control board upstage of the news desk. The results hit the screen superimposed between Marty and Ira. The entire viewing area around New York City read the results, "PERSON ID, dnareg34096778, 12/24/47 2:37 PM, VIRAL REP – POSITIVE - HIV-7B. 5Mil per liter."

People all over New York involuntarily held their breath in shock. Even the reality shows didn't go this far, because Pellet would have revoked their licenses.

"Herbie, have you plugged in your drives so we can show what we brought?"

Big thumbs up from Herbie, big hombre smile.

Ira leaned over his desk, his tongue hanging out of his mouth, trying to say something to get back control of his show. "It's okay Ira, sit back, we're going to play a clip that is synched up to both the central database and this bipod through the world clock entry sequences."

Herbie plugged in his headbandcam to the control board. A freeze-frame of Salem Jones popped on screen, standing next to Jamal and Maria, as she was about to begin her report and administer the biopod exam. But it was this moment when the world saw Salem Jones for the first time, so before he could press the play button, the entire studio went into an uproar, in unison with the entire viewing population all over New York. Space and time seemed to be re-rendered in ways beyond special relativity, with no quantum mechanics able to account for the gaping holes ripping into the cosmic fabric. Not even Maria in all her newfound clarity had thought about what would happen when this finally occurred.

The entire New York City-State was convulsing, as they watched Salem pick up little Jamal on the video. They listened to Maria, as they had in the past, narrate the mind-blowing visuals now happening before them. They heard her recite the prognosis from the biopod. They watched the clip as she broke down and sobbed. They plunged into deep communal shock as they witnessed Salem lick Jamal's tumors with his tongue, their reflexive groaning absolutely cacophonic citywide. Within the space of that collective gargantuan gasp, Salem looks up at them from Jamal's disease and stares through the lens into their riveted eyes, the celestial vibrato already running along its tonic down an octave and up to an amazingly graceful fifth . . .

The picture runs out. In the studio, Maria and Jamal are on camera with the two rattled anchor billionaires. "Can we administer another biopod exam please? Lorenzo?" The stage manager, also overwhelmed by the sight of Salem, somehow steadies himself, picks up the biopod and aims it at Jamal, pushing the button. The red light hits Jamal's wrist, the biopod beeps once, hushes, and instantly re-beeps twice, the results flashing immediately on the screens all over New York, "PERSON ID, dnareg34096778, 12/24/47 6:39 PM, VIRAL REP – NEGATIVE. 0Mil per liter."

NEGATIVE. NO DISEASE. With one bombshell after another leading into this one, the most unbelievable of all, the final mega-stunner completes the city's collective shock.

Pellet, tortured by the limitations of the physical plane, watches in his car in near paroxysm, veins about to burst out of the skin around his brain.

Sam shakes his head in astoundment and stares into the monitor. Through the lone camera left active by the technical director, he watches the ABCNN New York bureau in falling apart from witnessing the impossible. Producers and technicians wander about the room, lost about what to do next. Lorenzo attends to an overwhelmed Marty. Ira wipes his own sweaty brow with a handkerchief. Maria has her arms around Jamal's shoulders and the little boy is staring up at her like a baby chicken imprinting on his mother.

Herbie however, not missing a beat, bolts out of the control room door, zigzags around people in the hallways who have lost reality and are bumbling about in disorientation, and ducks out of view into an unlocked staircase exit.

Jack, savoring the miracle before them, emphatically embraces the celestial chorus now singing in glorious harmony all about his beloved city, and gallantly cheers it all on.

* * * * *

38

Sweet Lorraine. A woman who did not mind being built as the ultimate toy for a boy. In fact, she loved it. She lived for being sexy, even during the high tide of 1970's feminism, when the couture of a woman's liberation was measured by the amount of hair under her arms.

It was that grand and irreplaceable era when Herbie's dad was born in the backwaters of Harvard and MIT, upstairs in a Cambridge, Massachusetts, attic, amidst a dancing coven of new-wave, nouveau rich, recently emancipated, preppy witches from the suburbs. By then Lorraine had already decided she was to pick her own way the through the rapids in the river of time, damned if she doesn't make it, she drowns by herself. That's the kind of girl she was. Once asked at a party by some ultra-rich Harvard sophomore what she thought about original sin, she replied without a moment's hesitation that she certainly would like to have one.

If she had found one, she would have then started a search for yet more undiscovered peccadilloes, because she was that type of girl. It wasn't hard for her to find willing partners to assist her in this quest. She was young, she was beautiful, and if she liked you, she showed you.

Her preference ran to long-haired and sensitive musicians. It wasn't like she was a groupie or a plaster caster, she was an artist whose active sexual connections were more than just inspiration; they were fuel.

At first she dabbled in photography, but the price of the cameras, film, chemicals, and the darkroom immediately made it too constrictive for her scamper and rampant type artist's personality. She needed something more cosmopolitan, more sophisticated, more urbane, more mixed media, something more appropriate, like garbage sculpture. She roamed the streets of Cambridge, looking for anything of artistic, political, or sociological value in trash bins, construction sites, and deserted lots. All the rubbish she claimed would find it's way back to the back porch of Grandma's little rental house, which Lorraine had turned into her studio. There she worked, sometimes all night, hammering and sawing and chiseling and painting. What would eventually emerge was a garbage sculpture of how it was she really felt.

She was also really good at rolling joints. That made her a real love and kept her nicely stoned through most of the 1970s. Sweet Lorraine had a constant stable of guitar players and drummers who kept her well supplied and well fueled. She liked when they tripped on psychedelics. It made the experience deeper, got her motor going to get out in the street and collect more garbage to paint.

Grandma just laughed off her best friend's sexual bravado and kept her only liaisons for Bullmoose. Once at a beer and smoke fest at Perry Street, some hippie in the crowd hit on Grandma. After striking him out with her disarming charm, he asked her in a caustic, sarcastic, punk-ass kind of way what she had against sex. She laughed and told the silly boy that she had nothing against sex at all; as a matter of fact she loved sex, she once had forty-one orgasms in the same night. All purple. So, no thank you,

you can't beat that.

Returning to Boston from India, Bullmoose and Pranan stumbled out of the plane, jumped on the T to Central Square, walked the six or so blocks to Perry Street and knocked on Grandma's door with just the clothes they wore on their backs and Bullmoose's Martin guitar, albeit a bit dinged. Grandma, delighted, invited them in and fed them some homemade chicken and barley soup, along with a six-pack of Coors Light. They recounted to her their adventures, including the part with the little Gypsy and all its concurrent sordid details. It was somewhat surprising to Pranan that this didn't bother Grandma. But he was just beginning to learn that Grandma invented the open relationship and probably was the only person in history to ever actually have one.

Finally, she and Bullmoose drifted upstairs into her bedroom looking for purple and Pranan curled up to sleep on the couch in the living room. Above him he could hear Bullmoose and Grandma giggling, and the floorboards creaking from the bed rocking and rolling. Even though it was two a.m. when they arrived, without sleeping a minute from halfway around the world, the sounds of the amorous action upstairs kept him wide awake and, what was worse, made him horny.

He wandered with great continental disorientation up the stairs to the bathroom, tiptoeing past Grandma's door out of respect. He opened the bathroom door and there she was. This incredible white goddess, sitting on the john, fully naked, just completely and entirely bare butt naked, reading by candlelight what he later found out was the Kama Sutra. Lorraine, totally unfazed, looked up at him with a brief smile, made a dainty wipe, flushed, and left, muttering a pleasant how-do-you-do on the way out. She went back into her bedroom across the hall, leaving an astonished and smitten Pranan frozen in the hallway.

Agape and aghast, he heard a muffled young man's romantic voice behind her bedroom door ask, "Hey baby, where's the rolling papers?"

That image of her tender white nakedness never left his mind. Each day as Bullmoose and he continued to crash at Perry Street, it became harder for him to resist her allure and enchantment. He started to feel personally insulted by the neverending stream of longhaired and sensitive rock musicians who came and went day and night. It was like she was a librarian in a lending library where the only book available was the Kama Sutra, and one couldn't read it without her reading it to you.

It wasn't like it a personal snub. Mornings in the Perry Street kitchen, which retained an aroma of cheap red wine and whose greenish wallpaper was burnished by all the marijuana smoke, were always a great way to start the day. Grandma served him a breakfast bowl of granola and yogurt while a sleepy looking Lorraine cooed into the eyes of some anesthetized local guitar jock over a cup of cinnamon coffee. And those late night spaghetti dinners, with garlic bread, Chianti, and boxes of frozen shrimp borrowed from the Greek restaurant where Lorraine waitressed every now and then, were also warm and fuzzy, as she nibbled on the ears of the bartender drummer who helped her accomplish the heist. With Bullmoose pontificating and Grandma cooing over Herbie's dad, it was actually cozy, like a hippie family. That's the way Lorraine felt about him, sisterly. You don't fuck your sister.

She had no time for him sexually; her energy did not flow in that direction. Even if Pranan was a great and merciful East Indian god-like apparition, who looked so good he could have been the cover boy on her favorite book, she was just too busy researching her bathroom literature of choice with other guys who were musicians, longhaired and sensitive.

But, for Pranan, Lorraine was all he could think about. However, he stayed very polite and appropriate, because it was dynamite that Grandma let them crash there as long they needed to. Unlike his American teenage counterparts, politeness was how people from his part of the world always behaved in all situations. Most importantly, even though he was a really nice guy, it was because he was hopelessly lost in love or lust or both. He often lingered as long as he could by the upstairs bathroom door, in case he got another chance to watch her pee naked.

However, Pranan knew the count-on-able rules were working for him: nothing stays the same, everything is interconnected, and you never know what is going to happen next.

The genuine real article, the dropouts of the early 1970s, never had much money. That didn't really bother this hippie family because the life of a countercultural freak isn't supposed to involve much currency. In their household, those things important, mostly drugs, came as a part of the lifestyle. They were there, traded, bartered, re-traded and consumed without the exchange of much money of their own. Of course there had to be some money, for the man, you know, for things like rent and food. Money was a necessary evil, so you had to do necessarily evil things.

Often they dreamt about money, lots of it, and came up with crazy schemes about how to get it. Bullmoose was the best at it. He had crazy ideas like making a cup of coffee real fancy, like with shots of espresso, blended with soymilk and topped with caramel and lots of whipped cream. He'd give it a catchy name and sell it to everyone in America everyday for more than three dollars a shot. That would certainly make them a ton of the evil stuff.

But his friends just laughed at him, passed the joint and said how crazy he was. That could never happen; who would be so stupid to buy a cup of coffee for that much money?

One afternoon he thought they could make a TV show about the silly things they did in their house everyday and how they felt about it. They wouldn't need writers or actors or a plot, they could just let the reality happen. The audience would be entertained just by watching them do the simple things they routinely did everyday and then listen to them talk about what it was that they just saw them do. Maybe they could make up a game or two to keep them occupied, or do stupid and gross things nobody would ever do like eat the cockroaches that shared the love with them in their cozy little kitchen. Yeah, sure, they coughed. Which of the thirteen channels would go for that dumb idea? And what stupid American consumer would waste their valuable time watching something as boring as all that? People don't want reality they said.

Lorraine just rolled another joint, took a big toke and smiled. Bullmoose sighed, took a puff and resigned himself to having to do truly evil things.

To pay the rent they painted homes in Porter Square and waited on tables on Mass Ave., or they cleaned rooms for the Harvard Library Services, which employed people to maintain the libraries that were built primarily to extinguish insomnia from Harvard Yard. That was Bullmoose's favorite, wiping the dust off bookshelves, as rich preppies and foreign students, heirs to kingdoms in Africa and Asia, sat around thick hardwood tables and studied the Communist revolution in China as if it might have been at all relevant to the cultural movement going on in America at that time. To Bullmoose, those pinko Harvard guys, who thought quoting Robert's rules at the open meetings to strike against the university was going to get them girls, were equally as absurd as those MIT nerds, who believed the Big Bang was a way to get laid. His only response to them was, Robert who? And, what in heck came before that, and what before that?

Within a few weeks back in the States, Bullmoose settled for the lesser of all evils and was back up to his old tricks, which was waiting in a brown Boston cab at Logan airport for the Beantown bourgeoisie to come waddling up to the taxi stand to pay longhaired and sensitive young men to drive them to the outlying provinces. Thereby these young men in question could make a little cash before the end of the day so they could turn it over to evil supermarkets, evil landlords, and evil utility companies.

Wistful, Pranan knew some of them were lucky enough to have a lending library of their own to go home to that had an oral tradition of reciting and teaching the ancient ayurvedic sexual practices. But not Pranan, he didn't even have a job.

Oftentimes in the evenings when Bullmoose was gone, driving cabs for the evil stuff, the little house on Perry Street was quieter and somewhat more peaceful, but certainly not as entertaining. There were no sounds of electric guitars in the basement exploding caveman-like riffs that only white men imitating Jimmy Hendrix could come up with. There were no late-night philosophical dissertations with hygienically challenged college dropouts who came to pool their pocket change to buy beer and other soft drugs.

It wasn't a bad different, just a mellow different, which was hard to be when Bullmoose was home. But mellow could be an ambivalent thing. For Grandma, it was neither here nor there. She liked mellow; she liked chaos. It was all part of the great scheme of things. Lorraine didn't like mellow. She liked garbage sculpture; she liked mixed media; she liked nuttiness; she liked anarchy; she loved fuel. But for Pranan, an agnostic Muslim from a Hindu culture of everyone and everything having a distinct place in time, mellow actually gave him some much-needed space to be alone to think. He eventually came up with a plan.

Every morning, without fail, his best friend in the world, Bullmoose, gave him, quite unselfishly, a few evil dollars from the hard-earned tips he made driving the gentry all over Boston all night long. He'd just be getting home and Pranan would just be getting up. Over black coffee, Bullmoose would reveal his latest brainstorm concocted during the night. Everyone in the kitchen would smile, mumble and glance at each other with well concealed smiles when hearing these ideas. They wanted to tell him to shut up, but Grandma clucked something about being careful with the ones you love; so everyone just let him be.

Pranan, born appreciative about life, always accepted the few dollars Bullmoose supplied, albeit evil. Being a born ascetic, he used only what he absoultely needed, saving the rest for something special.

So on one otherwise undifferentiated morning, after Bullmoose re-defined the future of commercial TV, Pranan made his move.

Feeling charmed, Pranan wandered across Mass. Ave into a pawnshop in Central Square. He negotiated in the stubborn way only a native-born sub-continental Asian can, for an old Boehm silver flute displayed in the crowded window. The antique flute had once belonged to a classical flutist who used to be second chair in the Boston Pops before her heroin addiction became just too much.

Yuri Zeebeesteen, an Armenian who owned the pawnshop, also tried to sell him some high-risk car insurance. The deal was interesting to Pranan only in its intellectual possibilities. He turned it down eventually by telling Yuri that he didn't own a car. Of course, after that, Yuri tried to sell Pranan a car, which Pranan would have liked, since he missed his Ambassador. He envisaged it sitting at the curb by the passenger drop off in the Madras airport; it might still be there. Before they ran off to catch their plane, Pranan crawled back underneath the heroic little vehicle and retrieved from the driveshaft Bullmoose's magic ring that saved their lives. Bullmoose was wearing it now on his right hand, an historic gift from Pranan to his American best friend upon their arrival in the U.S. He was glad he did that now, considering how much Bullmoose had given him lately, which was just enough money to buy what he needed to become a longhaired and sensitive musician.

The only wrinkle in Pranan's wild and crazy cosmic plan was that he didn't know how to play the flute.

However, being truly resourceful and totally committed, it didn't take him too long to make a sound. It wasn't music; it wasn't pretty, but it was a sound that came from a flute. That was enough for rip-roaring congratulations from the assortment of hippies and street people who congregated at all times around Grandma's Perry Street nirvana, looking for leftovers, sometimes a place to crash, and maybe even a little piece of Lorraine.

That gave him all the encouragement he needed to continue destroying everyone's sound space. Granted it wasn't anywhere near as loud and annoying as a crappy electric guitar in the basement, but it certainly wasn't music yet. That didn't matter to Pranan because, as he practiced, day by day, he received a little bit more attention from Lorraine, whose ear for music wasn't quite as keen as were other parts of her body. The sounds may not have turned her on quite yet, but it seemed the effort to make them was just as important, so he felt he was on the right road.

Pranan had hope. He felt a quantum jitter in the universe that opened up this little seam and said, yes, you can sleep with Lorraine; all you need to do is seduce her with your tunes. He really didn't know how to make a tune, yet, but since the universe gave him reason to try, by Allah, he'd try. God is great.

He tried so hard that many times during the day he grew faint and lightheaded from lack of oxygen. He blew all he could into that thin little silver pipe until it grew hot in his hands. He knew nothing about music except what he liked: Van Morrison, Crosby, Stills and Nash, Jefferson Airplane. But theory, scales, arpeggios—nothing about that, nada. It seemed so simple, make a sound some stoned-out freak could like, and the world was at your command, well, certainly a young, sexually emancipated, upper middle-class, preppy witch or two. Golly, America was a great place, regardless of what they napalmed in Viet Nam.

Finally all that hot air paid off. But it wasn't without the usual intrigue. It happened one Saturday night. Grandma was away with Herbie's infant dad, off on a visit to Amherst to visit her Mom and Pop, who grew to accept the fact that their hippie daughter was a single mother without a job or a future they could see. They were relieved that at least she didn't marry Bullmoose.

Alone in Perry Street, Pranan drifted down to the basement where Bullmoose and his band practiced from time to time when they had enough grass. He turned on the PA and stood trembling in front of the mic that was set up for Bullmoose to sing into as he banged away on his Fender Stratocaster pretending he was Bob Weir. Yes, amplification could take the meekest of musical attempts and turn it into something to be reckoned with. That's what volume is good for. Pranan stood there spellbound and blew wavering and airy sounds into the electronic night, morphing himself into Jethro Tull. He opened his eyes and, to his full surprise, there was Lorraine who had just come home from flirting with her partner-in-crime bartender from the Greek restaurant on Mass. Ave where she sometimes worked. She had batted her eyes and giggled her way into a free souvlaki with dolmades and all the Pepsi syrup she could drink. Lorraine smiled at Pranan, and her teeth and the whites of her eyes glowed in the black light like some strobed-out vampire nymphet gone wild. To Pranan it was sex appeal saturated beyond imagination. Hey man, she said over the hum of the low-level feedback, not bad, not bad, where did you learn to do that? He smiled and shrugged and actually guffawed, and blew another triplet into the mic. They both laughed. A sweet, shared, first-time bond, first-time chemical transaction, and it all seemed so natural, let's get it on.

Just at that moment Bullmoose appeared at the bottom of the stairs. Far out, he said, dig that crazy flute. He grabbed his Strat and plugged it into his Fender tube amp, banged out a power E chord and gleamed, let's jam, brother Pranan. Lorraine, much to Pranan's surprise, gave a rebel yell and, reaching into her handbag, gave them each a tab of pure blotter acid that looked like a corner torn off of a piece of common copy paper. Pranan looked at her in dismay. She laughed and said there were enough milligrams dissolved into his piece to resurrect the entire Mayan Empire. Bullmoose swallowed his without hesitation, which brought a lecherous growling sound from somewhere deep inside Lorraine's throat, like she was a gasoline-starved Harley Davidson, needing to be gassed up. Not to be outdone, and sensing some barnyard competition about to begin, Pranan, the rooster, quickly shoved the tasteless piece of paper into his mouth and swallowed it down. Lorraine smiled and backed away to watch the show, her unbounding desire directed to these boys of the basement.

Pranan was thunderstruck with his own stupidity. He never jammed before. He didn't know how to jam. He didn't even know how to play the flute. To top it off he never took acid before. He has seen those high hippie clowns who took acid and stared obsessively at spots on the wall or laughed incessantly until they cried unremittingly. He certainly didn't want to turn into that clod who stood naked, hunched over in the Cambridge Commons during the local Sunday afternoon rock concerts, drooling and holding onto his own dick as if afraid it was going to fall off. To make matters worse, the instant Bullmoose plugged in, assorted freaks from all over the neighborhood started wandering down the stairs to check out what was happening. Wow, "far out," they all said. Joints got rolled in high frequency light speed time, Lorraine helping out with her share of expertise, and they were passed around with bottles of Wild Turkey and Ripple and Southern Comfort. Before he knew it there was a drummer and a bass player mixing in and some big electric sound was getting ready to go down.

All Pranan cared about was Lorraine. He watched her settle down on some pillows in the back of the basement to groove on the music, her long legs wrapped in a colorful peasant skirt, looking like the headliner in a pictorial for Playboy's issue of hippie girls of the Boston area. There was nothing this girl could do or wear that could take away her claim to being the sexiest chick in any room she was in. Amazingly, as assorted longhaired and sensitive types approached Lorraine to check her gas gauge, for the first time ever she completely ignored them. She only had eyes for Bullmoose and Pranan, her roommates, jamming buddies, world travelers, and defenders of the magic ring.

The acid that they all took a little earlier started warping things. Bullmoose took a very long time to tune his guitar. Even under sober conditions, it never sounded right to him. Especially the B string. Pranan stood in the flickering strobe watching Bullmoose turn different shades of blue and green as the string went flat and sharp and flat again. The guitar was wrapped around Bullmoose's body like a boa constrictor from Guyana trying to squeeze itself into tune. Bullmoose was huffing and puffing and tightening the string and loosening it and then tightening again and snap, it broke. That's where real time ended and the immutable laws you can always count on took over.

A groove kicked in and for some reason the backbeat seemed to reciprocate with a love and a lick for anything the bass had to say. For some unknown reason this all made sense to Pranan, who had yet to read the Kama Sutra. Bullmoose made some genuine magic by plucking one of his five strings left, somehow producing a symphony hall environment of just one note for Pranan to explore, breath by breath. Pranan could feel Lorraine's energy reaching out like some sultry double helix in love with her own design. He leaned into the mic and heard himself start playing things thaumaturgic inside the booming sonic architecture that Bullmoose was building. His prestidigital flute morphed into an extension of not only his lips but also his throat and tongue that looked real weird to his tripping eyes but sounded all right. The street hippies, always looking for a free buzz, seemed to genuinely dig it.

Most importantly, Pranan felt the current of intentional electrons from Lorraine's magnetic blue eyeballs zero in on him. He felt it tingle in his very special human place that adds soul to mere particles of matter, where the union of DNA, the stuff of eons, and DNA, the immediate message, gathers the most impact, reaches critical density and explodes as it recreates over and over again the original secret to why the universe needs eyes and ears to appreciate itself. In the midst of all this, he knew he needed to remember how he was playing what he was playing, so he could do it again.

After that, he couldn't remember anything. Until later, when he was pulling out of the long Perry Street driveway, behind the wheel of the VW minivan where Herbie's dad had been conceived several sun cycles ago as Grandma surfed the immortal and incomparable waves of purple. Bullmoose was on the passenger seat with Lorraine on his lap, tongues burrowing deep down into each other's throat. But Pranan was not jealous for he knew the night was young. There was going to be time for him. Although her face was lip-locked to Bullmoose, her left hand was mysteriously massaging peewee Pranan, still prisoner, locked up in the crotch of his skin-tight bell-bottom jeans.

It was 4 a.m. on a Sunday morning, and they were rushing to Singing Beach to catch the sunrise over the Atlantic. Pranan, the driver consummate from India, was driving with his own tenuous theory of, what the hey? what the hurry? Every streetlight they passed was a conical light show of infinite variation, every dip and bump in the road a three-dimensional challenge to maneuvering through the ever-evolving wrinkles of inflationary cosmology, and he hadn't even driven around the block. It was a darn good thing that later on no little blue meanies with flashing red lights stopped this unregistered motor vehicle on Route 128, driven by an illegal alien without a license doing bootleg psychedelics and going only ten miles an hour. There is no limit to the glory and grace of God.

At Manchester-by-the Sea, dashing over sand that whistled with the touch of their feet, they conquered land for Caesar and carved out fiefdoms of their own. As centuries shifted in the Atlantic wind, their tantalizing Guinevere lay breathless before them on the hard dry sand, watching them protect the kingdom as they ran along the dunes fending off dragons and dark sorcerers. Lorraine's long blond locks were dancing in the breezes blowing in from the sea. Her lovely long legs were spread outstretched on the sand with the cotton skirt draping between them with barely enough modesty. It lay oh-so-invitingly upon the softest spots of her smooth inner thighs, highlighting the direction to the tunnel to heaven these virile warriors most intended to go. Her marvelous appendages serenaded them as they galloped by on their knightly steeds, like sirens singing, "touch me, don't touch me, touch me, don't touch me, lick me."

A sharp crisp wind accompanied the glorious sun rising out from the mighty sea. The merciful fog rolled back in, darkening the early morn just enough to allow them to sneak back under cover into a sleeping Cambridge town.

Back in Perry Street, Lorraine undressed in her room. Her skin tingled and goosebumped as if it was on an independent search for a perfect match that would smooth every neuron in her body into one undulating wave of passion that could drown out every other need her soul had ever ached for, including painting garbage. The light brushing sound each piece of clothing made, as she removed them and dropped them to the wooden floor, echoed like a lone coyote in insufferable loneliness, howling from a desert peak into the glistening night for her mate to return home and bring her unbounded delight.

There in the early morning light, adrift in a sea of a first-time borderless and exotic sexual fury, Bullmoose stood shoulder to shoulder with Pranan in the bathroom across the hall from Lorraine's boudoir, both with the same empire-saving idea, which wasn't just to watch Lorraine pee. Behind the door in front of them was a nude, unbelievably sexy twenty-one year-old woman in wild love and passion for them both, whose wanton erotic aura could have been registered as a landscape point of light in the universal ledger of the stars. The smell of urgent sex permeated the entire house and billowed out into the street. Every united blood vessel in each of the two world conquerors was pouring juices into the same location of their young and powerful bodies, their hormones screaming at them to power through the door to where Lorraine was waiting and deliver themselves up to her incalculable concupiscence.

Bullmoose looked at Pranan, in whose eyes he saw the love, power, and destiny. He knew that Pranan, looking back, saw the lust, animal magnetism, and industrialized savage. You never do know what is going to happen next even when you are the one doing it, so, surprising himself in a knightly moment of utter and grand chivalry, smiling his infinitely most famous, and with the greatest of nobility, as if he was passing on the honor in history of finding the Holy Grail, Bullmoose stepped back and let his best buddy go it alone.

Pranan was about to open the door and enter the musky chambers of renowned literary pursuit, where Lorraine was surely putting the finishing touches onto a thick marijuana stogie, when Bullmoose made him pause. He looked him in the eye, tugged the magic ring from off his finger and handed it off with silent ceremony to his best pal in the world, Pranan. "You are going to need it tonight more than me, buddy."

Bullmoose would always say that she was more than capable of having them both that night, but he didn't want to ruin it for Pranan. Lorraine to Pranan was more than just a hippie fuck; he wanted her whole thing from bottom to top, inside and out. It was a change your nation, change your religion type of love, that he traveled half way around the world on what seemed like a whim to find.

He didn't need to wake up later that day and find her on her knees with his best friend, Bullmoose.

In that early red morning, wrapped in the soothing northeasterly fog, Lorraine's searing warmth enveloped his unbounded desire, which in turn pierced right through to a place in her soul that blossomed her life into something so absolutely brand spanking new.

Lorraine of course was ecstatic and in her intuitive heart knew her life had changed within the universal guidelines of number one: nothing can stay the same. Bullmoose was genuinely happy for both of them. It proved once again number two: everything is interconnected. When Grandma got back from Amherst with Herbie's toddler dad, and watched these two newly connected love birds swooning into each other's eyes, she relearned with glee all the wisdom of number three: you never know what is going to happen next. And the Defender of the Magic Ring from Mahabalipuram, India, who grew up everyday to the sound of clink-clink-clink cutting through the roar of the wind and the pounding of the sea, who came all the way to Massachusetts on a wing and a prayer as the chauffeur and best friend of the man who might have been the fully undocumented founder of the Mile High Club, where he refashioned the flute to insure the biological success of his own individual genetic existence, had finally gotten it. Pranan now fully believed and understood the count-on-able rule number four: there is truly no limit to the glory and grace of God.

* * * * *

But of course, Grandma had to have the last word, reminding them all that you have to be very careful with the ones you love. The story of Uncle Pranan and Aunt Lorraine, obviously toned down to a PG rating for young

Herbie's ears, always made him wonder why Grandma had to throw a little cold water over everyone after a great romantic story. After all, she was anything but a cynic. As an adult he thought maybe this was one place her conservative and pragmatic side showed through because of the trail of her own love life, and her difficult-to-manage entanglement with a bucking king alpha moose she met one night in a summer storm. Sometimes he wondered, when she was alone late at night, or maybe hushed around the kitchen table with Aunt Lorraine in some late afternoon evaluations of their interwoven lives, if she ever reappraised some of her earlier choices, whether she ever second-guessed those long ago instincts that bless us in youth and curse us in the years to come. Or maybe she was just reminding us all that even after happy endings, nothing stays the same.

* * * * *

The city moved on after its first view of Salem, and with an enormous outpouring of spiritual love caused by the mass mutual witnessing of a modern miracle it seemed like a happy ending indeed. But, heedful always of what his Grandma really meant to say, Herbie acted without delay.

He had a head start on everyone in the city when it came to seeing miracles. As clearheaded as he felt he had become, the miracle recovery seemed to make everyone else a bit woozy, in a giddy way, as though some psycho-bomb had gone off.

It was easy for him to get the stuff he needed out of the equipment room. He didn't even have to sign it out. The night guy, who was previously known to everyone to be a genuine prick, was glued to his TV watching the Salem clip Herbie had shot in Shantypark, over and over again. The station had put it on a loop and the ignorant brute was dumbfounded with fascination, as if once wasn't enough, there might be more the next time it went around. He didn't even look up or bat an eyelash at Herbie as he walked out of the room with two heavy equipment cases filled with remote field production gear. The man was in suspended animation staring at his screen, free fall talking into his head-gear, and non-stop banging out a constant stream of instant messages on his computer. His immediate response to today's amazing phenomenon was to talk to everyone on his buddy list on every device he owned about how he felt about what he just saw.

At the ABCNN garage, the story was the same. The company guard had simply upped and left his post and could be seen in the locker room near the public toilet by the exit ramp to Broadway, glued to the station's ongoing transmission, babbling nonstop to the mechanics and parking attendants. His response to the complete rearrangement of reality was to be hand slapping and back patting and talking jive with his pack of dogs about the coming kingdom of heaven.

Strange, but peaceful, like an eerie party with no rules, no form, but everyone at their weirdest. Herbie went about doing what he knew he had to do as fast as he could do it. You don't know what's going to happen next.

He pulled up and double-parked his commandeered Hummer outside the station's perimeter, waiting. The security was anything but secure. Every single one of the small army of private guards had left their posts and were off partying in the streets. Within seconds Maria emerged from the building with Jamal. She immediately saw Herbie as if she was expecting him to be right where he was, and they darted across the street. In an instant they were all in the protective vehicle rolling away.

Herbie smiled at Maria, a sweet smile. She smiled

back to him feeling so new and fresh, and cozy warm indeed.

Seconds after they pulled out and off into traffic, General Pellet's BMW limo screeched to a halt in front of the station.

Marty and Ira, descended from a long line of money changers and usurers, had recovered from their spiritual experience enough to know it was time to cash in. Marty was already on the computer in their adjoining offices logging in the non-stop hits for the orders coming worldwide for Herbie's Salem Jones clip, available now with the few amazing moments spliced in when the biopod in the studio revealed the healing. He heard a knock on his office door. Without stopping the directing of the uploads of these spectacular sequences to markets around the world, he heard General Pellet enter. He heard Ira make his usual pleasantries to the general, and then he was dead before his ears could hear the gun go off into the back of his head.

* * * * *

39

Squirrel killers on every corner tried to manage the traffic going uptown towards Shantypark. The televised images of Salem were drawing people closer to where everyone knew he had to be. Traffic congestion in the area was never a problem before the miracle, because ordinary people didn't go to Shantypark unless it was in an instance of being thrown in and not allowed back out. Now, more than a couple hundred thousand newly energized Salem proselytes were already encamped in the streets of no man's land immediately surrounding the park. The area had the feel of an outdoor church revival in an oncoming electrical storm, lightning striking the ground here would seem a likely occurrence. Ad hoc prayer meetings chorusing with hallelujahs were gathered around metal garbage cans lit on fire for physical warmth against the unusual cold. Choirs from neighboring cathedrals singing religious hymns written and produced for other generations with different considerations were performing impromptu in the streets and on the sidewalks. The edgy and disjointed Christmas Eve atmosphere was at the same time clogging the flow of all vehicular motion, and it was hard not to notice the menacing glints from the squirrel killers who patrolled in large groups with guns ready and unlocked on their shoulders. But the soldiers were tolerant of the relative peace the mob was exhibiting. They didn't need to kill Jones freaks yet, until of course they got the word from the general.

Inside the Hummer, Jamal gazed out the window in silent awe at a city in which he lived but never saw before. Herbie and Maria sat in silent reflection from the mind-boggling phenomenon that they not only witnessed but played such an instrumental part in unveiling. With so many people out on the streets to look at and so much more in their minds to think about, neither needed to speak. They did not need conversation to help water the garden blossoming in their souls.

Herbie drove with a gentle smile on his face that Maria had never seen before. It made her feel safe and secure; she realized she had always felt that way around Herbie. She always had the quiet confidence on the job that he was going to be there, to support her, and it had warmed her to think she never had to worry about that. Why in the middle of a modern miracle is she thinking about him in this way?

When they pulled up to Maria's luxury high-rise near the river, the streets were relatively quiet; all the commotion was in the middle of the island. Maria stepped out of the Hummer, Jamal naturally followed. All of a sudden reality kicked in. She looked at Jamal's imploring little baby face looking back up at her and Maria had a sudden moment of panic. She leaned back in through the passenger's window so Jamal couldn't hear. "What do I do now?"

Herbie looked at Jamal, mum in the glow of the streetlights, and gave him a fatherly smile, dredged up from some deserted shipwreck lying barnacled on the underwater plains of the ocean of his emotions. He twinkled at Maria, "Give him dinner. TV. A bedtime story. He's just a kid. Be like a mom."

"I really don't know how to do all that. I never did this before."

"It comes easy when you just have to."

"I wish you didn't have to go." She blushed because she meant it. "I could really use your help."

There was nothing else he would rather do than go up the elevator with this beautiful woman and play house in her warm and comfortable home. His soul had the kinetic charge of an entire school of salmon swimming up the rapids, knowing somehow that at the end of the journey there would be a cool mountain stream dazzling in pure sunlight, where creation in its grand wonder is transmitted with pure joy from one living body to the next. All he wanted to do was park the car, turn off the ignition, pull the key and follow her in.

"Don't worry. I'll be back."

* * * * *

40

The newsroom at ABCNN, which just shortly before was a riotous scene of anarchic jubilation, was now transformed into something very different. It was oddly disquieting, because this recent event was even bigger news than when the Jihad blew up the nuclear reactors at Indian Point in Westchester ten years after the Exchange. Back then, this newsroom was really hopping in anticipation of great revenue. But nothing close to what it was like today when it was center stage for modern miracle numero uno. Now almost all the techies, the producers, and the talent were out on the street marveling amongst themselves. Ira was left with only a forcibly conscripted few as crew. Pellet was at the podium, one solitary camera trained upon his face.

"Good evening. Today we witnessed a great changing point in our city's history. By the time the seditious transmissions were ended by the authority invested in me through the Emergency Statutes, we all witnessed the so-called miracle video. We heard the claims that the headbandcam and the biopod were both synched up to the world clock, verifying that a natural healing of an incurable disease took place today, right here in New York City.

My fellow citizens, there is no doubt that some of you might want to take solace in the false promise this kind of terrorism makes. But hear me out. I am not going to let my guard down for even one instant for the people of this city, this state, and this region. At this very moment, a team of experts are looking carefully at the memory stick on which was recorded the so-called miracle clip for signs of editing of any kind. Do not discount for one moment that our enemies take pride in being very clever in the ways they try to destroy us. As the commanding officer of the armed forces that are sworn to protect this city and all its law abiding citizens, I am not going to rest one minute until I can disprove the these unsubstantiated claims of a modern miracle in our midst."

Ira stared at Pellet's face on the monitor in the control room trying to not look as nervous as he felt. He ignored the sullen TV techie who was pulled at gunpoint from some spontaneous festivity celebrating the transcendental by some very persuasive squirrel killers demanding his special techie expertise. Ira's blood curdled from the laughter coming from his office down the hall, where several of these soldiers were now wiping Marty's brains off the walls.

* * * * *

Double-parking the Hummer in front of the pawnshop, Herbie in a headlong rush forced himself to pause, to take it in, to look about. On the streets all around him he saw the city in a state of collective shock. There were those hanging onto each other on the sidewalks, arm in arm, beaming like all Hosanna, faces to the sky, amen on the tips of their lips. Others were running helter skelter across streets and through the traffic now jammed at every corner. Extemporaneous oration erupted from benches and the roofs of cars, street priests preaching to crowds anxious to hear Salem's written words that they prayed would save them for all eternity. Some people were rejoicing as if they were just freed from any further burdens of survival or existence itself. But it was getting hard to tell if their ecstasy was chemical or Salem Jones induced.

He entered the store and immediately found the case he was looking for, but looking around, there was no one to pay. The owner of the pawnshop, who was usually so suspicious and wary of each customer that he kept a loaded piece plainly visible by the cash register, had just walked out the door and abandoned his business to join the instant holiday that was New York. Above the counter the TV was still on. Herbie looked up to see Pellet's talking head.

"In the meantime, I am dispatching units of the First Army to patrol the streets of the city in anticipation of the looting and rioting from the violent, anti-social elements in our city that will be sure to follow these acts of terrorism. My orders are very clear. My men are going to take whatever action is necessary to prevent and control any acts of a criminal nature against the people and property of this city that is now under my complete jurisdiction."

Herbie threw a fifty on the counter and galloped back to the Hummer. Grandma was right. The dark side did not take long to emerge. As the usual rules and regulations guiding a rigid society were suspended, much misanthropy was indeed breaking out. When just before there was only an angelic countenance to the smiles in the streets, now the other side of human nature was showing its snide and sneering self. For some this mighty day was a signal to spew perversion. Already he could hear the glass shatterings. People were running wanton in maniacal glee, smashing windows, violating storefronts and racing back out with their arms filled with unpaid-for stuff. There were shouts and screams, some in pain and terror, others cabalistic, coming from obscure alleyways and open doorways. Herbie could easily imagine squads of squirrel killers appearing on the scene and what they would do to these besieged people with their latest given orders. It was only a matter of time before overt violence on a larger scale would follow.

He had one more thing to do and then he had to get back to Maria. He split with celerity.

* * * * *

41

High above Manhattan, in her commodious apartment, all of her fears about entertaining a taciturn little boy from the ghetto dissipated before the can of chicken soup even came to a boil. The elevator up to the twenty-second floor seemed to fascinate him, never having been in one before, never having been above a ground floor. He was a little frightened with her view over the East River, but loved her state-of-the-art computer with the few games on it that he could play. He also was very impressed by the marvelous material comforts her apartment contained, mostly the big comfy bed in her guest room. The one she was tucking him into now because he was already fast asleep by the time she brought him the bowl of soup with a toasted English muffin. She smiled to herself as she watched his little body expand and contract under the comforter with each contented breath. She wondered how he understood the things that just happened. She shut the light and closed the door gently behind her. That was easy, she sighed. But, you never know what comes next.

For some reason both her cell phone and landlines were useless. She really wanted to call Herbie, but that was impossible now. She would just have to wait till he got back, and she hoped it would be soon. She wandered through her lovely flat not knowing what to do next, when her eyes landed on the blinking red light of the video answering device on her desk. For some reason the flashing seemed ominous, and because of the strange feeling, she didn't want to know who called. Whatever was waiting for her on memory in that hard drive may be something she didn't want to hear.

* * * * *

42

Milos, the mayor's Slavic techie, was still waiting to mumble his usual viscous goodbye and shut the door to the studio behind him. He knew the general's latest broadcast was not going to have favorable reviews with his boss. Besides he wanted to witness the streets firsthand. He didn't know if there would be sunshine or dark clouds outside of this safe room. More importantly he wanted to be near his wife and kids, and he couldn't get through with his cell phone. The emergency regulations seemed to have knocked the system out again. The general could be a real pain in the ass.

Milos had a job to do here, and he was the only one who could do it. Yet it wasn't easy getting a signal in from Singapore with all these brownouts. He kept trying to bounce a transmission off the few satellites that might be hot, but that took too long, and each attempt already failed. But what the fuck? Why should he care if New York could communicate with the rest of the world? The mayor looked like he was going to go into one of those goofy personal brownouts of his own soon anyway. He lowered the speaker from the operation room's volume so he didn't have to listen to the sound of Sam laughing.

He went back to searching the skies above the earth for a metal billiard ball to bounce a phone call off to the other side of the world, all the while worrying what Lydia and the kids were doing. He hoped they had the sense to lock their doors.

Notwithstanding the fact that monumental history was in the making, the whole thing was actually kind of ironic to Sam. He muted the volume on the general's special newscast after he heard it loop the first time through, but let Pellet's incendiary flapping lips go on silently ad nausea as backdrop to his own personal black comedy. He turned to Jack who seemed to be going again. "The pharmagiants will really want to wrap this guy's ass in a sling. They have been leading the world on for decades, dragging out the hope of a breakthrough cure for AIDS that could come from something they could package and sell, meantime they're the fattest cats on the planet offering snake oil to prolong the agony. I mean, look what's left of Africa. Then this totally random ex-con gets all this attention only one day out of the slammer by doing the impossible with just a heartfelt hug and a kiss. Does anyone have any real idea how many people are infected with some kind of incurable condition worldwide? All we do know is where they're going to come if they can get cured with just a big wet kiss! Zappo, there goes all that money, there goes all their power; and Shantypark, which has been one huge fomenting leper colony since its inception, now looks like the Garden of Eden. You know what? I think the chemical titans should have been working on their own holistic approach."

"Once the apple was bitten, there was no return to the garden." Jack barely grunted.

Sam stood up from the tabletop he was sitting on and wheeled 360 around on his heels. All the other monitors in the room, except the general's newscast, were dark. At a time like this Jack should have been in world conference mode with every leader in the Alliances. But he was silent. This time it wasn't all Jack's fault. The mayor had been ready to act, ready to lead. He knew that by now Milos could have by-passed the browns with the satellite technology installed here in this office, but there was something much bigger happening. This was Pellet's doing. There was a unilateral usurpation of power going on. Mutiny.

Jack shuddered as if ripped apart from a secret conversation. "Sam, you have to listen to me. You have to get out of here tonight. It's our only hope."

* * * * *

43

Returning to his apartment Herbie couldn't believe that only twenty-four hours ago he lived in this pigsty. Empty pints of tequila in soggy brown paper bags were rotting in the garbage, discharging a sour, fermented odor that made the room smell like vomit. Green, fetid water accumulating in the bottom of saucepans in the kitchen sink were breeding grounds for all kinds of life directly repugnant to man, now crawling through the crevasses of dirty dishes and hardened, rotten food.

Herbie grabbed the vintage guitar leaning against the wall and put it in the case he just bought at the deserted pawnshop. He looked the apartment over one last time with disgust and, without regret, closed the door behind him and walked out of there forever.

Back on the street he felt things were deteriorating. His cell phone was useless. He could try getting through on Maria's landline by dialing into the data banks and spidering through the coordinates, but that would take some time, which he didn't have. He figured the emergency regs would be in effect anyway, which would knock out any chance of picking up her security codes.

He put the guitar case in the back seat and pulled

the Hummer out onto Broadway. The crush of people swarming uptown towards Shantypark was hard to believe. Throngs were streaming across the wide avenue carrying backpacks and sleeping bags and paraphernalia towards Shantypark as if on a sacred pilgrimage. On the sidewalks however, it looked like a parallel planet in a visible sideways dimension; people were rioting and reveling in lawless abandon. Human yin and yang.

He couldn't even turn off Broadway and take the side streets, because they were also packed with people. He was just too close to Shantypark.

A rock hit the windshield. The bulletproofing absorbed the shock, but this was not a good sign. He heard another sharp thud against the side of the Hummer. If he floored it, maybe he could lose whatever maniacs were attacking him, although he would no doubt run over people doing so. He saw something through the rear view mirror that made his pulse quicken. Squads of SKs were moving in, most likely curious as to why a Hummer with the ABCNN logo was driving away and against the grain. Pellet had probably closed down all the media along with the cell networks, and here he was, the big and obvious fool, trying to sneak crosstown in the largest vehicle on the road with a huge ABCNN logo painted on all sides.

He had to move fast, so he put the Hummer in reverse, grabbed the guitar and one of the production cases and jumped out of the moving vehicle. It backed away, driverless, banging into parked cars in spaces along the parking meters, people screaming at him as they jumped out of its way. As he melted into the crowd he saw over his shoulder some miscreant fools trying to jump in to the big jeep to see what they could find inside before the squirrel killers took over. This could leave them as bloody messes all over the dashboard; but what else was there for some people to do?

Herbie moved as quick as he could, trying to blend into the teeming dusky night, carrying his gear the way the thousands brushing against him were carrying theirs. At this pace it could take him forever to get back over to the East Side. His concerns for Maria began to mount, but he got another good idea.

Herbie knew the entrance to the tunnel would be easy to find because he was part bloodhound and had been there once before. When Ibrahim had lead the way he climbed out of the dark onto an empty street only a few blocks away from their ABCNN home station. This time however, the streets were packed and squirrel killers were everywhere, several stationed right on top of the manhole cover. Shantypark was just a couple of blocks away, and these guys knew what kind of angry animal could come out of that hole at any time.

When the squirrel killers stationed there turned to sniff at him and cogitate about his suspect presence on this untouchable turf, he went into a quick act and seemingly careened off a parked car and into a wall as if he was freaking on some smizz and got himself lost along the way. He heard them snicker, "Dumb Jones freak," as he doubled back towards Broadway, losing even more valuable time, but still footloose and able to make his own way.

There seemed to be no other recourse. He'd have to go overland, around Shantypark and through the crowds. He would have loved a guiding hand from one of those newly anointed Shantypark saints that were lurking somewhere near him underground, but some things a man has got to do for himself.

* * * * *

44

Milos was glad he was finally allowed to go home. No matter what he did he could not find a satellite. There was something spooky going on and what it was he did not want to know. He tried to shrug it off hoping it was solar flares or something. He couldn't afford to take sides in this.

The armored door shut behind him and he was alone in the outer office. It was eerie, quiet. Unusual that there was no security present. Leaving the mayor unguarded, one of the most important people in the free world, seemed like more than just an oversight. It seemed like a breach of policy—like a desertion. But everything that made sense in this already mixed-up world was turned topsy-turvy in the last few hours. He had to get out of there.

Like everyone else, he saw the miracle clip over and over again. To say that he was stunned would be a pure understatement. Also like everyone else, he wasn't prepared for all the forces this event unleashed. Before he could say "human nature" three times and whistle Dixie, reports of the looting and riots began leaking in. Of course he couldn't see any actual footage of that, live or otherwise, because the general browned out the entire city. The browning was so complete, so dark; it was black. Creepy black. Where were the alliance partners? Wouldn't they want to know? Or did they already? He wouldn't put it past the general to have his own covert systems in place, in case he had to bypass the mayor. This made Milos shiver from within, so severely his body shook. He missed the warmth and comfort of his wife's sweet body more and more with each passing moment.

When he went through the deserted outer security post leading from the inner office to the administration rooms, he didn't notice the squirrel killer hiding in a doorway down the hall, who let loose a burst from the AK-87 that sent six bullets through his heart and lungs, killing him instantly before he could even feel any pain or greater fear.

* * * * *

45

Maria could never avoid her answering machine for too long, so after boiling water for some tea, she took the familiar place at her desk and punched the listen button.

It was her mother. Frantic. Shoot, she forgot, Mom probably thought she was dead. "My God, Maria, where are you? Your father and I have been crazy. We thought for sure you were gone. And now this. My baby, I am so glad you are okay. What happened to you? Is this thing real? Did you really meet Salem Jones? What is he like? I have so many questions. I have to talk to you, but we have to run. That nice General Pellet sent over an armored truck to take me and Daddy over to the command post where he said I'd be able to see you soon, so I'm running out the door. I'm so excited, being chaperoned by all those handsome soldiers and all. I'll see you soon, probably before you hear this. I am so happy. Love you."

Maria's state of mind was more than just a little discombobulated. Her mother's message seemed upbeat, confident, and genuinely happy. Maybe it was a good public relations move on Pellet's part to reunite them. Probably he was using Maria's connection to Salem to get as much public sympathy as possible for himself and his policies. She still couldn't reach Herbie by cell and she really wanted to talk with him. It felt strange to feel like she needed him.

She climbed onto her soft bed as if it was the first time, like she was a complete stranger to her luxurious bedroom and her privileged life. Her mind was such a confusion of feelings. These events left her dazed; everything she took for granted was turned upside down by Salem Jones. Too tired to take off her clothes, she lay on her big bed, not troubling to turn down the covers and take advantage of the world-class silk sheets.

She laid eyes open in the dark, perturbed, but tired and wanting sleep. Her hand slipped under her pants and lingered above the short well-manicured hairs as if to pleasure herself, as she had been doing all her life, especially at times when her wandering mind was trying to make sense of a mixed up world from which she needed reprieve. She thought of Herbie in so many new ways now. The smell of his sweat, so protective and sweet the way it covered her in the street from certain death. That could have been the last sensory comfort she would ever feel in this world. Now that memory signaled to her the readiness of the warmth and pleasures her own body could provide.

That connection seemed as powerful a sensation to her as Salem's glorious act of compassion in the ghetto. Herbie's aura, his presence, was so reassuring as they drove through the fantastical streets of Manhattan, as if in a fairy tale, with people in motion, slow motion, passing across the windshield, members of a cast of dreams in a movie that could save the world. Now the presence of his smile, in her mind, as if he were actually there in the flesh, surfaced as the predominant sensual stimuli to this simple physical release of tension she always enjoyed at the ends of unusual days.

Her free hand grazed through the thick hair on

her head and she thought about what it would be like if he was doing the touching. This was truly virgin territory she mused, no pun intended. Before while masturbating, she never gave faces to her fantasies. They were always some anonymous super male or males who were in worship of her wonderfulness. Basically it was sex turned on by success. She was the winner, the victor, so naturally she received the rewards and never gave them back. That couldn't work now, because there was a sexual feeling emerging that was directly linked to a certain man with an identity.

An identity. A mass of atoms that have been afloat in all corners of the universe since the beginning of time and, from across the unimaginably infinite, had somehow directed themselves to this lonesome part of the galaxy and incubated here on earth for billions of years in order to moleculize into this human being called Herbie. It was the vision of his face, with its hard, angular good looks, etched through time by thousands of prior exchanges of chromosomal matter, and then seasoned by the favors and scarred by the traumas of his individual life, that excited the nerve endings in her own body itching now to be attended to.

In her mind she saw his soft golden brown eyes flecked mosaic with those tiny tan tiles she never noticed before. She never could have. Now they cause her to excite, and to want that which she had only dreamed about before, and in such a puerile and undernourished way.

A tear rolled out of her eye, down her cheek onto her pillow. In the universe there is a conservation of all energy and matter; that which is destroyed is created in other forms. Her body, a reservoir of inspiration, realized its gain of spirit through the evolvement of an experience into an emotion, and loses some salt from an ancient sea to mark the spot of transmutation from one self to the next.

Even as that tear evaporates, her inner being propels her mind to someplace further. Her rhythmic breathing sounded to her in this semi-subconscious state that indeed she could be falling asleep, mercifully so, twenty-two floors above an island where millions were turning in equally as many directions towards a focal point in history that everyone could call their own.

This made her struggle. How could she sleep with all that is going on? Every now and then she forced her eyes open to glance at those incessant red digits blinking on her alarm clock, changing at whatever speed they chose.

She drifted in and out of a state of being that lifted her little speck of protoplasm into a photonic state where she could witness herself from the starlight streaming through the unknown void towards earth, able to observe the outcomes of battles large and small being waged between good and evil. Who was she now, watching that silly little clock with the elastic incandescent numbers, her fingers lying so near her vagina?

The curtains rustled and rippled in the dim and she sensed a presence in her room.

"Jamal is that you?" She thought she heard herself say, her conscious mind stretching for some reason practical. Maybe he woke up scared looking for some safety, some consoling words to ameliorate the horror that she could only imagine harassed his little brain. But how could her naiveté born into such advantage ever possibly relate to him and the depravity from which he sprung? Or perhaps he was just thirsty, looking for a glass of water or milk to pacify and settle himself back into a more secure uncertainty so he could go back to sleep.

"Hello, Maria." He stood by her bed, his body haloed by a soft golden light that seemed to be coming from within.

"How did you get in here?"

"I have been all around this world."

"Is it Jamal? Is he all right?"

"He is."

"Then what are you doing here?"

He took off his trench coat and laid it gently upon the floor next to her bed. He kneeled down before her, his face close to hers. She turned her head sideways on the pillow to look into his eyes. Even in the opaque light she could see how boundlessly clear they were. This time they were amber, a golden luster, the color of sand as the sea washes over the beach reflecting the rising sun. Was there a sadness there buried deep into his unfettered life of faith without fear?

The next thing she knew his mouth was upon hers. Was this a no, no, a silly no, no, like catching Mommy kissing Daddy in a Santa Clause suit? Or was it a real sin, like the priests in the shadows of the confessionals, wrongfully turning the inquisition against the innocent? Was she frenching a ghost, making out with a phantom, having a paranormal hallucination of her own narcissism gone berserk?

She could feel the soft short hairs of his beard as they tickled the corners of her mouth. The tips of their tongues darted in hesitancy around each other's, as his fingers smoothed the hair around her forehead, her ears, her neck, and slowly on down, removing her blouse and pants and bra and panties. She lay there before him fully naked, resplendent, as if she was the source of her own light from within the spotted urban dark.

His mouth moved off hers and down her neck tenderly, kissing its lean and strong velvetness. He moved lower along the bounty of her chest and up the voluptuous hillside of her breasts, finding the creases with his lips and locking onto the firmness of her hardened nipples, gently tugging them in.

She heard a soft timeless moan and imagined it came from her own satin throat.

He stood up and removed his clothes. His long lean body silhouetted in the sparkling night. He was erect and strong and pushing forth. She reached out and touched him and felt it was smooth and warm and lightly explored the gentle hairs around it with her fingertips and nails.

He climbed onto her bed, kneeling before her between her legs. She massaged the lips of her vagina with the tip of his cock, slowly rubbing the head of his penis against her vulva.

Moistened now, he entered her, and for a long undetermined amount of time he lie motionless within her, rigid in place, as if in prayer. Her mind was in a form of holy immersion, acknowledging that some body was inside hers and it seemed so unexpected yet so natural who it was.

They were enjoined there where they lay, and she thought that if time ever could stand still, this was the moment it had to.

* * * * *

Herbie finally arrived at her corner and stood down the street from the highrise, trying to figure out which window was Maria's. He counted twenty-two floors and scanned the windows of that level, thinking he saw some movement in the curtains of one with a terrace overlooking the river. He knew he shouldn't try to enter now, not with the contingent of squirrel killers stationed at the entrance and guarding the perimeter of the entire building. He settled in for the duration in an alley behind the shadows of a stoop and took the vintage Martin out of its new case. He began to tune the guitar, with care, so the good soldiers he thought of as bad dudes wouldn't hear.

Over his head, in the cloud enshrouded New York night, a helicopter roared into what was left of Christmas Eve, 2047.

* * * * *

46

Henry Lipton was an enigma from birth. Grandma thought he was born angry, said she thought he was looking for his dad from the gitgo, but only encountered some stoned ex-cheerleaders from the Boston suburbs who were acting like hellcats on Halloween. They strutted and whirled around like they were the ancient Hebrews on their first day of out Egypt, as Grandma lay there like a stoic and squeezed him out.

Bullmoose was in a cabin in Maine snoring off a Grateful Dead concert he attended the night before in Bangor, grooving with Pig-pen who was smoking the doobies tossed up to him on stage from the down east girls topless in the audience. He didn't think Grandma was going to deliver so early. Probably he didn't want to deal with the dancing she-devils he knew were going to dominate everything going on that day. He said they weren't really her friends, just fly-by-night wenches looking to get high and say angry, mean things about the men they really wanted to fuck but couldn't get because they made themselves so visually and psychologically undesirable. Within a year Grandma never saw any of them again.

The doctor, who her mother forced her to see the next day, said his constant crying and uncomfortable disposition was caused by a meconium plug in his lower intestines blocking his first crap. Bullmoose thought meconium was a houseware product you used to seal kitchen floors. Grandma, who never trusted doctors, knew this one was dead wrong. It was the distance between her two men that was to be a theme for the rest of their lives. In any case Henry howled bitterly for the first forty-nine hours, thirty-two minutes and nineteen seconds out of the womb before he fell asleep.

Henry was a born rebel. Except that he was a rebel born to born rebels, and rebels must have something to rebel against. That was a problem to the kids born to the counterculture. As he grew up he polarized from his dad, Bullmoose, and became ever more conservative, which was the enigma to his singularly Zen mom and his here-again-gone-again future rock-star dad.

He was one of those boys who you didn't hear too much about when he was growing up, probably because he didn't cause too many problems. He got straight A's, was a decent-enough athlete to make varsity soccer and tennis, didn't do drugs or alcohol, didn't get any girl pregnant, and never got into a car accident or had huge barn-burning house parties when his parents were away. To the outside world he was a good kid, kind of a nerd, but very bright. So good at school in fact that he graduated second out of Cambridge Latin straight into MIT. Grandma was so happy, thought of him as a genius and knew he had great things ahead of him in the scientific world.

However, his relationship with his dad was a cold one at best. The two never really got along and never shared the usual hallmark father-and-son activities like playing catch, going fishing or building model cars together.

He hated hearing the hippie stories Bullmoose

reminisced over with Uncle Pranan and Aunt Lorraine, especially the ones about India and their not-so-glorious escape from the clutches of the evil Durga. He couldn't believe his mom was not disturbed by the fact that Bullmoose was having sex with some pre-Bat-Mitzvah-age Hindu girl.

The deepest conversation they ever had occurred one day when he was turning fifteen. It was about women and went like this: Bullmoose asked Henry, "Do you know what a condom is?"

"Yes." Henry said.

"Use 'em."

Chalk up another bit of Bullmoosian perspicacity to live forever in the full and complete manual of practical and operative matters for all men.

Even though he went to school only a few miles from the house where he was born, Henry decided quickly and without question to move into an MIT dorm to escape the disdain he felt for his dad and those unannounced comings and goings of his, which, although they never bothered his mother, genuinely outraged the young Henry.

After a year of campus life, he moved into a studio apartment in Kendall Square that Bullmoose never visited, but Grandma came as frequently as he would allow, to decorate and help keep it clean. Regardless of her motherly devotions, the small apartment was spartan at best. It was just big enough for a queen-size bed covered with the afghan comforter that Grandma knitted herself, and a desk shoved into a corner with piles of paper and books surrounding Henry's monster computer and keyboard. Dingy linen-like curtains were always closed over a window whose only view was the tracks of the subway that ran above the Charles River. Passing trains shook the building at night. As pathetic as it might have appeared to others, it was a magic kingdom for Henry.

When Henry finally found that special girl, it was no surprise that Bullmoose was left out of the equation. She was a dark-haired beauty that he spied early in his first year at MIT. He watched her in the computer lab, the reflections of the LCD on her black horned-rim glasses cast spells of enchantment on the inexperienced Henry. After class, he often positioned himself behind a tree near the sidewalk where he could admire her from a distance as she waited for the bus that took her back where she lived with her mother in Dorchester amongst the working class immigrant Portuguese families.

It took three years of being in the same advanced theoretical physics pipeline for them to finally have the courage to simply say hello to each other. Finally Henry got the nerve to ask her to share a bagel one day after they counted pions and bosons and other antiparticles during their afternoon session with the atom smasher. Afterwards they careened back to his Kendall Square pad under the premise to study the uncertainty theory and its historical implications in the discovery of black holes. Instead they fell madly onto the afghan comforter Grandma had knitted to keep Henry warm through the lonely Cambridge nights. Together they played out years of mutual longing and withholding by making the sweetest of sweaty and pungent love all through the night and into the next day. Needless to say, once initiated, that activity continued as often as possible. From that moment on they shared everything together. They were a couple now, both slated for abstract mathematical history, on a mutual march through academia, towards their intended destination into the small but highly coveted membership in the international club of theoretical physicists.

Of course, it was a club Bullmoose had no regard for whatsoever. He was the true nonbeliever in anything scientific. In his opinion, it was arrogant that physicists dared to give answers to those things he felt were outside the ability of human beings to understand. He believed the attempts of science to determine exactly when the universe began, were feeble at best, even though the most dedicated scientists say they can trace the beginning of time back to the first millionth of a second. Bullmoose would scoff and say it's obvious that the closer we get to the beginning with these dubious theories, they all break down in failure. Therefore, the question looms so large. What was before that millionth of a second, man, and what was before that?

A millionth of a second was not good enough for Bullmoose, however it didn't stop him from liking Dolores. She was sweet, and beneath those bulky sweaters of hers lurked a killer body that did prove to him that the universe was curved. Bullmoose was built in such a way that he couldn't help himself.

It was a weak moment when Henry actually let Grandma talk him into bringing Dolores over to Perry Street so she could be formally introduced. After a couple of glasses of wine Henry stormed out in a rage over some inappropriate remarks by Bullmoose in front of his girl. Even though both Grandma and Bullmoose protested and said that it was just his way of trying to be charming and there really was no harm, no foul, Henry was too sensitive to his dad's incomprehensible social graces and inescapable reputation. He fumed out of Perry Street with Dolores in tow, vowing never to come back again.

To Bullmoose's credit, he persevered. He made repeated overtures for forgiveness to his son even though he was rebuked again and again. He called, he faxed and he emailed even though he hated computers. He stood out in the rain waiting for them to come home to their love nest by the T only to be violently ignored by his son who would unlock the front door, hustle inside and stomp up the stairs, slamming the door behind him. Dolores gave Bullmoose a wispy look over her shoulder, not really understanding the problem. Admittedly he said some off-color jokes that night that most people would consider highly questionable considering the circumstances, but Dolores found him cute, unique in a middle-aged way. She really didn't find the disrespect in his slightly tipsy comments that Henry did. But no matter how gentle she was trying to convey this simplicity to that brilliant mad theoretical physicist she was totally in love with, he refused to listen. The boundaries of family feuds, powered by those particular emotions, know no logical constraints.

The awful silence continued until that fateful graduation day. Grandma sat alone near the back as her son accepted his diploma, magna cum laude. Cautious, she approached them after the commencement, and couldn't help but detect the difference beneath the caps and the billowing gowns. Sensitive to the explosiveness embedded into the personality of her son, she tried to make small talk with both of them, but they acted more cryptic than usual. Dolores had a furtive and nervous look about her. After a few minutes of awkward nothing talk, they excused themselves saying to Grandma that they had some parties to attend. They disappeared into the blazing and dazzling hullabaloo of academic costumes.

A mother is nothing without her innate bundle of instincts. Grandma hustled over to Kendall Square and hung out in a Greek diner across the street from their apartment and nursed several cups of coffee until she spied them walking up the street.

Henry's proud arm was tenderly wrapped around Dolores' shoulders and her lithe little hands were proudly holding her very rotund and pregnant belly. Well, of course! How could Grandma help herself then? She left some change on the counter, thanked the counter girl in demure tones and sprinted across the street.

She caught them at the moment of entry into their humble apartment that overlooked the subway as it emerged from underground, just as Henry's key was inserted into the lock, opening the door for his expectant woman.

There on the noisy and dirty street below their little love shack, the tears of exhalation and exultation came running out and mighty hugs followed. Grandma was always a cut above the rest. There was nothing she did to intend or provoke guilt and no contrition was made. Just the joy of new family and the jubilance of the grand mystery of life came streaming forth from within this special woman, and this was something even these cool, budding clinicians who professed to be unraveling the origins of the universe could appreciate now. Grandma was now zooming into her own, through her son, her fate and destiny now made apparent by the fecundity of the moment.

Grandma made no mention of marriage, far be that from Grandma, but she was delighted to hear that the kids were intending to get married at city hall before the baby was born. Henry made mention of this with subtle references to his own bitter feelings of illegitimacy, which Grandma never could deter. Now wasn't the time to make a case for how very loved Henry was and how certainly he was wanted. A marriage certificate could never have changed any of that. To her this was about the reconciliation and reuniting of her family over the impending arrival of its newest member, her grandchild. She didn't want to get into any sticky past issues.

Even though he was mollified by the emotions, Henry was still stubborn and resisted any meetings whatsoever with his dad. However he had to back away from these feelings and learn to honor the wishes and emotions of the women in his life, who always dominate when it comes to basic family matters like childbirth, since they were the ones doing the real work.

Against his wishes he agreed to a little baby shower, but he wanted Dolores' relatives present as well, since it was a joining of the two families that was being celebrated. In his tender young mind it would serve as a much-needed buffer between himself and his father. A date was set for an intimate family get together with the newly expectant, their parents and, of course, Uncle Pranan and Aunt Lorraine, the only other close family for Henry.

It was a long summer night at the end of June. The coastal North Atlantic haze and humidity had settled over Boston, making it feel more like sub-Sahara Africa than Massachusetts, everyone retreating to air conditioning, their nerves already frayed.

Pranan and Lorraine had arrived early with their kids so they could help with the preparations and were surprised by Bullmoose and his new and moderate demeanor. Genuine in his desire to patch things up with his son, he was determined to be on his best behavior. He even cut his hair and shaved. His signature ponytail since 1969 was gone, leaving only an inch or two below the ears. He was clean and sober, not even a token puff of pot for a week. Pranan was astonished and Grandma was so proud. Her anticipation of this evening was intense and now her expectations were going to be exceeded.

Henry and Dolores arrived a bit late. He helped her out of the front seat of their little Hyundai, like actors from Central Casting auditioning for the life insurance commercial that asks first time pregnant parents if they thought about how they were going to pay for the kid's college education while preparing for their own eventual deaths.

They were followed into Perry Street by Dolores' mom, Sonia, a smallish woman, Mediterranean in complexion and slightly hunched. She walked with pride but showed the wear and tear of the hard life of a single mother and an immigrant. She looked warmly upon Grandma and gave her a big hug, two women from different continents about to be united through the issue of their loins. She was effusive and agreeable with Pranan and Lorraine, but when she greeted Bullmoose with all the open mindedness she could conjure, a look of puzzlement flashed across her face. Sonia was wise enough to see that beneath his simple nature and natural good looks there was a more complicated free spirit lurking within. What was there she didn't want to know and hoped she wouldn't find out.

The evening started off well enough. Pranan's good-natured soul added to the ease and familiarity the night needed. They sat in the small living room talking away. Lorraine babbled to Sonia about her three kids, who had already excused themselves and went down to the basement to fool around with Bullmoose's electric rock and roll instruments of pure antiquity. Her fourteen-year-old girl was impossible to talk to, angry at the whole world, and acted like she was already nineteen, online all the time and caring nothing about nothing except for her friends. The eleven-year-old girl was just the opposite. Brilliant in school and always cast as the lead in the school play, she was interested in a career in acting and kept her room as clean as a whistle. The seven-year-old boy was the apple of his daddy's eye. Pranan always wanted a son, that's the way it was with macho men from India. Sonia just smiled through all this kid talk. Lorraine got a little embarrassed by coming across as such a typical American parent, overindulging her children and re-living her own imperfect childhood vicariously through theirs.

Before Sonia could interject a word of her own, Henry turned the conversation around and back to themselves. He brought into the living room a chilled bottle of champagne and everyone giggled at the sound of the cork popping free. Tonight was such a special night. The baby's due date was only a couple of weeks away and both parents had received notification that they were awarded graduate fellowships at the California Institute of Technology. They would teach several classes a week and play with a world famous particle accelerator while studying with Richard Feynman's associates as they tried to unlock all the secrets to the unified theory of the universe. Pranan and Lorraine smiled in genuine pride and Grandma poured the champagne.

Bullmoose was overtly quiet, trying hard to force himself not to say anything as to how or why anybody on earth could think they could decipher unfathomable mysteries of anything by playing with silly little neutrinos and bosons that were spun off by the vibrations of some equally unobservable tiny quantum string system that nobody ever really saw or actually could prove existed. To him any science that said that the act of observation would change the results of the experiment couldn't be very accurate at all, now could it? That actually ran contrary to the time-honored tradition that science is science because theories can and need to be proven by actual experimentation.

Of course Henry jumped all over his dad's first adversarial utterance, which Bullmoose delivered with a slightly cynical tone, and demanded how anybody living at this point in time could, as mankind roared towards Y2K, deny the fact that modern physicists, due to background cosmic radiation left over from the Big Bang, have been able to determine the origin of the universe down to a nanosecond approximately fifteen billion years ago, and only fossilized Neanderthals and anachronistic aging hippies could still apply miraculous interposition to the origins of life on earth.

Bullmoose, not to be outdone, took another long

draught of his champagne and retorted that if his narrow-minded son, myopic in his own overly intellectual way, and blinded by the bindings of academic physics, thought that his own father believed that God placed all creation on earth only a few thousand years ago, then he was as ridiculous as those creationists who actually did still believe that. And if ignorant and stupid men believed they were created in God's own image, then even more ignorant and stupider men worshipped a God that was created in man's own image. Which was what Henry and his cohorts were trying to prove with their self-inscribed prayer books of abstract reasoning written in a language of mathematics that nobody except for the few contributing authors could understand or would even want to understand.

Henry leaped off his chair that was next to his rotund and doting wife who was beginning to look worried over the intensifying heat of the discussion. He stood over his father and replied that it was similar to a criminal investigation, where forensic experts could piece together events that nobody ever did witness, yet still come to an accepted belief about what went down in that crime scene during that unobservable period in the past.

Bullmoose jumped out of his seat and stuck his nose in his know-it-all son's face and replied that there was a unifying system of physical laws with which the universe operated, and there were no accidents within the mystery of the universal count-on-able rules; nothing stays the same, everything is interconnected, and we don't know what's going to happen next. That proves that even though evolution seems like random natural selection to scientists, their had to be something that actually set these forces in motion so that self-important men could evolve out of the primordial muck on earth and search for these so-called unified laws of the cosmos and pompously name them after themselves.

He sat back down and sipped on his champagne, the little bubbles bursting in his brain. Everyone in the room tried to ignore him but Sonia sensed a darkening cloud form as he brooded in his favorite armchair with the cigarette burns on the arm rests.

When the champagne ran out, Pranan opened a bottle of Cabernet that he said he was saving for a special occasion. Since he was now through having kids of his own, what better way to celebrate than with the coming together of these two families and the imminence of their latest issue nigh upon the planet. His eyes watered when he said Bullmoose and Grandma were his family, and he toasted to that.

Everyone drank as he refilled their glasses and the room grew cheery again for some, and bleary for all. Henry made a point of kissing Dolores deeply on her mouth, partly out of affection, but partly out of some sense of triumph. Grandma tried to ignore that, as everyone chatted on about the oncoming change in history when the dates they would write on their personal checks would change from nineteen hundred to two thousand.

Grandma went into the kitchen to tend to her cooking while Lorraine began telling Sonia how Pranan and she met. She left out of course all the long-haired and sensitive young men marching in and out of her bedroom that kept her engine fueled for garbage sculpture, and the part about how the first time Pranan saw her she was peeing naked in the bathroom just at the top of the stairs reading the Kama Sutra. Pranan took it further back and explained how he met Bullmoose and he showed Sonia the magic ring they came upon in India and how it saved their lives, glossing over the part about the little Gypsy and how old she was when Bullmoose knocked her up.

That's when the rules really take over and the glories have to be taken completely on faith, which means besides believing in the things you don't know, you must also live through the things you never thought you could. With an alarmed look on her face, Sonia seemingly levitated off her chair and crumpled forward to the floor on her knees. Bullmoose thought she had simply drunk too much and rushed to her rescue. He got down on the floor and put his hands under her head and lifted it up. Kneeling, they gazed into each other's eyes and everyone in the room witnessed the recognizable horror that was there, as Sonia communicated in a nonverbal way that although she lived in a Portuguese community, she never said she was Portuguese.

Bullmoose fell back on his butt on the living room rug stunned.

Pranan rubbed his face, stupefied as twenty some odd years melted away in an instant.

Grandma held her breath as she felt some psychic earthquake reach out through time and wrench the ground beneath her life, throwing the people she loved into the air and tumbling them back to the earth, to get up again as strangers to each other as well as themselves.

Unable to cope with the gargantuan moment, all Henry could do was grab Dolores and pull her up out of her comfortable seat on the couch, uttering, "I'm outta here." Before anyone had the strength or the clarity of mind to do or say anything to stop them, he had thrown his pregnant lady back into his Hyundai and was insanely screeching back out of the driveway.

The little Perry Street living room was left in worse shape than an explosion inside a vacuum. It was a whirlpool of nihility, completely sucking the reality out of everything that could have meant anything to any of them. The enormity of their consequences stemming from the count-on-able rules was staggering. Nothing now could ever be the same, and how could this interconnectivity find such a convoluted connection, and what could possibly happen next?

Grandma sunk to her knees beside the little Gypsy and put her arms around her, gently squeezing her quaking body closer to hers, sisters in some surreal psychotic plot that only the angels up above could ever hope to understand. Bullmoose staggered out the door.

All left in speechless terror, pondering the depths of the glory of the grace of God.

* * * * *

As the unseen helicopter roaring away overhead switched to stealth, Herbie tightened the B string just a bit too much and it snapped. He unraveled what was left on the tuning peg and stuck it in his pocket. It always was the hardest string for him to tune.

* * * * *

47

December 25, 2047. 6:00 a.m.

The armored office was deathly still when Theodore blinked onto one of the cold, blank monitors, filling it up with his magnificence. The mayor looked up from the throes of tortured contemplation and smiled at his dad, this was truly a fine Christmas present.

Teddy was dressed in his holiday best, the dark brown suit with tan pinstripes, a dark blue shirt with matching handkerchief in the breast pocket, and the red silk bow tie with the little dark green spheres in a pattern, like Christmas tree ornaments. He looked the personification of holiday cheer, complete with the crackling fireplace, strings of homemade candy popcorn, and the smells of hot apple cider laced with the best Barbados rum. His smooth and clear brown skin belied his age, so it was his mustache peppered with silver that gave him the distinction of his years, adding the right visuals to the wisdom of his words. But this time, for once, Theodore Roosevelt Storm didn't say anything at all. He just beamed down on his son Jack who was sitting by his computer, swiveling back and forth on an office chair as if he was a little ten-year-old boy.

Jack has heard silence before. He was in the thick of the deafening crack of collective dismay when the total will of all good men was sucked out of their lives by a vengeful satanic warlord, descending on the jugular of all mankind. He was a crafty demon. Beaten back time and again away from the warmth and safety of the community fire, and cast out into the cold and dark to eat or be eaten, he had always found a way to return. Evolved now, time worn, tested and ready, he had come once more to collect his revenge on an unworthy and thankless species. How else could hundreds of thousands of people die in one blink of an instant? That is the sound of silence.

It wasn't the quiet in his operations room that spooked him; he actually liked it and was genuinely grateful for it. It was the city out there full of humans that depended on him that made him sad. People who leaned on Jack in the worst of storms, who would watch him grapple with torrential bursts of wind and tsunamic crashing waves, and after conquering these extreme forces, they would cheer as he sailed with quiet valor into a clean harbor of protected waters.

But today he was not the captain. Today he was alone, locked up in his own office tomb. The only water warm and cleansing . . .

* * * * *

48

Her sensations were all comfort on a seashore of pleasure, her gentle lapping dreams were oceanic, like she was drifting on an inflatable cushion in a balmy Caribbean cove, when the sense of an assassin nearby roused her out of the sweet sea in which she was buoyed.

She opened her eyes looking down the barrel of a 35-millimeter, behind which was Gregor's scarred and smirking face, saliva and blood dripping off his jagged and broken teeth, as he fondled his erection inches from her startled face.

She lunged for the blankets to cover her nakedness, but in her panic she realized that she was fully dressed, which was perplexing considering the freshness of the previous night's dramatic intercourse. When did she put her clothes back on? When and where did Salem go?

She sat up on the bed in her empty room, utterly discomposed, but entirely grateful. What could this mean she supposed. Did she dream of a god and the devil all in one night? The last few days were a roller coaster, it was hard for her to believe any of what happened was real, and if some of it was, which part?

She remembered it was Christmas morning and

there was a little boy sleeping in the guest room, and she had fallen asleep waiting for Herbie. Maybe it was just her subconscious life trying to keep pace with what was happening to her in the physical world, which was admittedly turning more dreamlike by the minute. It was the perfect time for a cup of fresh coffee.

She left her bedroom and entered the kitchen. When she saw General Pellet at her breakfast table, it only compounded the oversaturated surreality of the recent events. The general was seated looking out the kitchen window at the East Side of Manhattan, now daubed with a burnish of tainted snow, waiting for the clouds to dissolve so the morning sun could put some sparkle to the city's patina.

She begged to herself that this had to be another dream, like Salem or Gregor; Pellet couldn't really be there.

But the blunt nudge of an AK-87 in her ribs made her realize the disturbing truth. The squirrel killer behind her in full combat gear leaned against the kitchen cabinets, his gas mask and goggles hiding every identifying facet of his facial features, like an anonymous terminator, part of the performance, this fear provoking aura they worked to perfection. With a gloved hand he gestured wordlessly for her to sit down. She noticed there was coffee already made and another squirrel killer with sergeant's stripes was pouring some. He placed the cup on the table in front of her. She blinked several times, still hoping beyond hope this was just another crazy dream.

Finally Pellet spoke. "Excuse me for talking the liberty of making my own while you were in repose." He took a sip. "Have some."

Maria didn't know what to do, so she hesitated. She didn't think the general would be so melodramatic to have poisoned her coffee. But what made her think of that anyway? She didn't do anything wrong. The whole world saw. She associated his smarmy smile to those porn sites she visited in her early teens, those pictures of armored warriors screwing naked young lasses up the ass. What a guy. Somehow that manly and hearty dick escapes through all that hard steel and penetrates her rectum exactly to the point where she can't control her infinite pleasure. What was she thinking now? Maria was putting very little together that made sense at this point and felt extremely weak in her knees. She was getting shaky and she actually felt like sitting down, so she did.

"I know you must be somewhat befuddled about all this. But to put it plainly Mz. Primera, you have broken a few of the most important laws in this city and unfortunately we are going to have to deal with that. As of late you are a person of very high profile, so I felt I had to handle this delicate situation personally."

Maria in the seat facing him closed her eyes, rubbing the bridge of her nose with her thumb and index finger. Her ability to intellectualize seemed to have disappeared in Shantypark along with her former skills of disputation. She was at a genuine loss of words and did not feel too good.

"I'm glad you slept so well, considering the ordeal you have been through. Myself? I couldn't sleep a wink last night. Didn't even try to, worrying what was going to happen to my city now this latest terror attack has incapacitated the entire population and rendered it's most popular mayor stricken and incapable of decision."

"General, what are you talking about?"

"Oh, by the way, your parents are safe with me. For the time being. I couldn't let anything happen to them after you endangered their welfare, exposing yourself as a principle in this nefarious plot to allow the infected legions of Shantypark to invade our city."

* * * * *

49

Christmas snow had fallen in the night. At the dawn's ghostly graying Herbie's eyes jerked open, realizing he had fallen asleep. That couldn't be good. Things didn't feel so right, especially when a powerful hand grabbed his mouth and a knife was precipitous against his throat. The slightest pressure could draw instant blood and he would watch his life spill out into the alley.

Herbie was pulled by his hair into a standing position and stood up, his face pushed against the wall. Two men held his arms behind him, and a third padded him down for weapons, which made him realize how stupid he was not to be carrying any. Satisfied that he was clean they turned him around and there, to Herbie's shock and chagrin, he faced a gloating Ibrahim who was calmly picking his fingernails with the sharp edge of a pearl handled twelve-inch blade.

"You double-crossing snake." Herbie spit out the rusty grit from the building that smeared his tongue and lips.

Ibrahim glared at Herbie for an instant as if deciding whether to cut off his head first or his balls, and then broke out into a roar of laughter. The two strong men restraining Herbie did not relax their grip.

When Ibrahim finally composed himself, he rested

the point of the blade on the hollow of Herbie's neck just underneath the Adam's apple. He pulled his face up so close Herbie's could smell his gizzards. "Maybe I'm just teaching you a lesson for falling asleep while watching over that very important mama upstairs in her crib. Besides, I thought you might get violent when I woke you up. I didn't want you to make too much noise and attract those SKs over there. I'd have to kill them before they killed us." He stepped back, giving Herbie some space to really see him once again. Ibrahim beamed a silent smile, the unconditional love of an older brother carrying out his self-appointed filial responsibilities, no need for thanks.

His captors also smiled at him and released his arms. Herbie recognized them from the Council, men who now shared newfound values and goals.

Embarrassed, Herbie first looked at his pretend enemies and then peered around the corner of the building to the front entry of Maria's highrise, as if he could salvage some of the time he lost when he was supposed to be staking it out last night. He was just in time to see some soldiers in anti-contamination outfits leading Jamal out the front entry.

His adrenalin ignited. His knee-jerk response was to run to Jamal's rescue, but once again those burly arms constrained his futility just in time before he did something really stupid. Once again Ibrahim released another smooth laugh, more serious, yet still patient, all-forgiving. "We are going to have to work on your first instincts, my brother. You see, doing battle by committing suicide never works. It is up to me to make sure you don't get killed. Let Salem handle this other little problem."

Herbie wondered why it could still surprise him to see Salem in the alley behind him as if he materialized out of a shadow.

* * * * *

50

"I know that it's not your fault, Maria. I don't think you have the brains to create a plan like this. You were just a reporter deluded by the prospects of a great story, a victim in this like the rest of us. However the major role you have been playing in this incredible hoax has been acted out in the entire planet's living room. What am I to do, considering the extraordinary dimensions of the crimes you have committed? What am I to say to all those people out there who are now calling for your head in a bucket?

"These are troubled times, Maria. People ask if Pandora is out of the box. I believe there is a threshold spot in society, a ground zero where all order breaks down and there is only the law of the wild. In times like this the strong kill or be killed until there is nothing left to fear, except for the savage loneliness of being the last one standing on the edge of history, the last life left.

"But don't worry my dear, I'm not there, yet. I love this city; I love my people. So, to protect them I am going to have to put you in the safest place I know, until I can deal with your case through the channels the Alliance will eventually decide."

Discovering some poise, Maria took a sip of

the coffee. "General, with all due respect, and no one is questioning your loyalty, you are operating with very poor intelligence. Salem Jones is no threat to your security. Quite the contrary. I've been there."

"You were under the influence of the strongest drugs, administered to you by his henchmen."

"The miracle is on disk, registered to the world clock."

"Prestidigitation! Any sorcerer with only few skills can prepare an illusion like that."

"But Jamal . . ."

"What about the boy? You don't have to concern yourself with him now; he is under my protection. He's an unwitting accomplice like you. In a nice world he would serve as a never mind to this whole thing, but he is not living in a nice world and is guilty of different perpetrations than you."

Flashing on Jamal sleeping in her guest room made Maria jump up from her chair. "What do you mean? What have you done to him?" The harsh muzzle of an AK-87 jabbed into her kidneys. Two SKs grabbed her shoulders and, to her shock, handcuffs were clamped around her wrists, binding her arms behind her back. The soldier with the gun in her ribs was trying to prod her back down into her chair, but she didn't feel like sitting anymore.

"You do know the penalty for being caught outside Shantypark without the proper blood ID. The boy can infect an entire city. What were you possibly thinking bringing him out knowing what you know? To me that is the real crime; his was just an unfortunate accident of birth."

"But he's not sick anymore!"

A hand from behind plunked her back down, her cuffed wrists bruising against the back of the seat. Then, it dawned on her and she got really scared.

* * * * *

51

The last few squirrel killers on the pavement closed the door behind Jamal and jumped in through the back hatch of the armored truck. The driver gunned the motor, grinding the gears as he shifted into first. The heavy vehicle trudged forward on the snowy street. Fearful passersby, avoiding looking directly at the scene, scurried by in the early monochrome morning. The driver dropped it into second gear and the truck belched out an oily groan.

Salem stepped into the middle of the road. The sun broke through a crack in the clouds and tinged golden the misty air above his head.

Everyone culpable of being caught now out on the street couldn't help but watch, as Salem strode unflinching into the path of the oncoming truck. The armored vehicle lurched and Herbie could see the surprised driver shift into third, picking up speed and inertia, not sure what was going on in the road ahead of him in that sparkling spotlight.

As all sixteen tires of the mighty war machine picked up speed, Salem held his arms out in front of him, as if to stop it and hold it fast. Just before it would have knocked him down and crushed him, the driver jammed on the brakes and the truck screeched to a hydraulic halt a scant few inches in front of him.

Squirrel killers jumped out of the truck from all sides, their deadly AK-87s pointed at Salem, one twitch of the finger and he would be an instant bloody carcass. Salem just smiled at them and voiced not a word. But his eyes were talking, connected like a bluetooth fused directly into the center of each soldier's brain. They circled him for a long drawn moment, when one lowered his weapon and lifted the tinted shield covering his eyes. He peered with a quizzical expression at Salem, who looked back with great love and faith, and the soldier, astonished, dropped his gun in a clatter to the gutter and removed his helmet. With a humbled grace he bent down to one knee.

Ibrahim turned to give Herbie another brotherly look, but Herbie knowing he should be recording this was already headed back into the alleyway to retrieve his headbandcam from the equipment case. The soprano jumped an octave.

Back on the street the bystanders were now tripping over each other to see what was going on. By the time Herbie returned with the camera, all the professional soldiers who were trained to kill in a myriad amount of ways had abandoned their helmets and jettisoned their instruments of death. Each was kneeling before Salem.

Salem beckoned towards the alley. Herbie grabbed his guitar and his gear and followed Ibrahim and his men. He climbed into the passenger seat of the armored truck, and Jamal jumped on his lap. They hugged.

Together they watched through the windshield as Salem engaged the would-be warriors. He touched each upon his head and, as he did, their teary eyes uplifted into his, grateful for the release of the overbearing weight they had been carrying all this time.

As the soprano glided down to its fourth, Salem departed from the ring of peaceful soldiers. Without looking back, he strode to the rear of the war vehicle, stepped up and in. As the doors closed behind him, Ibrahim, who was in the driver's seat, shifted into first. The armored truck lumbered forth once more, leaving behind Pellet's squirrel killers circled up in the street in the patch of golden sunlight. They were kneeling in the fresh New York snow on this Christmas morning, arms draped around each other in great relief, giving thanks in a way they had never done before.

* * * * *

52

Mayor Storm emerged from the bathroom in the operations room showered and shaved, wearing his best and most conservative black three-piece suit, as if he was dressed for a state funeral. The armored door was fully engaged and the controls to operate it fully disenabled. He heard explosions coming from the secret escape routes, and the door to the roof was sealed tightly shut. Pellet missing not a thing. The phone lines were dead and his cell phone was useless. The T3 lines were cut so he couldn't communicate over the Internet or the Alternet.

However, Jack's computer was very busy, for as he walked around in his office prison, Teddy watched him from the screen following with silent, but joyous, eyes, snatches of sweet lullabies and gushing babies gurgling in the background. Yet, Jack didn't feel much like talking. Tired, he laid down on the burgundy leather couch by the coffee station. Using the armrest as his pillow he stared up at the ceiling. Trapped, but at peace, his mind began sudsing, his heart slowed and his breath shortened.

The ageless tones of a wise and ancient flute surround-sounded Jack's inert body sepulchered on the couch, echoing through the many blank monitors designed for other things. The choir began, soft and humble, and their consonance swirled therein purging, scouring the misery off the temporary walls of who he was, calling him home.

Amazing Grace, how sweet the sound, that saved a wretch like me,

I once was lost but now I'm found, was blind, but now, I see.

Whispers like so much sunlight, dripping with strength so vastly refined.

" . . . and so my darling I miss you more than words can say, than hearts could beat, than blood could pour. We have always been together and will always be."

". . . Well son, you know sometimes you just gotta get your butt off the floor and give it one more good shot, which I know you still got."

Through many dangers, toils and snares, we have already come,

Twas Grace that brought us safe thus far, and Grace will lead us home.

" . . . you precious and marvelous man amongst men, I will always be yours, waiting in eternity for eternity if needs be . . ."

" . . . Stick your nose to the task at hand, Jackie boy, you've done that over and over so well so many times before. Now focus, boy; focus on the one thing, the one and only imperative thing above all others that will save us all."

Twas Grace that taught my heart to fear, and Grace, my fears relieved.

How precious did that Grace appear the hour I first believed.

" . . . That's right, son, you duke left and drive right; they have to go for that fake, it's human nature boy, it's what we're made of, what we are all made of . . ."

" . . . it's his heart, Jack, it's his soul, you'll recognize it, you will, you'll have to because it is yours, the beauty of which your eyes still can't see, but it will be so easy soon . . . "

Amazing Grace, how sweet the sound, that saved a wretch like me,

I once was lost but now I'm found, was blind, but now, I see.

" . . . It's the stars that shine at night, boy, you got that right, and you ain't never been afraid of the dark."

He wanted to follow the clean water as it roared to the sea and, as the last breath was let go, a tear, adding barely an instant to his life, slowly rolled over the cool flesh of his cheek. The rush in his soul was brilliant counterpoint to the stillness in his heart and the settling of his blood into standing pools within his vessels.

He has heard silence before, but not the excellence of this.

That primordial flute, so resonant with the infinite, leaped up an octave and then a fifth and down a third from there . . .

* * * * *

"John Kennedy Storm."
"Here I am."

* * * * *

53

The war vehicle moved slowly through the deserted streets toward Shantypark. Ibrahim stared out the windshield, serene, as if absent of thought. Not so Herbie, whose brain was churning, trying to absorb the inexplicable events of this morning that he was too late to record. He shifted Jamal, the essence of acceptance, over in his lap so he could put the headbandcam in his pocket.

From deep within his stunned reasoning he realizes how distracted he was from all these amazing changes. If squirrel killers were coming out of the building with Jamal in custody, there must be others inside the apartment with Maria. Duh! His heart leapt with fear, just as Salem climbed into the cab from the back of the truck.

"This is a good place to let me out."

Before Herbie could utter a word, Ibrahim applied the brakes and the heavy machine slowed to a halt in the middle of the block. Salem opened the side door and jumped out. Herbie handed Jamal off to Ibrahim and tried to follow. Salem turned him back. "Herbie, you must stay and watch over Jamal."

"Ibrahim can watch him. I can't sit here doing nothing when Maria is back there."

"Herbie, don't worry. The universe doesn't answer worry. Have faith. I will always be with you."

They watched him through the windshield as he disappeared around the corner. When Ibrahim pulled the truck up to the intersection, he was nowhere in sight.

* * * * *

54

Rodney Pellet could never cope with the emotion brought upon by failure. Once perceived, it drove him crazy to the heights of the same criminal insanity that he deplored in the enemies of his world that he hunted night and day. Standing outside Maria's apartment building he felt the beginning tremors of that exact fury right now as he stared in disbelief at his once-proud recruits cringing in fear from his impugnment. They were crouching, disarmed, against the wall of Maria's building.

"So, what I understand is that you all say Salem Jones, North America's most wanted, Salem Jones, was right here, a few minutes ago. And you just put down your guns and watched as you let him drive away in your truck." None of the soldiers could answer; it sounded so absurd.

A jeep pulled up to the curb armed with machine guns turreted on its roof and pointing out the side windows. Pellet looked away from his once-proud recruits and signaled the gunners. They opened fire and in seconds the men were shattered, blown apart into tortured and disemboweled positions, pieces of torsos in pools of blood, body parts and fluids scattered on the sidewalk and splattered on the wall.

A second lieutenant was taking pictures from the passenger window. Pellet gave him an order. "Email these photos to every soldier and every officer in this army. I want them to see what they are up against. We cannot miss another opportunity like this." He grabbed the throat of the lieutenant squirrel killer assigned to his personal command and whispered with a great threatening chill into his earpiece. "New standing orders. If anyone approaches within fifty feet of this vehicle on your way to the prison, and I don't care if they look like your mother, you are to consider them the enemy and shoot to kill immediately and without question."

He turned to a shocked, handcuffed Maria as two soldier goons pushed her into the back seat. He leaned over her through the open door, "I am through with the niceties, my dear. I am keeping you alive for one reason. My boys are going to take you to a state prison where they are going to closely guard you until tonight, when at prime time for a Christmas special, you are going back on the air. You are going to apologize to this city and the entire world for your part in the evil you perpetrated. With a prepared statement that is being composed at this very moment, you are going to extol my leadership and the bravery of my men. If you don't follow my every order and command, your parents will die very slowly and painfully with the methods of torture I have learned first hand while fighting to keep pathetic bleeding hearts like you free. When you do exactly as I say, then I will let them continue to live."

As the jeep with Maria roared off down the street, the general's armored BMW sedan pulled alongside the curb to pick him up. He sat down and transmitted an all-points alarm. Seek out and destroy the armored truck on the Upper East Side that was hijacked by the gangs from Shantypark and reported to contain the terrorist Salem Jones.

* * * * *

55

Ibrahim pulled the vehicle up to the median on Park Avenue and was able to see the barriers that were hastily set up on the corner ahead, blocking his entry. Pythons stationed by the barricade immediately took notice. Glancing into the rear view mirror he could see a squad of SKs on the move, approaching from behind, several loading their shoulder-mounted rocket launchers as they scrambled towards him.

The loyal men of Shantypark riding in the back immediately helped themselves to some AK-87s stockpiled in this mobile armory and began firing at the oncoming targets to their rear. Instantly, some squirrel killers went down and others took cover. They began to fire back. Hard sharp sounds of lead projectiles pounded into the armor protecting the truck. On the barricade in front of them a howitzer was raised into position to fire. Ibrahim shouted at Herbie and they threw open their doors and flung themselves out with Herbie pulling Jamal in tow as the missile hit the truck and blew it up and backwards into the air in an eardrum-crushing explosion.

Herbie was on the ground next to Jamal. In that sharp crack, the truck and the men in it were destroyed, left in a blaze of fire and smoke. In the turmoil he could see soldiers advancing from both the front and the rear, firing bookoo lead into the debris. Through the smoke he heard Ibrahim yelling for him and he grabbed Jamal and ran through the smoke and devastation towards the shouts. Bullets thudding all around, the absurd thought actually crossed his mind that he was getting pretty good at this.

Ibrahim gestured to a spot close by in the street on Park Avenue that had erupted with men carrying automatic weapons of their own. They sprouted up through a manhole, firing on the squirrel killers advancing on them, taking several of them out. As Herbie dropped Jamal into the tunnel, splatters of blood from these brave dudes, who were now being killed, splashed onto his face and neck. He let himself fall into the hole after Jamal, and then Ibrahim landed on top of him with a bone thumping. In the little tunnel more men from Shantypark pushed them out of the way and clamored out onto the street firing their weapons at indiscriminate targets as they emerged. What Herbie couldn't see at that time was how quickly they were terminated by the posse of SKs that descended on them from all sides. They were anonymous and cruel and nobody liked them, but these Marines were good at killing people.

The tunnel branched off into several directions. Ibrahim shouted at Herbie to follow, so he grabbed Jamal and did. As he ran away from the battle, Herbie turned to look back for an instant. He saw squirrel killers descending through the hole, firing into the murky light. Men on both sides were pierced and screaming and dying around the bottom of that hole. The fight had been taken from the street into the tunnel and even in his panic Herbie knew what this meant.

Herbie pulled Jamal out of the other end of the tunnel just south of where the old Model Boat House would have been in ancient Central Park days, where aficionados of this simple pastime spent leisurely afternoons with their grandchildren playing with remote control ships in sculptured renaissance fountains. Today a terrific explosion from back where they had just come ripped through the narrow passageway and spewed forth a volcanic rush of dust and smoke that blew out all over them. Gagging, they fell to the ground. Herbie rolled over to see Jamal. He was covered with dirt, but smiling. Merry Christmas, Herbie thought.

Ibrahim wasted no time rousing them. "That explosion killed many men but it will buy us some time. It'll take some time for the SKs to bring in heavy machinery and clear the tunnel, but there are many other places from where they can come. We have to hurry. This thing has started."

In the last couple of days Shantypark went from insane diabolic paranoia, to born again and saved, and now suddenly thrown back into a declaration of full-scale war with an outside enemy. Chaos. People were running in all directions in panic, others were huddled together lamenting. Where to go, where to hide? If the tunnels were breached where could they go to survive aerial assaults?

Most of the hobbled and sick couldn't do much but opt for whatever ridiculous sense of security their tents and shacks had to offer. But those healthy enough and able to keep their heads, moved toward the one place that could give them some strength. Herbie, along with Ibrahim and Jamal, kept a desperate pace with them towards Reginald Square, where they knew the Council would convene. But where was Salem? What would he do?

* * * * *

56

Hundreds of thousands of pilgrims and proselytes clamored together in No Man's Land just outside the walls of Shantypark. Their collective sounds bordered on braying, driving the overly paranoid squirrel killers crazy.

News of the firefight spread in an instant through the First Army and tensions ran high; no one knew when the next outbreak would come. Pellet's orders, shuttled through the personal communications gear inside their helmets, were clear. The pictures of their slaughtered comrades butchered by Salem Jones and the terrorists from Shantypark were even clearer.

Pellet wanted to end this thing once and for all. That was his message to the Alliance members who were coordinated into neat little windows on the large monitor in his command car.

"You don't get it, Chancellor," said Pellet. "This latest violation of the non-aggression agreements clearly indicates that these are not isolated instances from some renegade gang. This is already the beginning of a well-coordinated plan by the terrorists to take over this city. Salem must have been in communication with them from jail, the same way he wrested control over large portions of the population with this subverted form of born-again mind control. In my estimation Shantypark is ready and poised for a major outbreak. Obviously, Salem is in command."

An extreme and delicate pause. The Sony Korean stared from behind his leaden scopes out into the virtual cyber conference, while the middlesex man from Microsoft seemed to be fidgeting with something in its pocket. The Excellencies in The Hague clinked the ice in their brandy around in their tumblers while the Queen of Singapore played with the hair on her eyebrows. The only sounds came from the princes in Abu Dhabi hiding all expression behind dark mirrored sunglasses, clueless in their opulence, grunting something in Arabic, which might have been nothing but exhortations to some well-imprinted deity from decades gone by. Pellet was irritated.

"I am closing in on my threshold of patience with all this. I have soldiers dead and dying. Right at this moment I am clearing the area around the park to try and avoid unnecessary casualties, but I need you to know that is not my main consideration. I want you to understand that my objective is one hundred percent clear. I am going to get to this Salem Jones in whatever way I can, and terminate him. Then and only then can I subdue this revolt from Shantypark and gain control back to the city government.

The man from Sony finally said something from behind his dark cyberglasses "General, I assume the mayor has been consulted about this intended course of action?"

"Chancellor, the mayor has been incapacitated. I'm afraid we won't be privileged with any of his esteemed counsel anymore."

Deep, long-distance silence. "General," finally it was the tree snake Queen of Singapore, "my sympathies are for the mayor, but we are unanimous in support for you in all things, you know that."

"Of course, I know that. You need me in many ways."

"Yes, of course, but you still need us as well. This tiny world keeps us too well connected I am afraid. Since we have no other choice now but to put our full trust in you, all I can do is implore you to keep the body count down as much as possible. Once this is over, world opinion will still matter. We cannot have reports of massacre. We cannot have reports again of armies bombing their own cities. You know what kind of panic that will start worldwide. We can't afford outbreaks of violence like this in other places. Besides you have the girl and she will cooperate. She will read our statement and, when this is through, she will have put a somewhat palatable spin on this unfortunate turn of events. That is what we want. So keep it swift; keep it quiet, and keep it on the ground. Unfortunately, you must take no quarter, for at the end of the day we can only have one point of view."

* * * * *

57

At that instant, as New York prepared for battle once more, Maria was thrown into a dark prison cell, banging her head against the cinderblock wall. She crumpled into a corner as her head rescinded consciousness.

In the ensuing vision she saw her mother, who looked very self-assured and at ease. She was sipping raspberry iced tea through a long green straw. Surrounded by squirrel killers she seemed in her element, secure, composed. The barracks she was confined to for her own safekeeping wasn't quite her choice in interior decoration, but she was confident that the general was doing the right thing; this would only be a temporary staging spot before he moved her to a different more tolerable location for her and her husband. He was in a different room, and she supposed he was answering the same questions about Maria that they just asked her. Stuff about her childhood, her career. The questions about her sex life were nasty, but easy to answer, because, as far as she knew, Maria didn't have any. She agreed that this generation had a strong price to pay, but it was better than the alternatives. Besides she told them that she had enough sex in her life for all of her family.These guys did look cute in their combat gear.

When Maria opened her eyes, charcoal shadows were moving about in her cell, some exchanging grunts and metallic snickers in her direction. The SKs who brought her in were stationed in the prison corridor; even more were in position inside her cell. They were going to take no chances. There would be no terrorist action, real or supernatural. These soldiers were ready, tightly wound, primo killers. They knew this mission was of paramount importance to the general. In this man's Marine Corps nothing else mattered.

The squirrel killer guards hunkered down for what they thought should only be a couple of hours. Besides, after she did her thing at the TV station, the general wouldn't care if they had a little fun . . .

* * * * *

58

Grandma sat in the twilight zone of her living room and gazed at Sonia who drifted off to sleep after Grandma gave her the Ambien. Pranan and Lorraine put the kids to bed upstairs. The children wanted to know what happened and why weren't they old enough to understand. It was hard for Pranan who always liked to be frank and forthwith with his kids, but he knew nobody could ever be old enough to understand this. So he just hushed them to sleep with a stern but loving not-right-now. He sat in the tiny green Perry Street kitchen with Lorraine, nursing a cold cup of green tea and honey, waiting, not knowing what to do.

It was hours before the telephone rang, shocking the awful stillness. Nobody dared to move. Pranan lifted the receiver from its base on the kitchen wall. At first Grandma could only make out a few inaudible mumbles but then she heard him try to hold back a gasp.

He hung the phone up and, with Lorraine's help, they guided Sonia off the couch. The four of them climbed into Grandma's Volkswagen minivan, the very same in which her son was conceived, and Pranan drove them to Mass General.

Bullmoose had seen it all. He had walked all the way to Kendall Square to try and set these things gone haywire with his overwrought children somewhat straight. Not unexpectedly, he couldn't. Dolores couldn't stop crying and Henry screamed and yelled and actually punched him hard in the face. Bullmoose took the blow, and his eye was swollen and black when they met up with him in the hospital's emergency waiting room.

When he had gotten off the floor in Henry's apartment, head pounding and vision blurry, he stumbled down the stairs and watched them get into their double-parked Hyundai in a state of emotional turmoil. With his unswollen eye he watched Henry kick the little car into gear and screech off into traffic to get slammed by that passing bus on its route towards Government Center.

The paramedics and police arrived as soon as possible. They worked with blowtorches to pry them from the twisted wreckage and then rushed them both by ambulance to the hospital. For poor Henry, it really wasn't necessary.

The five old friends were huddled in a state of grief and shock when the doctor stepped out from the operating room. He looked at them with a long mystical, quizzical stare. I'm sorry he said, tears misting in his eyes; we did all we could for her. But, miraculously, we managed to save the baby. Congratulations everyone; it's a boy.

As the tears flowed and the grief howled, Pranan slid the magic ring off his finger and placed it on the pinkie of Bullmoose's picking hand. "You're going to need this now more than me, buddy."

* * * * *

59

By the time Herbie reached the outside edges of the mall, all of Shantypark was a raging tempest. Angry waves of people heaved and swelled upon the bandshell, like a hurricane surge foreshadowing an oncoming deluge. Off in the distance from all directions were heard large, muffled explosions, and people could feel the ground shaking beneath them. Up above they heard the blades of the Apache choppers hovering off and away, just out of eyesight. Their deadly discharge could be upon them at any moment. The precarious prisoners in Shantypark were in full-blown panic.

Herbie knew the real reason the choppers were there, ever vigilant. They were searching, detecting, and then blowing into pieces unauthorized transmission sites wherever any may be. Pellet was tightening the noose and keeping it private with one bold military move.

Up on what was left of the stage some heavily armored men kept the crowd at bay. Behind them he could see the Council engaged in animated discussion. In the center of it, as always, Marcus and Gregor were standing across from each other, facing off.

Ibrahim pushed his way through the fuming mob

with Herbie and Jamal hanging on in tow. The crowd, although in a chaotic tumult, recognized them and allowed them to pass through, everyone looking for a sign from Salem, greatly disappointed he was not there.

When they reached the stage Herbie saw that hostilities had intensified since the firefight outside Shantypark in which Jamal and he narrowly escaped with their lives. Marcus wandered off wild-eyed into a corner of the bandshell shouting into one of his cell phones, “It is imperative that you keep those SKs locked down all the way to Douglass Circle. Fan the brothers out in a defending arc all the way from the 7th Avenue gate to 106th Street. I’m sure Pellet’s lookin’ for a way in behind us for a possible surprise attack and that’s the way he’d come. Now hang up before they spook onto this line, next time use the bootleg N-Tel IIIs.” He flipped the phone off and walked like a wounded jaguar back to Gregor, who stood silent and unflappable amongst his boys, his arms folded on his chest like he enjoyed all this. All were waiting for his next words because, despite his ugly appetites, he had a way with crowds.

“You losers,” he took a drink from a flask and wiped his mouth with his sleeve, “you gotta look on the bright side or we’re all gonna die right here. The one good thing about them blowing up our tunnels is that we don’t have to defend them. They’re telling us they’re coming in on the ground. So I say before they can concentrate into an area and overwhelm us, we choose our own spot to fight.”

A man so white he was almost albino, with a huge earring made of bone and an illustrated body, smacked his big-barreled sidearm, which could blow a hole through the side of an elephant, against the palm of his hand. “But Gregor, what if those fuckheads come from the sky, like last time? At least then we had the tunnels to hide in. We were powerless against their bombs then; what's gonna stop them now?"

"I'm not waitin' to find out. We gotta get outta here before they attack, because the best defense is a good offense, asshole. I'm gonna go for the museum."

A short but brilliant hyperstunner of a pause as the Council grasped what Gregor was proposing. They were desperate just to stay alive, while Gregor was planning a full-scale revolt.

"We've got more than enough explosive shit to blow a couple of huge holes in those walls they built near the drive. Then we pour on in and take them by surprise. They are going to be really weak in there, because most of the SKs will be out in the streets patrollin' the crowds, getting ready to bust on in. They'll never expect us to hit first. Bang, bang, and we blow on in from two sides, straight in, hand-to-hand the old fashioned way, the way we used to do it. Then we take out those chickenshit squirrel fuckers, cause, nobody is ever going to take my stani boys in a fight like that. Once we're in, we got the heart of Uptown. Pellet's army is spread out in a circle around Shantypark, our best chance is to concentrate everything in one spot and punch on through."

Gregor took another big swig from the flask in his pocket and turned to his troops. They were busy smizzing and drinking and getting ready for whatever Gregor had in mind. He took another long pull from the bottle and laughed. He glared at Marcus with zealotic fever. "We can use your boys already uptown as a diversionary action. When I give the word, you tell them to attack, then we go the other way."

"You're going to hang them all out to dry, Gregor."

"Do you want a chance of getting outta here alive or not?" Gregor turned to the Council. "The time to strike is right now, when those numb nuts out there think they got us on our heels. I promise you they'll never know what hit 'em."

A huge explosion just to their south, just outside Columbus Circle, rocked Shantypark, sending huge plumes of smoke belching into the sky. People everywhere were screaming and crying. Just standing there on the bandshell, doing nothing, they all knew they were soon to be goners. Thus the Council was swayed.

Ibrahim was helpless. He looked over at Marcus and muttered, "I wish Salem was here; he'd know what to do."

Hearing that, even in the midst of the end of their world looming down upon them, Gregor broke out into the deepest uncontrollable, smizzified hysterics, like conjured demons up from the dead, spitting in the face of faith.

The Council stared at him in fear. Even though they hated him, this was the time they needed him to be somewhat sane.

"Salem-fucking-Jones? Are you fucking completely fucking outta your fucking mind? I told you from the beginning that guy was bullshit. Look at the mess he got us into now with this peace and love holy fucking crap. Fuck that! People are going to be dying like crazy today, and the dude who brought all this bullshit down on us has totally disappeared."

Marcus couldn't summon a real challenge to Gregor's livid revilement, but he tried. "There has got to be a reason for that. He would never let us down."

"Bullshit. He sweet-talked you all into making this your last Christmas. What are his sweet faggot words going to do for you now when the squirrel killers come riding in here with their armor and shit, burning and killing and ripping up this garbage heap we live in. Pellet's been wanting to wipe us out for years, and now Salem has given him the reason to do it in front of the whole fuckin' world. Salem Jones is fucking bullshit!

"I say we do what we were born to do. If we are going to die today, let's do it like men and go out in a blaze of glory!"

* * * * *

60

Sam knew things were not adding up. He had been trying all morning from the safe house to get through to the mayor's office, but there was no available line of any kind, not even the powerful T3s. That's when he began to fear the worst. As he approached Manhattan airspace, his automatic pilot overrode his every effort to fly, as if it was taking them somewhere as fast as it could with a will of its own. From what he could see, New York looked deserted. Sam assumed everyone was either off to Shantypark or was hiding in their apartments glued to ABCNN. The chopper banked low along the East River, flew under all those bridges still standing and ended up in a hover over City Hall. Sam's heartbeat rifled over the top when he saw the motionless body on the roof.

The helicopter descended faster than its human operator would have attempted. The instant it touched down upon the tarry surface Sam leaped out. He bolted over to the door that led to the operations room elevator. A body was wedged up against it, blanched and still. Sam leaned over his boss, his friend, and put his ear down to listen for his heart. He let out a reflexive gasp, there was a beat, albeit weak; but, thank God, Jack was alive.

Several young Iroquois men appeared at his side, and without spoken words they picked Jack up, put him on a portable stretcher, and transported him over to the chopper. Sam watched them carry off the mayor's body. He tried to open the door that led down to the armored office but it was locked from the inside. How did Jack get up here?

Sam wasn't built to wait for an answer. As the mayor was lifted onto the back of the helicopter, Sam pulled out his pistol and fired two shots into the elevator shaft door lock and forced the door open. There was nothing there, certainly no elevator. He bolted as fast as he could down the eight flights of stairs leading to the armored office.

At the bottom of the stairwell he found the elevator was waiting, trashed beyond recognition, someone dropped a grenade into it. The door to the operations room was also locked from the inside.

He paused to reload. How in hell did Jack get up on the roof, especially in his condition? There were some things Sam knew he'd never understand, but he felt forces at work here beyond the pale of politics. So he said a prayer, something he hadn't done in years, since his belief in God exploded with all those nuclear weapons. He fired into the lock and kicked his way in to the office where he spent his entire professional life.

The room was empty, unscathed. However, if there was any real air left in there, it seemed to be thick with carbon monoxide. He covered his mouth and nose, whirled back around, and flew up the staircase as if he was the turbochopper and not just a well-trained pilot.

By the time he got back up to the roof, Jack's stretcher was secure in the rear of the helicopter, and Deganawida was holding his headphones up in the air signaling him to hurry up. There was an urgent beckoning signal on the GPS and Sam better get on the chopper or it was going to lift off without him.

* * * * *

61

Maria sat taut, fearful to move, barely breathing amongst the squad of soldiers standing guard in her shadowy dark cell, the handcuffs behind her back excruciating. In this position she could see into some corners of the small room and in others she knew there were ominous soldiers standing. Her mind was working at a furious pace; doing the only thing she could think of, trying to summon her own Christmas miracle on this day of extraordinary and unprecedented events. Locked up, she was frantic that she couldn't do anything to protect the people she loved from something she was powerless to stop.

She must have been in there for an hour or two without moving, not wanting o squirm or show her discomfort, afraid to attract any attention, because time here was lubricious, and these petulant soldiers had nothing to do but stare at her helpless female form.

In every conscious moment she was trying to mentally telepathize warnings to the people in her life who mattered. Her mom. Her dad. Herbie. But to no avail. She wasn't the miracle maker. She was just Maria Primera, a reporter of miracles. But if she ever needed a supernatural phenomenon, she needed one now.

Instead, a squadron of salacious terminators surrounded her cell blocking any attempt of escape, young Americans who have lost all sense of their birthright that had at one time come with freedom and liberty. What was the general doing? Did he really think he was protecting the world from the next round of religious conflict? Or had he lost his mind, gone power crazy and become unfit for command?

No more time for self-pity or futile efforts at mental telepathy, because the SKs were gathering themselves together in the hallway outside her cell. The electronic door opened on command and the lieutenant marched in. “Okay bitch, time to get up.”

He grabbed Maria by the waist and lifted her off the floor. He leaned in close from behind and put his arms around her, grabbing her breasts. She tried to struggle, he held her back by her crotch, but she broke free. “What are you doing, asshole?”

The lieutenant tried to smack her, but an SK guarding Maria inside the cell stepped out from a shadow and grabbed his wrist before he could strike. The two soldiers glared at each other. “Who the fuck are you?” asked the lieutenant. The guards in the hallway pointed their AK-87s at the intruding officer who kept silent. The lieutenant noticed the two silver bars by his collar. “You know the orders, Captain, delivered right into my face by the general himself. I’m supposed to trust nobody, and you certainly don’t look like my mother.”

The captain squinted behind his faceshield, his finger tickling the trigger of the pistol at his side. “You know the mission, soldier. This lady’s going on TV in a little while on the general’s command. He doesn’t want the whole planet to see her bruised. That would mean my ass, since I’m the ranking soldier in charge here, sent personally by him to watch over you and make sure nothing goes wrong like it did earlier today. And, as I just saw, he was justified to be concerned. So, either I report you for disobeying his direct orders, or you let me do my job. I suggest you stand down soldier."

The lieutenant took a deep breath, looked at his squad behind him and took a sullen step back. The captain continued, "Besides, my fine rodent-killing marines, after the broadcast, she's all yours."

The SKs snickered through their mouthpieces and pushed Maria out of the cell. They escorted her down the dim and somber hallway of the dingy penitentiary, while withered, scabby fingers of the depraved and undesirable tapped frantic messages on the bars of their ghastly prison cells as she passed.

The world had gone completely crazy and there was no trust left between people, but as she moved through these passageways of attrition, the captain sidled up behind and removed the unbearable handcuffs from her wrists.

* * * * *

62

Gregor pranced up to the thick stonewall, silent, undetected. Several of his men wearing bulky vests under their parkas followed several steps behind. Unspoken, with quiet coordination, they removed their outer garments and revealed the packets of high-powered explosives. Years of training as suicide bombers left them cool and comfortable in the presence of body-obliterating substances. One with glee in his eyes started chiseling away at the mortar cementing the stones together. Ibrahim ran up behind with Herbie and Jamal.

Gregor had a minute to goad. "So Ibrahim, you motherfucking turncoat. How do you like your new boss? Where is your wonder boy now that this whole city is at war because of his pure bullshit?"

"You know, Gregor, I used to love you. Like a father. But then a real brother opened my eyes. He opened my eyes cause he made me realize that we all have the same father. And it ain't you. I was a stupid ass."

Gregor liked that and laughed as the demolition boys removed the stones and started packing the hole with explosives. "I could kill you right now, but what would that do? A lot of people are going to die today. You're a good fighter, let's see you fight your way out of this one." He pulled a pipe out of his vest and put some purple smizz into the bowl. He struck a match against the wall, lit the drugs, and took a big hit. He offered the pipe to Ibrahim, and then Herbie and Jamal who blankly refused.

"But I realized my love for you, Gregor, was really more like fear. Some people have trouble distinguishing between the two, love and fear, especially with authority. But not with Salem. Through him it is simple and easy, if you really want to see. That's where you go wrong my old friend, with all your power and shit, you still don't see."

Gregor took another big hit of smizz and the whites of his eyes turned a dull and glassy yellow. "You know what I see, asshole? I see a world of pure bullshit and pain. I see a world where the strong survive and the weak bend over on their knees." He took another big hit of the drug and his eyes lit up sulfuric. Then he broke out into that place smizz freaks love, that chemical place of momentary personal enlightenment. "I've read it all, the Q'uran, the Bible, the Bhagavad-Gita, and you know what I learned, fuckface? Get ready; cause this is it. I learned that there ain't nothing out there, dude. There's just us. We are born for no reason, and we eat, shit, fuck and kill for no reason. And that, asshole, is it. And why? I'll tell you fucking why. Because that is it! Do you understand? So fuck you, and let's get on with this."

Gregor signaled his suicidal boys who couldn't wait to get to work and send as many people to hell as they could. He called Marcus on the N-tel III, and they heard a large booming explosion about two hundred yards away. Pointing at his fearful sons, a deafening explosion rocked their area. Before the smoke cleared, scores of insane stanis equipped with the latest attack apparatus went screaming through the breach towards Allah. With weapons going off and men starting to die, Gregor ran through the hole after them, howling in ecstasy.

Ibrahim looked at Herbie and gave him a wink and a brotherly squeeze to his shoulder. Herbie picked up Jamal, and they followed after Gregor and his hordes, through the hole in the wall of the ancient museum, into the first, and most likely last, declared battle of the third New York City gang war.

* * * * *

63

Salem stepped through the arch in Washington Square Park. The early morning snow, still unmelted, refracted the brilliance of the sun, and rainbows scintillated about his body like suckling stars at the end of a spiraling mother nebula. In an instant the awareness of something vast and colossal flashed the itinerant, hungry population of homeless and helpless who clung to life in this frigid, inanimate patch of urban space.

He walked amongst them, the infirm and the sick, and touched them and offered words of hope and cheer. Those who were faithful and worthy were enabled to see him, really see him, and his offering, the healing, took them to the splendiferous, far past their gnawing hunger and afflictive diseases. They were now able to find the strength to get up off the frozen turf and feel the warmth.

Salem moved and they began to follow. They formed behind him in a procession, whose quintessence was the celebration of his being there. It started with a few humble steps, through the time worn Memorial Arches honoring the first president of an erstwhile nation that failed in its own promise of freedom and opportunity. It headed straight uptown on Fifth Avenue. While all along the way, the weak and the hobbled, and all that were needy, joyously joined in.

By the time Salem crossed 23rd Street, there were thousands of souls stretched out behind him. The people living on the streets, the cold and hungry, were empowered by his presence to raise themselves from the dregs and follow him up the avenue.

From windows above in the quiet affluent apartment buildings, protected by private security people packing assault rifles, innocent but inquisitive young children peered down with glee at the curious Christmas parade going on below on the snowy streets. Their mothers and nannies, not as sure as they, pulled them back and closed the shades. The nervous guards holed up in their reasonably secure lobbies fingered the safeties on their automatics, some wishing they could chuck them aside and join in, others thinking they should be looking for an open shot on this deceiver of men.

As Salem strode uptown, he gave his blessing to those he passed, and many found within themselves a place of healing. They affixed themselves to his host, and marched under the golden glow as if they all were one.

* * * * *

64

After a short journey avoiding the masses crowding around Shantypark, the small convoy pulled up to the security zone at the ABCNN building near Lincoln Center. The SKs escorted Maria to the checkpoint, now guarded by squirrel killers. The general had replaced the ineffectual private security force that allowed in the contagious terrorists from Shantypark with his own men. Ira had to stand by helplessly as Pellet made the station his own.

As each SK passed through the checkpoint, they rolled up their sleeves and subjected themselves to an identity check. Their fellow soldiers on security duty flashed the lasers from their biopods onto their wrists. It all went smoothly until the captain escorting Maria was tested. A red light flashed on the detection device and a loud alarm buzzed in the SK guard's hand. They all turned, somewhat stunned, and stared at the officer. Without a moment's hesitation the captain turned his AK-87 on the security guard and murdered him with a stream of bullets. At the same instant, two other SKs close to the captain opened fired on the rest of the squad. In a second there were eight dead marines surrounding them, littering the sidewalk.

Without a word between them, the captain and the two remaining soldiers grabbed Maria and hustled her into the building.

Just inside the front door of the ABCNN headquarters, Maria heard the running boots. The detachment of marines that had been guarding Ira in the control room dashed around a corner in the hallway toward the source of the attack and nearly plowed right into them. The captain raised his hand and shouted, "There is a force of terrorists just outside who are trying to stop the broadcast. Take up position and take them out while we get her inside."

Without any hesitation, the marines followed his orders and ran toward the entry door. The two SKs rushing Maria into the studio let her go, turned, and gunned them down. In an instant their bodies were splattered into bloody puddles swelling on the floor, their guns clattering away onto the tiled hallway now slopped by little pieces of their flesh. Before Maria had a chance to react to this carnage, the two murdering SKs grabbed her once again and continued to press forward, following the captain who already entered the main studio.

As they forced her through the soundproof door she saw the captain pointing his weapon at Ira, cowering behind the main console. "Don't shoot, man, don't shoot. I haven't done anything wrong man; please don't shoot."

The captain showing him no regard, seemed to scowl at Ira through the dark eyeshield of his helmet, and did not lower his weapon pointing at his head. The two SKs holding Maria slammed the door shut behind them and locked it.

A dark stain started spreading over Ira's pants by the crotch. "Don't shoot me. Please. I'm just waiting for the general's orders. He said he's going to email me the statement he wants her to read. It's going to be here any minute, and we are going to broadcast Maria upon his command. I'm following his orders, I'm doing the right thing; I swear to you, please don't shoot me!"

The captain kept his gaze fixed upon Ira. The TV exec's panic was apparently amusing him, like some comic marionette from an old-time puppet show. He appeared to be lost in thought as whether to cut him in half with a power burst, or put one well-placed bullet through his forehead.

"Shit man, I don't want to die. Please don't kill me. Tell me what to do. What do you want me to do?"

Finally the captain moved. With one hand he slowly lifted his faceshield and removed his helmet. He was much older than Maria thought, bald with one eye covered by a patch.

Gino smiled at the quailing media giant and said, "I want you to prepare yourself. We're all gonna be called soon, my man."

* * * * *

65

After the gangs breached the outer walls defending the museum and killed off the few marines guarding the perimeter, it was easy to enter the building. But once inside, a couple of stubborn SKs had enough time to mount some resistance to the surprise attack on their compound. Huddled behind some sandbags they neatly took out Gregor's boys as they entered the old grand room which once housed artistic marvels. It was now looted, emptied and riddled.

Taking cover out of the kill zone of the SK machine gun, Gregor sat down whistling a happy tune, reached into his parka and pulled out his pipe again. As some of his men who were blinded by the glory of martyrdom made another suicidal attempt to destroy the machine gun nest, he lit the smizz and took a deep hit of the potent drug. Herbie watched the scene with disbelief, ducking low as the marines that were hunkered down in front of him kept peppering bullets into the wall above their heads. Gregor just blew smoke rings and sighed with pleasure. No matter what was happening, he was going to enjoy this. He took another big toke and, without warning, jumped out into the hallway, diving over the bullets hitting the floor. He flipped a hand grenade into the makeshift bunker and blew those Marines into many bloody pieces.

He signaled the all clear and Ibrahim, Herbie, and Jamal ventured out after him into the ransacked historic room, smoky with the smell of war.

Gregor wiped the dust off his face. "Wow, I love this shit."

* * * * *

From the moment the explosions rocked the museum, the streets outside Shantypark became a stampede of terror. Salem followers waiting in No Man's Land for a healing glance or touch shrieked and fled from the sounds of combat, trying to find safety in the landscape of the city. But there were so many, they fell over each other as they tried to get out of harm's way.

The SKs patrolling the crowds reacted in a well-rehearsed defensive drill. They took positions behind their armored vehicles, guns ready and pointed at the scarred façade of the once-majestic landmark.

One of the large doors to the old museum creaked open. Several well-armed stanis charged out in several directions, but the SKs quickly cut the attackers down, their bodies twisting into macabre contortions as the bullets blew through their muscles and organs. They fell sprawled into their final postures over the stone steps leading down to the once elegant and fashionable Fifth Avenue sidewalk, portraits in a portfolio of violent death.

Gregor loved it when men readied themselves to die on his command. He sat down inside the huge metal doors and settled in, more intense, focused. He flipped on his N-tel and punched a number. "Get your niggers on the move, Marcus. On my orders I want them breaking out and giving the army boys up there hell. We want these shit-for-brains SKs to think we're the diversion and the attack is going to the West side and to the river. So we're going to lay low here for a while and lull these bastards into thinking we ain't coming out. Then we'll hit them with everything we have."

Herbie grabbed Jamal and tucked him under his arm. Now that the gangs were busting out, there was no turning back. He realized it was nigh time for him to die.

* * * * *

After the deadly shots dispatched the first few marauding stanis to the concrete steps, a tense quiet ensued. The crowd of Salemites began filtering back to Fifth Avenue, making the connecting streets too dense for the elite Pythons to clear a path. Pellet had to get out of his bulletproof BMW limo at Park Avenue and hoof it the rest of the way. Surrounded by a ring of Marines with titanium shields, he headed towards Fifth Avenue. He enjoyed this. It was his style to be in the middle of the action. He was going to be there personally when they cornered Salem Jones and whacked his terrorist ass out of existence.

There was a sharp crack behind him, a quick whistling sound, and then a large pounding explosion coming from the top floor of a nearby building on the east side of the Park Avenue divider. The tinny radio voice in his helmet confirmed what he suspected. One of his Apaches had hooked onto the signal of a news crew trying to patch onto a subcarrier going into the ABCNN satellite. Most likely it was those prying LAFox people using proxy talent that couldn't be tied back to them after an investigation. They would have done the same to him if they were browning out the true extent of the damage from their latest earthquake or torrential rains.

Huge blocks of building stone slammed to the ground across the way, followed by pebbles and dust that sounded like rain. He thought to remember to give a medal to those boys in the air when this mission was through.

Abruptly the tree snake zinged in on his left ear, and her low res picture pixelated on his glasses down by his right nostril. "General, what's your position? What is going on down there?"

What do they want now? Why are they meddling in what they know nothing about? "I'm on what used to be 83rd and Park. It's a madhouse here. The bad news is the gangs commandeered the museum. The good news is we have them pinned down inside. They'll never get out alive; we have too much firepower in the area. Unfortunately this place is saturated with civilians. It will be impossible to keep the collateral damage light because they are all insane. Salem Jones has them brainwashed, like they are all on some community death wish."

The Sony CEO from Pyongyang interrupted, blinking in by Pellet's left cheekbone. "Oh, yeah, now I see you. Stay where you are, General, we're coming down."

What? Pellet couldn't quite believe it as he shot a look back up at the Apache, which was now banking in a tight aggressive one-eighty, making a rapid descent onto the divider on Park Avenue. The general could see the anxious faces of the Alliance through the tinted glass.

Damn, this complicates things! He didn't need some rich and powerful pansy-ass bleeding hearts to screw this up. He was the true commander. He knew when to sacrifice the limb to save the body. He knew that clemency was the road to disaster in situations like this. He didn't need some meddlesome committee horning in on his authority here. Not now, not when the future of the world should be in his hands.

Pellet intuitively reached for the holster on his hip, his finger lingering on the trigger inside. There were always certain options that were definite and clear, and once they were executed, there could be no return.

* * * * *

66

The turbochopper flew up the deserted concrete gap of Broadway. Stealth in place, keeping low to the street to further muffle the sound of the blades. With all the Apaches in the air and the explosions on the ground, Sam knew there was no way they could be detected. Besides, all the SKs would be surrounding Shantypark and they wouldn't think twice, figuring it was one of their own. Anyway this wasn't even his call, since the aircraft was flying itself on automatic. At this point he could do absolutely nothing about it. Sam was relearning the meaning of faith his own way.

The helicopter touched down on the street outside the ABCNN building, which seemed strangely unguarded. The Iroquois, still on the same telepathic page, unstrapped the stretcher with the unconscious mayor from the floor of the aircraft and lifted him out the side door. Without a word between them they hastened towards the building, following Sam and Deganawida close behind.

Once inside, they walked the gory corridors towards the studio, stepping over body parts and smears of blood. As they came closer to the control room, a lone SK waved them inside with a smile turning from murderous to earnest.

Maria exhaled a long slow breath when she saw them enter. Even with the events of the last few days, she was still not prepared to keep up with each new and unexpected happening. She embraced Sam and Deganawida as comrades even though they barely knew each other. Now they were like a team, and their smiles were charged with the deep responsibility they all felt at this moment. But when Maria saw the mayor carried in on a stretcher and placed on the floor, her heartbeat jumped and she ran to his side.

He was stirring, emitting soft moans, maybe dreaming he was somewhere else, someplace better, a place of joy and of peace, a luxuriant land of sunshine and harmony, a rich and gentle country of creamy milk and the sweetest honey . . . with swift running streams of warm purifying water . . .

* * * * *

67

This time when Bullmoose left home to travel, he was gone for a long, long time. Longer than he was ever gone before. Where he went, nobody ever knew. Not Grandma, not Pranan. He didn't phone; he didn't write; he didn't fax; he didn't email. When he returned he never talked about any of it, his travels, or the incident. Never. They assumed that wherever he went he must have worked out the unbelievable grief that he had to carry.

During the time he was away, back home in Cambridge, through a lot of hard work, time, tears, and all-night sessions at the kitchen table, slowly but surely, Grandma and Sonia worked out their own versions of the devastating loss just enough for themselves to survive. Of course, raising Herbie helped deflect the pain, his babyness the principal factor in their eventual recovery.

Unlike his father, he was the sweetest little thing from birth. He was the sunshine that cut through the storm clouds, raising the rainbow that bridged the distance from the broiling seas of despair to their lovely little family picnic blanket. Sitting there in the pot of gold was a gurgling, playful, smiley, Herbie baby boy.

Those years that Bullmoose was gone, Herbie lavished in grandmotherly love twixt Grandma and Grandma Sonia. With regular doses of boy brought in by his Uncle Pranan and Cousin Max, he was raised as regular and as normal as any baby could be in a twenty-first century non-nuclear, hyper-extended family.

Although he was born into extreme and dire tragedy, this gentle toddler personality, coupled with the unprecedented and singular kind of love he was given, developed into a golden boy extraordinaire. He was Grandma's Dali Lama, Lorraine's long-haired and sensitive rock-and-roll god, and Sonia's beautiful teenage boy, strumming guitar in the moonlight like a manifestation of Vishnu incarnate, the energy that makes all the universe aglow.

It was all going so well for the young Herbie when right before his middle school graduation, Bullmoose returned home. That's not to say that Bullmoose intentionally tried to shake up his home life; it's just that according to the count-on-able rules, with nothing staying the same and everything interconnected, Bullmoose being around meant what ever happened next would always be out of the ordinary.

When he finally did show up that fine sunny day in May on the Perry Street driveway, they shelved their misgivings because they were all delighted to see him, except for the little Gypsy. Her past life with Bullmoose had caused her too much sorrow, and that heartache still played a major part in all her almost unbearable present-life pain.

When he hurried out of India, he abandoned her to a world that rewarded unmarried pregnancies with a funeral pyre. Durga, enamored with his favorite daughter, spared Sonia that awful fate, but scandalized, he banished her from his family to the lower classes as an untouchable. She had to fend for herself for months, finally giving birth on the muddy floor of the temple made of sand with the orange man as the midwife, babbling benedictions and cantillating invocations, but useless for anything else. Reduced to a beggar, she raised her little daughter without any money whatsoever, save the charity of Cudalore Cathy and the handouts from well-to-do tourists who threw rupees into her tin can in the Mahabalipuram town square.

She finally saved enough money to immigrate to the United States, because her future in India as an unwed mother was absolutely no future at all. Sonia had to hold down two jobs a day just to afford the flea-infested rat trap she rented in South Boston, and had just enough money leftover to feed the two of them white bread and baked beans. It was a life of drudgery, privation, and sacrifice.

Even though it wasn't directly Bullmoose's fault for the tragic events that took the lives of Herbie's parents, there was nobody better to blame than him. It wasn't easy for the little Gypsy to be around him, without feeling that he was responsible for tragedies in two successive lives. Even though Grandma tried to take care of the ones she loved and provided her rare trademark warmth in super-sized doses to the third grandparent of her only grandson, sweet Grandma Sonia started drifting away from the hippie family roost. She was only seen at seldom holidays and the occasional birthday celebration.

At first, the novelty of a man living in his house was a cool change of pace for the pre-teen Herbster. Bullmoose was fun in an oddball, erratic sort of way. To be sure, he was the one who did get him started on the guitar, however usually of the five-string variety. Bullmoose gave Herbie his very own Martin to learn on, the same one he played on the beach as a younger man, strumming at the juncture of the endless motion of the universe, jamming to the melodies of life.

The first year or so wasn't so bad. It wasn't until the Lipton family jewels descended, and hair started growing out of Herbie in the usual suspect places and his voice turned a squeaky kind of alto, that the first signs of danger manifested themselves.

For some reason Bullmoose decided to take over Herbie's upcoming transition from teenager to young man. According to Grandma, it was to replace the son he lost, the one he almost never had, that caused Bullmoose to push Herbie to grow up too quickly. Bullmoose always replied with his usual wisdom, "Nah, that's bullshit. It's 2014; kids grow up much faster than when we were kids." With that he was not wrong.

Bullmoose's role model madness reached the peak of insanity when Herbie was just a sophomore in high school. He took it upon himself to teach Herbie how to drink. He rationalized with Grandma using irrefutable Bullmoosian logic: Herbie was drinking anyway, or was going to do it soon enough, so he might as well learn under the safety net of the best, his very own grandfather. One day Bullmoose met him after school to prepare his young grandson in the ways of the sybarite. They were going to drink vodka together out of his flask and wash it down with Coke Zero.

That evening early in June, they got a late start and arrived at the end the day to Bullmoose's favorite spot down on the shores where Harvard had met the River Charles for more than four hundred years, between the Boylston Street Bridge and the walk bridge by Kirkland House. There on the banks of the brown, muddy river one would always find Harvard students hanging out, hooking up, throwing Frisbees, or sneaking hits of the latest designer weed people were calling smizz. But that crowd had already thinned out, most of the preppies and foreign students had gone off to their mahogany-paneled dining halls to eat their privileged pie and talk about William James as if anything he said was still relevant to this crazy century. If they only knew what this planet was spinning them to.

The sun was sinking low into the dirty Boston twilight, like a scoop of raspberry sherbet melting into a bowl of oatmeal, curdling on the edges and sticking to the buildings on the horizon. Bullmoose sat them both down at a spot near the bank of the river and they settled in cushy and comfy to relate.

Some water rats were swimming unseen under the river's scum, but Bullmoose and Herbie could hear them break the surface of the water as they pushed their noses out to gather air, very upset to find the two humans sitting so close to the entrance of the sewer that led to their lair. They knew how hated they were. Bullmoose toyed with them by throwing the still-burning butts of his Lucky Strikes into the water, trying to singe the hairs around their grotesque little snouts, warning them that people were about, and water rodents should not dare try to trespass. There was something beginning to smell rotten in that night.

Bullmoose's past travels in India, when the world was so much bigger and people so much slower and there was so many less of them, were no secret to anyone, at least the PG version. In fact, the story of the little Gypsy was a favorite amongst Herbie's fellow geeks in the electric shop, his favorite class even though he excelled in science and math. With a watchful eye on the water rat he rambled to Bullmoose his classmates' post-pubescent theories of how they thought the Little Gypsy was just a little street whore, or who was his grandfather kidding?

Tonight, as the vodka burned down the guardians of truth in Bullmoose's brain, he took offense at this complete misinterpretation of an innocent time once so sweet and dear to him. He cranked his mouth open just long enough for his foot to get stuck and muttered to

Herbie what a dastardly thing that was to say about his own Grandma Sonia.

As the last bits of raspberry sun melted into the artificial sticky red syrup that laced behind the gentrified Cambridge skyline, Herbie's young mind put together a reality that he had no hope to accept, even in this absurd perverted generation in which he grew up. He sat in miasmic silence as Bullmoose realized what he said.

Herbie's young brain felt like a slab of turkey bacon spluttering in a frying pan, bursting random globules of trans-fatty-less oil out onto the stovetop, messing it up. He felt the broiling heat of incomprehensible loneliness, and the fuel of long-term deception, ignite by this spark of recognition of his not so simple conception. Each moment's pained realizations felt like fire.

They crept home together, in the shadows of the silence of those indiscretions. The sky was now so solid it wedged itself between the stars, shunning out the imploring moon, and blanketing the town with an impending sense of doom so full of poison that even the grisly water rodents now scurried out of the sludge and into their filthy holes to escape the greater evil and nurse their hairless young, away from the inflicted and polluted night.

Back up in his Perry Street attic bedroom where his daddy was born, Herbie shut off the lights and smoked up his stash of smizz until his brain turned into a dead fish, undulating with maggot activity. As the whites in his eye turned a sickly yellow-green, he calmly tipped the candle over and watched the little flame run the rug, and then go dancing up his bed sheets, and rush roaring up his curtains, and why should his life have very much more meaning . . .

Bullmoose burst into the flaming room with a blanket, and threw it over Herbie's protesting body trying to wrap him up within it. But Herbie did not want to leave.

He pushed Bullmoose away and he fell. The fire crackled up the ponytail, his clothing igniting. As he got back up, he was pushed back down again hard, now conflagrating.

Herbie heard his name being screamed and that he loved him so and he was so sorry and knew it could never be enough but we have to go on regardless of the whatever. Bullmoose finally knocked him down the stairs and dragged him out of the house screaming. Herbie collapsed on the asphalt to watch from the driveway as their little house where he had spent all of his life melted into the fire from the top on down.

That next day at the hospital with Grandma, his Grandfather was so wrapped up in gauze he could hardly see. Bullmoose pushed the little metal ring that the nurses slid off the melted flesh of what was left of his picking hand over to the edge of the hospital's bedside tray towards Herbie. He managed with the rest of his strength to say something that sounded like "You're gonna need this more than me, buddy."

Grandma almost succumbed in pain so acutely scorching. Was she too careful with the ones she loved? With searing tears she grabbed Herbie's hand so unscathed and pushed the ring onto his finger, crying that maybe its special charm could still be found.

For saving Herbie's life and giving up his own, no greater love could ever be shown. Maybe that was just enough for the wandering defender of the magic ring, to enter the limitless glory and the unbounded grace, with only five of his strings.

* * * * *

The gleeful warring stanis gathered in the museum lobby under Gregor's animated exhortations of Allah, infidels, and virgins. The mujahedin shouted back and brandished their weapons, raising them to the heavens in supplication.

Huddled along the wall with Ibrahim and Jamal, Herbie tugged on the little copper ring he wore on his right hand ever since that fateful day. He felt thankful, grateful for Bullmoose albeit in a way so taboo and impure, for nothing stays the same, and they were so incredibly interconnected, and who could have thought that would have happened next?

He wondered now how his tiny human identity was connected to the one and the all. Which was the missing part of this puzzle? There was little time left to learn. The mystery of his life was now on the final leg of its journey, sailing through the furious rapids of the river of time, towards the white and foamy waterfall waiting at the end of his days.

* * * * *

68

The squirrel killers on 57th Street were surprised to feel a warm misty yellow on their necks. When they turned to look, they were fully shocked to see a host of people of all colors and kinds marching up Fifth Avenue so close and undetected.

The clothes the people wore were torn and bedraggled, but not so their countenance, which was strong and uplifted. Many among them were silent but others were almost singing, humming a mixture of an Om and a soft, sweet melody, the kind sung before music could be recorded. They possessed little, most seemed very poor, but they carried themselves with grandeur and the richness of spirit.

If this procession had any hostile nature to it, these well-trained, murderous SKs would have blasted them into hodgepodge bits of flesh, hair and bone. But they had none. Zero. No threatening anything. They were childlike, docile, intent on something far away and nebulous, like yellow itself. Not a single soldier amongst them even thought to shoot. In fact, the troops took slow steps back away from the avenue, astonished, allowing the throng to continue forward unimpeded.

It was the beginning of a day hard to fathom for these lifetime professional killing machines. What was really strange to these SKs was the silence on their radios, and their inability to contact the general, who was only a mile or so away. It was as if the golden fog floating above the heads of the procession was running interference, blocking outside detection.

Oddly, none of the soldiers at that corner ever reported seeing any of the alleged yellow protective fog. When later questioned, none were able to say they actually saw Salem. But they said they knew he was there; they felt him all around as the procession advanced steadily forth.

* * * * *

A squad of Pythons with their titanium shields assembled into a ring around the side door of the chopper, and the Alliance stepped out into their protection. Once all the esteemed members were on the ground, they moved off as a unit through the gathering crowds of fervent neophytes and curious onlookers, all who were eager to see Salem Jones. For the moment they settled for observing these mysterious dignitaries who landed amongst them with so much self-importance.

These people, swarming in the street with some collective undersense that something heavy was to happen there soon, were mostly from the middle class and scraped enough crumbs off rich tables each day to live in real apartments with heat and running water. Not the type to rise to violence. They were angry but not enough, and a bit too scared. However, just by being there, everywhere and all around, they created a tense and claustrophobic mood, which heightened as the crowd grew thicker and more insistent by the moment. They rabbled around the Alliance, watching them with their silent anger, turning more resentful as the nervous VIPs flinched behind the Python shields, ducking their heads low as if taking cover from psychic snipers in the crowd.

The large and immediate presence of the military, scurrying about with great mechanical noise and jostling of armor, plus the ominous explosions of tunnels being destroyed and buried off somewhere in the distance, made everybody in the area skittish, twitchy.

Pellet watched them cross Park Avenue, iron-like, rigid, body language telling it all. He knew in their paranoid condition it would be hard for them to think rationally, hard for them to reach a consensus about anything. It was foolish, and certainly a big mistake, that they came. The armored marines ushered them through the mass of people to the general on the other side of the street. Before they could say a word he was upon them.

"Who is responsible for this outrageous decision to come here? Do you know what you are doing? You are putting yourself and therefore my men in grave danger. This is a battle zone."

The Queen of Singapore, usually the seductive tree snake, glided out from the protective ring and slithered in front of him, somewhat wavering. Although lacking her usual strength, she was able to make a stand. "Of course, General, but we felt we needed to see this for ourselves. Certainly you understand that considering the high level interest these developments are creating around the world, the blackout you imposed couldn't satisfy everyone in the Alliance's native curiosity for the truth on the ground."

Pellet scowled at them all. He knew they were making it up as they went along. Here, on the street, confronted by the physicality of the people whose lives they controlled, these animals with unsavory smells making discomforting sounds, the inadequacy of their collective will wavered. He knew which ones in the Alliance had voted to come here in the first place but were kicking themselves now for being so stupid. He fired back without hesitation.

"You know the deal. The girl is now getting ready to broadcast the statement you prepared. And that's enough. We don't want to, and should not want to, show any of the mess that's here or might likely occur here today, do we? And as importantly, I was hired to protect this city and to protect you. I can't take the chance that if guns go off you could get hit."

"Sincere sentiments, I'm sure, General," the brave tree snake said stretching herself, "I know the plan. But I thought you said the situation was well under your control? That the terrorists are pinned down in the museum?"

He could see them all squirming behind the shields, their eyes glancing away from making contact with his. "It seems like you don't trust me, or my decisions. Funny, because, up until now, I've been leading your group with the same consistent policy direction I have taken since the beginning of this crisis."

"Truly." Her deadly serpent eyes now glazed with alarm. "But now I fear that the situation may have gotten out of your expert hands. Perhaps there is something about this whole thing that you haven't taken into account. Maybe it's somewhere above the sphere of what is considered natural. Are you sure, General, that Salem Jones is even with the terrorist gangs in the museum?"

Pellet's lack of rebuttal did not conceal his disdain for her ignorant presumptions.

She continued, "I'm distressed because, while flying up the East River, some of us saw a strange golden cloud moving up Fifth Avenue, that neither our heat sensors, radar, or optics had tracked. It was like a huge living mass that was completely unnoticed by anything electronic."

She twisted her body as if without a spine and peered over her shoulders towards downtown, obscured by the burnt-out buildings before her. Pellet remained silent, baffled. "Even more bizarre, only a few of us in the aircraft could even agree that there was a disturbance out there to see. Now I am truly concerned, because this very odd thing is very close and I was sure you had to be aware of it."

Pellet's body language twisted like he stepped into an unseen hole in the ground.

"But no, General, now I see that you do not know. How very, very strange."

He cleared his throat trying to find something to say, but she wouldn't allow it. "No, General, please no more discussion, let's move on. I am afraid of many, many things. But as of right now, we're still in this together."

* * * * *

The scouts from the roof brought Marcus in the museum lobby some grievous news. Pellet had established a strong defensive position surrounding them on the Fifth Avenue side. Large vehicles placed concrete barriers in strategic positions on the street. On the rooftops above, the Pythons had set up their versatile titanium sniper posts. From these positions, the SKs could launch a deadly crossfire at any attempt to break out the doors, while guarding against any movement on the museum's roof. Of course, Apache attack helicopters were buzzing angrily above them in the sky, and each alone had enough missile power to launch a devastating salvo that could bring down the building.

If that wasn't bad enough, his boys uptown were being cut to pieces by Pellet's Street Hawks who seemed to be waiting in ambush for Gregor's diversionary tactic.

The brief messages he was getting on the N-tel seemed like the army had already knocked them out of position where the old Blockhouse used to be, and that the fighting was fierce up by the Great Hill. Marcus knew that, as valiant as his brothers were, they wouldn't be able to hold off the intruders for too long. That meant the army would be howling up his ass shortly. He imagined the terror in his people's hearts as they fled their tents for downtown, many falling under the indiscriminate deadly fire of the AK-87.

He knew Gregor had taken them on a suicide mission, but it was out of his control then, as it was now. But was this inevitable? For the truth was that Salem's arrival and subsequent actions, although miraculous, had put them into this dead-end in the first place. And truly, where was Salem now? Could Gregor be right, that he had abandoned them? He looked over at Jamal, and somehow Marcus couldn't get himself to believe that. Seeing the calm in that young boy's demeanor, this recipient of an amazing miracle that he himself had witnessed with his own eyes, Marcus couldn't accept the fact that this was the end. Salem said to have faith. Yes, it was a matter of faith. Jamal had faith, so, Marcus will have faith.

* * * * *

The titanium barrier with the wary Alliance ensconced within moved through the throngs of agitated bystanders, pushing random people out of the way who did not move quick enough. Pellet refused to walk behind the shields and led the way in front. His Hawks were making short work of the resistance uptown, and were already into Shantypark and fighting their way across the North Meadow. The point of outbreak was going to be the museum. Of that, Pellet was sure. So that's where he was headed. He liked to be close to the action, to make sure it went down the way he wanted. Damn these pompous fools who think they can tell him what to do. Let them tag along if that's what they want. Their presence here cannot affect the outcome he has arranged. He won't allow it.

However, he still wasn't able to raise any communication south of 66th Street. What was this new kind of interference device he did not know about, this undetectable yellow fog or cloud?

As the clock in his face shield flashed 4:24 p.m. a buzzer went off on his headgear, everything was still going according to plan, and this was right on time. Better get down to it.

* * * * *

69

A little red light flashed on Ira's monitor. Maria and Sam were in deep discussion, Deganawida observing and nodding, the mayor still out on the floor, Iroquois shaman attending. Ira touched a button below the flashing light and the insignia of the First Army blinked on the screen. "Maria," Ira said, "Maybe you should come over and take a look at this."

Maria looked up at Ira with consternation, gave a sideways glance at the monitor, and moved over to the console to get a better look, Sam and Deganawida following. She was missing someone. The last couple of days had brought Herbie deep into her thoughts, her heart, her life. She ached that he wasn't there to help her, that he wasn't there for her to lean on. A fleeting chill shot through her body when she thought that he might be dead out there in the brooding violence.

She took a deep strengthening breath and crinkled her eyes. "Go ahead."

Ira hit the play button and the general's face appeared, slightly distorted on the studio monitor because of the wide-angle lens of the webcam embedded in his helmet. Although fisheyed, his image was still imposing and caused a sensation of deep apprehension to everyone who viewed it, all those in the studio tensing and tightening up along with Maria.

"Okay, Maria, it is time. At exactly 4:30 p.m. Eastern Standard Time, the whole world will be waiting by their televisions for some word from you about what is going on here in New York. They will finally get what they want. Your statement has been downloaded into the teleprompter in your studio. Give yourself a minute to get ready, because I want you at your best. Convincing and sincere. I truly hope you remember what I told you earlier. But for added motivation, or because I think you might be foolish enough to think I'm bluffing, I want you to take a look at this."

The screen flashed to an interior of an army barracks. Maria gasped. A man who looks like her father is tied to a support beam in the center of the floor. She hears a rustling sound and some SKs enter the frame. The man starts to shake and flail against his ropes. No, no, no, he is shouting though his mouth gag. The SKs stare at him like he is a pathetic little skunk snared in a hunter's trap set for bigger game.

The screen flashed back again, Pellet is looking at her from behind his combat helmet. "If you don't do what I say, we finish this and do your mother next, except with her we have a lot more fun. You have five minutes."

* * * * *

70

Ibrahim edged closer to Herbie and Jamal as the stanis finished their silent communion, petitioning in their own vicious way to a convoluted Allah for the violent deaths of their enemies and a glorious martyrdom for themselves. The attack was imminent and Ibrahim needed to take some measure to insure their safety, even though he knew it was just about futile. They were surrounded by intense firepower and had little chance for survival. He knew they had to go forward, there was something out there in their destiny and he was going to guide them to it.

He looked at Jamal imperturbable in the face of disaster, and Herbie, usually intent and highly charged, now had an almost poised sense about him, like a big cat in the jungle, on a stake out, waiting all night for that one perfect moment to strike.

All three had looked death in the face together before and came out alive, maybe with a black eye and some cuts and bruises, but alive. This time . . .? We all have an end game to play out, but never know how much time before the final whistle blows.

Gregor, kneeling, rose to his feet before the now reverent stani gang and they followed, standing before him. "My brother warriors, my blessed mujahedin. We came to rot here in the bowels of this foul and heathen city in what was once America, from the sweet mountains of our ancestors halfway around the world, where the disease dwelling within our midst brought destruction on our homelands and forced us here. Now we are imprisoned in the center of the evil empire that as children we were brought up to hate and vow vengeance against. So now we rage against the evil infidel in his home. It is through this great jihad that we now find ourselves together once more as brothers in combat. We are perched on the sunset of our destiny, with a chance to go down forever in history as men of great valor and of the highest nobility. I say we make the most of this moment, for he who dies fighting, will certainly live forever in the bosom of Allah's bounty."

* * * * *

71

Witnessing the imminent execution of her father had a profound emotional reaction on Maria, just not the one Pellet intended. Now for the first time since Salem's release from prison, she found herself grounded, centered, like she knew herself better than ever before. Maybe it was the culmination of so many life-changing events one directly after another, but she really didn't have time to psychoanalyze herself right now. Not only was her parents' life on the line in the next five minutes, but most likely the city itself.

As she read through the Alliance's prewritten statements that she was about to deliver to the entire world, she knew things were still changing in ways entirely too fast and therefore totally beyond her conscious understanding. By the end of the day Shantypark would probably cease to exist. Pellet was intent on going in and eradicating any gang power that existed in the search and destroy Salem Jones mission. What would happen to all those poor people? And if he achieved his loathsome goal, the loss of Salem after the world had only just found him would be cataclysmic. From what she saw first hand, his unique power was a true gift this world could not afford to lose.

But what was she to do?

Ira was no help, just twittering away about work-related technical nothings, satellites in the air, beyond commission, beyond repair, drifting out of control. Sam was the opposite. He was speechless, unable to create the plans he had always been able to make with his uncanny knack of finding the lowest common denominator in every situation. And Deganawida, always good for spiritual support, seemed to be lost in some kind of meditative prayer, as if he was trying to contact dead ancestors for advice. And Herbie? Where was Herbie?

Mayor Storm sat upright, lasered out of unconsciousness, but babbling and jibbering, talking in tongues.

They all drew close to him, surrounding him on the floor. He opened his eyes and his jabbering stopped. He looked at them with a relaxed twinkle in his eyes, as if all this was just a silly little joke they could now share together, like he simply fell asleep at an inopportune moment during a routine briefing.

But for Maria, it was another shock in a sequentially shocking day to see him recover so quick. It didn't help with her clarity of the situation when Gino, Esteban, and Lucas started laughing amongst themselves. True, they raised Salem from an infant, and they were heroes for her up to this point, breaking out of prison and rescuing her from the SKs, but let's face it, all three were known killers of men throughout their lifetimes, including all the bloody mess they perpetrated a little while ago back in the studio hallways.

Maria also did not find it funny when Jack stood up like there was nothing wrong and walked over to Ira, who was breathing with difficulty and peering into the flashing monitors on his control desk. The mayor put his arm around the tired old TV exec in a friendly gesture, smiled with his usual nonchalance, and suggested to Ira that to help set things straight, he ought to start searching the scopes in the east for the star that was going to rise in the sky.

* * * * *

72

At the same time Salem crossed 72nd Street, an SK runner in full combat gear, who somehow enabled himself to break free of his presence, sprinted up the avenue and found the general standing behind some of the armored vehicles that created a barrier of protection from the gangs waiting inside the museum just across the street.

Before the soldier could catch his breath to speak, the Lady of Singapore clutched at her throat. Staring south above the roofline, she cried out. "There do you see it?"

Bewildered, but not wanting to sound shaken, the general muffled his voice into her ear so that no one else could hear what he said, "What in hell are you talking about?"

She turned to him, frightened, and grabbed his burly shoulder and slightly shook him. "Above the trees, above the buildings, that yellow shiny fog. Do you see it?"

"General, sir," the exhausted soldier blurted, "It's him, sir. It's Salem Jones. He's just walking straight up Fifth Avenue right towards us, sir," he panted for some more air, "and there must be thousands of people walking behind him."

At that instant the broadcast started, which saved the general from looking like an immediate fool to everyone.

Maria's face popped up on the screen inside the general's face shield, and on every face shield of every SK in the city. It also blinked on all the biopods and other personal communication devices of everyone else, believer or not, who was out jostling for position on the streets of Manhattan. The broadcast reached deep into every home in New York and throughout the Northeast Alliance of Cities and City-States, all over North America, across the oceans, and onto every seaside, mountaintop, and river valley on every continent, and anywhere there was a TV monitor in the whole living, breathing, waiting world.

* * * * *

73

"Ladies and Gentlemen, it is 4:30 in the afternoon here in New York City on Christmas Day, December 25, 2047. I am Maria Primera, broadcasting to you today from the ABCNN headquarters here in Lincoln Center. Sadly I have to report that tensions have reached a peak here. Earlier this morning there was a second ambush in as many days on a platoon of First Army regulars by terrorist gangs from inside Shantypark, resulting in the brutal execution-style massacre of twelve Marines and the hijacking of an armored vehicle. Many eyewitnesses on the street reported seeing Salem Jones on the scene.

"Shortly after that incident the army located and engaged the hijacked armored vehicle in a firefight and destroyed it just outside no man's land, killing all the hijackers. Gang fighters from Shantypark then breached their borders and attacked the city via the underground tunnels. They too were repelled. At the moment we can hear the army destroying all other known subterranean routes out of Shantypark, sealing them off.

"In fact, war between the city and its Shantypark gangs has just now been officially declared by General Rodney Pellet, commander of the First Army, acting under contract of the Northern Hemisphere Alliance. General Pellet is known as the sworn protector of the free world, and to be a man of character and dignity, one whose name is synonymous in keeping the peace here in New York and around the world."

Maria paused and looked down off camera. All the world watched and waited through this brief unintended instant. The clarity she felt and the focus she found went way beyond the words, it spiraled forth from that singular human intelligence that stems not from logic but from the synthesis of all intuitions firing in the human heart. With calm resolve she lifted her head back up, eyes now deadlocked onto the center of the lens.

"A short while ago I downloaded a statement onto my teleprompter which was written to tell you that everything is under control and the First Army is suppressing the radical terrorist forces organized inside Shantypark. In the physical sense that is true. But you are going to have to make your own mind up about today because nothing is what it seems. Usually what we say to you and what we show you here on the air is only what we want you to know. It isn't really the news, never the whole picture, and certainly not the truth."

What is she saying, this bitch? We didn't write this. He punched a button on his phone and relayed a message to several waiting sets of ears, "Plan B. Eliminate her."

"What I know for a fact is, that as I speak, a division of the First Army is sweeping from the north through Shantypark, massacring the outgunned retreating gangs and routing people from their homes. They are spearheading towards the Upper East Side where the Council is believed to be holed up inside the old Museum of Modern Art, which the terrorist gangs had commandeered in a daring raid a short while ago. They are threatening at this point to break out from there into the city in hostility.

The bulk of Pellet's forces are dug in firmly around the entire block on Fifth Avenue and the streets behind. Army spokespeople are confident that these troops are fully prepared for any eventuality. If we had cameras we would show you that the whole place is also packed with Salem Jones supporters who are everywhere, seemingly heedless of their own personal safety."

Pellet barked into his transmitter, "Shoot her. Kill her now." But of course the command fell on recently dead and butchered ears lying in bloody puddles in the hallways of the ABCNN studios.

"But what is most amazing in the middle of this battle for the control of the city and possibly the entire world, is that those who truly believe are able to see a huge procession that is following Salem Jones, moving uptown on Fifth Avenue, on a direct collision course with both the army and the gangs from Shantypark. How Salem and any of those people arrived there is unknown at this time.

"I believe it is important to know that the battle being fought here today will not be won with guns and bullets. The outcome of this conflict will be decided in each one of our individual hearts. We all must take a firm look at what is really happening in the streets of New York City today and make up our individual minds about what the results should be. Because it is these determinations within our collective souls that will decide the outcome in this war."

The missile from the attack helicopter ripped into the transmitters on the rooftop with a mighty roar blowing the building apart, and Maria's face in the picture on every TV screen around the world sizzled off and died.

The Alliance registered the general's barely audible grunt over the intercom and was troubled by his ambiguity.

The proselytes murmured between themselves and that began a dangerous din that unsteadied the squirrel killers who were trying to follow their orders without any confusion.

The stanis gazed in fearfulness at Gregor whose eyes drifted off the biopod and rolled up into his head.

The soldiers back in the barracks heard the words they had often liked to hear. Plan B. The lady didn't look too bad for a middle-aged chick, especially when they tore the burlap bag off her cardio-ripped body and saw her naked and trembling on her knees before them.

But when the SK reinforcements on the ground broke into the main studio at ABCNN all they found was a dumbstruck babbling old fool playing with a video recording device, amongst many images of that woman reporter frozen on several computer and studio screens. He just looked at his executioners, took a deep breath and told them it was too late. Even they couldn't stop a star. Luckily for him he was finally composed and at peace with himself when the burst from the AK-87 tore across his neck and split his head off. It thudded as it hit the studio floor, rolled a turn or two away and stopped against a wall, with a shit-eating grin on its face staring back at his killers like he was the winner here.

The mayor was already hustling back down Broadway, aided by Gino and the other two disciples from Rikers, Esteban and Lucas. He was thanking them profusely and was very excited, and looking forward to getting back to his office, when the missile struck. They were so close the force of the explosion knocked them to the ground. With debris still settling around them, the four men lifted themselves up from the street and dusted off their clothes while feeling for broken bones. Finding none, they smiled the fond smiles of men who just shared near-death together and continued back on down the Great White Way, the mayor knowing there was going to be a lot of work to do at the end of this day.

Sam was in the pilot's seat but once again the helicopter's GPS had taken control and flew itself west and away from the battle. He and Maria had gotten out just in time, lifting off just as the missile zeroed in and blew off the roof of the TV studio. The stealth technology on the turbochopper kept them out of the crosshairs of any other possible bad guys. But where were they going now he wondered as they hovered over the Hudson River.

Maria looked through the chopper's window back at the smoke and fire raging on what was left of the ABCNN building. Now that her recording was smashed, she had bought all the time she could. From now on it was all about what went down on the streets, where she knew Herbie had to be. She stared down at the blank monitor where her face had just been trying to warn the existing world, and wished with all her heart and all her soul that something would appear.

* * * * *

Herbie watched the screen on Ibrahim's biopod go black just as the doors of the museum blew open and the stanis charged out. His body went cold with fear for Maria's safety when he saw the screen go dead. But now he could only tuck Jamal close to him and run as fast as he could, following Ibrahim out, believing there was a reason they were still in his hands. His body tensed up as he ran out into the indefensible open air, expecting at any moment to feel bullets pierce through his flesh. But, there was only deafening quiet.

Instead of the ear-shattering sounds of modern war filling the air with instant death, he heard the preternatural hush of an immense mass of silence coming from so many amazed people. Down the steps and in the streets by the museum there was no fighting, no violence, only massive crowds of the motionless, and the sounds of their breathing and their hearts beating, and that soprano music he swears he has heard before.

The attacking stanis ahead of him were now standing still by the curb of the sidewalk, looking puzzled at their soldier counterparts instead of trying to slaughter them. The squirrel killers directly across Fifth Avenue had their weapons lowered to the ground and were paying the stanis absolutely no attention back. Everyone was just staring at the man from the very heart of the universe, standing in the middle of Fifth Avenue.

This man in the long trench coat was pivoting in a great circle, captivating every individual in his presence, peering directly into all their souls. With lightstream eyes as bright as the Christmas sun beginning to set in the New York sky, thus spoke the Manhattan Prophet.

* * * * *

74

"You ask me who I am and why I cause you this trouble. Well, my brothers and sisters, I ask you the same. Who are you, and who were your parents, and who were the parents of your parents and those that came before them? Are they those who chose to defile our mother earth and destroy the harmony of this blessing, this miracle of life conceived here in this hallowed part of the universe so very long ago?

"Since mankind crawled out of the oceans and the mud and self-proclaimed dominion over every species on earth, there has been a slow and determined decline towards these days of affliction. And now, standing here on the brink of extinction, I ask all of you, why did you bring on this disaster?"

Pellet stood just off the curb of the street corner, a step or two ahead of the leaders of the Alliance who cringed behind him, stymied, overpowered. He was speechless, stonewalled. He wanted to shoot Salem dead but he couldn't. Like everyone around him he was transfixed, powerless, like grass blowing in the wind.

But not so Ibrahim who pulled at Herbie's elbow and guided him and Jamal down the steps towards the street, silent, unobserved behind the halted stani marauders.

"We have been warned so many times before," Salem continued, "There has not been a nation of people anywhere on this planet, large or small, with many gods or just one, that has not spoken of the universal spirit that lives deep inside each one of us. This one infinite source of life has been blazing since before the beginning of our feeble and inadequate idea of time. But, even so, with every turn of the earth we have been pushing it further and further away with our arrogance. In our insolence we actually think we can do better. As if the majesty of our creation needed our approval. How dare we? I ask you, can we still not build a tower that reaches the heavens?"

At the bottom of the steps Ibrahim found a spot in the stani front line stalled at the curb and gathered Herbie and Jamal in close. Everyone around them was spellbound. No one noticed the three of them as all eyes were upon Salem. Except for Jamal, who was looking up into the twilight sky.

"We were born into a daunting world, but were given everything we needed to help ourselves grow, be fruitful and multiply, as long as we accepted that we were the children, created by love to give love. But no, we have turned our back on creation and instead we make false gods to worship.

"In the beginning of civilization we were pagans trying to find order to the chaos, creating a god out of every force of nature we couldn't understand. As we evolved so did these gods into the oppressive and rigid regimes of the pre-scientific world. Now, after the technology of the last few centuries, we bow down to a religion called the global economy. We choose amongst our favorite gods, be it money, pleasure, power, or fame. Deep inside that false temple of earthly things, we venerate the most insidious god of all to reign supreme, the god of science and technology, and we empower it to forgive us all our transgressions and sins.

"Well I ask you, where are all those gods to which you have built your temples? Let them arise and save you now in this hour of great turmoil and despair. It will take great faith to be able to get back where science can help save you."

Herbie knew there was one thing he had to do. He reached into his pocket and pulled out the headbandcam and held it down in the palm of his hand, out of view, not wanting to arouse any attention, for it was his anointed role. Ibrahim scanned the crowd for any sign of danger. Jamal's eyes were still upon the skies.

"Yes, my brethren, I am greatly pained to the very core of my soul. Here now, standing amongst you with all human life in the balance, my beautiful mother, my earth, lies ravaged and spoiled, and her sons and daughters die daily by violence, leaving widows and children starving and diseased. Yet we still choose not to seek redemption or correction. Nor do we even try to hear the sweetness of the voice that sings within. We have rejected the truth we have always known and have placed science as the obstacle in the narrow path towards faith.

"This is a generation in which evil regales and abounds. We have sickened the earth with poisons and have made it hot and swelter. The oceans rise and swallow great parcels of land, while from the skies great floods and mighty winds bear down upon us. The ground shakes beneath our feet, rocking the very foundations of our lives. Most sadly of all, the devil walks amongst you without fear, claiming your souls for agony on earth, and condemning you to a meaningless and horrible death.

"Every prophet from every age has sounded the alarm, to warn that this evil will befall upon us, our cities will perish and no one will be able to escape. But did we listen? Or did we turn into pillars of salt?"

With one-pointedness of mind, Herbie sought out the receiver. Realizing there was none in sight, he reached for the B string in his other pocket knowing that as an antenna, it could extend the range and possibly find one. Using their three bodies to keep it out of sight from prowling SK eyes, he attached it to the transmitter. Those all around Herbie, Ibrahim, and Jamal could not see, because they were mesmerized by Salem maybe ten scant yards away in the center of Fifth Avenue, watching his hands reach up to the heavens beseeching the sky.

"Today I see people from all ends of the world who cry unto me saying, surely we have inherited the lies and the sickness and the disease from our fathers? How could our parents deny thee? Hear me, oh spirit of all creation, where may these people now go to know you? I pray they shall find thee, and love thee, and that they shall dwell within your glorious house."

Pellet turned his back on Salem and screamed out his horror and distress to the Alliance standing behind. "Do you not see? Do you not hear? Does this man not pretend he is a prophet of God? This has always led to religion and wars and untold suffering and death! We must end this now before he can ruin us again."

Salem hearkened these words and turned upon the general. "This world was not created by religion, General, nor was religion here when it was created. It was lost children of the light seeking shelter in the dark who found only their own ignorance and superstition. It was they who gave us the religion of this world. As if they could announce rules and regulations in order to decide who can join or who to be denied. But there are no rules and regulations you or anyone else can invoke. There are only the unalterable workings of the universe and that which created it. There is only one constant yet ever-changing state of being of which we are just one small part."

He continued to circle around, looking into the eyes of the people convened on the street, those staring back in wonder from the truth and beauty he possessed, and those scowling in confusion or in anger. Yet he saw them all with only love, and Salem's face brightened with joy.

"We are such a grand part of the spirit! We are the flower and the fruit at the end of the branch. We have been graced with hands and brains to refashion the bounty provided here on earth. We have been endowed with eyes and ears so that creation can appreciate itself, and our mouths are to sing songs of its wonders."

Herbie glanced at the tiny blank screen on Ibrahim's biopod. They were still out of range of a receiver and the world was already at a loss without this, he needed to do something fast. He looked over at Jamal who was still scanning the heavens when a feeling of unfathomable awe grabbed Herbie and filled him up. He gazed up into the fleeting sky with his singular great intuition.

"What have we done with these awesome gifts in the name of religion? Look around you, for the bones of people slaughtered in the name of these false gods are like the sands of the shore that rumble under the waves of a roiling sea. But can we find redemption while those who commit the gravest sins still strut about with nary a thought for absolution? I don't think so. No, I don't speak of religion, General; I speak of life! I speak of the one true source, the spirit, the light. It is you and your kind who give us modern idolatry forced upon us by the threat of death."

The people let out a mighty roar hearing this, those who believed and those who did not.

"Did you hear him? Can we continue to listen to this heresy? We must end this now. We must remove him from our midst!" cried the general.

"Kill him! Kill him!" screamed Gregor, whose eyes were turned up into his head, the whites of which were now black and red and looked as if they were seeing from someplace dark and low. His horde of ignorant and fearful men stamped their feet in approval and shouted. "It is he! It is Salem who now brings us death and despair! Kill him; kill him!"

The multitude behind Salem grew loud and grim. "How base are these men?" they shouted back, "that they cannot see the glory of the new age upon us!"

As the crowds assailed each other with curses and maledictions, each accusing the other of treachery and blasphemy, the Queen of Singapore took a cautious step forward next to the general and turned to all who were around her. "What are we accusing this man of? I see nothing that he has done for which we should take his life."

But she had to hold her breath and step back as the hordes of nonbelievers shouted out even louder to kill him. As they screamed for his blood, a legion of black-robed wraiths slipped amongst them and spread themselves throughout the crowd, eyeing Salem with hollow sockets. When the multitude saw evil in great numbers before them, their cries for justice equaled the shouts for his death, resulting in a great deafening clamor.

In the middle of the cacophony Herbie saw a dim light moving in the sky and Jamal saw it, too. They stood spellbound in this spot at this sight. Herbie knew what was coming and accepted the odds knowing that only he had the power, but from where could that come?

Without any conscious thought he removed the ring made of copper from his finger and placed it directly under the lens of his headbandcam still nestled in the palm of his hand, to increase the power of the signal to the satellite dying in orbit like a slow shooting star over the eastern sky. Ibrahim and Jamal huddled closely to him and the three became as one. In the midst of the madness on the street they created a space of prayer to transmit the scene through the miracle of Herbie's identity.

Thus connected, Herbie panned the reckless avenue, holding the headbandcam close to his hip and out of sight from those who would do him harm, and he focused in on Salem standing tall in the middle of the street.

In the helicopter, Maria saw the blank screen snap on with that famous image of Salem, arms raised to the New York City skyline, embroiled in the portentous twilight.

Pellet growled in anger and the Queen in simultaneous astonishment.

Jack put his arm around Gino and uttered a very thankful, "Ah-hah."

Graced by Herbie's rising star, every screen, in every village, town and city, on every mountain and valley, on every continent all over the earth, flashed on the picture of Salem at exactly the same instant. With that breathing image now in place for all to see and hear, a heavy silence descended over the angry factions. In that reverent space, came Salem's voice, so loud and strong and appealing.

"I say to all of you, those who look to me and those who look to kill me. Whether you walk amongst shadows in the valley of the night, or you bathe in the sweet and fresh running waters of the cool mountain stream, you must believe in the light and the spirit from which it comes, and then you shall have the truth.

"It has been said over and over, time and again, love one another as you would love yourself. When we begin to truly do that, we can all be as one. I put forth to all of you today; there is no better place to be, than to be one with that one.

"My brothers and my sisters, rich and poor, old and young, black and white and every race of man, those who follow me and those who want me dead, now as my time draws nigh, from this moment forth and forever, do not ever doubt or disbelieve. Because as I stand before you today, I can truly say that I love you all."

In the quiescence of that all encompassing heavenly hush heard around the world, the shot rang out, and we all saw the bullet pierce his heart.

Everything became instantly meaningless. As if all mankind was lassoed by one giant superstring yanking on the mother lode of DNA, coursing it back through its own continuum extending far beyond the physical, and landing it on that sacred crossroad that sets humans far apart from all the other living creatures on earth, turning us now into a different sort of beast.

Everyone, everywhere on earth, for an interminable second, was as one.

Thus wounded, Salem Jones, with outstretched arms, turned his head towards the three who now were so wise straightaway, and he beheld their loving eyes. Peering into the camera that Herbie held in the palm of his hand, he spoke his last words to the awestruck world. "I pray now for the one who comes after me, that if Jesus was the first to die for your sins, let me be the last."

Blood spouted forth from his body like a fountain from his heart, and he collapsed to the ground.

The mightiest tumult that ever arose from men broke like a thunderclap over the crowd. Men and women scrambled over his body, some to administer to it and to venerate it for the ages, and some to defile it and to use it as an instrument of repression and terror. Pandemonium amongst humans exploded, and the madness was all consuming.

In the chaos, General Pellet could see that it was Herbie who carried the eye of the world into the midst. Herbie panned his headbandcam back to look for the source of the shot, and everyone all over the world saw the smoke coming from out his gun. The barrel rose once more and pointed at Herbie's chest. Herbie raised his hands over his heart as if he could stop the shot, and the people of the world watched the bullet burst forth and rush, as if headed between each one of their beholding eyes.

Crack and through the lens, the bullet entered his vulnerable mortal body. Herbie crumpled to the ground. All the screens went dead.

A great battle between men ensued upon this spot, between the armies of the empire, the legions of evil, and the host of proselytes, all who witnessed the moment when Salem Jones was martyred.

Herbie lay on his back on this cold, snow-sprinkled Christmas Day in New York City, his blood making a steaming puddle on his chest. Jamal and Ibrahim looked down; their faces grew dim. A swift white light descended upon him with a roar and a fury devouring all his senses, and then he could not see or hear.

* * * * *

75

"Grandma?"

"Yes, my little Herbie baby boy."

"Is this what it's like being dead?"

A soft pause. "Yes, my little rainbow pot of gold."

"It's different than I thought."

"Yes, it is."

Moving as everything does, now he knows the answers that Grandma never really had to give . . . and the sweet celestial soprano glissandoed up to its tonic and then its fifth, and through its variations and into a crease of light glowing golden bright, and Danielle, she's pregnant, she's holding her belly, baby head beneath, she's abundant, just right . . . and then the great modulation in the universal breath . . . and it's okay, my Daddy, I'm so glad you're home . . . and she's pig-tailed and vibrant and energy pure, and he knew what he'd been missing, can't hold on even here . . . and Henry smiling with Dolores on his arm . . . shining forth hundreds of generations of identity before. . . and somewhere in the gentle mist Maria is smiling through grateful tears and he wants to reach out and hold her forever . . . the great exhalation shuttles him into the wrinkle where Bullmoose sits . . . strumming his guitar at the juncture of the endless motion of the universe . . . jamming to the melodies of life . . . he looks up at him twinkling and melts into it all . . . and it goes on and on . . . and never the same . . . and always interconnected . . . and nothing happens next when its always now in the unbounded glory and the limitless grace . . .

* * * * *

76

"Herbie Lipton."
"Here I am . . .

* * * * *

September 22, 2069. 6 a.m.

The silver haired man steps from the shore of the lake, crosses the moist sand, and proceeds with great purpose up the wooded embankment. The morning is embossed with the lush moistness of autumn's first dew. It brushes against his pants and his sleeves and dissolves into the purl of mist clinging low to the ground plants in the chirping forest of colorful songbirds and hidden crickets. On his way to the top he pauses several times to face the orange sunrise and deep breathe in this life-repairing ether, and to marvel, through the braided branches of the forest, the rustic palace he helped build many winters ago.

At the end of the path the trees give way to the clearing that surrounds the lodge, on which sleek solar panels follow the sun without apparent effort across the expansive blue sky. On the great front lawn the tribe assembles. Ibrahim beckons him with a grin.

Deganawida looks up from his wheelchair, smiling, his spirit as present as the day he was born, his body slipping back to his ancestors. Grand wonder is upon his face, and his wise eyes are fascinated on the handsome youth standing by Maria, his younger brothers and sisters standing beside him in a row, each shorter than the other by a few inches or a head, and Tadodaho and Jamal, packed and ready to go, towering behind them all.

Herbie walks across the lawn and stands with his wife by his side, and their family, and all the tribe gathered around. He speaks to the young man. "Nothing ever stays the same, my son. The more you grew towards this day, the more your mother and I knew it was inevitable."

Maria smiles, takes Herbie's hand, and pats it. Looking into her son's eyes she says, "As parents we wish it wasn't so, but that power you feel growing within, which we see so clearly, is much to be expected, considering your birthright, which we had to conceal from the world until now."

All notice the breeze whistling through the leaves like something new settling in.

Jamal speaks to the tribe. "It is time. They need us now. They all must know."

Herbie continues, "You see, everything is interconnected in ways so perplexing and intricate, yet so wondrous and clean. Even though you are my son, I am not your father. I am very sure the one who is, is most proud of you today.

"Each one of us can spend our entire life wondering how and why we got here, this place in time and the people who we are. But can anyone ever grab hold of a miracle?

"And no matter how hard we continue to try, none of us will ever know what is going to happen next. But I do believe that each one of us is significant, and we can know what is happening now."

Herbie pulls his old headbandcam out of his pocket. He unfolds it and takes the small copper ring that was nestled inside and slips it over the fourth finger of the young man's outstretched hand. His son's green apple tree eyes gleam with pride seeing Bullmoose's magic ring, the very one which helped open the eyes of the world and stopped the bullet just enough so the Iroquois shaman on the chopper could save his step-dad's life.

The soprano glides up an octave as Herbie smiles into those sunrise eyes. "Pay heed my son, as you travel through this land of seemingly endless night, always seek the light that shines inside to show you the way. Accept the miracle that brought you here. The amazing gift of your life is all the proof you need, there are no limits to the glory and the grace of God.

* * * * *

Jake Packard has been in the creative business all his life. He currently lives and works in the New York City area. He welcomes any comments at TheManhattanProphet.com.